DARK DESIRES

"Tell me, what would you do if I kissed you, my dear Miss O'Connor? My fiery Cait of the shamrock eyes." He took a step closer.

"You would not dare, sir!"

"Oh, I dare, Cait, I dare almost anything. I am not lacking in courage or in bravado. Besides, I'm Irish!" He laughed softly. "We are known for our recklessness—and for our romantic hearts! Humor me, little Cait. What would you do?" His sapphire eyes danced with wicked merriment. "If I could not help myself? If I kissed you until you could not speak?"

She stared at his sensual lips, wondering how they would feel if he succumbed to his dark desire—and she to hers. Wondering, if truth be told, how it would feel to be kissed speechless.

How would his lips feel if he tasted her? Kissed her?

Warm? Insistent? Arousing?

She looked down at his hands. At broad palms and long skilled fingers. Such strong, masculine hands. Capable hands. Knowing hands that were no stranger to the soft curves of a woman's body. How would they feel on her bare skin, touching her, stroking her?

Other books by Penelope Neri:

MOONSHADOW
HIGHLAND LOVESONG
KEEPER OF MY HEART
SCANDALS
STOLEN

Obsession

PENELOPE NERI

LEISURE BOOKS   NEW YORK CITY

A LEISURE BOOK®

April 2003

Published by

Dorchester Publishing Co., Inc.
276 Fifth Avenue
New York, NY 10001

ISBN 0-8439-5081-1

The name "Leisure Books" and the stylized "L" with design are trademarks of Dorchester Publishing Co., Inc.

Printed in the United States of America.

Visit us on the web at www.dorchesterpub.com.

For the wicked wahines of the Romance Readers Anonymous gang at Borders Waikele Store, Hawai'i—Leslie Galloway, Carol Kahalewai, Margaret Mizuta, Kathy Preeg, and Karen Wong, With love from your "Reader Leader." May you always 'embrace the addiction'!

Ballad of Jack the Ripper

It began in the autumn,
Eighteen eighty-eight,
Scotland Yard and Whitechapel
Were in such a state.
Five drunken 'unfortunates'
Jack sent to hell
Without even so much as
A "Fare-thee-girls-well!"

He killed Liz, Catherine, Annie.
Mary Jane. Mary Anne.
"Catch me, coppers," he taunted,
"Buckle me, if you can!"
One by one, they tripped
Into the shadows with Jack—
Five went into the fog,
But *not one* drab came back.

For instead of the 'tricks'
They expected of him
In return for the coin
To buy porter and gin,
Jack pulled out his knife
With a thwackety-thwack—
Then escaped in the fog
Without once looking back.

There was panic in Whitechapel,
Murders galore!
Stout padlocks and bars
Barricaded the doors.
Vigilantes and bobbies
Were scouring the place,
But there weren't any clues
To Jack's name or Jack's face.

Some thought him a surgeon,
Still others, a prince.
Or maybe a copper—
Watch Abberline wince!
He *cannot* be English—
Perhaps he's a Jew?
Does he come from Poland?
From Russia? From Crewe?

The Autumn of Terror,
It came to be called,
And the Queen and her Empire
Were rightly appalled.
Yet a century later
Jack's legend lives on,
Although written in blood,
'Tis remembered in song.

For although Jack was hunted
For weeks, night and day,
And although Scotland Yard
Vowed he'd not get away
But would swing for his crimes—
All of London would see!
Jack had the last laugh.
Mad or not, he went free!

Sometimes in Whitechapel,
On foggy fall nights,
As tourists are flocking
To see London's sights,
A shadowy spectre
In black will appear.
Miller's Court to Buck's Row—
Jack the Ripper's still here!

—P. Neri, 2002

Prologue

Death was no stranger to London's Whitechapel that terrible autumn.

It lurked in the foul brown water that spewed from pump and tap to thirsty mouth. It ran in filthy gutters that were choked with rotting waste, and in the bite of flea-bitten rats. It rode the air in the suffocating smoke and soot that blackened lungs, and in the foul miasmas that carried disease: consumption, which whittled down even the strongest man and had him spitting blood into his kerchief. Or cholera and typhus, which turned his bowels to water.

Death also stalked the rookeries of the East End that autumn wielding a blade. The murderer, christened Leather Apron, then Saucy Jack by the press, had taken the lives of as many as four 'unfortunates' by the

1

end of September, or perhaps as few as two.

God alone knew how many more murders were to come, but that there would be more was never in doubt.

Death prowled the workhouses and the hospitals, too, where it gorged on the poor, the sick, the down-trodden, who overflowed the fourpenny doss houses and dirty tenements.

Irish, Polish, Jewish, Russian, American, they teemed like sewer rats through the courts and dens of the East End, desperate to escape the famine and persecution of the lands that had given them birth.

Arriving in London starry-eyed, they dreamed of a better life for themselves and their children. A life in which Death had no part.

Instead, they found only disillusionment awaiting them, and an even greater horror: the death of dreams, and of hope.

Polly had once been such a woman, he thought. She came over on the ferry from Ireland to England, wed to a shiftless bricklayer when she was barely sixteen because she was in the family way. She'd been a fresh-cheeked country colleen then. Unspoiled. Innocent. Lovely. Full of the sheer joy of life.

Poverty and disease had long-since destroyed poor Polly's claims to beauty and innocence. Death had finished the job with particular violence.

She lay on her back, the dirty ticking mattress beneath her dark with blood, her lifeless blue eyes fixed on the scarred ceiling above, with its stained continents of damp and mildew. Her long auburn hair streamed across the pallet, an explosion of color in an otherwise colorless room.

The stench of blood and burned wax made his belly heave. His gorge rose up his throat.

Obsession

She was not the first. Nor would she be the last, he reminded himself, bloody hands clenched at his sides. He should have grown accustomed to this, long ago. Death was, after all, an inescapable part of life. Of his chosen trade.

But in his deepest heart, he knew he would never grow used to it.

"Forgive me, Polly," he said thickly as he washed his hands in a basin. The water turned cloudy, then red. "It should not have ended like this. You deserved better."

Throwing a cloak over his shoulders to hide his bloodstained cuffs, he pinched the reeking candle flame and left the fourpenny doss house, plunging out into the inky rookeries of London's East End.

The shadows swallowed him up like the jaws of a monstrous beast, closing behind him as if he'd never been.

I am panting as I hurry through the rabbit warren of courts and alleys, past sweatshops, slaughter-yards and boardinghouses that double as brothels.

Moments ago, a horrified carter found a pile of old rags in Dutfield Yard, off Berner Street. Discovering it was not rags, but a woman's body, he drove off to fetch the coppers, squealing like a stuck pig. Not knowing I was only inches from him. That Death waited, only a breath away.

I hid in the shadows until he left, then fled into the night, just as Big Ben struck one in the distance. Seconds later, the first police whistle shrilled its strident alarm.

I chuckle to myself. By now, coppers are combing the streets, going house to house in their efforts to find me. They will not succeed. I am God's Instrument, invisible in my cloak of righteousness. In obedience to His Divine Will, I have been chosen to punish the daughters of sin. To make the city's whores and jezebels pay for the filth and disease with which they contaminate righteous men.

As they once contaminated me.

As His chosen Instrument, God hides me from the hunters. Like the wolf in sheep's clothing, I go out amongst the frightened flocks to do my bloody work. wearing the guise of a harmless shepherd.

Lusk, the leader of the vigilantes, claims the women were brutally murdered, then mutilated. That blowhard fool! What does he know of such matters? Those women were not murdered. They were sacrificed, their blood spilled in atonement for their sins.

Like her sisters in death, the woman tonight was a whore, a diseased vessel, used by men for their pleasure.

I slit her throat like an animal's in an abattoir as she bent over before me, palms braced against the wall, awaiting my pleasure.

I smile as I duck into a dark court to catch my breath. Killing her . . . slitting her throat . . . ah, that was sweet pleasure indeed.

My pleasure.

At first, I thought Long Liz would fight for her life. Half laughing, half frightened, the stupid bitch asked what I was up to as I hooked my arm around her throat from behind.

"Oy, oy, cock! Not s'bloomin' rough," she protested, her voice slurred with gin. "I'm willing."

But then she looked over her shoulder, into my eyes, and she knew.

Somehow, the whore knew.

I smelled her fear. Rank. Intoxicating as perfume.

4

Obsession

I watched terror shrivel her pupils to pinpricks, long before the shining blade appeared like magic in my fist.

"You?" she whispered incredulously. Her face drained of color beneath the gaslight. "Gawd, no!"

Shuddering, I close my eyes and lean back against the rough brick as I touch myself. I am growing hard again as memories of the slut's terror revive my lust.

Raising my hands to my nose, I sniff them. Blood. The scent of life itself. It is everywhere—in me, on me, surrounding me, filling me. My jacket cuffs are soaked in it. There is more red beneath my nails, encrusted in the seams of my knuckles, trapped in the deepest creases of my palms, smeared over my brass buttons.

So much blood, although I wiped my hands on a scrap of the whore's apron before I vanished into the night.

'Long Liz.' Not the best, perhaps, but good. Very good. She uttered a single gurgling squeal that was abruptly cut off; then gouts of hot, purifying blood washed away her sins forever.

But alas, as good as she was, her sacrifice did not bring about the release I crave. I fear it was too hurried, too hastily done, cut short by the clatter of hooves that warned me someone was coming. Ah, yes. The carter's sudden arrival forced me to abandon the ritual before it was fully completed.

Now, only half fed, my hunger has quickly returned. It gnaws at my innards like a monstrous rat, its razor teeth gnawing . . . gnawing.

My terrible thirst is likewise unquenched.

My aching need unfed.

Only blood can appease that need. That lust. Hot sweet perfumed blood.

God will understand. He will condone it. A second

sacrifice is necessary. The next one shall be His reward to me, His loyal Instrument.

If one will not do, there perforce must be two!

I smile, pleased with the silly couplet I have composed. Perhaps I shall include it in my next letter to the newspapers? Neither the Boss, as I affectionately call Inspector Abberline, nor Scotland Yard, has any idea who I am, nor how powerless they are to catch me.

I am the proverbial needle in a haystack. The bad penny in a town of 'coppers.'

I am Leather Apron. Saucy Jack. And now, Jack the Ripper! They call me monster, butcher, insane. I am all of these and more. So very much more.

My letters to the newspapers, horribly misspelled, badly penned, have thrown the blundering fools off my track. They are so desperate to catch me, they cannot see the wood for the trees.

Quietly, confidently, I leave the alley, making my unhurried way down cobbled streets slick with drizzling rain, as is my nightly custom. I am rendered invisible by my very visibilty.

Tonight there will be a double event, as I promised the newspapers in my letter. A sensational double murder that is guaranteed to sell the scandal sheets!

Emerging from the shadows, I stroll down Goulston Street to Mitre Square, where the whores and their strutting bullies ply their dirty trade. I am swinging my trusty stick as I go.

As I approach the corner, a woman sidles toward me, wearing a coy smile. The odor of gin and stale sex surround her like perfume.

The rank stench of sin.

Another filthy whore!

I reach inside my coat. The tide is rising through me

again; ruby red, piping hot. I shiver with anticipation as cold steel slithers between my fingers.

Icy. Phallic.

"Evenin', gov'na," the woman greets me throatily. She runs a finger down the forearm of my black coat. "Lookin' for a bit o' sport, are you, luv? 'Cos if you are, I'm yer gel, eh?"

Like the others, she is no longer young. Old enough to know better, I tell myself, fighting the urge to jerk my arm away in disgust.

Instead, I force myself to look at her in the gaslight. At her upturned face, gray with hunger and exhaustion. The years and the flesh trade have not been kind to her. Unlike Long Liz, her hazel eyes are fearless, glassy, bloodshot. Too much gin . . .

I lick my lips.

Strands of dark hair stick out from under the brim of her shabby straw bonnet. Like its owner, it has seen better days. Her long dark jacket is trimmed with moth-eaten fur.

"So? D'ye like my jolly new bonnet, gov'na?" She flirts with me, her fists on swaying hips as she smiles up at me. "Gawd knows, ye've looked me over long enough, you cheeky sod!"

"What do you think?" I ask her. I am breathing heavily. My voice is thick with excitement. Never mind. She will take it for lust.

She snorts. "As if you care what I think, cock!"

"You're right. I don't."

She grins. "Honest cove, ain'tcha?"

A faint smile ghosts my lips. "I do my best."

"That makes two of us, then. So, what'll it be, cock? Name yer poison! A quick French? The old in 'n' out?"

"Not yet. Tell me your name first."

"Why?" She grins saucily and nudges me with her

elbow. *"Not fixin' t' buckle me, are yeh, cock?"*

I ignore her question. "I like to know who I'm tupping—before I . . . you know."

"Ohh, I know, all right, you naughty boy. What will your missus say if she gets wind of this, eh? It's Catherine. Me name's Catherine. Kate, if ye like."

"I prefer Cath-er-ine. Tell me, Catherine. Have you no fear of the killer who stalks these streets? The papers are full of Jacky's . . . doings."

My voice cracks with mounting excitement, but it no longer matters. It is only a matter of time now.

"Me, frightened o' saucy Jacky?" Catherine scoffs. "Not bloody likely! I'd give Old Nick a poke fer a nice glass o' gin, I would! Aye, and a French too, if he wanted! 'Sides, I've got big strong blokes like you t' protect me, ain't I, luv? So, what's your pleasure?"

I tell her.

The stupid whore laughs. She thinks I'm funning.

But I'm not, Cath-er-ine. Far from it.

Catherine is still smiling as I leave her. Smiling for Saucy Jack.

Smiling ear to ear.

Chapter One

Huntington House
Huntington Square, West End, London
October 1, 1888

"Here we are, miss," the cockney cabby sang out. "Number thirteen, Huntington Square."

The Fitzgerald residence stood apart from the other large houses fronting the park, Caitlynn O'Connor saw as she peered through the hackney's murky window. It was as if number thirteen had offended its neighbors by some shameful act and been cast out. 'Twas a fanciful thought for a woman who prided herself on being practical, she thought with a wry grin.

Perhaps the house only seemed so alone on the square because the property was so much larger than the houses on either side of it. Or it could have been the way the wrought-iron palings and high hawthorn hedges walled off the grounds like a fortress.

Whatever the reason, number thirteen stood imperiously alone. Her green conical turrets rose from between old trees, rambling gardens and a rockery that, in this season, were as bereft as a jilted bride.

Withered leaves lay in faded heaps beneath ancient oak trees that stretched bony fingers to the charcoal sky in silent supplication. There, flags of smoke from London's countless chimney pots mingled with the thickening fog and turned the sky a grimy gray. It would be a pea-souper before long. Ah, for the crisp, damp chill of Ireland's misty autumn evenings . . .

Caitlynn shivered as the cabby handed her down from the carriage, drawing her cloak more closely about her.

Not a trace remained of the sweltering summer, when, according to newspaper reports, record temperatures in London had frayed tempers, incited riots, and created an abundance of rats in the stews of the East End.

Quite the contrary. It was exceptionally cold and damp on this, the first of October, 1888. The wind had a bite she felt deep in her lungs with every breath she drew.

Caitlynn forced a smile for the cabby as he hefted her trunk down from the roof. "Thank you kindly, cabby." Her lilting voice was as Irish as peat bogs and shamrocks. "How much do I owe you?"

"Tuppence ha'penny, miss."

She fished in her drawstring bag and dropped five copper halfpennies into the cabby's paw with a noisy 'chink.' "Thank you."

"Likewise, miss." The cabby swung her two bulging carpetbags down to the wet pavement, beside the large trunk, which he did not offer to carry to the door for her. He seemed edgy, anxious to be gone. And who could blame him, on such a nasty afternoon? "A good afternoon to ye, miss."

As the blinkered horse clip-clopped away, Caitlynn squared tired shoulders.

Well. Here I am, she thought, glancing up at second-story windows veiled in lace and velvet like the eyes of an Eastern odalisque. *Now, if I can only find Deirdre, this journey won't be in vain.*

Picking up her bags, she pushed open the wrought-iron gate and marched smartly up the flagstoned path to the front door, aware of a shadow at one of the upstairs windows as she went.

Caitlynn could feel eyes upon her with such intensity, the fine hairs on her neck rose and stood straight up. But the prickling sensation lasted only a few seconds, before both it and the shadow were gone. She shivered, then gave a rueful smile. At least someone in the house was aware of her arrival.

A housekeeper answered her knock. The woman frowned as she looked Caitlynn up and down.

"Yes? What is it you want?" the tall, blunt-featured woman asked briskly. Her hands were primly folded beneath her bosom, as if Caitlynn were a common tradesman who'd come to the front door rather than using the servants' entrance, and so deserved a sharp reprimand for her impertinence.

The housekeeper's hair was scraped so tightly back into a bun, her blunt features had acquired an Asian cast. Perhaps her unpleasant demeanor was caused by pain, Caitlynn thought, resisting the urge to giggle—a reaction she blamed on sheer exhaustion.

The Irish Sea had been rough, the crossing choppy. She had lost what little food she'd eaten over the ferry's railing before they were halfway across the Irish Sea to England, discovering belatedly that she was no sailor. The train journey to London had sapped the remainder of her strength.

Disapproving gray eyes flickered over Caitlynn's modest cloak, noting the unruly strands of dark brown hair that had escaped bonnet, pins and combs during her long journey from County Waterford.

Caitlynn, although weary, was not easily cowed. She met the housekeeper's critical inspection with unblinking green eyes.

"Good afternoon, ma'am," she began firmly. "The Kelly Agency sent me. I'm—"

"Kathleen O'Connor. The new lady's companion. Yes, I assumed as much. But look at the time! Where can you have been?"

"It's Caitlynn, ma'am," Caitlynn corrected. "And 'tis sorry I am to be so late, but the journey took longer than expected. That's all. There was no help for it. I came as soon as I could."

She shivered as a gust of wind flattened her cloak to her spine, chilling her to the bone. Behind her, dry leaves skittered across the flagstones. From here, they sounded like a huge animal's claws. "It's bitter out. Might I come in, Mrs. . . . ?"

"Montgomery. Mary Montgomery. I'm Dr. Fitzgerald's housekeeper."

"Mrs. Montgomery. Yes. 'Tis a pleasure, I'm sure," she murmured, trying to be the subservient lady's companion that the woman so obviously expected, though it was not a role that came naturally to her. Far from it! "Might I come inside, ma'am? 'Tis cold as charity out here, it is."

"Oh, well, yes. I suppose you must."

"I have a trunk. Out on the pavement, by the gate . . ."

"Very well. I'll have Tom fetch it for you. Just come

in, for now. You're letting the draught in." She stepped back, waving Caitlynn inside with an irritable, impatient gesture.

Caitlynn passed between double doors that had stained-glass lights on either side. The doorway was more than wide enough to accommodate her skirts and fell just short of being grand, as befitted a doctor's residence.

She found herself in a spacious wood-paneled foyer. A mirrored mahogany hall stand stood with its back against the staircase, facing the main door. The polished hardwood floors were strewn with Turkish rugs in burgundy, cream and dark blue. The effect was comfortable without being fussy, much like Lough House, her family home in Waterford, Ireland, she noted with a twinge of homesickness.

"Dr. Fitzgerald will be wanting to meet me, I expect?" Caitlynn observed, removing her gloves, finger by finger, teeth chattering as she did so. Was it the wretched weather she'd heard so much about, or an attack of nerves? she wondered. "To go over my duties?"

"Not today," Montgomery said firmly, her brisk tone implying that she would decide when and where such a meeting would take place. "Dr. Fitzgerald makes his rounds at St. Bart's—St. Bartholomew's Hospital—every afternoon, before he comes home for his supper. We'll not see him much before seven this evening, at the earliest. Miss Estelle takes her supper with him, whenever he's dining at home, so any entertainments or outings you plan for her should be finished well before then. Remember that in the coming weeks, Miss O'Connor."

"Oh, I shall, ma'am, you can be sure. And where am I to take my meals?" She'd already guessed where her position in this household would probably fall, if the housekeeper's overbearing attitude was anything to go by. She seriously doubted that a lady's companion would be dining *en famille* with the doctor and his fifteen-year-old invalided ward!

"Why, in the kitchen, with the rest of the staff, Miss O'Connor! Where else?" Montgomery said crossly. "Or you may choose to have a tray sent up to your room, if you prefer, as I do. I'm sure Mrs. Larkin will oblige you. Now. I expect you'll be wanting your tea before you go up?" There was disapproval in her tone.

"Tea would be very welcome, yes, thank you," Caitlynn accepted, ignoring the woman's grudging tone.

"It is served promptly at four here, or I'll know the reason why. However, I suppose we must make an exception today, on account of your tardiness. Let's hope the others have left something for you."

"Oh, I'm sure there will be more than enough, ma'am. I don't eat much more than a bird, or so my mother always says. Thank you, Mrs. Montgomery. You've been very kind." The woman had barely been civil, but Caitlynn was a firm believer that more flies were caught with treacle than with vinegar. She forced a smile.

"Yes, well, leave your bag there and come along."

Her room was on the second floor, like those of the family and Mrs. Montgomery herself, she discovered, rather than a cramped garret up in the attic with the two maids, Bridget and Annie. There was a connecting door to her young charge's room, which was in one of the two witch's turrets. To her relief, there was a key in the lock, should she choose to use it. The room's only window looked out over sprawling Huntington Park across the street.

Caitlynn drew aside the draperies and peered out, much as the mysterious figure at the bedroom window had done earlier.

Although it was already dusk, she could see copses and allées of trees, arbors and undulating lawns, meandering pathways confined by tall, spiked iron palings.

Curls and wisps of fog drifted over the grass like smoke, playing hide-and-seek with the metallic glint of a large body of water—a pond, perhaps, or an ornamental lake. The palings and ornate iron gates must enclose several hundred acres of open parkland, she thought.

She unpacked her trunk, which must have been carried up by a servant while she was having her tea, and hung up her clothes. Two cups of hot tea, buttered toast with blackberry jam, and a generous slice of poppy-seed cake, pressed on her by the cook, a kindly soul named Rose, had done wonders to revive her flagging spirits. She was feeling almost her old self when the upstairs maid, Bridget, came in to light her fire.

"Why, there you are again, miss," the girl greeted her, smiling. "I hope you like your room," she added, bobbing her a curtsey. "Mrs. M. put you next to Miss Estelle, in case the darlin' girl needs help during the night. I'll just light the fire, an' you'll be warm as toast, aye? Look half frozen, you do, miss, and you such a tiny wee soul."

"Please, Bridget. Call me Caitlynn, not Miss O'Connor."

The maid's blue eyes widened. "Oh, but I couldn't, miss . . . ma'am. Really, I couldn't. It wouldn't be right."

"Nonsense. Mrs. Montgomery has made it quite clear that I'm not to affect airs and graces while I'm here." She screwed up her face, making Bridget laugh. "So, plain Caitlynn it is and must ever be."

"*Miss* Caitlynn, then."

"All right. Miss Caitlynn it is. For now, anyway. You're Irish, too, I'm thinking, Bridget, if that brogue's anything to go by. Where are you from?"

"Connemara, ma'am . . . I mean, Miss Caitlynn. Aye, most of the servants here are Irish, like Dr. Fitzgerald himself, and Annie. That's Annie Murphy, the other maid." Bridget wrinkled up her nose, as if she didn't much like Annie. "And you, ma'am?"

"County Waterford."

"Waterford, is it! I hear it's beautiful there. The place where all the pretty crystal comes from."

" 'Tis heaven on earth, t'be sure," Caitlynn agreed softly, overwhelmed by a sudden pang of homesickness. "Tell me, Bridget. How do you like being in service here?"

"In London?" Again, Bridget wrinkled up her nose. "I don't, much. Like it, I mean. Londoners are a hard lot. They don't like the Irish at all. But my family's here, aye? And a big one it is, too."

"And what about the Fitzgerald household? Does it suit you?"

"That's a funny question to be asking. The way I see it, it doesn't much matter where you work, does it now? Being in service is the same anywhere."

Bridget smiled, her freckled face pretty beneath her white cap as she arranged the coals. There was a smudge of soot on her cheek. Caitlynn smiled, liking the girl instantly. She knew that many Irish girls in domestic service in London were little better than 'unfortunates,' as prostitutes were so delicately termed. Poor wages and terrible living conditions forced many decent yet desperate young women into the oldest pro-

16

fession, in order to improve their lot, or to put food in their bellies. But somehow, she did not think the girl before her was one of them.

"...hard work, long hours and precious little t'show for it," Bridget was saying.

"And the doctor? Is he a good man?"

"Oh, Dr. Fitzgerald's wonderful! We couldn't ask for a better master."

Caitlynn smiled, noting the girl's flushed cheeks, her eager smile. Clearly, Bridget was sweet on her employer. "I'm glad to hear it."

Bridget rocked back on her heels and fed the last shiny lumps of coal to the fire. "There. It's caught. 'Twon't be but a wee while now, and you'll be warm as toast, Miss Caitlynn."

"Hmmm. I can feel it already. Thank you, Bridget. You are a dear. Now. Tell me a little about Miss Estelle before you go, will you? What's the darlin' girl like?"

Bridget thought before answering her question. "Sure, she acts as if butter wouldn't melt in her mouth, she does. And she looks like an angel. But we all know the young miss for what she really is. A spoilt little—"

"There you are, you wretched girl!" Montgomery exclaimed, swooping in through the door Bridget had left ajar like a striking hawk. "Hasn't that fire caught yet? What can you have been doing all this time? Not gossiping, I hope." Bridget's cheeks deepened to a telltale crimson.

"I'm very disappointed in you, Bridget. You were warned more than once. If you must exchange idle chitchat with Miss O'Connor, then do so on your own time, not when you are supposed to be working. If I

catch you gossiping again in this fashion, you will be
let go. Do I make myself plain?"

"Yes, ma'am," Bridget mumbled, scrambling to her
feet. She bowed her head. " 'Tis sorry I am, ma'am."

"As well you should be, my girl."

"Yes, ma'am. May I go now, ma'am?"

"You may. Run along. I trust you have everything
you need, Miss O'Connor?" The housekeeper turned
to Caitlynn, her tone cold as Bridget thrust past them
and fled. "If not, please ask me for what you need, in
the future. Or Rose. Not the maids."

"Bridget wasn't to blame, ma'am. I was. I'm afraid
my curiosity got the better of me. She was only being
polite by answering my questions."

"Nevertheless, Bridget knows better," the housekeeper insisted.

"Really, ma'am, she did nothing wrong," Caitlynn
said firmly.

"I'll thank you to let me be the judge of that. You
see, Miss O'Connor, until the doctor says otherwise,
I'm in charge of this household. Not you, and certainly
not Bridget." At the door, the woman paused. "You
were most fortunate to find this position, were you not,
Miss O'Connor?"

"I was, yes."

"Correct me if I'm wrong, but I understand certain
. . . strings were pulled by the doctor's father?"

"Yes, ma'am. Indeed they were." She had been recommended to the Kelly Agency for this position by
none other than Dr. Joseph Fitzgerald, young Dr. Donovan Fitzgerald's father.

A country doctor from the neighboring county, he
still made his rounds on horseback, the old-fashioned
way.

However, neither Dr. Fitzgerald knew that the lady's

companion Caitlynn was replacing was her own cousin, Deirdre Riordan. Sweet Deirdre, who had vanished from this very household two months ago and never been seen or heard from since.

"That being the case," Montgomery continued, "it would be a pity if your . . . obstinacy caused you to be let go so soon after your arrival, would it not?"

Caitlynn flushed, but wisely made no comment. The ill-concealed threat required none.

"Your duties, if indeed they can truly be called duties, are far from taxing, after all," Montgomery added with a sniff and a toss of her head, her hands still primly clasped beneath her bosom.

The woman looked, Cailtynn thought irreverently, much as she imagined a witch might look, with her scraggly hair pulled back into a severe bun, and a long nose and chin.

"You have merely to provide suitable daily companionship, guidance and entertainments for a young woman who has the misfortune to be an invalid. Miss Estelle is unable to walk, you see. She is confined to her bed or a chaise most of the time."

"I see," Caitlynn said politely, although she'd known that much from Deirdre's letters.

"It will be your duty to entertain her, and to provide such companionship and conversation as she requires, and as befits a young lady of her position in life. In return, you will receive a generous stipend of five guineas a month, and your room and board. More than adequate compensation, wouldn't you agree?"

"Oh, yes, I would, ma'am. Most certainly." *Play the game, Cait,* she reminded herself. *Remember why you're here, what you came to do. . . .*

"I'm very glad to hear it. That being the case, please keep in mind that Dr. Fitzgerald will have no difficulty whatsoever in finding a replacement for you, should you prove unsatisfactory in any way. There are, after all, many impoverished Irish and English gentlewomen who would jump at such an opportunity."

"Indeed there are, ma'am," Caitlynn agreed, tight-lipped. "You're quite right."

"Refrain from gossiping with the servants, who have proper work to do, remember your place in this household, and you will do well enough. Do I make myself clear?"

"Yes, ma'am. Clear as glass." Caitlynn, more accustomed to ordering servants about than being one herself, again bit back the sharp retort she longed to make. But it went against her nature to stand there, her proud dark head meekly bowed, defiant green eyes downcast. How her brothers would laugh if they could see her now, the young devils!

"Good. Then I shall leave you to rest after your long journey, and to reflect upon what I have said. Tomorrow, after breakfast, you will meet with Dr. Fitzgerald and Miss Estelle, and we shall go on from there."

Caitlynn closed and locked the door in the housekeeper's wake, muttering, "Oooh, what a miserable old bitch you are, t'be sure!"

Going to the connecting door between her room and that of her new charge, she locked that door, too, very quietly, deciding she'd met quite enough people for one day. Mrs. Montgomery, the cook, Rose Larkin, and the maids, Bridget O'Riley and Annie Murphy—more than enough new faces for the time being.

The room was spartanly furnished by the ornate standards of the day, made so popular by Her Majesty, Queen Victoria.

There was a desk, on which stood a milk-glass chimney lamp and a leather ink blotter, an oak armoire, a dresser, and a brass bed, spread with a white tufted candlewick counterpane. The gas lighting she had noticed downstairs had apparently not been extended to the upstairs of Huntington House yet. Nor had she seen or heard a telephone anywhere. There was, however, a bathing room, with a huge claw-footed tub and a water closet, both much more modern than in Lough House.

She unpacked her inkwells and pens and arranged them on the desk, then stood the two silver-framed ambrotypes of her family on top of it.

A smaller portrait, this one of her cousin Deirdre, she tucked into her drawstring bag, carefully wrapped in brown paper and string. It wouldn't do for anyone to make the connection between the two lady's companions just yet.

A pair of oval silhouettes framed in gold lacquer, one male, one female, hung facing each other above the brass headboard. A wing chair, upholstered in rose-flowered chintz, and a matching footstool with a ruffled skirt were pulled up to the fireplace, where Bridget's fire now burned cheerfully behind a polished black grate. Braided rag rugs softened the bare wood floor before the fire and beside the bed.

A porcelain chamber pot, discreetly covered by a linen cloth, was tucked under the bed, hidden by the folds of the candlewick bedspread.

A rose-flowered china ewer and matching washbasin stood on a small table beneath a needlework sampler that read "CLEANLINESS IS NEXT TO GODLINESS" in painstaking cross-stitch. Estelle's handiwork probably. It was the sort of boring busy-work that governesses and nannies set restless young hands to producing. Caitlynn wrinkled up her nose. To her way of thinking, such pointless projects were an utter waste of time, and served only to dull keen minds. Or was it that she had no patience for such things herself? The nuns had often scolded her, insisting she was too impulsive, too restless, an undisciplined hoyden.

She sat down on the edge of the bed and bounced experimentally. It was wide and comfortable, much like the brass bed she'd left behind in Ireland. Another wave of homesickness for her big and boisterous family swept over her.

She already missed her four older brothers, Timothy, Kevin, Sean and Ryan, and her younger sister, Margaret, or Little Maggie as everyone called her, who shared her bed. And Patrick, the baby of the family at four years, had been like her own child rather than her little brother.

Removing her wrinkled traveling ensemble, Caitlynn washed, then changed into a warm woolen dressing gown before she brushed out her hair. She would rest for a half hour, she told herself, then go down to take supper with the other servants. She was one of them now, after all, and everyone knew that the servants knew all the goings-on in a household. Bridget, Rose and the others would help her to find Deirdre, whether they realized it or not.

But her thoughts kept returning to what Mrs. Montgomery had said while she was having tea in the kitchen.

"The last companion had ideas far above her station," the woman had said about Deirdre, Caitlynn recalled as she lay there, staring up at the ceiling. "She expected to be dining with the family. The very idea of it!"

"Perhaps she wasn't sure what was expected of a lady's companion?" Caitlynn had suggested gently, trying to get the housekeeper talking about the young woman she had come to England to find.

Mrs. Montgomery bristled. "Oh, our Miss Deirdre knew, all right. 'Still waters,' that one was, despite her wide-eyed innocent look. But then, that's the Irish for you! It came as no great surprise to me when she up and left without so much as a fare-thee-well to anyone. Ungrateful chit!"

Caitlynn swallowed her protests.

"She left?" she echoed innocently. The less anyone knew about her relationship to the former lady's companion, the better. "Just like that? How very odd! You mean, she wasn't sacked or anything?"

"No. Well, not exactly. There were . . . circumstances, of course."

"Oh, I quite understand," Caitlynn said, not understanding at all. What did Montgomery mean by 'circumstances'? "How long had the woman been in service here?"

"Almost two years."

"That long! And no one thought it strange that she gave no notice?"

"No. As I said, she was secretive."

Not secretive at all, but sweet and on the shy side, Caitlynn corrected silently, her temper fraying and ready to snap. Not half an hour in this house, and already she itched to do battle with the old dragon! To tear out her gray hair and scratch her horsey face. But she must learn to curb her temper, at least on the surface, if she hoped to learn anything useful.

"You could never tell what she was thinking," Mrs. Montgomery added.

"Apparently not. And has there been no word from this young woman since she left here? Nothing to explain such odd behavior?"

"Nothing. But that's hardly surprising, considering

her—oh, my word!" The housekeeper peered suddenly at the face of the tiny gold fob-watch pinned to her flat, heavily starched bosom. "Look at the time!" she exclaimed. "The doctor will be home for his supper at any minute. I'll send Bridget up to light your fire."

With that, the woman had abruptly left, leaving Caitlynn's mind churning with unanswered questions.

Irish indeed! As if being Irish explained anything! Montgomery's casual insult smarted. Still, Caitlynn should have expected as much. Before she'd left Ireland, Father had warned her that the English had no liking for the Irish who'd swelled the numbers of the poor crowded into London's East End since the Potato Famine thirty years ago.

More recently, Irish Nationalists had staged uprisings in London, demanding an end to British rule in Ireland. Such violent demonstrations did little to endear the Irish living in the country to their English neighbors.

Caitlynn had laughed and told her Father she was quite aware of that, reminding him that she was a grown woman. One of the New Women, moreover, who were independent and spoke their minds. He and Mam needn't worry about her.

Even so, Da's warnings had not prepared her for the sting of firsthand prejudice.

Never mind. Let the English and the Mrs. Montgomerys of the world say what they would. She would do what she'd come here to do, which was find her missing cousin, then take her home to Aunt Connie and Uncle Dan in Ireland. Once that had been accomplished, Devil take the lot of them!

When Deirdre's weekly letters had abruptly ceased three months ago, Caitlynn had known immediately that something was very wrong.

She and Deirdre were cousins, but closer than most sisters. Growing up in the same small village, they had been best friends, doing everything together, whether it was attending Sacred Heart Convent School, taught by sour-faced nuns they'd made fun of, or playing in the woods along the banks of the lough.

She and Deirdre had also shared their dreams and their secrets. Deirdre's dream had been to see something of the world beyond their village. When her family fell on harder times, becoming a lady's companion to the ward of an Irish doctor living in London seemed the perfect opportunity to kill two birds with one stone.

Uncle Daniel was in poor health. He could hardly support himself and Aunt Constance, let alone provide for two well-educated, gently raised daughters who showed no inclination toward either marriage or starting their own, separate households.

Deirdre's older sister, Catherine Margaret, had been the first to leave. She'd become governess to the eight children of a wealthy widower in County Sligo, and was now sending money home to help her parents. Her letters hinted that marriage to the wealthy widower was also in the offing, and would be welcome.

Soon after Catherine Margaret's departure, Deirdre had left Ireland for London to take up her own position.

At the time, Caitlynn had been betrothed to Mr. Michael Flynn, Esquire, the only son of the grand Michael Flynn, Senior, who owned the White Horse Hotel in Waterford. Their wedding had been set for the first Saturday in June, 1888.

But in May of this year, just a month before their wedding, Michael had run off to America, leaving behind a note saying only that he was not ready to be

married. That he wanted more from life than a wife
and a brood of children, or running the fine old hotel
that had been in his family for centuries. He had gone
off to make his own fortune in the gold and silver
mines of America. He would not be coming back.

Caitlynn had been numb with shock at the sudden-
ness of his defection. But to her surprise, she'd quickly
recovered. Relief, and with it, a different Caitlynn, had
emerged from the ashes. A stronger, more independent
person who knew what she wanted from life. And
what she wanted was not Michael Flynn, nor anyone
as shallow and materialistic as he. She wanted a man
who cared about others. A man who had ideals and
principles, and cared more about those than he did
about money.

What she'd felt for Michael had been affection
rather than true love; she understood that now. Their
engagement had been the end result of a childhood
friendship. Being betrothed to the man had been comfortable, easy, like wearing a well-worn shoe; unlikely
to leave either blister or callus. But there had been no
fireworks on either side. No fierce sparks, no breathless
passion or desire. No deep conversation nor any sharing of plans or ideas.

The next time around—if there ever was a next
time—she wanted a very different kind of love, with a
very different kind of man. One who would treat her
as his equal in every way, and celebrate her passionate
nature instead of trying to curb or tame it, as Michael
had always tried to do, even when they were children.

Life, she had written to Deirdre, pouring her heart
out after Michael's departure for America, was too
short to settle for anything less than what she wanted.
She saw that now. How could she have been so blind?
But Deirdre had never responded to her emotional

outpouring by so much as a single word. Even worse, her own letter had been opened and returned, postage due, with the cold comment "No such person at this address" dashed across the envelope in the bold, sure hand she now recognized as the doctor's.

Standing in the hallway of Lough House, staring at the returned letter, she'd grown suddenly cold, as if someone had walked over her grave.

Something was very wrong in London. Deirdre would never have ignored her letter, not in a million years. And especially not this letter!

For the two years she'd lived away, Deirdre had written often, her letters filled with lively anecdotes of her life in London as companion to Estelle Marsh, the fifteen-year-old ward of physician Dr. Donovan Fitzgerald.

There had been nothing in those elegantly written pages to indicate anything amiss. Nothing that would suggest Deirdre was unhappy, let alone planning to leave the doctor's household, never to be heard from again. Or at least, nothing that Caitlynn could discern. Quite the contrary, in fact.

Reading between the lines, she'd sensed a bubbling joy in Deirdre's letters that started in early spring of that year, and she had wondered—a little hurt, if truth were told—when Deirdre would finally see fit to share her newest secret.

I'm afraid for you, Dee, Caitlynn thought, her eyelids drooping with exhaustion. *Where are you? Please, God, let me find you, safe and well. . . .*

Chapter Two

Caitlyn slipped effortlessly into sleep, and from sleep, into dreaming.

She found herself in an unfamiliar house, wandering through a bewildering maze of stone, searching for her missing cousin.

"*Deirdre!* Where are you?" she called as she stumbled down passage after passage. "If you can hear me, answer me!"

But she heard only her own voice, echoing on the stillness.

Undaunted, she stroked the darkness with her fingertips, learning the empty shadows, the twists and turns of the house, by feel alone, reaching for new ways to go, like a blind woman learning a new face.

"Dee Dee! It's me, Cait! Where are you?"

"*Cait. . . . Oh, Cait. . . .*"

Cait's heart leaped with joy. Deirdre, at last!

Her cousin's voice shivered on the darkness, fading

28

gradually into profound silence once again.

"No, wait! Don't go! I'm here! I've come to bring you home! Where are you, Dee?"

Frantically she tore aside the garlands of sticky cobwebs that choked the passageways like waterweeds, reaching toward the sound of Deirdre's voice like a swimmer, reaching through dark fathoms of water to treasures buried just out of reach.

But, in the manner of dreams, she could get no closer, although she walked until her limbs felt like lead weights.

"Cait . . . oh, Cait . . . !"

"Dee! Thank God!"

She held her candle aloft. Through the veil of cobwebs that brushed her face and clung to her bare arms, she could see Deirdre's shadowy figure, as if she were seeing her through a rainy windowpane.

Deirdre's dark eyes were like great empty holes in her pale face. Her fair hair streamed past her shoulders to her waist, long strands of it swirling and lifting on the currents. Her generous mouth was turned down in sorrow. One arm lifted, fingers curved to beckon Caitlynn closer.

"Here I am, Caitlynn. Come to me."

"I can't, Dee Dee . . . I'm sorry . . . My legs . . ."

"Find me, Cait! Please. You must find me!"

Suddenly the candle guttered and went out with a soft hiss that was like a woman's sigh, plunging Caitlynn into obsidian darkness. The ground beneath her feet fell away, and she was falling through yawning blackness. Twisting and tumbling like a feather, head over heels through nothingness, knowing that when she hit bottom, she would die.

"Nooo!" she screamed, and sat bolt upright in her bed in the same instant as she would have landed.

29

Her heart was pounding in terror. Her face and throat were bathed in clammy sweat, although the room was far from warm. It was still quite dark, except for the banked fire behind the grate, which cast its ruddy gleam on everything.

Still trembling, she glanced fearfully at the connecting door. Was it her imagination, or had it closed just as she woke up? Imagination, she decided, shaking her head in self-disgust. It must be. Hadn't she locked the connecting door before retiring? Of course she had. She was behaving like a frightened child, seeing monsters and bogeymen where there were only shadows.

"Only a nightmare, ye blathering fool," she chided herself. "Just a bloody nightmare."

There was no Deirdre, and no cobwebs. Only the aftermath of a frightening dream, brought on by anxiety, hours of exhausting travel, and sleeping in a strange bed in a strange house.

Deirdre, like her nightmare, had vanished.

Where are you, Dee Dee? she wondered as she drifted off to sleep again.

Where?

She met her employer for the first time the following morning, when she literally ran into him in the foyer after breakfast.

At six feet, he was taller than she expected. Tall enough that she at five feet and six inches, had to tilt her head back to look up at him.

"Oh!" she cried, startled, grabbing his lapels for dear life to keep her balance

"Whoa!" He held her upper arms to steady her. Lively, dark blue eyes that snapped with intelligence searched her face. "Slow down . . . Miss O'Connor? It *is* Miss O'Connor, I presume?"

He wore his hair combed back, the wild black waves tamed except for several locks that fell across his brow. More inky strands brushed the starched wing collar of his snowy shirt, in fine contrast to his dark topcoat, trousers and knotted dark tie.

His features were fine yet stern in a lean face, the lower half of which was beard-shadowed, which gave him a swarthy, disreputable appearance. He had a slim masculine nose and a generous mouth that looked ready to smile but was thinned now in annoyance.

His most striking features were his eyes, framed with black lashes and topped with brows like hasty pen strokes, dashed across his forehead in scowling black ink. Both added wicked punctuation to a startlingly handsome face.

Indeed, he had all the attributes of a most attractive man. The good Lord knew he'd certainly knocked the wind out of her sails, and had her staring at him like a gaping fish. Unfortunately, he also looked as impatient as the Devil, and as bad-tempered as sin itself.

"When you're done with your inspection, madam, I have a sick patient to tend to," he snapped.

"Then go, sir, by all means. It's not as if I'm stopping you!" she shot back.

"I beg to differ, madam. I can go nowhere unless you first let go of my bloody coat."

Belatedly, Caitlynn realized she'd grabbed his lapels to steady herself when they collided—and was still hanging on to them.

"Oh! Forgive me!" she exclaimed as she released him. Brushing off his coat fronts, she held out her hand in forthright fashion. "You must be Dr. Fitzgerald. I'm Caitlynn O'Connor—"

"—and I'm late," he rasped. "You'll find my ward through there. Good day," he snapped, nodding at the dining room's double doors as he turned on his heel and strode away.

"Overjoyed to meet you, too, I'm sure, Doctor," Caitlynn tossed snippishly after his retreating back, all caution thrown to the winds in her annoyance.

To her horror, Fitzgerald froze, then turned slowly about to face her. He looked even taller and more ominous than he had at first glance. A dangerous light had kindled in his eyes now, too. A murderous light. Despite it, he inclined his dark head, one side of his mouth curled up in a scornful twist.

"Much as I'd enjoy exchanging pleasantries with you, Miss O'Connor, I cannot. I have a dying man who needs me."

"Ready, sir!" an older man sang out, sticking his head around the open doorway. He was brandishing a carriage whip.

"I'll be right there, Tom. *Bridget!* My bag!"

"Coming, Dr. Fitzgerald!" Bridget flew down the stairs, her face flushed, her eyes dancing. She was carrying a physician's black instrument bag. "Here you are, sir."

"There's my good girl. I can always count on you, can I not, Bridget?" The doctor cast Caitlynn a withering look, intended, no doubt, to remind her of her own shortcomings.

But instead of blushing with shame, she bristled. And, when their eyes clashed, her green to his dark blue, she refused to meekly lower her gaze. To her delight, in the end it was he, not she, who turned aside, though she fancied it was only the urgency of his mission that forced him to look away.

"Sir?" Bridget bobbed her master a curtsey, glancing uncertainly from Fitzgerald to Caitlynn as she handed the doctor his instrument bag. Obviously, she sensed the crackling current that ran between them.

"Thank you, Bridget." Straightway, Fitzgerald was through the door, gone to wherever doctors went in emergencies, leaving the air unsettled in his wake.

"St. Bart's Hospital," Bridget supplied, as if she could read Caitlynn's thoughts. "St. Bartholomew's, that is, over by Smithfield Meat Market. The hospital's messenger came to fetch him a few minutes ago. He's a very dedicated man, is Dr. Fitzgerald."

"A veritable saint, perhaps—but not a very nice one, I'm after thinking, for all his pretty looks."

Bridget's lips tightened. She did not like to hear her hero maligned. "You just caught him in a rush, ma'am—Miss Caitlynn. He's a good man, is Dr. Fitzgerald. Thinks nothing of leaving his dinner or getting up from his bed of a night t'take care of someone who's sickly, rich or poor alike. An' he teaches medicine, makes morning and afternoon rounds, and has clinics for the poor and needy besides, God bless him. Ye won't catch one of them Harley Street doctors lifting a finger t'help the likes of us! 'Bog Irish,' that's what they call us, looking down their long English noses at us."

"Indeed? Then I stand corrected," Caitlynn said, amused by Bridget's eagerness to defend her handsome employer. "For the man must surely walk on water, since you're saying it's exhaustion that makes him so . . . abrupt?" She threw up her hands. "No, don't answer that. Mrs. Montgomery will have your guts for garters if you gossip to me about 'The Family.' It's high time I met Miss Estelle for myself, I do believe. Wish me luck."

With that, she waved away any comment Bridget may have intended to make, took a deep breath and sailed into the dining room, hoping she looked the part of a proper lady's companion.

The bodice of her snowy blouse was accented by a deep lace flounce, its high collar set off by a small oval cameo. Her trim waist was hugged by a hunter-green skirt, and beneath it, two layers of petticoats rustled crisply as she walked.

Caitlynn's expectations of the doctor's ward evaporated within minutes of meeting the girl.

She'd fully expected her charge to be the spoiled brat Bridget had described, a demanding invalid who nagged and whined to get her way, ruling the household from her bed. But Caitlynn was pleasantly surprised.

Estelle Marsh was a sweet-natured, angelic young woman with a mass of golden ringlets and a flawless complexion. Although she was pale, her cheeks bloomed with delicate shades of pink. Her eyes were the powder-blue of forget-me-nots, and just as lovely and innocent.

"Oh, good morning! You must be my new companion. Or should I say, my newest friend?" she greeted Caitlynn, smiling sweetly in welcome as Cait entered the room. She was seated in a wicker bathchair on wheels, which had been pulled up to the dining table. Her legs were covered by a plaid carriage rug. "I'm so happy to meet you, Miss O'Connor. It *is* Miss O'Connor, isn't it?"

"Indeed it is. And it's a pleasure to meet you, too, Miss Marsh." She offered her hand in forthright fashion, delighted when Estelle accepted it in the same manner.

" 'Miss Marsh'! Oh, please, you must call me Estelle. Dee Dee always called me Estelle. I do so hate to be formal and proper, don't you?"

Caitlynn's heart skipped a beat with excitement. *Dee Dee!* "Yes, yes, I do, Estelle. Who is Dee Dee?" she asked, feigning ignorance.

"She was my last companion. Miss Deirdre Riordan. She left without a word to me, and never came back." Sadness crossed the girl's lovely face. "I still miss her so. I told Donovan—Uncle Donovan, that is—that I did not want another companion. That no one could ever take her place. But he insisted. You won't do that, will you, Miss O'Connor? Leave me, I mean. I couldn't bear it if it should happen again."

"I shall never leave without telling you, not if I can possibly help it," Caitlynn said frankly. "Is that good enough for you?"

She did not believe in making promises she might not be able to keep. When she found Deirdre, she would persuade her to return to Ireland and her frantic parents, unless Deirdre insisted on staying here in London for some reason.

"Oh, yes," Estelle said, favoring her with a dazzling smile that was more adult than child. "More than good enough. I do believe I can trust you to always tell me the truth, Miss O'Connor. You have honest eyes, and don't make promises you cannot keep. I like that."

"You can trust me, Estelle. Always."

"Tell me, have you had your breakfast yet?"

"I have."

"Good. Then you shall sit here beside me. We'll talk and get to know each other better while I finish mine, shall we? Mmmm, Rose's strawberry jam is just scrumptious, isn't it? Won't you have some?"

"I couldn't, really, but thank you for asking." Caitlynn sat in the chair Estelle indicated, warming to the young woman's engaging manner immediately.

"Tell me, what shall we do today?" Caitlynn asked later, as Estelle dabbed crumbs of her toast and strawberry jam from her lips. "Would you like me to read to you, or sew, or do something else entirely?"

"Something else entirely. Let's go out. We'll drive through the park and feed the ducks. It's my very favorite thing to do, and I haven't been there since Miss Dee Dee left. The poor things are always hungry, especially when the weather turns cold."

"But . . . can you? Go out, I mean?" Involuntarily, her gaze dropped to Estelle's lower body and the wheeled chair. The young woman could not help knowing what she must be thinking, Caitlynn realized, her face reddened by embarrassment. "I'm sorry, but I don't want to do anything that will endanger your health."

Estelle laughed. "You're quite right, of course. I cannot go out on my own. These silly old legs of mine don't work very well. But if you ask Tom to ready the pony and trap, he can carry me down to it, just as he carries me downstairs for my meals."

"Who's Tom?"

"Rose Larkin's husband. Rose is the cook here. Didn't you meet her at breakfast? The Larkins live over the carriage house. They are such dears, and very kind to me."

Tom must be the older man who drove for the doctor and did the work of handyman about the house. "Very well. But . . . will your guardian permit such an outing?"

A peal of laughter followed her question. "Of course he will! He bought me the pony and trap for my birthday last year. He says being outside is good for my constitution. He encourages me to go out and get as much fresh air as I can. He's very clever and modern in his thinking," she added proudly. "Quite the finest doctor in all of London. Other doctors think he is mad, but he isn't. He's brilliant."

Caitlynn smiled. Obviously, his bearish temperament notwithstanding, Dr. Fitzgerald had captured the heart of every young female in the household—with the exception of her own. Personally, she found him bad-tempered and unnecessarily brusque.

"Very well, then. An outing in the park it shall be. You finish your hot chocolate. I'll ask Rose for a stale loaf and fetch our cloaks and bonnets."

"All right. Miss Caitlynn?"

"Yes, Estelle?" She turned to look back at the girl from the doorway.

"I do like you very much. And I think we're going to be great friends."

Caitlynn retraced her footsteps. Reaching out, she touched Estelle's cheek—she couldn't help herself. "So do I, darling girl. So do I."

"Bravo! But what of me? Am I to be included in your friendship?" demanded a voice from the doorway.

"Hello, Uncle Declan," Estelle sang out, laughing.

"Hello, minx. And hello to you, too, miss," the tall newcomer declared as he came in, turning to Caitlynn with an appreciative grin. He looked her up and down. "Ahh. You must be the long-awaited new companion. Enchanté, mademoiselle."

The man with laughing brown eyes took her hand, drew it to his lips and kissed it. "I'm Declan Fitzgerald, barrister-at-law. Donovan's younger, very successful and much more handsome brother," he added with a wicked wink. "What a pity I can't accompany you to the park, but I'm due in court at nine. Estelle, mavourneen, will you share a bite of that toast and jam with your old uncle?"

"Why? Has your serving woman left you again, Uncle Declan?"

"Hmm. Something like that," Declan agreed with an airy grin, helping himself to a triangle of buttery toast. He winked. "Hmmm. Blasted woman expected to be paid. The very nerve!"

Chapter Three

Estelle loved Huntington Park, Caitlynn thought as the girl drove the small dogcart through the park gates and along the winding pathway for what was surely the fifth time in as many weeks.

They had come here at least once a week since Caitlynn's arrival at the beginning of October. It was now November, yet Estelle showed no signs of tiring of the place. She much preferred driving the dogcart through the park to staying at home and doing decoupage or marquetry, playing pianoforte, embroidering fire screens, or any of the other new pastimes Caitlynn offered to teach her. She had even rejected suggestions that they choose another destination for their drives, claiming she was afraid to wander too far afield.

"Perhaps you are unaware of it, Miss Caitlynn, coming from Ireland as you do, but a murderer has been roaming the streets of London for over a month," she explained in the adult, world-weary voice that so reminded Caitlynn of Little Maggie, her thirteen-year-old sister.

"He calls himself Saucy Jacky and has killed at least three women so far. *Wicked* women. It is all any of the newspapers can talk about." Her blue eyes shone with a mixture of lurid fascination and girlish horror. "And Scotland Yard is quite baffled."

"Is it indeed? And how is it you know so much about such terrible goings-on, miss?" Caitlynn asked, trying to sound stern.

Estelle laughed. "Don't look so cross. I hear all the gossip from Rose. Dear Rose! She tells me everything. And what she leaves out—the juiciest, bloodiest parts!—I read about in Mrs. Montgomery's penny dreadfuls."

Cait's eyebrows rose. "Montgomery reads the penny dreadfuls?" The lurid scandal sheets carried graphic accounts of the murders, accompanied by garish pictorials. By no stretch of the imagination could she imagine the formidable Montgomery poring over them—though that did not mean Estelle was lying. Mrs. Montgomery struck Cait as the sort of woman who might indulge in any number of strange vices in secret.

"You wicked child!" Caitlynn exclaimed, but she laughed nonetheless. "Don't they give you nightmares?"

"Not at all, Miss Caitlynn. Why ever should they? We're still going to the lake, are we not?" she asked anxiously, adroitly changing the subject.

"Of course we are. A promise is a promise.

Caitlynn suspected that Estelle loved the park so very much because when she was handling the reins of the pony cart, she was almost like everyone else: whole, healthy and well in control of her life, no longer an invalid to be pitied for her wasted legs and confined to her bed or the bathchair, unable to go anywhere unless someone carried her.

Here, she was free as a bird, just like any of the other pedestrians strolling through the park with their dogs, or the nannies that promenaded their young charges in gleaming perambulators during the summer months.

It saddened Caitlynn to see such a lovely young woman denied a normal existence. She was still determined that Estelle's jaunts should have a wider scope someday, but for now, a drive through the beautiful old park, once a royal hunting reserve, would have to serve.

They drove between an allée of horse-chestnut trees with branches that almost met overhead. From time to time, Estelle halted the pony so that Caitlynn could climb down to gather handfuls of the prickly green horse-chestnut seeds scattered over the pathway or hidden in the frosty grass. When split open, the seed pods revealed the shiny reddish-brown 'conkers' so beloved by little boys—and girls.

"Why are you gathering those?" Estelle asked, watching her curiously with her fair head cocked. "Horse chestnuts aren't good to eat, you know."

"I know. I'm not going to eat them. I'm going to fight with them."

"Fight? But how?"

"You'll see when we get home. You make a hole through the middle of the conker with a meat skewer, then thread a piece of string through the hole and knot it at one end, so that the conker can't fall off. Then I take my conker by its string and swing it at yours. If I can break your conker in half, I win. If you can break mine, you win."

"What a silly game!"

"Silly, perhaps—but great fun. Do you want to try when we get home?"

Estelle wrinkled her delectable nose. With her angelic face framed by a fur-trimmed scarlet bonnet, she was drawing the eyes of more than one of the young men who happened to ride or walk past them. And Caitlynn was convinced the precocious minx knew it, too!

"Aren't conker fights just for little boys?"

"Not just boys, no. I used to have conker fights with my brothers every autumn when I was a little girl. So what do you say? Will you be a good sport, Miss Marsh, or a sniveling coward, afraid to match her puny conker against my robust champion?" Caitlynn, looking very fierce, brandished the biggest conker aloft.

"Very well. Challenge accepted!" Estelle agreed, laughing. "Get up there, Buster!"

The fat little pony trotted past the arboretum which, in warmer months, promised to be a charming spot to stop and enjoy the sundial and the tiny waterfall. There were mossy statues rising from the banks of a water-lily pond, lichened chubby male cherubs for the most part. Unusual trees and exotic climbing plants grew wild up and over the trellises, and all around the wrought-iron benches.

Today the enormous ornamental lake gleamed dully, like an antique glass of polished silver. A thin layer of ice covered it in places, but it was not nearly hard enough for skating. The lake's irregular borders were fringed by irises, rushes and skeletal trees, mostly silver birches and weeping willows. The trees' delicate branches and pale trunks traced a fragile pattern against the gunmetal sky and cast shifting shadows on the surface of the water.

There was a stone bridge across the narrowest portion of the lake. Just below it squatted a small wooden boathouse.

"That's where they store the skiffs in winter months," Estelle had explained the first time they'd gone there. "In summer, we can take them out and spend the afternoon rowing on the lake."

Today, however, a ragged lad of about thirteen was standing by the boathouse. A catapult dangled from his fist. Loaded with stones, the weapon had already proven deadly. The limp body of a duck lay huddled on the grass beside him.

"There he is again, that wretched boy!" Estelle exclaimed excitedly. "Look! He's always hanging about and staring at me!"

Caitlynn was about to scold the boy for his thievery when he suddenly spotted them. His freckled face blanched. Grabbing the duck by its neck, he hared off across the park, headed for the gates.

"Filthy little ragamuffin!" Estelle spat out. "He was poaching—did you see, Miss Caitlynn? He had a dead duck by the neck."

"I saw it. But he's gone now. And I'm sure the poor duck gave its life for a good reason." The boy had been barefoot despite the weather, ragged and thin beneath his too small clothes.

"Reason! What possible reason could there be?"

"Not every child in London has a doting guardian to care for his or her needs, as do you," she pointed out. "Perhaps the duck will feed a hungry family tonight. A poor family that has nothing to eat."

"Hmm." Estelle seemed unmoved. "Miss Dee Dee and I used to come here all the time, you know."

"You did?"

"Yes. Rose used to pack us a picnic basket. Sometimes Miss Dee Dee would manage to get me into the boat and we'd row on the lake. Or else we'd lie on the banks and read or play Patience. We had so much fun." A wistful shadow flitted across her lovely face.

Caitlynn nodded in understanding. Her cousin had always loved the water. She could easily imagine Deirdre enjoying herself here, decked out in a sailor collar and saucy sailor hat, rowing one of the little skiffs, just as they had once rowed Timothy's dory about on the lake at home, laughing and sharing girlish secrets. Her throat constricted. Would they ever share such idyllic times again? *Oh, Deirdre, where are you?*

"I know. But we'll have fun, too, once the weather is warmer," Caitlynn promised huskily. Estelle must have been very close to Deirdre.

"Promise?" Estelle whispered, her lower lip trembling. Tears made her eyes bright. For once, she seemed younger than her fifteen years. A sad and lonely child, rather than a beautiful young girl on the brink of womanhood.

"If I'm still here, yes."

"If? But why wouldn't you be here?" Alarm widened Estelle's blue eyes. There was panic in her voice.

"I don't know, darling. Anything could happen. Mrs. Montgomery may have sacked me by then," she teased.

"No, she won't! I won't let her. I'll tell Uncle Donovan to let you stay forever and ever, and to sack her instead, the nasty old thing. I hate her!"

With the little boy and his slingshot gone, swans, geese and ducks, sighting the pony cart and anticipating a feast, paddled or came waddling toward the path, quacking noisily.

Their wings clipped, the comical birds were unable to fly south to warmer climes like their wild brothers.

44

Obsession

Not surprisingly under the circumstances, the young women, with their generous rations of stale bread and currant buns, were welcome visitors.

Estelle reined the pony in close to the water's edge, while Caitlynn got down from the smart black-and-gold trimmed dogcart. She broke the stale loaf Rose had provided into pieces, handing some to Estelle.

They laughed as two of the boldest ducks noisily fought for the same scattered crumbs that bobbed on the shallows, quacking loudly. Their beating wings hurled crystals of icy water in every direction.

"Miss O'Connor! Estelle, my dear! What a charming picture the two of you make."

"Dr. Fitzgerald. Good day." Caitlynn inclined her head politely, but felt no real pleasure at seeing her employer so unexpectedly in the middle of the day, for all that he cut a handsome figure in his dark tweed greatcoat and woolen muffler.

She and the doctor had got off to a bad start the morning after her arrival when they collided in the foyer. The somewhat stormy interview that followed the next morning in the doctor's study had not helped.

"Ah, Miss O'Connor. Please have a seat. This will only take a few minutes, and then I will let you resume your duties," the doctor began that morning.

"Very well." She inclined her head and sat with her hands folded in her lap, staring at him without smiling, in the way that used to unnerve her brothers. He had been rude to her when she accidentally ran into him the day before, and she did not have a forgiving nature. No. She carried grudges, her brothers had also discovered. To her way of thinking, the doctor owed her an apology.

"Yes. Well, I wanted to discuss your duties with you after you'd met Estelle. You knew when you accepted

45

Penelope Neri

the position that she was an invalid, did you not?"

His voice was deep and dark and made her think of Irish whisky.

"Yes. They told me at the Kelly Agency that Miss Marsh is bedridden."

"Yes, well, that's not exactly true, though it's close enough. Estelle has a weakened heart, and because of it, she tires easily, so I expect her to rest most afternoons and not overexert herself."

"I quite understand. Quiet pursuits, such as needlework and watercolors, as long as the colors aren't too bright, or the needles too sharp, of course." Try as she might, she could not keep the sarcastic edge from her voice.

"Er—yes. Exactly." His scowl said he wondered if she was making fun of him. "On the other hand, I don't want her confined in an airless sickroom with the draperies drawn for hours on end, waited on hand and foot like a hothouse lily."

"No?" She couldn't quite suppress a twitch at the corner of her mouth.

"Quite the contrary. I believe fresh air is good for everyone, invalids included. I encourage Estelle to go out several times a week, unless the weather is very bad. I believe such excursions are good for her, and good for her temperament, which can sometimes be a little . . . demanding."

"I couldn't agree with you more, Doctor. I very much enjoy the outdoors myself. I used to take long walks in the hills and around the lough. Back home in Ireland, that was, of course."

"Hrumph. Yes. Well. The other matter I wished to discuss with you is the problem of . . . attachment."

"Attachment?" She laughed. "What on earth do you mean by that, sir? Attachment to what?"

46

"It's not a question of what, but a question of *who*. Estelle became very attached to her last companion. But after two years with no complaints, the woman left my employ quite suddenly, without giving a moment's notice to anyone, including Estelle. My ward, needless to say, was devastated. I must ask you to give me your word that you will not engage Estelle's affections while you are here. For her sake." He eyed her expectantly.

"No. I think not."

He blinked. "No?"

"That's what I said, Doctor. *No.*"

"No, you won't give me your word, or no, you won't enagage Estelle's affections?"

"Both!"

"But it is in her best interests that you agree to this, Miss O'Connor. It is for her protection. Surely you see that? I should not like t'see her hurt again."

"What you are asking me to do is to maintain a polite distance from the girl. To be cold. To never respond to her with an affectionate hug or a kiss. To deny her all the little pleasures of having a friend. The person you want for your ward is not a companion, Dr. Fitzgerald, but a keeper. I suggest you go to Regent's Park Zoological Gardens. Good day." She got smartly to her feet and marched to the door, skirts crisply swishing.

"Where the devil do you think you're going?" he exploded, jumping to his feet.

"Back to Ireland, sir, since 'tis quite obvious you don't need me here."

In the end, he had agreed to let her stay on her own terms. To her satisfaction, he had also grudgingly muttered his apologies for his brusque manner the day before, his lips saying one thing and his eyes entirely another.

There had been precious few opportunities since then to change her unfavorable opinion of the man, however. In fact, she rarely saw him, which was exactly as she liked it. She had noticed that he went out frequently at night, and she wondered at the purpose of those nocturnal jaunts.

Estelle, who took her supper with her guardian whenever he was at home, felt no such reticence toward him. She reached down from the pony cart and hugged him about the neck, kissing him squarely on the lips. "Hello, Donovan."

"It's *Uncle* Donovan, Estelle," he reminded her sternly, untangling her arms from about his neck and looking somewhat embarrassed as he did so. "You look very fetching today. Scarlet becomes you. Have you been helping Miss Caitlynn to settle in?"

"Of course I have, *Uncle* Donovan," the girl teased, her blue eyes sparkling. "Haven't I, Miss Caitlynn?" She looked imploringly at Caitlynn for confirmation. "I've been the perfect hostess."

"She has indeed, sir," Caitlynn murmured, self-consciously tucking a wayward curl inside her bonnet.

"I'm very glad to hear it," Donovan Fitzgerald said gravely. "Just as I'm delighted to see you both out and about. Estelle knows the benefits of being outdoors, don't you, poppet? The fresh air does wonders for the constitution. Just look at the roses in your cheeks!"

His comment included both young women, but he was staring at Caitlynn as he said the latter, and his grave, thoughtful expression belied his words and was oddly disturbing to her.

What was going on behind those long dark lashes?

she wondered. What did the doctor think of her, if he thought of her at all, which she doubted.

Declan had been wrong for once, Donovan thought with surprise as he regarded Estelle's new companion. The O'Connor woman was no beauty—at least, not in the classical, accepted sense of the word, he realized, staring at her as if he were meeting her for the very first time.

She was, however, quite lovely, her loveliness a combination of glowing complexion, good bones and radiant good health. These, coupled with intelligence and strength of character, were more alluring than fashionable claims to beauty.

Her shamrock-green eyes sparkled beneath tawny arches. Those eyes, he noticed, the few times he'd seen her, changed whenever her mood changed, as mercurial as the sea; a dreamy green one moment, and the next, an electric emerald that threw off sparks as her temper flared. Her flawless creamy complexion contrasted well with her hair, which was the deep dark brown of luxurious sable. A small, well-shaped nose offset a surprisingly carnal mouth, with lips that were ripely defined, and totally at odds with both her simple loveliness and her occupation. No proper lady's companion should have such wanton lips. Nor such bewitching eyes . . .

Exhaustion slipped from him like a bad dream.

"Is that a conker you have there, Miss O'Connor?" he asked teasingly as he reached for the prickly green ball. It was all he could think of to say. "How odd. I've lived on the square for years and never noticed the horse-chestnut trees before."

"Sometimes we look but we don't really see, Doctor," she murmured, drawing her hand away and

49

sweeping the conker out of his reach. "Much like those who listen but never really hear."

The woman spoke in riddles! "Please. May I see it?" he demanded, annoyed that she would whisk the bloody conker out of reach.

"No, Doctor," she refused in her lilting brogue, acting on impulse and looking not in the least bit sorry. In fact, she was smiling as she said it. "If it's a conker you're after, you'll have to find your own. *Sir.*" The 'sir' was an obvious afterthought, as if she was not accustomed to calling anyone 'sir.'

"Surely you're joking." Although he laughed, he was irritated.

"Indeed, no. If you want to challenge either of us to a conker fight, you must find your own weapons, sir. These conkers belong to the ladies' team. Estelle and myself."

The teasing green eyes that met his sparkled with challenge—and mischief.

Out of the blue, he caught himself staring back at her, slack-jawed, enchanted, annoyed all at the same time. The infant he'd delivered last night was forgotten, along with the fact that he had yet to go to bed, or that a night's growth of beard had undoubtedly given him a more evil cast than usual.

For once, he forgot all about his patients. Forgot his physician's oath. He was just a man, with a man's needs, in the presence of a highly desirable young woman who, by God, was laughing at him!

Tired eyes narrowing, he wondered how her sparkling green eyes might look darkened by desire. Or how those laughing lips might taste crushed beneath his own. Or how—

"Oh, go on, Miss Caitlynn! Let Uncle Donovan see the conkers, do!"

Estelle's pleading voice interrupted his brief but highly pleasurable reverie. For once, he could cheerfully strangle the brat.

"He's far too busy with his horrid patients to bother with our silly games, aren't you, Uncle dear?" Estelle pouted prettily.

"I am, yes," he heard himself agree, sounding like some stuffy old boor. "Much too busy. Please, ladies, carry on. Enjoy your outing, Estelle. Miss O'Connor."

Tipping his hat to the young women in turn, he beat a hasty exit, continuing his shortcut across the park to his residence, and cursing his cowardice with every step he took.

He could feel the O'Connor woman's eyes boring holes into his back as he went, blast her!

Lovely or not, she was every bit as prickly as her bloody conkers. Like a damned hedgehog.

"Now look! You frightened him off!" Estelle accused, sounding annoyed for the first time since Caitlynn's arrival. "He would have stayed and fed the ducks with us if only you'd let him look at the silly conkers."

Caitlynn shrugged. "I'm sorry. I didn't expect your guardian to take offense over some harmless teasing." Arrogant clod. He'd acted like a spoiled child denied its sugar teat.

"Well, he did, and it was all because of what you said."

"Well, I can't unsay it, can I, now?" She smiled, trying to coax a smile back to Estelle's face. "'What's done is done and can't be mended,' my mother used to say. So, since there's nothing we can do about it, let's enjoy ourselves, feed the ducks and forget about him, shall we?"

Bloody miserable devil, Caitlynn thought, flinging

51

stale bits of bread with such force, the hungry birds
were forced to duck or be brained. Donovan Fitzgerald
was as big a baby as her little brother, Patrick, hurrying off in a pout because she hadn't jumped to do
his bidding. The devil she would apologize to him, despite what Estelle seemed to expect of her.

"Feeding the ducks would have been much more fun
with Uncle Donovan," Estelle said stubbornly, staring
down at the dark lake.

"More fun than we're having? I doubt that," Caitlynn insisted brightly, prepared for a rough day of it.

But within a few moments, Estelle was throwing bits
of bread to the ducks and chattering blithely, the silly
incident forgotten and Caitlynn quite forgiven.

*Thank God the child isn't given to moods, like her
guardian,* Caitlynn thought later that afternoon as she
climbed aboard the pony cart for their short drive
home.

Not for the first time, she found herself wondering
about the relationship between the doctor and his
ward.

Was Fitzgerald Estelle's uncle by blood—the daughter of a dead sister, perhaps—or her uncle by marriage? Or was 'uncle' merely the respectful way the
doctor preferred to be addressed by her, although he
was only her legal guardian? Or . . . could he possibly
be her natural father? It was unlikely but far from impossible, now that she thought about it. The doctor
was surely no more than thirty, thirty-three at most,
which would have made him only a lad of fifteen or
so at the time he sired the child on his mistress, child
bride or whatever.

She shook her head. Her imagination was running
away with her again. What nonsense she was thinking!
Estelle was right. She was being silly today, sounding

for all the world like a character from one of the
Brontë novels she so enjoyed reading.

"Hang on tight, Miss Cait!" Estelle clicked the pony
into a speedy trot, laughing in sheer delight as the wind
ruffled the blond ringlets that streamed from beneath
her scarlet velvet bonnet.

Caitlynn grabbed hold of the seat to steady herself
just in time. The pony cart bowled through the frosty
park at a spanking pace, red wheels spinning over the
hard ground.

Watching her charge, Caitlynn could not help thinking about the magnificent, vital woman Estelle could
have become had she not lost the use of her legs. What
cruel God could have taken both parents from her, as
well as the mobility that would have allowed her to
live a normal existence?

That evening, while the doctor and Estelle dined on
roasted mutton with capers and mint sauce and all the
accompaniments, Caitlynn enjoyed Rose Larkin's tasty
lamb stew with herb dumplings and green tomato
chutney in the congenial company of the servants,
Tom, Annie, Bridget and Rose herself.

Mrs. Montgomery had a tray sent up to her room
every evening, preferring not to socialize with the others, whom she considered beneath her. The arrange-
ment was very much to everyone's liking, since to a
man, the others preferred not to socialize with *her*.

"Can't abide her superior ways, I can't," Rose observed, ladling savory lamb stew into sturdy earthenware bowls.

"Plays merry hell with my appetite," Tom agreed,
flashing his wife a grin. "Dyspepsia, the doctor calls
it."

"Heartburn, more like," Rose clarified. "Whenever

that Mary Montgomery comes down here, my poor Tom gets heartburn."

"Did Miss Riordan take her supper here with you, or alone in her room?" Caitlynn asked casually.

"In her room most evenings," Annie said quickly. "Thought she was too good for the likes of us, she did."

"Now then, Annie, that wasn't it at all," Rose chided. "Miss Deirdre was on the shy side, and Mrs. Montgomery couldn't abide her from the very first. Never missed a chance to find fault with her, she didn't. I think the poor love kept to her room as much as possible just to keep out of her way. It had nothing to do with any of us. Always nice to us, she was."

"Was that why she left here, do you think? Because the housekeeper had it in for her?"

"Hardly. She left because she knew that if she didn't, she'd be dismissed. Pass the 'taties, if you please, Mr. Larkin," Annie cut in quickly, ignoring Rose's glare. "Well, it's true, Mrs. Larkin, is it not?"

"No. I don't know that it's true at all," Rose said sharply in answer to Annie's comment. To Caitlynn, Rose said, "Annie had no business saying what she did."

She glared at the maid. Annie bowed her head as Rose turned back to Caitlynn.

"I suppose you might as well know. What she means is, some of Miss Estelle's pretty trinkets disappeared just before Miss Riordan left us. Nothing very valuable, just one or two little bits and pieces the doctor'd given her over the years. Our Mrs. Montgomery found out about it. She was convinced the girl had . . . well, that she'd pilfered them. Mrs. Montgomery threatened Miss Deirdre. Said she was going to tell the doctor all about it the next day, and have her sacked for stealing. Miss Riordan was so upset.

"She was out all that day with Miss Estelle; then she retired very early that night without her supper tray. None of us saw her after that. In the morning, she was gone."

"And she never came back," Caitlynn said softly.

"Never." Bridget said. "While we were cleaning out her room, me and Annie found Miss Estelle's missing bracelet in a drawer amongst Miss Deirdre's things," she said with obvious reluctance.

"But if she ran away, why wouldn't she take her own things with her? It makes no sense," Caitlynn mused aloud, looking around the circle of faces. "When she left, she obviously expected to come back here, unless—she didn't send someone for her belongings, perhaps?"

Bridget shook her head. "No. After a week or two, Mrs. Montgomery told me to box everything up and have Mr. Larkin take her things to the poorhouse, or give them to the rag-and-bone man, did she not, ma'am?" Bridget looked to Rose for confirmation.

The woman nodded. "Aye. Said it was on the doctor's orders. To be sure, there wasn't much by way of belongings to worry about."

"Miss Deirdre once told me she had only one thing of any value, and that was her diary," Bridget said. "'Twas a gift from her cousin in Ireland, she said. Like sisters, they were. She was always writing in it."

A chill trickled down Caitlynn's spine.

"A five-year diary! Oh, thank you, Cait! It's just what I've always wanted!" she heard a younger Deirdre exclaim in her memory. *"Sure, an' 'tis the happiest birthday I've ever had—and the very best present!"*

"*Look, Dee Dee. There's a little key on a ribbon. A fairy key. It opens the tiny lock.*"

"*So it does.*" Her wide brown eyes were shining. "*Now my secrets will be safe forever and ever, darlin' Cait.*"

"Oh? How very . . . odd," Caitlynn said aloud, controlling her emotions with the utmost difficulty. "And what happened to the diary when Miss Riordan left?"

Bridget shrugged innocently. "Far as we can tell, Miss-Deirdre took it with her. It was the only thing of hers that was missing, except for the clothes on her back, of course."

"And the crucifix," Annie reminded them.

"Oh, that's right. I'd forgotten about the cross and chain. Pretty piece it was, too. Real gold. It was never found," Bridget added.

"Stolen from her last employer, I shouldn't wonder." Annie snorted.

"Annie Elizabeth Murphy! Is there not an ounce of Christian kindness in you? I'll put up with no such spiteful talk at my table!" Rose scolded. "If you've nothing nice to say, then off to your room with you, my girl."

The atmosphere in the servants' hall changed tangibly after sulky Annie flounced off. It was as if a cloud had lifted, to let the sun shine through.

"We have to be careful what we say in front of Annie," Bridget explained to Caitlynn in a low voice. "Never a nice word about Mrs. M., Annie hasn't, but she's always first t'go running to her with tales about everyone else's doings. How about some nice custard on that blackberry crumble, Miss Caitlynn?"

"Mmm, please! Why did Mrs. M. dislike De—dislike the last companion so much? Do you know?"

"Jealous of her, I always thought," Rose said.

"Didn't you, Bridget?" The maid nodded her agreement. "See, Miss Estelle loved Miss Deirdre, she did. That's reason enough for Mrs. M. to have had it in for her."

"You watch out for yourself, miss. Don't go letting the old battle-ax run you off, too," Tom Larkin warned in his gruff voice, removing the pipe from his mouth for only as long as it took to offer the rare comment. The hand gripping the pipe stem was liver-spotted with age. His hair, moustache and brows were as white as snow, yet his eyes were a lively gray and his body whipcord-lean and still as spry as that of a much younger man.

"Don't you worry, Mr. Larkin. I'm made of far sterner stuff than your poor Miss Riordan. I don't frighten off so easily."

"I'm right happy to hear it."

"Is there a Catholic church close by? I really do need to find a church. I haven't been to confession in weeks."

"There aren't many Catholic churches hereabouts," Rose said. "The closest would be St. Anthony's in the East End. That's where I go. Miss Riordan went to church there every Sunday, regular as clockwork."

"Did you go with her?"

"Not me," Bridget said. "Oh, I wanted to, but Montgomery wouldn't give me Sundays off, so I go to evening mass on Saturdays instead."

Tomorrow was Thursday, and Caitlynn's own afternoon off. She decided she would spend her free time talking to cabbies and priests, showing Deirdre's picture to anyone who might have seen her after she left number 13 Huntington Square.

As long as she was home by dark, the East End was as good a place as any to begin her search, surely?

Chapter Four

"You'll want to be getting home before dusk, miss," a police constable warned her late the following afternoon. "After dark, these streets are no place for ladies."

"Not for any decent woman by day *or* by night," his companion warned grimly.

The two police constables wore tall 'bucket' helmets and dark uniform jackets and trousers. Sturdy truncheons swung from their belts, as did whistles on chains.

The constables, PC Johns and PC Reece, were just one of many two-man police patrols assigned to comb the East End day and night, going house to house and asking questions in the hope of finding the Whitechapel Murderer before he claimed another victim.

Several of the Ripper murders had been committed right under the noses of these police patrols, and yet the murderer had somehow managed to escape.

"Shall I whistle you up a cab, miss?"

"No, thank you, Constable Johns," Caitlynn murmured, favoring him with a grateful smile. "I have to go into St. Anthony's first. I shan't be long."

"Right you are, miss."

Smiling, she turned away and started up the few steps to St. Anthony's wooden door, covering her head and bonnet with a black lace veil before going inside.

It was gloomy and smelled musty inside the church, which was empty except for an old woman and a shabbily dressed younger woman in her twenties. The scents of candle wax and flowers were familiar, comforting ones, a link of custom and faith to the family she loved across the water.

Genuflecting, Caitlynn made her way down the aisle to the front pew, where she knelt and closed her eyes.

Deep in prayer, she fervently asked God to watch over her family, and to help her in her search for Deirdre.

She was still praying when she heard footsteps on the tiled floor. Opening her eyes, she saw a priest wearing a black cassock.

"Forgive me for disturbing you, my daughter. I must prepare for Evensong."

"Not at all, Father. To be honest, I wanted to speak with you," she said, rising and walking toward him.

"On a matter of faith, my child?"

"No. Not this time. It's about my cousin, Deirdre Riordan. She's missing, Father . . . ?"

"Robert. Father Robert," the assistant priest said. "What did you say your cousin's name was?"

"Deirdre Riordan."

The priest frowned. Obviously, the name was not familiar to him. "I'm sorry, my child. There's no one by that name in our congregation. Did someone tell you you might find her here?"

"Rose Larkin, the cook at the household where I'm employed, said Deirdre used to come here for Sunday services. I was hoping that perhaps you'd seen her." She turned her head. "My cousin was last seen on July ninth of this year at number thirteen Huntington Square. She often came here on her afternoon off. She was about my height, but had brown eyes and fair hair." She fumbled in her drawstring bag and withdrew the ambrotype of her cousin. "This is she."

"A very pretty girl."

"Very."

"I'm sure I would have noticed her if she'd been here. I may be a priest, but I'm still a man. We never lose our eye for a pretty lady." His brown eyes twinkled. "I'm sorry, my child. I wish I could help you, but I can't. Why don't you come back when Father Timothy is here? He may be able to help you. I'm only his assistant, you see."

"I will. Thank you, Father."

It was late afternoon. The sky was a lowering charcoal, streaked with a malevolent sulphur, as she left the church. The light had already begun to fade, but the lamplighter was nowhere in sight and the gaslights were as yet unlit.

Crossing the street, Caitlynn walked briskly westward, her head up as she passed rows of rookeries, sweatshops, factories and public houses. The old buildings rubbed shoulders with men's social clubs, slaughter yards and breweries.

The doorways and courts between the rookeries were crowded with frowzy washerwomen or poorly dressed 'unfortunates,' gossiping or arguing or soliciting passing men with crude catcalls that brought a blush to Caitlynn's cheeks. Most such women were to be pitied rather than condemned or blamed, she believed. From what she had read, such women were not so much immoral as desperate.

At the entrance to one dark court, surrounded on three sides by buildings with grimy yards, she saw a crowd of onlookers. They were staring at a spot on the pavement, ignoring the constables' urging for them to move on about their business.

From the scraps of conversation she overheard as she passed, the spot was where one of the latest murder victims had been found. Horrified, she quickened her pace.

Dirty, ragged children ran between the carts and wagons that trundled along the streets, dodging horses' hooves, wheels, thundering horsetrams and unsympathetic pedestrians alike with amazing agility—and even more amazing good fortune.

These little ones, filthy and poorly dressed, most of them barefooted, risked life and limb with neither nurses, nannies nor mamas anywhere in evidence to see to their care or to keep an eye out for their safety.

She had heard that many of these urchins headed into London's wealthier West End each morning to pick deeper, more affluent pockets, or to steal produce from the costermongers' barrows in Covent Garden, or meat from Smithfield Meat Market to fill hungry bellies or eke out their family's income.

"You bleeding little sod! Come back 'ere! Gimme back that bloomin' pear or I'll take off yer bloody nose!" one barrow boy bellowed after a young thief.

The little girl—about nine years old—tore past Caitlynn, cursing a blue streak as she went. Her face was grubby, her nose running like melted candle wax.

"Stop, thief!" came another yell.

As she passed a coffee stall, Caitlynn saw a freckle-faced lad fly across the street, his dirty bare feet pounding the wet cobbles, a loaf of bread tucked under one arm. She frowned. He looked like the same urchin she'd seen poaching ducks in the park. His pinched face was gray with terror, yet hard as flint beneath a ragged thatch of red hair as he made good his escape,

"Laidy! Laidy! Hold your horses, then, do!"

Caitlynn walked on briskly, ignoring the voice, unaware for several moments that the 'laidy' the female was calling was herself.

When a scrawny hand closed over her elbow, she reacted, certain she was warding off a female pickpocket who was after her purse.

"Oh, no, you don't, you wicked creature!" she cried, swatting the hand away.

"Wicked? Me? Hold yer blooming horses, laidy. I ain't after stealing nothing!"

Caitlynn saw that the indignant woman was about her own age, shabbily yet tidily dressed. She looked familiar.

"No? Then what are you after?" Caitlynn demanded, clutching her drawstring bag.

"Oh, I'm after yer money all right, don't get me wrong." The woman grinned. "I'm selling information."

"Oh? About what?" she asked warily.

"The woman you was asking the priest about. You know—the missing woman. Brown eyes, fair hair? But we can't do business out here in the street. It ain't . . . it ain't . . . appropriate. Tell you what, I'll let ye buy me a nice glass o' porter over at the Britannia. We'll talk there, all right, ducks?"

Without waiting for Caitlynn's answer, the woman turned and marched across the street toward the run-down building. She obviously expected Caitlynn to follow her if she wanted to hear what she had to say.

Caitlynn hesitated, then hurried after her.

It was not the first time she had been inside a public house. It was, however, the very first time she had been inside one with the Britannia's dubious reputation.

A popular rendezvous for prostitutes and their bullies, the Britannia was also a home-away-from-home for assorted pickpockets and thieves, judging by the look of the raffish clientele bellied up to the bar when the two women entered the pub.

"Double porter. Laidy's payin'," the woman told the bartender, elbowing her way up to the beer-stained bar. She jerked her thumb in Caitlynn's direction.

With that, she turned and wove her way through the crowd of standing drinkers to a small table in a corner. That left Caitlynn to fumble in her bag for the required coins, thank the leering publican, and follow with the woman's double port wine.

She knew, in that moment, what it felt like to be a butterfly, pinned to a slide and examined under the lens of her father's microscope.

Every male eye—and most of the female ones, too—were on her as she made her way to where the woman was sitting. They were hard, too-bright stares that assessed and speculated as if she were a racehorse about to run a steeplechase and they were avid gamblers.

She heard more than one lewd comment about her person as she passed between the drinkers. She was also almost certain she felt a hand upon her derriere, though surely nobody would dare touch a decent woman's posterior in so coarse a fashion, and in public, with so many police constables about.

"Is it always so crowded here?" she asked the woman, breathless as she took her seat.

"It is lately." She grinned. "Folks reckon there's safety in numbers."

"Safety from what?"

"Jack." When Caitlynn looked blank, the woman tsked and repeated, "Jack the Ripper. Saucy Jacky. The Whitechapel Murderer. Leather Apron, or whatever you want t'call him. This ain't your fancy West End, you know. Here, you're on Jacky's turf, like it or lump it, ducks."

Caitlynn bit her lip. "About the woman I'm looking for—" she began.

"What woman?"

"You said you heard me in the church. The woman I was asking the priest about?"

"Oh, right. That woman. What about her?" She took a long swallow of port and smacked chapped lips in pleasure. "Aaah, that's a lovely drop o' porter. Ta ever so, ducks. It's wetting my whistle a treat, it is."

"Don't mention it. She was about my age, fair hair, big dark brown eyes, very pretty. She was Irish, like me, with a soft voice."

"Right. Soft voice. Lemme have a look at that picture you was showing Father Bob." She peered at Deirdre's likeness. "Looks like her, all right." Another long swallow. "What was her name again, ducks?"

"Deirdre Riordan. She liked to be called Dee Dee."

"Aah. Ain't that sweet," she said without sincerity. "And when was it she went on the game?"

"On the game? I don't understand?"

"The game, the game," the woman repeated impatiently, clicking her teeth in annoyance. "You know, when she became a prosser."

"You mean a prostitute?" Caitlynn asked in a faint voice. She swallowed down the protest that begged to be made on Deirdre's behalf, keeping silent for the sake of finding out what she'd come here to find out. "Well, it—it would have been around the second week of July."

"Right. And do yer know the name of her bully, or did she work in a house, like?" The woman drained her glass with a gusty sigh.

"I have no idea. I—I was hoping you could tell me."

"Aaah. Well, so happens it's yer lucky day. I have a few connections, I do. People I can ask questions of, if you know what I mean." She tapped the side of her nose. "I'll need a bit o' blunt fer the answers before I go ferreting about."

"Blunt?"

"Lolly, ducks. *Money*." The woman smiled. When she did so, she looked pretty, in a hard, conniving sort of way.

"I see. Yes, well, here." She nervously placed a pound note on the scarred tabletop, which was ringed with glass stains.

"'S that all you got, then?"

Something about the woman's excited tone warned Caitlynn to answer in the affirmative. "Yes. Every last farthing. Take it or leave it."

"Ah, well. I dare say it'll do for starters." Her eyes shifted away from Caitlynn's. She snatched up the pound note and tucked it down her bosom. "There we go. Safe as the bloody Bank of England. Kitty's lockbox, I calls it!" She winked. "You wait here. I'll see what a quid will buy you on the street, ladybird."

Caitlynn nodded. "Go on, then."

When she looked up again, Kitty had melted into the raucous crowd as if she'd never been.

Caitlynn sat at the stained table in the corner with her eyes downcast at first, waiting patiently for Kitty to return. Ten minutes came and went. Fifteen. She began to fidget anxiously in her seat. Twenty-five minutes. A half hour.

Dare she hope that Kitty—or whatever her name was—would really have information about Deirdre and where she might be? Or was she insane to put her trust in a woman like that?

From anxiously waiting, she began to wonder if the woman would ever return at all. With every passing minute, she became more and more convinced that Kitty had duped her, taken advantage of her desperation and made off with her pound note.

Dare she even wait any longer to give the woman the benefit of the doubt? The longer she sat here, the darker and more dangerous it was getting outside. The warning the police constables had given her, about being off the East End's streets before dusk, loomed large in her memory now. Her stomach felt queasy.

She looked around, catching the eyes of several coarse-looking men and quickly glancing away.

Some of the men were porters or fruiterers from nearby Covent Garden market, judging by their flat caps and the kerchiefs knotted around their necks. Others were bummerees from the Smithfield Meat Market. The meat haulers' white clothes were smudged red from the massive carcasses they carried on their backs.

But it wasn't their obvious poverty or their attire that she found so disturbing. Not in the least. She knew from experience that poor people were not to be feared or mistrusted simply on account of their poverty. It was the predatory gleam in the patrons' eyes that scared her. The hard, calculating edge to the smiles. The desperation and death of hope apparent in their faces.

Deciding that a spirited offensive was probably safer

than any defense, she sat up straight in her chair and glared at them one by one, rather than meekly bowing her head, until they looked away.

All of them eventually did so, except for one bold fellow at a nearby table. When she shot him a green-eyed glare, he grinned wolfishly and tipped his bowler hat to her.

"Evening, darlin'," he greeted her with a heavy Irish brogue. Getting to his feet, he strolled over to her table.

Thumbs tucked into his belt, he looked down at her, his foxy face sharp and alert, keen eyes missing nothing. "Liam O'Sullivan's the name. Looking for a bit o' company, are you, then?"

"I certainly am not, Mr. O'Sullivan, as well you know. I'm waiting for a—a friend. So please go away."

" 'Go away,' is it? Tch-tch. Hoity-toity piece, ain'tcha, colleen? And fresh off the boat from the auld sod, I wouldn't wonder. Well, that's fine. You'll come around."

"I don't think so."

"You will. Even good Catholic girls fall sooner or later—and they fall harder than most. I'm thinking you'll be well worth the wait, darlin'. West End gents'll pay handsomely fer a real 'lady.' " He grinned. "Irish or not."

Her face burned. The man was obviously what Kitty called a 'bully.'

"I asked you to leave, sir," she repeated as coolly and calmly as she could, praying he would be too busy watching the fire in her eyes to notice her knees trembling. "Do so before I summon the publican. As I told you, I'm expecting someone. That person is certainly not yourself!"

"I heard you the first time, darlin'. But a word of

warning. If it's Kitty Abbott you're waiting for, you've got yourself a bloody long wait."

"I have? Why is that?"

"Because she's halfway to the next pub by now, our fine Kitty is. Loves a tipple, ye see?" The lout reached out and chucked her beneath the chin in a familiar way. "Let's hope she don't run afoul o' Saucy Jacky, eh?"

Caitlynn jerked her head away, batted at his hand and glowered at him. He laughed.

"Aye, you're a fetching piece an' no mistake. Spirited, too, just the way men like 'em. When you're done waiting for your 'friend,' I'll be back, me darlin' girl."

Caitlynn was trembling as the man moved away. The women watching her wore different expressions now. They were no longer merely curious but openly hostile. Obviously, they were not happy that O'Sullivan had spoken to her.

Nervously she glanced down at the tiny gold fob-watch pinned to the front of her cloak. It was a full forty-five minutes since Kitty had left her. She didn't want to admit it, but that awful man was probably right. Caitlynn doubted Kitty would be coming back now. She had been robbed of her pound note by a clever trickster with less effort than it took to take a sugar teat from a baby.

She stood and pushed back her chair, furious with herself for being so gullible.

"Oy, oy, watch it, gels. The Queen of bloody Ireland's on the move!" one of the women jeered. "Make room, you lot! Make way for her blooming majesty!"

Ignoring their spiteful catcalls, Caitlynn breathlessly forced her way through the crush of drinkers, heading for the public house's main doorway.

As she squirmed her way past the crowd holding up

the bar, her eye fell on a group of laughing young women gathered around a striking dark-haired man. A man who looked very familiar.

A second peek over the head of the bald fat man in front of her confirmed her initial impression.

The man at the bar, the handsome devil laughing and downing a glass of beer with a group of 'unfortunates,' was none other than her employer. The oh, so very respectable Dr. Donovan Fitzgerald of Huntington Square! She was so shocked that, for a second, she froze and simply stared.

At that moment, the doctor happened to turn his head in her direction. For a fleeting second, their eyes met over the heads of the crowd, and held.

The doctor's eyes widened in startled recognition. But before he could react, she ducked and bolted out the door.

Fresh air smacked her cheeks and stole her breath away, icy and bracing after the gamey sweat-sawdust-and-beer atmosphere of the pub.

As she feared, it was already full dark outside. It was also raining, a miserable drenching rain that chilled her to the bone in minutes. A shiver ran down her spine. She walked a little faster to reach the next puddle of gaslight, then the next.

The click of her button-boot heels on the cobbles seemed overly loud, somehow sinister on the uneasy wet hush, as if made by someone else. Was she being followed? she wondered, her breathing unsteady now.

She darted a quick glance over her shoulder, but there was no one there, unless her follower had ducked into a shop-front or courtyard when she turned to look.

The streets of the East End were gaslit for the most part, but the areas between the lamps were cloaked with deep shadow and practically deserted. The only pedestrians about at this hour were men hurrying home to their sorry lodgings in crowded boarding houses after a hard day's work.

She darted a glance over her shoulder, wondering if the doctor had been sufficiently sure of her identity to follow her out of the Britannia. But there was no one behind her. Not Donovan Fitzgerald, nor anyone else that she could see, thank God.

Walking briskly, she was back at St. Anthony's in a matter of minutes, but there was no sign of the friendly Father Robert now, and the church's doors were closed. The gargoyles that glared down at her from the eaves were frightening.

Pulling her cloak more tightly about her, she quickened her pace, all but running past the cemetery with its mossy headstones and lichen-covered angels, grotesque and otherworldly in the fading light.

Half running, half walking, she soon left both church and public house behind her. But still ahead lay yet another hazard: the railway arches. She would have to pass beneath the menacing black caverns of the railroad bridges to get home to the West End and Huntington Square.

As she drew level with the soaring brick arches, she heard scuffling in the shadows. Muffled squeaks or whimpers. Animal or human? She froze, her hand over her mouth to silence a scream. Oh, God, *rats!*

Or was it something worse? Something even more frightening?

Chapter Five

As she stood there, too terrified to move, straining her ears for a sound of some kind, she heard the scrape of a boot. A low moan. A gasp. A breathless giggle. Then there was a masculine grunt, followed by a satisfied, "Up he goes! Aah, that's the way of it!"

Caitlynn dropped her drawstring purse with a frightened, "Oh!"

At once, two startled faces swam out of the deepest gloom beneath the bridge. Pale moons turned in her direction. A man and a woman. But what the devil were they doing, hidden in the shadows?

Her lips pursed. A courting couple—or something more sinister? Sweet Mary and Joseph! Could it be the Ripper and his latest victim?

Her heart hammered in her breast. Her hands were icy. She hardly dared to breathe or move for fear of drawing the man's attention. Yet she dared not stay.

He might leave whatever it was he was doing and come after her.

She edged away carefully, inch by tiny torturous inch, painfully aware of just how alone she was, and how very vulnerable. The man could be anyone . . .

Her fingertips pressed to the grimy brick wall at her back for guidance as she moved. She could hear the slow trickle of rain down the sooty railway arches. The reek of train smoke, of cat urine, stale beer and dead things was so strong it made her eyes water.

"Wait yer turn, luv," the man told her hoarsely, leering in her general direction. He was, she saw now that her eyes had adjusted to the gloom, a soldier, dressed in his brown Army uniform. The metal buttons on his jacket glinted slyly in the meager light. "I'll get to you in a bit, never fear, eh, Sal?"

"The devil you will! Shove off, you cow," the woman snarled at Caitlynn over his shoulder. "This 'un's mine. Go earn your doss somewhere else, why don't ye!"

Belatedly, Caitlynn realized what the pair were up to. The woman was braced against the wall, skirts and petticoats hiked up about her waist. Her lower half was quite naked except for her garters, stockings and boots, which were clamped around the soldier's waist.

"I said, scarper!" the woman hissed. "Else I'll scratch yer bleeding eyes out. Come on, Bertie. Get on with it, do, ye great lout. I don't have all bloody night, not for your lousy tuppence."

The soldier needed no second urging. Nor did Caitlynn. With his first grunt, she took to her heels and ran, all decorum abandoned.

A quarter mile and two dozen streets later, she spotted the rain-caped and helmeted bobbies she'd spoken with earlier, PC Johns and PC Reece. They were standing beneath a gaslight, enjoying a smoke. Both constables carried bull-nose lanterns as well as truncheons.

They turned at the sound of her running feet, their lanterns' broad beams cutting a swath through the darkening street like knives.

Thank God! My guardian angels! She almost wept in relief as she reached them.

"What is it? Someone after you, miss?" The bobby flashed his torch in a broad arc around him, casting monster shadows of his companion on the far building's walls.

"No one. I just . . . well, I just panicked, I suppose. It was so dark under the railway arches, you see—"

"God in heaven, miss! What were you doing by the arches? You don't ought to be out in Whitechapel after dark, you don't," the older of the two men scolded her, "let alone down there."

"Stay away from here during the day, too," the younger bobby cautioned. "Not much difference between the two, you ask me, miss."

"Why don't I have PC Johns here call you a cab, miss?" Police Constable Reece suggested.

"Would you?" she asked, so relieved she almost wept.

Within moments, the constables had summoned a hackney cab and seen her safely handed into it. Then she was on her way, headed west to Huntington Square, with Whitechapel and the East End safely behind her.

As they rumbled around the next street corner, she saw a solitary bobby standing in a shop doorway, caped and helmeted against the rain, like his fellows. There was no sign of a partner, however.

As the hack drew alongside him, he raised his head. Despite the inky shadows cast by his helmet, which

Penelope Neri

rendered him blank and oddly featureless, she could feel his eyes. He was staring directly at her!

It was such an unnerving sensation, she hurriedly shrank back against the leather banquette, trying to melt into the concealing shadows of the coach's interior. It was an oddly unsettling encounter, and several minutes passed before she recovered her composure.

"One is for sorrow," went the old Irish saying about seeing a solitary magpie. Did the same rule hold true for police constables? she wondered.

It was such an odd thought, she couldn't get it out of her mind. Proof positive, she believed, that her foray into the East End had badly shaken her nerves.

She should have laughed at her foolishness, for that was all it was. But rather than laughing, she shivered.

"You're late and have missed supper," Mrs. Montgomery announced with ill-concealed glee when she let her in.

"That's quite all right, Mrs. Montgomery. I'm not in the least bit hungry," Caitlynn lied, a hand pressed to her growling stomach as she swept past the housekeeper, who looked decidedly disappointed. *"The Queen of bloody Ireland,"* the women in the Britannia public house had called her. Perhaps they weren't far wrong, she thought grimly as she sailed up the stairs. Hungry as she was, she wouldn't let Montgomery know it.

But her brave facade crumbled the moment the door closed behind her. Brave words notwithstanding, she was cold, exhausted and starving!

Almost immediately there was a tapping at her door. She tensed but opened it anyway, to see Bridget standing there, a finger pressed to her lips. She carried a tray.

"Here you go, miss. Rose said to eat up and enjoy,

74

and never mind what old Montgomery says," she whispered. "She remembered this was your favorite, aye?" The covered tray was laden with dishes of delicious-looking food.

"Shepherd's pie! Oh, yes!" Pleased, Caitlynn took the tray from the smiling girl and carried it over to the desk. There was not only shepherd's pie, but Brussels sprouts and treacle pudding with custard, too. A small pot of tea and a buttered crumpet rounded out the meal. A feast fit for the gods—or perhaps the Queen of Ireland, she thought with a smile.

"You and Rose are darlings. Thank you both from the bottom of my . . . stomach!" Bridget laughed. "I'm starving, but I refused to give that wretched Mrs. M. the satisfaction of knowing it."

Bridget grinned. "Me and Rose said as much. 'She'll be proper starving on a bitter day like this, poor lamb,' Rose said. 'Bridget, take Miss Caitlynn this tray.' So here I am."

"Everything smells divine. Close the door. We'll talk while I eat. Sit down, do. Make yourself comfortable. You're finished for the day, aren't you?"

"Yes." Bridget gingerly sat in the overstuffed chair by the hearth, obviously not accustomed to relaxing. "The doctor's not coming home until the wee hours, so I'm done early tonight. Off to a dinner party, he is. . . ."

Bridget chattered away while Caitlynn tucked into her supper, realizing belatedly that she was not just hungry, she was ravenous. The shepherd's pie was delicious.

"So. What did you do on your afternoon off? Where did you go?" Bridget asked at length.

"Oh—" She shrugged casually. "Nowhere really. After I bought the sewing supplies I needed, I explored a bit. I like walking. In Ireland, we didn't have a pony and trap, so I walked everywhere. There was a used-book shop I rummaged about in for quite some time. Hatchard's, I think it was called. But I didn't buy any books."

Bridget wrinkled her nose. "I'm wanting to go to a music hall, but Mrs. Larkin says they're no place for a respectable young woman. It's awful hard, being respectable. No fun at all." She sighed wistfully.

"Are you walking out with someone?"

"Not yet. But there's a lad I like. He's in service at number fifteen. His name's Sean. His smile could make the angels weep, sure it could."

"Speaking of angels, I stopped by St. Anthony's."

"Where else did you go?"

"Nowhere really. You know how it is. Time flies on your afternoon off, but it plods by on leaden feet when you're working. Mmm, this treacle pudding is heavenly! Tell Rose she's a darlin' woman, will you?"

After Bridget left, Caitlynn fed fresh coals to the fire, then turned up the oil lamp, resigned to spending a quiet evening doing her mending now that she had the darning needles, wooden mushroom and wool she needed.

She was almost finished darning the holes in her stockings—never a favorite pastime—when she realized how smoky the room had become. So much so, the back of her throat felt scratchy.

Unless she was mistaken, the fire was drawing badly. Something must be blocking the chimney, keeping the smoke from escaping. Perhaps it was blocked by an old bird's nest that had blown down the chimney.

Kneeling on the hearth, she peered up the chimney. Something was hanging out of the lower part of the chimney, into the hearth. It was cloth, rather than a bird's nest.

Caitlynn reached up the chimney. The object was quite bulky, wrapped in fringed cloth. With a quick tug, it fell free, showering sparks over the hearth. She carried the sooty bundle to her desk, where she opened it.

A chill of recognition ran down her spine.

It was the five-year diary she'd given Deirdre all those summers ago.

Using a hatpin, then a button-hook, with shaking hands she forced the tiny lock to yield.

Unharmed by either smoke or fire, the diary's pages fell open to an entry dated June 11, 1886, over two years ago.

"*Today,*" she read, her eyes filling with tears, "*Caitlynn told me she is to marry her Michael. I smiled and tried to be happy for her, but in the end, I could not keep up the pretense. Instead, I made an excuse to come home early.*

"*Dear Diary, my cousin is so very precious to me. The two of us are closer than Catherine Margaret and I have ever been, for all that we are true sisters. But, although Michael is very handsome, and although he belongs to a fine upstanding family, and although he seems genuinely devoted to Cait, I fear he is not the husband she needs nor the caliber of man she deserves.*"

Tears spilled from Caitlynn's eyes. Deirdre's entry recalled the day Michael had proposed to her as if it were only yesterday.

There had been honeybees buzzing in the apple orchard, and the air had been thick and lush with the scent of sunshine on dewy grass.

She had been riding the tree swing Da had made for

them when the boys were little. Michael had pushed her higher and higher, up and up into the sea of pink and white apple blossoms, toward the bright winking eye of the golden sun.

"See that golden ball, mavourneen? I'm going to catch it for you! I'm going to lay a fortune at your feet, you'll see!"

"Forget about the fortune. I'll settle for your heart, Mr. Michael Flynn!" she'd replied, laughing at him.

How right her cousin had been about Michael Flynn, she thought with a sniff, hugging the diary to her chest. But the tears were not for herself, nor for Michael. They were for Deirdre. Caitlynn was even more worried about her since she'd found the diary. It was proof positive, as far as she was concerned, that Deirde had not left the house of her own free will. She would never have done so without her precious diary.

She leafed through the pages until she came to the final entry, written at the beginning of July.

"Dear Diary: I have tried my best to please her, but daily she grows more impossible. I believe I know why she is so intractable, but am at a loss as to what to do. After all, who will believe me? I am just the hired companion here. To that end, I have decided to speak with her this afternoon. I no longer have a choice. Matters cannot be allowed to continue in this fashion."

Who was the woman Deirdre meant to speak to? Caitlynn wondered. Annie? Mrs. Montgomery? Probably the latter. Rose had said the housekeeper 'had it in' for Miss Riordan. Then there were the missing items. Were they the 'circumstances' the housekeeper had mentioned? Had Mrs. Montgomery accused Deirdre of the theft, then threatened to tell the doctor? Was that what drove her cousin away from the house on Huntington Square? Was she so shamed by the woman's accusations, however untrue, she had not dared to stay and fight her accusers, let alone contact her family, or take her beloved diary with her? So ashamed, she was still out there somewhere, trying desperately to survive? Because if not, *where could she be?*

The alternative was too terrible to contemplate.

As she brushed away a tear, her gaze fell on another, earlier entry.

"Dear Diary: D was here this morning. As always, my day was made brighter by his dear face and the warmth in his brown eyes."

Then, a few days later: *"Dear Diary: I dined this evening with E and D. Oh, how we laughed! It was such fun, I hardly remember what Mrs. Larkin served."*

More entries in a similar vein followed. Caitlynn frowned as she leafed through earlier entries. Taken singly, Deirdre's casual comments about 'D' meant nothing. But together, the entries painted a remarkably clear picture.

Deirdre had been in love with Donovan Fitzgerald.

An image of the man flashed into her mind's eye as he'd looked in the park.

There had been a kindling in those thick-lashed deep blue eyes that had betrayed the doctor's awareness of her as a woman, despite all his actions to the contrary.

Had Fitzgerald seen Deirdre as a woman—or as just another servant? Had he, perhaps, taken advantage of his position as her employer to force his attentions on her?

"I wonder what part, if any, you played in my cousin's disappearance, Doctor?" she asked the room.

Unease still simmered inside her as she thoughtfully returned the diary to its sooty hiding place.

Bridget had mentioned that the doctor was not expected home until very late. He had sent a messenger over from the hospital to fetch his evening attire, with instructions that the staff was not to wait up for him as he would be dining with some colleagues from St. Bartholomew's Hospital and expected to be home very late.

Hmm. Dining with colleagues—or consorting with a bevy of prostitutes in the East End? Caitlynn wondered, annoyed out of all proportion to the situation.

Perhaps tonight was as good a time as any to search the doctor's study.

Chapter Six

"Ah, there you are, Fitzgerald, skulking behind the potted palms. Glad you could join us tonight. How've you been?"

"Very well, thank you, sir."

"Good to hear it. And how's that father of yours?"

"In perfect health, thank you, sir. And you?"

"Splendid, splendid. Is Joseph still practicing?"

"Indeed he is. Seeing more patients than ever, and making house calls all over the county, rain or shine." Donovan grinned. "He says the Grim Reaper will have to carry him off kicking and screaming if he wants him."

Sir Charles Townsend, an elderly, white-haired Harley Street physician, chuckled. "That sounds like the Joseph I remember from medical school. Always the dedicated country physician, when he wasn't raising hell! You attended medical school in Edinburgh, too, if memory serves?"

"I did. Edinburgh University's School of Medicine. It was what Father wanted. Nothing but the best for Declan or myself. Fortunately, it was what I wanted, too."

"Well, it shows. You're a damned fine doctor, Fitzgerald. Just like Joe. I hear good things about you from my colleagues at St. Bart's. You should be in private practice in Harley Street, with me. Not squandering your God-given talents in some overcrowded public hospital. Give some serious thought to joining me, won't you, my boy? With a practice in the City, you'd have a guaranteed income of seven, eight thousand guineas a year, if you saw the right patients."

Donovan smiled. "By that, I presume you mean the wealthiest ones, do you not, Sir Charles?"

"And what if I do, eh? What's the bloody difference?" the older man demanded, tugging on his white moustaches. "A painful gut is a painful gut, don't ye know? Needs doctoring, whoever's gut it is, rich man's or poor man's. Now, how about a cigar, m'boy?"

"Thank you, sir. I'd like that."

"Good show! I need all the allies I can get. My Cecily detests the smell of 'em, God bless her. I keep 'em in here."

As he talked, Townsend led Donovan into a paneled study, to a humidor placed prominently on an inlaid marquetry table.

"These little beauties are Cuban. The very best that money can buy. I think you'll enjoy them."

"I'm sure I shall. Thank you, sir." Donovan selected a cigar from the box Townsend offered him, and sniffed it, enjoying the fragrant aroma of expensive tobacco.

"They roll the leaves on the naked thighs of Cuban *señoritas*, don't ye know?" Townsend winked and nudged Donovan, who grinned. "Do give some thought to joining me in private practice, m'boy. After all, a patient is a patient. If you want to practice medicine, it makes no difference whether you cure a rich patient or a poor one, so why not cure the rich? Far more rewarding, what?"

"Financially, yes," Donovan allowed. "But not in other ways. My patients need me, Sir Charles. That they do gives me great personal satisfaction. With all due respect, sir, that's more important to me than being wealthy."

It was the driving reason he had chosen to begin his practice here in London, after he graduated from Edinburgh University's prestigious School of Medicine, rather than returning to Ireland to become a partner in his father's country practice. It was also the reason he'd decided to stay on at St. Bart's, a training hospital, after his residency ended. At St. Bart's, he was able to treat the poorest of the poor in the stews of London's East End, where Irish expatriates outnumbered the British two to one, and were, if anything, even more despised.

"You're a hopeless bleeding heart, Fitzgerald. But it can't be helped, I suppose. It's the Irish in you, and that's how you people are. Emotional, full of poetry, music, ideals, and what-have-you, but bloody little common sense! Have you heard the latest?"

"About what, sir?" Donovan asked, snipping the end from the cigar he'd selected. He was far too accustomed to hearing the British opinion of the Irish to feel slighted by such prejudice any longer.

"Scotland Yard's saying the Ripper has medical knowledge. That he may well be a doctor, even a surgeon. Who knows? Perhaps the depraved brute's one of your students?"

Donovan smiled. "Oh, I sincerely doubt that, sir. But what's brought Scotland Yard to such a conclusion? Have there been new developments in the case?" he asked, curious.

Fear of the Whitechapel killer had held the East End locked in its paralyzing grip since late September, when it became apparent that someone was killing prostitutes in a ritualistic fashion. It was impossible for the doctors not to speculate on the identity of the murderer, when their patients—many of them women, many of them 'unfortunates' who lived and worked in the area where most of the victims were discovered— talked of little else. They were horrified, scared and fascinated, at one and the same time.

"According to Philipps and Blackwell—both medical examiners as well as colleagues of mine—the women's autopsies suggest that the murderer mutilated their bodies with some degree of surgical skill, after he first cut their throats, removing various organs and what-have-you. Furthermore, he did so in poor or no lighting, in an extraordinarily brief amount of time. Such speed and dexterity imply considerable anatomical knowledge, wouldn't you say?"

Donovan frowned. "Not necessarily. There's been endless discussion among the staff at St. Bart's, too. The popular opinion there is that the murders of these poor women were committed by a sexual sadist. A butcher, perhaps, or a knacker who slit their throats, then removed their organs willy nilly as his rage and fancy took him. He takes sexual pleasure in the bloody acts themselves."

"So, what are you saying?"

"That in my opinion, he's more likely to be a butcher at one of the abattoirs in the East End, or a

bummeree from Smithfield market, than any physician."

"Interesting. I, er, I hear you've been spending nights
in the East End yourself, Donovan? Buck's Lane. Mitre
Street. All over St. Giles and Spitalfields." Townsend's
gray eyes were no longer mild, but penetrating as polished steel.

A guarded look filled Donovan's eyes. He puffed on
his cigar but gave no reply for several seconds. "I
have," he admitted at length. "I go where I'm needed.
What of it? Who wants to know?"

Townsend shrugged. "People talk. They read the
newspapers, put two and two together, and come up
with five."

"Do they, now? Exactly what are you trying to say,
Sir Charles?"

"Simply that certain people wonder what you, a re-
spected physician—and an Irish physician, at that—
could be doing in the slums, at all hours . . ."

"Aah. Then you're saying the police consider me a
likely suspect?"

"No, no, of course not! If they did, they would have
taken you in for questioning long before this, like that
Leather Apron fellow. But . . . I do have it on good
authority that your name appears with alarming fre-
quency in the constables' nightly blotters. The dates of
record include at least two of the—er—the nights in
question. Perhaps more."

"You mean the nights when these murders were
committed?"

"Yes. I'm afraid so."

His jaw hardened. "With all due respect, Sir Charles,
I would suggest that 'they' mind their own business,
and leave me to mind mine. Which, incidentally, is not
the business of murder, but of practicing medicine."

"Oh, indeed. Point taken. And don't think for a minute that I believed you could ever be the . . . well, you know what I mean. Still, I can't help wondering why you're spending so much time in the stews, my boy. Truth is, I'm concerned about you, Donovan. I think of you as the son Cecily and I never had. Rest assured, anything you choose to confide in me will go no further."

"I'm sure it won't, sir, because there is nothing to confide."

The steely edge to his tone left the older man in no doubt that, as far as Donovan Fitzgerald was concerned, the matter was closed.

"Donovan, I—"

"Why, there you are! What are you two rascals up to? Smoking those dreadful cigars, I see! Discussing those wretched murders, too, I shouldn't wonder. Nobody talks of anything else these days. The art of witty conversation is dead. Charles, do come back to the drawing room. Our guests are wondering what has become of their host."

"Oh, I very much doubt that, Cecily, dear," Charles protested as his wife attempted to shoo him out of the study and back to their dinner guests.

"If you'll excuse me, Sir Charles, Lady Townsend, I really should be getting home," Donovan said.

"So soon? Oh, please, do stay a little longer!" Sir Charles's wife implored.

"Hope it wasn't anything I said, m'boy? If so, I trust you'll accept my apologies?"

"No, it has nothing to do with you, Sir Charles. I really should be on my way."

"But you can't leave yet! I have a special entertainment planned for later, Donovan. One that I went to enormous trouble to arrange, with you and the other

86

scientific fellows in mind." She patted her husband's arm.

Lady Cecily Townsend, reed thin and elegant in gray satin, black pearls and osprey plumes, pouted like a young debutante and fluttered her lashes at Donovan.

"I arranged for a mummy from the Valley of the Pharaohs to be delivered here this very morning!" she announced triumphantly. "Isn't it exciting? Tonight my honored guests are going to witness an unwrapping."

"Oh, good Lord, Cecily!" her husband exclaimed with a shudder. "Tell me you didn't!"

"Oh, stop making that horrid face, Charles. Mummy unwrappings are all the rage in high society, don't you know? And if it's good enough for them, it's quite good enough for me. By this weekend, my little dinner party will be the talk of the town!" Her faced glowed. "Donovan, be a dear, dear man and say you'll stay? For me?"

Sir Charles was unaware of it, but Lady Cecily had approached Donovan privately on a medical matter a little over a year ago. Sadly, he had been unable to offer her much hope about her condition; it was only a matter of time. However, he had agreed to keep her secret and let her decide when to tell her husband.

Her sweetness and courage in the face of such a daunting enemy filled him with admiration. How could he refuse such a valiant lady this one small request, so easily granted?

"Very well, Lady Cecily. I shall stay for your so-called 'entertainment,' as macabre and ghoulish as it sounds. I never could refuse a beautiful lady anything!" He lifted her hand to his lips and kissed it, murmuring wickedly, "Ahh, Lady Cecily, if only you were not a married woman—"

"Oh, you flatterer!" Lady Cecily exclaimed. "Be warned that if you continue in this fashion, my husband may have to call you out, sir! He's really quite jealous, you know."

"What's that? Who's calling on us, m'dear?" Charles asked, confirming Donovan's impression that the older man was growing hard of hearing, though he would never admit it.

"I'll tell you later, Charles, dear," said Cecily, smiling a conspiratorial smile at Donovan. "After the unwrapping."

Caitlynn opened the study door just wide enough to slip inside. Quickly closing it behind her, she raised the candle aloft in its brass holder and looked around.

The fire had been banked for the night. Coals glowed dull orange behind a gleaming black grate. The heavy velvet draperies were drawn, so that the study cum library lay in ruddy shadow, dark as any tomb. She could barely make out ceiling-to-floor bookshelves ranged along two walls of the spacious room. The spines of the leather-bound books gleamed with gold leaf.

Using a paper spill, she lit the oil lamp, turned up the wick and replaced the milk-glass globe. Her giant shadow accompanied her across the masculine room as she carried the lamp over to Fitzgerald's desk.

Praise be! Its little drawers were unlocked. After a moment or two, she overcame her qualms about invading her employer's privacy, and opened the first drawer.

Inside were bills: from a haberdasher, a wine merchant, a tailor, various tradespeople, a lawyer. Correspondence from other physicians. Letters from his family in Ireland, from friends, and thank-yous from grateful patients.

Caitlynn methodically began sifting through the correspondence, one drawer at a time. In due course, she found both of the letters Uncle Daniel had written to the doctor, one in late July, the other at the end of August, inquiring about Deirdre's whereabouts. Reading them now, four months later, brought tears to her eyes. There had been no news then. There was still none now.

There was also a letter from the Kelly Domestic Service Agency, advising Dr. Fitzgerald that a Miss Caitlynn O'Connor, a 'spinster and gentlewoman of good reputation, sterling character, and of the highest moral standards,' had been recommended by the doctor's own father, physician Joseph Fitzgerald, to replace the previous lady's companion who had left his employ so unexpectedly. Miss O'Connor would be arriving in London on October 1st. Dr. Fitzgerald should expect her then.

She stifled a nervous giggle. And here she was, Miss Caitlynn O'Connor of 'sterling character' and 'good reputation,' rifling through her employer's desk like a common thief!

The third drawer yielded a rather grubby, well-folded sheet of foolscap, signed by one Lily Perkins of 92 Chapel Road, St. Giles, London. Written in an almost indecipherable scrawl, with many spelling mistakes, inkblots and crossings-out, Caitlynn read:

"In exchange for the Sum of Ten pounds, I herewith relinquish any and all Lawful Rights to the Female Child, Stella Marsh, age 9 years."

It was dated March 5, 1882. Six years ago. Estelle was fifteen, almost sixteen, now. Had the Perkins woman been Estelle's mother? she wondered. Surely not, if her name was Perkins. Besides, what mother would sell her own child?

Rather than explaining the doctor's guardianship of Estelle, the note only raised more questions. Had he fathered the child on this woman, or—

What was that?

Caitlynn's head snapped around at the sound of a loud click. Her hand in a drawer, she froze. The brass doorknob was turning. Someone was coming into the room!

Who would it be? she wondered, sick with apprehension. That horrid Mrs. Montgomery? If so, she'd be sacked for sure. Dare she hope that Tom, the coachman, had seen the lamplight under the study door or between the draperies, and come to surprise the intruder with his billy club, knowing the doctor was not at home?

Hastily stuffing the note back into the drawer, Caitlynn darted away from the desk and all but flung herself up the rungs of the library ladder.

There, she selected a book at random and stared blindly at its pages, pretending rapt fascination with the contents. Hand shaking, heart beating like a terrified bird in her chest, she froze in horror and fascination as the door slowly opened inward.

Chapter Seven

"Well, well, Miss O'Connor! To what do I owe the pleasure of this visit?"

Donovan Fitzgerald stood on the threshold, looking up at her with a grim smile.

His coal-black hair was burnished with blue lights, like the glossy wings of a raven or a lump of polished obsidian. Both fire and lamplight cast his striking features in shadow and mystery. He looked like a Celtic hero, stepped from the pages of a history book or an epic poem about Brian Boru. Mysterious. All-powerful.

He had obviously come straight in from outside, for the folds of his swirling black cape were sodden with fog and rain. Indeed, a layer of moisture covered the inky fabric. Each drop caught the light in miniature rainbows, so that, with the glowing fire behind him, he seemed like a dark angel, cloaked in misty light from head to foot.

"Why, Dr. Fitzgerald," she managed to stammer offhandedly. "Good evening. I do hope you'll forgive the intrusion. I couldn't sleep, so I took the liberty of—"

"—coming down here and raiding my library?" He frowned. "No, Miss O'Connor. Absolutely not."

"No?" Her tawny brows shot up in surprise and confusion. "You mean you won't forgive me?"

"I mean, no, I don't mind in the least if you borrow one of my blasted books! Unlike someone else, I might add, who selfishly refused to share her blasted conkers."

He smiled, and it was like the sun coming out after a storm. Disarming. Devastating.

He was, she realized belatedly, repaying her in kind for teasing him in the park. Rather than being annoyed, or even flustered, she found herself staring at his lips, as if he were about to speak in tongues. Or at the very least, breathe fire.

"I see you have found something to your liking, Miss O'Connor. What can it be, I wonder? *The Compleat Book of Conker Fighting*, perhaps?"

In two lazy strides, he was standing at the bottom of the library ladder. Reaching up, he turned over the book she was holding so that he could read the title for himself.

His fingers brushed hers as he did so, skin to skin. A deliberate touch, she thought.

The brief yet sizzling contact sent unexpected shock waves dancing up her arm. Her skin tingled as if she'd been stroked by lightning. She immediately wanted to rub the prickly spot his fingers had brushed.

"Aha! I see I was quite wrong. Thurlow's *Male Anatomy For the Apprentice Physician*. How clever you are, to read it upside down. I had a hard enough time of it the right way up," he observed drily.

"What!" She turned the book over, horrified to see that he was right on both counts. The book *was* upside down—and alarmingly graphic about the male anatomy.

"A somewhat unusual field of study for a young lady like yourself, I must say. And hardly what I would have expected of you, my dear Miss O'Connor, with your delicate sensibilities." His dark brows lifted in wicked inquiry, but true to form, he did not smile, although the glint in his dark blue eyes hinted that he wanted to.

"Oh! How silly of me! I must have pulled out the wrong one." Flustered, she withdrew another small gold-leafed volume from the shelf and quickly replaced the slim anatomy book in the slot from which she had withdrawn it. "This—this was the one I really wanted. Miss Brontë's *Wuthering Heights*. Thank you."

"Ah, indeed. The dark and brooding Heathcliff. Much more fitting." He grinned knowingly, and her cheeks grew hot. "Then if you have made your final selection, allow me to assist you." He offered her his hand.

After a moment's hesitation, she accepted, and let him take her slender hand in his own.

When she reached the bottom rung, he let go of her hand, yet made no move to step aside nor permit her to step past him. Rather, she was forced to stand there at the bottom of the ladder, pressed so close to him that his wet cape dampened her flannel dressing gown.

"I see it is raining out." She desperately wanted to move, to defuse the explosive tension in the air, yet could have kicked herself the moment she spoke. It was such an obvious comment to make, not clever at all. He would think her an utter dunce! It was suddenly very important to her that he think her clever, witty.

"It is indeed. Raining cats, dogs and even the occasional mouse," he agreed with great solemnity. "It is also bitterly cold. I decided to walk home after my dinner engagement. Not a wise decision, in retrospect. I thought I might have a brandy and warm up by the fire before going to bed. Would you care to join me, Miss O'Connor?"

She blinked.

His tone was low and sensual. Almost intimate. "I beg your pardon?"

"In a nightcap," he clarified.

"A what?" She had the sudden vision of the sort of headgear an old man might wear to bed.

"A brandy, Miss O'Connor. A harmless drink! Far more effective in achieving sleep than your romantic novel." His voice was black velvet.

She reached up to touch the back of her neck. It tingled. "I don't think so, no. But thank you anyway, Dr. Fitzgerald." She turned as if to go.

"Come, come, my dear. Just this once won't hurt, surely? Don't think of it as liquor at all, but as medicine. A prescription for insomnia, prescribed by your personal physician. Please, do sit down."

His tone, while still low, was quite firm and brooked no refusal.

He indicated one of the leather wing chairs on either side of the fireplace.

Despite herself, she sat, perched precariously on the very edge of the chair like a white-feathered bird poised for immediate flight.

Leaving her momentarily, he draped his wet cape over the coat hook on the back of the door, before moving over to a large globe set in a finely carved wooden stand.

He wore evening attire—black cutaway coat, waist-

94

coat and trousers set off by dazzling linens and a perfectly knotted silk tie. The stark black and snowy white attire was the perfect foil for his fine dark looks, she thought. Just watching the spare, efficient way he moved, the way he carried his handsome head, caused a flutter in her belly. A treacherously pleasant flutter.

He rubbed cold hands together, then fiddled for a moment with a mechanism on the side of the globe. To her surprise, the top half lifted off like a lid, revealing an array of sparkling crystal decanters inside.

Selecting a small brandy snifter, Fitzgerald splashed an ounce or two of cognac into a balloon glass, a more generous amount into a second glass, and carried both to where Caitlynn sat, squirming uncomfortably on her padded perch.

"My dear." He handed her a glass. Their fingers brushed. "To a sound night's sleep!" he toasted, raising his own. "Your very good health, Miss O'Connor. 'May sweet dreams attend thee,' " he quoted.

"And you, Doctor."

Their eyes met. Held. Flustered, she looked away . . . looked down . . . looked anywhere but at him. God, what was it about him that caused this turmoil inside her? He was, after all, just a man, however attractive.

"Thank you. Have you had brandy before?"

"Never."

"I thought not. I recommend cupping the glass with your hand, like so." He demonstrated, placing his hand over hers. "The warmth of the hand warms the brandy, you see." But the warmth of his hand was warming far more than just the brandy. Rosy heat filled her, stole through her veins. "That's right." His voice was a velvet mist. An Irish mist that curled around the senses and ensorceled them. "Now swirl your glass a time or two, and drink."

95

She touched her lips to the hard rim of the glass, very conscious of his dark eyes upon her, as she did so, of his lips, pursed in concentration.

"Splendid."

Rather than taking the wing chair opposite hers, he remained standing. One hand cupped his brandy glass, while the other rested comfortably along the marble mantel as he warmed his coattails.

She could not recall ever being alone with a man before, except for her father or brothers. And even then, she had been fully dressed, not wearing only her dressing gown and night chemise, with her hair tumbling loose down her back.

Although her nightclothes covered her quite modestly, she felt naked sitting there at dead of night, drinking strong spirits with a handsome devil of questionable character and the morals of a tomcat!

After all, he—a bachelor—had apparently purchased a child—another human being, an angelic, beautiful little girl!—for God-only-knew what sinister, probably immoral purpose. He also frequented public houses of the lowest sort, and kept company with prostitutes. She must be out of her mind to meekly sit here and do his bidding, let alone allow him to touch her hand! And yet . . .

. . . what options did she have, really? He was the master of the house, her only link to Deirdre and whatever had befallen her. She told herself she must commit such small indiscretions if it helped to find her cousin.

And so she obediently sipped the ginger-gold liquid, then swallowed.

Liquid fire coated the back of her throat, sent heat singing through her veins, sizzling through her innards. She gasped as the brandy hit her belly like an exploding rocket.

"Oh, my stars!" she sputtered hoarsely. "It is rather . . . potent, is it not?"

"Indeed it is, yet as smooth as only the very best cognac can be."

The heat in his eyes as he said 'smooth' made her bones melt. Her stomach muscles clenched. "Hmm," she murmured incoherently. "Smooth."

He smiled. "We've had little opportunity to get to know each other since your arrival, Miss O'Connor," Fitzgerald murmured as if they were casual friends meeting at an afternoon tea or an evening soirée, rather than master and servant.

Tactfully ignoring the way she was sputtering and fanning her flushed cheeks with her hand, he added, "I'm afraid I was somewhat overbearing at out first interview. I have been wanting to make amends ever since. Finding you here tonight was a happy coincidence, don't you think?"

"Delirious," she agreed, unhappily. Perhaps even a little tipsily. "However, I—um—I really should retire, sir."

"All in good time, Miss O'Connor. You have barely tasted your brandy. Tell me, how do you like us so far? Or perhaps I should rephrase that. How do you like my ward?"

"Estelle is an intelligent young woman. She is also lively and charming. I like her very much indeed."

"Good. I understand she feels the same about you. It was very wrong of me to ask you to withhold your affection toward her, Miss O'Connor. I hope you'll accept my belated apology for doing so. However, Estelle was very resistant to having another companion. I did not want her to be hurt all over again."

"Yes, she told me as much. She was attached to Miss

Riordan, and very distressed by her untimely departure, exactly as you warned me."

He frowned, dark brows drawing together. "How now? What's that I hear in your tone, Miss O'Connor? Disapproval?"

"I don't know what you mean, Doctor," she insisted. The brandy had caused her to lower her guard.

"Come, come. Don't play the innocent. There was a decided note of disapproval in your voice, your eyes. Why? Surely you don't think I was somehow responsible for Miss Riordan's 'untimely departure'?" he exclaimed suddenly. "Is that what Estelle has told you? That I was to blame for her beloved Miss Dee Dee leaving?"

"No, not at all, sir. However . . ." She paused. "Oh, never mind. It's not important."

"On the contrary, it is very important to me. Go on. Out with it! Tell me. You don't have to mince words, Miss O'Connor. I much prefer that you speak your mind."

"Very well. I did hear that there was a possibility Miss Riordan was going to be sacked by you at the time she went away. A matter of some missing jewelry?"

"Yes, that's right. But the matter was between Mrs. Montgomery and the young woman. As my housekeeper, the responsibility for hiring and firing the staff is ultimately hers. By the time I was informed of the problem, it was a fait accompli. Miss Riordan had already left us."

"Really?" Caitlyn sipped again, feeling braver, bolder by the minute—thanks, no doubt, to the false courage of the brandy. She did not entirely believe him, but she could hardly call him a liar to his wickedly handsome face. "And were you surprised to hear that she had done so? Left, I mean?"

"Very much so."

"You were?" She knew she sounded startled but couldn't help herself.

"Of course. Why shouldn't I be? Miss Riordan struck me as a serious, responsible young woman. She came to us, like yourself, on my father's highest recommendation. What's more, she seemed an excellent influence on my ward. Also, like you, she complied with my wishes that Estelle be encouraged to go out and enjoy the fresh air as much as possible, although it is a somewhat revolutionary idea in medical circles. I was deeply disappointed when I learned Miss Riordan had seen fit to leave us so abruptly, and why she had done so. I feel sure if she had not taken matters into her own hands and acted so precipitously by leaving us, the problem could have been resolved to the satisfaction of everyone concerned."

"I see." He was lying, of course. He must be.

"Miss O'Connor. Caitlynn. Have you ever cut your hair?" The odd question spilled from him almost involuntarily.

Immediately, her hand rose to her head in a self-conscious gesture. "My hair? Why, yes, several times. Why do you ask, sir?"

"Idle curiosity, I'm afraid. A bad habit of mine. It's quite beautiful. Like sable silk."

The muscles in her stomach contracted again. That odd fluttery feeling stirred in the very pit of her belly. Heat filled her cheeks as her lashes swept down, modest dark fans to conceal her wayward thoughts. "Thank you for your compliment, Doctor."

He frowned, hesitated. "I have the distinct feeling you don't like me, Miss O'Connor."

"That's not true." It was her turn to lie now.

"No? What is the truth, then?"

"I . . . well, you are my employer, Doctor! I don't think of you in terms of liking or disliking, to be honest. Or as a man—as a person—at all."

"How very flattering." He grimaced.

"What I mean is that I always think of you as my employer. As Dr. Fitzgerald."

"Always?"

"Always. To me, you are just . . . well . . ."

"There? Like part of the furniture?" he prompted. "Is that what you were going to say?"

"Yes," she confessed. "In a way."

"Liar!" He swirled the brandy in his glass, regarding her over the rim with dark blue eyes that smoldered like the hot blue flames that danced among the coals from time to time. "You are not indifferent to me at all. Quite the contrary. Dislike crackles all around you, like a layer of frost on a wintry morning! But why, I wonder?" he mused, tugging on his chin in a thoughtful way as he regarded her soulfully from deep blue eyes set in a face that was handsome enough to make the blessed Virgin weep. "What have I ever done to make you dislike me, my dear lovely Miss O'Connor of the sable tresses and the shamrock eyes?" There was a hint of mockery in his voice now.

"Nothing . . . nothing at all," she insisted, jumping to her feet. She felt hot and cold by turns. Somehow, the wretched man had a way of making his words touch her like the most intimate caresses. Or maybe it was a combination of the brandy, the ruddy shadows and her state of undress. She felt so—so naked, so very vulnerable, yet breathless with excitement, all at the same time.

"With all due respect, I believe you are a little the

worse for drink, Doctor. So, if you will excuse me, I shall go up to bed—er—to—to my room—now." She crossed the study and thumped the empty brandy snifter down on his desk with rather more force than was necessary. "Good night, sir."

"Running away again, Miss O'Connor?" he challenged, coming to stand very close to her. "How odd. I didn't take you for a coward. Yet this makes the second time today you've fled me."

"Second time? I don't know what you mean."

"You ran from me at the public house this afternoon, remember?"

"I have no idea what you are talking about, sir," she lied. "I do not frequent public houses."

"Oh, come, come. I think you do, miss."

"No, really, I don't."

"No?" he said in patent disbelief. "Then it must have been your *doppelganger*. They say that everybody has a double somewhere in this world, do they not, Miss O'Connor?"

"Perhaps. However, I spent my afternoon off exploring St. Paul's Cathedral. St. Paul's is some distance from the Britannia."

A faint smile hovered about his lips at this. "Did I mention the Britannia?"

She could have bitten her tongue off the moment she said it. Had he mentioned the name of the public house? No. She didn't think so.

"St. Paul's, indeed? What a coincidence, then," he said, clearly unconvinced. "The woman I saw had hair exactly like yours. Sable silk, like a nightingale's wings. And shamrock eyes."

"Please, Dr. Fitzgerald, you really should not pay me such extravagant compliments—"

"It's Donovan, Miss O'Connor. And give me one

good reason why the devil not?" he asked huskily, staring at her mouth, then dropping his gaze to the fluttery pulse that throbbed in the shadowy hollow at the base of her throat. At the swell of firm round breasts beneath nightgown and wrapper.

"Because I am a—a servant here, nothing more, Dr. Fitzg-"

"Call me by my given name. *Donovan.*"

"I cannot," she whispered. "Don't make me. Please."

"Just this once, Caitlynn. I shall never ask you again. Never command you."

"No?"

"No. Because, you see, the next time you whisper my name, 'twill be because you want to. Because you cannot help yourself." The lilting cadence of his voice was hypnotic. Mesmerizing.

Dangerous!

"Very well," she said, trembling and desperate to escape, not so much in fear of him but in fear of herself and what else she might succumb to. "Donovan. Donovan. *Donovan!* There. I've said it."

"Indeed you have. And it has never sounded sweeter than it does on your lips. Tell me, what would you do if I kissed you, my dear Miss O'Connor? My fiery Cait of the shamrock eyes?" He took a step closer.

"You would not dare, sir!"

"Oh, I dare, Cait, I dare almost anything. I am not lacking in courage nor in bravado. Besides, I'm Irish!" He laughed softly. "We are known for our recklessness— and for our romantic hearts. Humor me, little Cait. What would you do"—his sapphire eyes danced with wicked merriment—"if I could not help myself? If I kissed you until you could not speak?"

She stared at his sensual lips, wondering how they

would feel if he succumbed to his dark desire—and she to hers. Wondering, if truth were told, how it would feel to be kissed speechless.

How would his lips feel if he tasted her? Kissed her? *Warm? Insistent? Arousing?*

She looked down at his hands. At broad palms and long, skilled fingers. Such strong, masculine hands. Capable hands. Knowing hands that were no stranger to the soft curves of a woman's body. How would they feel on her bare skin, touching her, stroking her?

Strong. Enflaming. Caressing.

And how would she react if he touched her, held her?

"What would I do? I would scream, Doctor. I would scream loudly and insistently, for a very long time," she declared firmly, unable to meet his eyes lest he see her lie. A flush rode high on her cheekbones. There was an ache deep in her belly now. A yearning.

"I would scream so long and so very loud that my cries would rouse this entire household, and possibly every household on the square. Then I would leave, sir. Leave and never come back, and remember you ever after with loathing, as a lecher and a reprobate." She looked him full in the eyes.

"Sweet Lord, would you really?" He sounded amused, admiring and also a little sad. "What a formidable young woman you are, Miss O'Connor! I should have known. Then it appears I must steel myself to resist temptation, for your departure from my household would be far too harsh a punishment to bear. Fly, pretty bird!"

So saying, he stepped back, his arms spread wide.

Caitlynn flew across the room, bolted through the study door and up the staircase in a heartbeat.

She was too shaken at having escaped unscathed

from the wolf's lair to recognize the deflated feeling in her stomach for what it truly was, until much later, when she was alone, in her bed.

Disappointment. That's what she'd felt, though she hated to admit it, even to herself. *Disappointment.*

God help her, she'd *wanted* him to kiss her!

Caitlynn's headlong flight from the study did not go unnoticed.

The watcher shrank back into the shadows until the door to Caitlynn's room closed behind her, then tiptoed out to peer over the balustrade.

The study door opened. Donovan came out. The watcher sucked in a gasp. Smoking a slim cigarillo, he strode across the entryway to the foot of the stairs and just stood there, staring up at the staircase, as if willing Caitlynn to come back down by his thoughts alone.

Seeing his expression, the watcher bit back a sob of denial. Not three months in this household, and the O'Connor woman was working her wiles on the doctor, just like the last.

Something would have to be done about the slut.

Chapter Eight

"Do be still, Miss Caitlynn! How am I to draw your profile if you keep moving?"

A sheet of white drawing paper had been pinned to the dining room wall with drawing pins. Beside the paper sat Estelle, armed with a lead pencil with which she was outlining the shadow of Caitlynn's head and profile.

Caitlynn sat on a straight-backed chair a few feet away, the oil lamp behind her so that its light cast her shadow on the blank paper.

"Hurry, then! It is not in my nature to sit still for long." Caitlynn laughed, trying very hard not to move. "I have a restless spirit."

"What you will have, my dear Miss Caitlynn, is a witch's silhouette with a very large nose and a pointed chin," teased Estelle, "unless you stop moving about so much."

The two young women laughed, enjoying each other's company.

With December only a month away, Caitlynn had suggested they make silhouette portraits of each other to frame and give to loved ones as Christmas presents. Estelle had eagerly agreed.

"I shall give one silhouette to Donovan," Estelle declared. "And send another one to Grandfather and Grandmother Fitzgerald." She wrinkled her nose. "Although I don't think they like me very much. Grandmama says I'm difficult."

"That's a wonderful idea. And don't be silly. I'm sure they like you. Why wouldn't they?"

"They are jealous, because Donovan is very fond of me, you know. Who shall you give yours to? Are you betrothed to anyone?"

"Not anymore, no."

"But you were?"

"Yes."

"How exciting!" Her blue eyes shone like stars. "I never dreamed you had a tragic past, Miss Caitlynn," she added thoughtfully.

"It is hardly tragic!"

"Your fiancé did not die, then?" She sounded disappointed.

"No, thank goodness."

"What a pity. It would have been so much more interesting if he had. . . . But if he didn't die, what happened to him? Did he find another woman?"

Caitlynn was about to say that her past was none of Estelle's business when she thought better of it. Surely many invalids lived their lives vicariously, through the stories of others. Where was the harm in telling her?

"It's not a very exciting story, really. Nor that tragic. In fact, you'll probably be disappointed."

"Tell me anyway."

"Michael simply decided he didn't want to be married, not to me or to anyone else. There was no scandalous other woman. He simply went away to America to find his fortune in the goldfields there."

"Oh, how awful. Then you were jilted—left at the altar in your wedding gown, just like Miss Haversham in Mr. Dickens's *Great Expectations*?"

Caitlynn rolled her eyes. "Not exactly, no. He wrote to tell me some weeks before our planned wedding day. There was no wedding feast left to molder and gather cobwebs."

"Oh. And when was this? Years ago?"

"Just this past June."

"And were you terribly sad about it? Do you pine for him still? Are you sick and sleepless with longing for him? Shall you grow pale and wan?"

"Not at all. When I think of him, it is with fondness and the hope that he has found his heart's desire, whatever it may be. To be honest, I am relieved that we were never wed."

"Relieved? Not me! I would be so ashamed and angry if I were jilted, I couldn't bear it!" Estelle sighed and theatrically clutched her hands to her heart. "I would have followed him to the very ends of the earth and forced him to marry me!"

Caitlynn smiled. "I considered it. To be honest, I *was* quite upset at first. It seemed as if my entire world had come to an end and crashed down around me. But it was more a case of being in love with the idea of being married than true love itself. Once I thought about it, I realized I'd never loved Michael at all. I only thought I did. Feeling that way, it would have been a disaster for me to spend the rest of my life with him, don't you think?"

"No. What I think is that you are a very silly woman, Miss Caitlynn," Estelle said seriously. "Imagine not knowing whether you loved someone or not. The idea! I'm so glad I know my own mind. I know whom I love." She smiled, her face radiant. "There, your profile's finished. Now it's your turn to do mine."

When Caitlynn was done tracing the girl's profile a few minutes later, Estelle asked her to push her wheeled wicker chair over to the table.

Taking the chair beside her young charge, Caitlynn began the enjoyable task of cutting out Estelle's profile with very tiny, very sharp nail scissors. Once transferred to stiff black paper, the finished likeness would be cut out, then mounted on heavy cream-colored paper and framed in gilt.

"There! See what a lovely girl you are!" The silhouette showed Estelle's face, caught in sweet profile. She wore her long fair hair pulled back on either side of her face, then tied behind with a scarlet bow.

"Do you really think so? Uncle Declan says I'm a mudlark and as ugly as sin. If I were his ward, he swears he'd make me scrub the floors *and* empty the chamber pots."

She giggled, her blue eyes sparkling. That afternoon, she looked irresistible in a cherry-red and black plaid wool gown. A dark green carriage rug was thrown over her frail legs for warmth.

"Uncle Declan's so funny," she added.

"He certainly seems to be," Caitlynn agreed, her lips pursed in concentration as she carefully snipped along the intricate outline of Estelle's profile.

Declan Fitzgerald was a frequent visitor to Huntington Square. Estelle said he used to live with them but had moved into his own lodgings last May.

"Did your Miss Riordan like him?" Caitlynn wondered aloud.

"Miss Riordan, Miss Riordan, Miss Riordan! Why do you ask me so many questions about her, I wonder? Is it because you are jealous of her?"

"I really don't know," Caitlynn lied. Had she really been so obvious? "Perhaps it's because she was your companion before me, and nobody knows what happened to her? I expect I'm curious, that's all. I wouldn't want to make the mistakes she made and have to leave," she covered, choosing her words carefully, while wishing with all her heart that she didn't have to lie to the girl. No good ever came of lies.

"Then it's not because you're wondering if Uncle Declan had a tendresse for my companion?" Estelle asked archly, her eyebrows lifting in a way that was more seasoned woman-of-the-world than girlish. "She was very pretty and charming."

"Tendresse! You know far too much about such grown-up matters, miss," Caitlynn scolded, pretending shock.

"More than you would ever dream, my dear Miss Cait," Estelle said with a mysterious smile, but ruined the effect by laughing.

"Nevertheless, your answer is no," Caitlynn said. "I am not wondering anything of the sort about Mr. Fitzgerald. Why would you think that?"

"Because you always laugh at Uncle Declan's silly jokes, and you always seem pleased to see him. Montgomery said he is a 'fine catch' for some young woman. She'd snap him up herself if only she were younger, the old battle-ax! But enough of Declan. Let's get on with our silhouettes, shall we? Look! I've finished yours!"

Estelle held up her paper cutout.

The young woman had made good on her threat, Caitlynn saw, taken aback. Her own profile was almost spitefully rendered, spoiled by a hooked nose and a crone's long, pointed chin. It was cruelly yet cleverly done, for it retained enough of her real likeness to be easily recognizable despite the additions.

Although she knew Estelle meant no real harm by her prank, she felt a twinge of hurt.

"Tell me, my dear Miss Caitlynn. Who will you give this lovely silhouette to?" Estelle crowed, laughing at Caitlynn's expression.

Caitlynn forced a smile. "To someone very special," she murmured. "And my silhouette, matted and framed, will be the *only* gift she finds in her stocking this year. From me, anyway."

"Really? And who is this special person?" Estelle demanded eagerly.

"You, you horrid child!" Caitlynn replied, smiling as Estelle's gleeful grin faded into dismay. Perhaps being repaid in kind would teach her charge that teasing was no fun for the victim. "After we finish your guardian's present, let's ring for tea, shall we? I'm starved."

Caitlynn fell asleep in an armchair by her bedroom fire that evening, still fully dressed, an open copy of *Wuthering Heights* forgotten in her lap.

She was dreaming of the tormented Heathcliff, who now had the doctor's face and was bent on doing any number of deliciously wicked things to her, when an alien sound woke her.

Springing to her feet, she hastened to the door and pressed her ear to the jamb. After a moment's hesitation, she slipped out and crept along the empty landing.

At the top of the stairs, she crouched down and

peered over the balustrade into the foyer below.

Despite her haste, she was in time only to see the top of the doctor's dark head before he donned his hat, and to catch a swirling glimpse of his dark cloak before he plunged out the door and into the night. There was a rush of cold air against her cheek, then the click of the door as it closed behind him.

Her decision was made in a heartbeat. Hurrying back to her room, she threw on her cloak and bonnet, snatched up her gloves, then hurried down the stairs as fast as her skirts would allow.

Despite the doctor's comment about her 'delicate sensibilities,' she prided herself on being a New Woman, and a New Woman was one of action! A New Woman would not continue to sit idly by, twiddling her thumbs and wondering where the doctor went at night, and why such secrecy shrouded his nocturnal jaunts, and if they could in any way be connected to Deirdre's disappearance. Or even the recent murders. No. A New Woman would follow him and find out for herself, whatever the risk. She owed her cousin that much, she thought with a frightened little shiver.

Praying no one would hear her, she ran lightly down the stairs, unbolted the front door and let herself out into the dark, rainy night.

The moon was full, yet shrouded by tattered remnants of clouds and a light veil of rain. The gaslights on this side of the square shed oily puddles of light on the wet cobbles, which were black as pitch at this late hour.

In the pools of amber gaslight, she could see that the square was quite empty in both directions, and her heart sank.

There was no point in trying to follow the elusive

doctor unless she knew in which direction he had gone. For the time being, she would have to forgo her pursuit, admit defeat and return to her room. But the next time, he would not escape her so readily, she vowed.

She pushed open the iron gate and started back up the flagstone path to number 13's front door. As she did so, an owl flew over the park railings. On ghostly white wings, it glided only a few feet in front of her as it pursued its squeaking quarry into the darkened gardens of number 13.

The owl's hooting was so low, so melancholy, so eerie on the damp hush, the fine hairs on her neck and upper arms stood up. Almost simultaneously, icy chills trickled down her spine. And with the gooseflesh came a sudden, sad thought. A bone-chilling possibility she had not dared to contemplate till now.

No matter what she did, she might never see Deirdre again.

It is a dreary night, cold and drizzling as I make my way through the darkened streets of Whitechapel toward Miller's Court.

Every step I take draws me closer to my quarry. Closer to my final sacrifice. First there was Polly. Then Annie. Long Liz. Catherine. And now Mary Jane. Can you feel me, Mary? Can you? I am very close. Have you any inkling that Justice will find you even there, locked in your sorry bolt-hole? Do you confess your sins, Mary? Will you make atonement with your blood to save your immortal soul? Or do you believe yourself safe from retribution, protected by the ugly fortress walls of your little doss?

I chuckle to myself as I watch her window from the mouth of a dark alley across the street. She has a fire lit, does little Mary, and its flickering pattern plays

*across the walls. I smile. I am saving you from flames
far worse than those, Mary Jane. From the fires of hell
and from the flames of eternal perdition.*

The tide is rising again as I cross the street to her
lodging. No one accosts me as I go, although there are
people about. No one asks what I am doing there. My
kind are many on these darkened streets since Polly's
murder. And in their great numbers, there is a certain
anonymity. No one will remember me afterwards. I am
but one of thousands, caped in righteousness, an
avenger, a warrior. God's own champion, I knock
upon her door.

"Who is it?" she asks. There is fear in her voice.
"Joey, is that you?"

"No. It's me. Everything all right, Mary?" I ask, the
soul of concern. "I thought I heard something. A cry,
perhaps. A shout. Something."

She opens the door a crack. Peers out. She is younger
than the others, dark, and surprisingly pretty. "Oh, it's
you. I thought it was . . . well, never mind."

She expected her husband, Joe. Or the landlord, after the overdue rent.

"Anything wrong?"

"No, nothing. I was singing. That's all."

"You're sure? There's no one in there with you?"

"Gawd, no. I'm sure."

"Good. I thought one of your callers might be the
worse for drink—"

"No, everything is all right. I don't have a caller,
not tonight. Never again. I've given it up, I have." Her
decision was swayed by drink.

"It's a cold night, Mary. A wet night for a man to
be out. That fire looks warm." I nod at the hearth
across the room. There's a big black kettle on the hob.

"So it is."

"A warm fire and a nice cup o' tea. Got the kettle on, too, I see."

"So I have. I thought my Joe might come home, see."

"Do I have to ask, Mary?" I say in a wounded tone. "Do I have to beg? Is that what you want me to do? I was worried about you, Mary. Remember—that cry I heard? I thought the worst. That Ripper bloke! You never know. I was worried for you, pretty Mary, so I came. Won't you ask me in?"

Embarrassed, she smiles. "I shouldn't. I really shouldn't. You should know that, better'n anyone."

I laugh. "If you're not safe with me, then who are you safe with, eh, you silly girl, you!"

My laughter works the charm.

"You're right. I'm being a proper twit," she agrees, flinging the door wide. "Come in for a cuppa."

Like that, I am in, as smoothly as a hot knife sliding through butter. The rest will follow, as surely as day follows night.

"I'm going to make you famous, Mary Jane," I murmur under my breath as Big Ben chimes three in the distance. "A hundred years from now, the world will still be talking about you. I'm going to save your soul. . . ."

"What's that, luv?" she asks me.

"Nothing, Mary," I tell her, smiling as I draw the knife from my sleeve. "Nothing at all."

114

Chapter Nine

"God help us!" Rose exclaimed over breakfast on Friday in the kitchen of number 13. "He struck again." Her rosy face, plump and creased as a winter apple with worry, peered over a copy of the *London Telegraph*.

"Who did what, Mrs. Larkin?" her husband asked around the ham he was chewing.

"The Ripper. He struck again last night!"

Caitlynn dropped her fork with a clatter. She immediately felt sick. "Last night? You're sure?"

"Oh, yes, miss," Rose confirmed in a lurid tone. "It says so right here in this morning's *Telegraph*. 'Monster Claims Fifth Victim in East End Bloodbath.' "

"How awful!" Caitlynn said, remembering. Last night she had stood at the top of the stairs and caught a glimpse of the doctor as he left number 13.

A swirling black cloak.

A rush of cold air.

The ominous click of the front door closing.

A dedicated physician hurrying out into the foggy night on an innocent errand of mercy? Or a vicious killer gone to stalk his helpless prey?

She shivered. Dread lay like a stone in her belly. Something awful was going to happen. She just knew it. "Who was it? Where did it happen?"

"The woman's name was Mary Jane Kelly. Another of those sort. She was found in Miller's Court off Dorset Street. Killed in her own doss, she was, not like the others!"

"He used her own lodgings for his dirty doings?" Tom exclaimed. He shook his white head. "The bastard—pardon me language, miss."

"Aye, and took his time about it, by all accounts." Rose shook her head in disgust. "It says here the poor gel was naked, her innards draped about the room like—like bunting!"

"Holy Mother of God!" Bridget crossed herself. She looked pale. "Miller's Court's not far from your family's lodgings, is it, Annie?"

"Just a few streets. But she asked for it, I reckon. Wicked women like that sort . . . well, they deserve a bad end, and that's just what she got. You reap what you sow in this life," Annie said darkly, looking at Caitlynn. "And all of us know what the wages of sin are."

"Then I hope to God you're as lily-white as you claim to be, miss!" Rose declared. "Oh, there now, will you look at Miss Caitlynn, gone just as white as whey, she has, the poor love. Me and my big mouth. I should never have said anything. Take no notice of me, sweetheart. Just enjoy your breakfast, there's a lamb."

"I couldn't eat another bite, really, Mrs. Larkin. It was delicious, truly it was, but I've lost my appetite."

Caitlynn managed a wan smile. Was he the one? Was Fitzgerald the ruthless killer that Scotland Yard was hunting for? A butcher? A lunatic, wielding a knife?

And she had wanted him to kiss her!

The thought of how close she'd come made her feel sick.

Annie's eyes sparkled with malice. "Oh, you poor love," she mimicked Rose. "I expect it's all that sleep-walking you do. I reckon it's taken away your appetite."

"Sleepwalking?" Caitlynn frowned. "I've never walked in my sleep."

"No? Must be me imagination, then, mustn't it?" Annie shrugged, her expression crafty. "Could have sworn I heard you up and moving around last night. Last week, too."

Annie must mean the night she'd searched the study and been surprised by the doctor. Then again, just last night when she tried to follow him. What else could she mean? She would have to be more careful, if Annie was watching her so closely.

"You must have been dreaming, Annie," she denied glibly. Her cheeks were warm with guilt, yet she forced a breezy smile. "Besides, even if I was sleepwalking, it's not likely you'd have heard me from up in your garret, is it?"

Unless Annie was up and about herself at that hour, Caitlynn thought, frowning. Had the maid been watching her? And if so, why?

A sudden thought occurred. Had Annie once watched Deirdre as closely as she appeared to be watching her? If she had, Annie might know more about her cousin's disappearance than she let on. How could she pry that information from her, Caitlynn wondered, without drawing suspicion on herself? Annie had made it quite clear that she disliked her.

"Enough about those horrid murders. Who's going to the Lord Mayor's Show today?" she asked the others.

There was a chorus of "I am!'s" and Caitlynn breathed a sigh of relief that the subject had been changed so easily.

The Lord Mayor's Show had been an important London tradition since the twelfth century, when London was first granted a City Charter by King John. Accordingly, Dr. Fitzgerald had given permission for all the staff to attend the colorful procession, provided their work was done.

A week ago, over the objection of Mary Montgomery, Caitlynn had persuaded the doctor to permit Estelle to attend for the very first time.

The invalided girl would be able to watch the entire procession comfortably from the Fitzgerald coach. Caitlynn planned to tell her about the surprise outing this morning when Estelle came down to breakfast.

On this day for over eight hundred years, the Lord Mayor of London traveled by coach from his residence in the City to the Royal Courts of Justice in Westminster. There, sumptuously robed in historic fashion, and with all due pomp and circumstance, this year's Lord Mayor, James Whitehead, would kneel to pledge his allegiance to his sovereign lady, Queen Victoria, as had so many before him.

Rose told Caitlynn that thousands of people would line the route the two-hundred-year-old coach would pass through, followed by soldiers, sailors and horse-drawn flower floats decorated by various guilds and businesses. People came from all over England to witness the color and pageantry of the procession. And this year, Caitlynn vowed, Estelle would be one of them.

"You'd best make haste, Miss Caitlynn," Tom said. "It's past seven already, and the procession starts at eleven sharp. You'll have to be there early t'get a good spot."

"Where will you take us, Tom?" Caitlynn asked.

"We'll find a spot by St. Paul's, miss. It's close to St. Bart's Hospital, and the old cathedral's right on the Lord Mayor's route."

"I'd best get on with my work if I'm going," Rose observed, pushing back her chair and bustling about. "You young ladies will be needing a picnic basket to take with you. I hope there's enough cold ham in that pantry for three."

"There will only be two of us, Rose. I'm sure there'll be more than enough."

Rose looked unconvinced. "I hope so. Annie, get to work, now! You, too, Bridget! Both of you, look sharpish!"

"This is so exciting. I've never seen the Lord Mayor's Show before. Thank you for bringing me, Miss Caitlynn," Estelle said. She threw her arm around Caitlynn's neck and hugged her. "You always have the best ideas."

"You're very welcome," Caitlynn said with relief. She'd often suggested outings that would take them farther afield than Huntington Park, but Estelle had never wanted to go. Caitlynn had been afraid the girl would refuse to go to the Lord Mayor's Show as well, but to Caitlynn's surprise, she'd been delighted.

As Rose had promised, London's streets were crowded with excited onlookers. Everyone from clerks to peers of the realm were in attendance. Ladies and gentlemen craned their necks from carriage or coach, or from the upper windows of nearby buildings, while urchins, chimney sweeps and apprentices perched on stone pillars or dangled from the gaslights like monkeys.

The grand old stone or brick buildings, soot-stained and grimy, were festooned in rosettes and red-white-and-blue streamers that fluttered like pennants on the chill November wind. Even the lofty wrought-iron gates of ancient St. Bartholomew's were hung with ribbons and flags, giving the hospital's austere gray walls an oddly festive air.

The citizens of London had outdone themselves with their decorations and their gaiety. They seemed determined to throw off the pall of terror that the murders had cast over their city all that terrible autumn.

"Ooh, look at the horses! Aren't they beautiful?" Estelle exclaimed. Her blue eyes danced with pleasure as she watched the grand procession rumbling past the coach's open door. "Six dappled grays and a golden Cinderella coach! Just like a fairy tale."

"Complete with happy ending, I trust?" finished her guardian, catching his ward's breathless comment as he appeared like magic in the coach's doorway.

"Donovan!"

"Hello, poppet. Enjoying the show?"

"Oh, yes! I'm so glad you could come. Now everything's perfect!"

"I told Tom to find you a spot close to St. Bart's so I could join you both for luncheon," the doctor explained, casting Caitlynn a look that was oddly sheepish.

"What a wonderful idea. I don't see you nearly enough you know, Donovan." Estelle scolded her guardian before Caitlynn had a chance to speak. The girl frowned like a little old woman. "You are hardly ever at home lately, you know."

"I know, poppet. But it can't be helped. There are so many sick people who need me. And by the way, that's *Uncle* Donovan to you, miss," he corrected her, climbing into the coach with them.

He dropped a kiss on Estelle's brow, then grinned at Caitlynn, who had grown silent with surprise. Inclining his dark head to her with mocking gallantry, he murmured, "Good day to you, Miss O'Connor."

He rubbed his cold hands together. Despite the nip in the air, he wore no greatcoat, no cloak, muffler or gloves over his coat. "Now, where's that picnic hamper I was promised, ladies? Don't tell me you've eaten all the food?"

"No. We didn't start yet. Tom has the hamper up on the box. I'll get it. Um, did Mrs. Larkin know you would be joining us, Doctor?" Caitlynn inquired coolly. The cook's comment about there being three for lunch suddenly made sense.

"Oh, I think she had a bit of an inkling, yes," he admitted. A disarming smile and twinkling blue eyes replaced his normally somber expression. "Did I miss the Lord Mayor's coach?"

He had to shout to make himself heard over the din of cheering onlookers, the rousing oom-pah-pah of the brass marching band, and the noisy clatter of hooves, which sounded like the rattle of gunfire.

On the River Thames, far beyond the sea of waving Union Jacks and fluttering pigeons, water cannons were erupting, shooting fountains of water high into the air. Great ships anchored in the Pool were blowing their whistles, as if it were midnight on New Year's Eve instead of November.

Estelle scowled. "Yes. Mayor Whitehead passed by

just a few moments ago. He looked very grand. Did *you* know Uncle Donovan was going to join us?" she asked Caitlynn suddenly.

"Miss Caitlynn had no idea," Donovan cut in before she could answer for herself. "In fact, I believe it's safe to say that, given a choice in the matter, Miss Caitlynn would have preferred I stayed well away."

Although he was speaking to Estelle, he glanced across at Caitlynn as he spoke. She did not return his look, but kept her eyes down. How could she feel such an attraction to him when everything within her screamed that he was dangerous?

"It was a secret between Rose and myself. A surprise. I had to let her in on it so there'd be enough to eat when I joined you. Now, let's see what she packed for us, shall we? I'm starved. Hungry enough to eat a horse. I don't suppose there's one in there . . . ?"

At their request, Tom hefted the hamper down from the box and placed it on the coach floor, between the two leather seats. Caitlynn reached for it, but, despite her infirmity, Estelle was quicker.

Leaning across the banquette, she swung the heavy wicker basket up onto the seat beside her as if it were a feather. Quickly lifting the lid, she handed out folded linen serviettes and plates. "No horses in here, I'm afraid. Will you have a ham sandwich or a salmon-and-cucumber sandwich?" she sweetly asked her guardian.

"Ham," he said quickly, "with mustard."

"There you are. Ham with mustard. And you, Miss Caitlynn? What will you have?" Estelle asked prettily, the perfect hostess.

"A salmon-and-cucumber sandwich, please."

This was no dainty afternoon tea but a substantial meal, designed to satisfy appetites whetted by cold fresh air, and fill hungry bellies. They lunched on crusty slices of bread stuffed with savory fillings of salmon and cucumber, or ham, cheese and mustard pickles, washed down with lemonade. Rose's ginger-snaps, cream buns and jam-filled biscuits followed.

As they ate, the parade streamed past them in a blurred frieze of colors, accompanied by a cacophony of sounds. There was cheering and applause, the rousing, steely blare of brass bands, rumbling flower floats on red or yellow wheels.

Drays from various breweries followed, pulled by magnificent shire draft horses that stood eighteen hands high from their withers to their feathered hooves, which struck the cobbles like hammers striking anvils.

There were military troops, too, rank upon rank of uniformed men marching smartly behind their baton-wielding drill sergeants, boots striking the road as one.

Weaving in and out of the crowds that lined the route were pickpockets up from the East End, ragged little boys, girls, grown men and women. These rascals worked the unsuspecting crowds with such sleight of hand, even a magician would have marveled at their cunning.

"There's a fireworks display later tonight," Donovan said, seated casually opposite Caitlynn. "They set off the fireworks from barges anchored in the Thames. It's really a sight to see."

His left arm lay along the back of the banquette, behind Estelle, who had become very animated since her guardian's arrival. They made a handsome pair, Caitlynn thought idly, she so angelically fair, he so devilishly dark. Day and night. Light and darkness.

Good and evil?

She shivered, as if someone had walked over her grave.

"Fireworks!" Estelle exclaimed. "Oh, I'd love to see them!" She looked up at Donovan beseechingly. "They must be magnificent."

"They are." He seemed annoyed and uncomfortable now. "Very beautiful. On crisp cold nights, the fireworks reflect off the Thames like a mirror. You should see it."

Estelle's face glowed. "I'd love to," she said quickly.

But it was not to Estelle that Donovan was speaking, but to Caitlynn.

"I'm sure it's wonderful," Caitlynn murmured at exactly the same time as Estelle said, "I'd love to."

She eyed the girl, concerned. Estelle had a crush on her handsome guardian. That much was obvious. Had he noticed? she wondered. She thought not. Men! They could be so dense about such matters, and unintentionally hurtful.

"Would you like to? See the fireworks display, I mean?" he asked, looking straight at Caitlynn.

"Oh, yes!" Estelle exclaimed eagerly.

"I'm sorry, poppet. I was asking Miss Caitlynn this time. Perhaps you can come with me next year. Well? Would you care to see the fireworks display, Miss O'Connor?"

"Ye-e-es," Caitlynn begun doubtfully, noting the abject disappointment on her charge's pretty face. How could she gracefully refuse her employer's invitation? "However, I—"

"I'm not doing a very good job of this, am I?" Donovan cut in. He sighed. His smile, always rare, had vanished now. "Let me try again. I've been invited to a dinner party tonight at Sir Charles Townsend's residence on Harley Street. The Townsends are old friends of my father's. They've urged me to bring a dinner companion. You, Estelle, lovely as you are, are not nearly old enough for tonight's gathering. Sorry, poppet. I'd intended to go alone, but then I thought . . . well, I was hoping *you* would do me the honor, Miss O'Connor."

"Me!"

"Yes. We could leave the Townsends' early, then stop off somewhere along the Embankment to watch the fireworks display before going home? What do you think?"

Her heart fluttered in her breast. "It—it's kind of you to invite me, Doctor. However, I have nothing suitable to wear on such short notice. Really. Thank you, but I must refuse."

She inclined her head prettily. Had his usual companion let him down at the last minute? Was that why he had turned to her? Out of desperation? Or . . . did he really want her to accompany him?

"Were you wearing sackcloth and ashes, Miss O'Connor, you would still outshine every woman there," he said in a husky voice, as if it were an effort to speak. "Won't you reconsider?"

"You really should not badger Miss Caitlynn, Uncle Donovan," Estelle broke in crossly. "The poor thing's been jilted once already this year, after all. She's decided to remain a spinster for the rest of her life. Haven't you, Miss Caitlynn?"

"Not exactly, no," Caitlynn amended hastily, shooting Estelle a quelling look. Estelle's eager face dropped. Reaching across, Caitlynn squeezed the girl's hand to show she was not upset with her. The girl meant well, but the things she said! Was that how she seemed to the young woman? A pathetic creature, resigned to being a spinster for fear of being hurt again?

"If your invitation is still open, Dr. Fitzgerald, and if you are sure you will not be ashamed of me, I accept," she said quickly, before she could change her mind, adding, "with thanks." It was not as if they were going to be alone, after all. Tom would be driving the coach, and there would be other dinner guests besides the two of them. She had nothing to fear. Nothing but her own responses, which had proven wildly unpredictable in the doctor's proximity. And if he was in a relaxed and unsuspecting mood, she might be able to quiz him about Deirdre's disappearance.

Estelle sharply withdrew her hand from Caitlynn's as the doctor's normally grave face was transformed by a broad smile. Could the girl feel the current that crackled between them? she wondered.

"Splendid! I'll have Tom ready the coach for us at seven. Meanwhile, I still have patients to see and rounds to make. Until later, Miss O'Connor. Cheerio, poppet. Enjoy your outing."

He chucked Estelle beneath the chin and was gone, munching his half-eaten sandwich as he went.

"You should not read too much into his invitation, Miss Caitlynn. My guardian is something of a womanizer, and very popular with the ladies," Estelle said in an oddly clipped voice when they were alone again.

"Oh?"

"Yes. He has had any number of mistresses, all of whom were ravishingly beautiful. One was mistress to the Prince of Wales before she met my guardian. Donovan keeps her in a little house in Chelsea now, and visits her whenever he wants to share her bed."

"Really, Estelle! That's enough. I do not care to discuss your guardian or his personal life." Her tone was sharp.

The girl's remarks were probably due to jealousy.

Perhaps it would have been wiser to refuse the doctor's invitation, if accepting caused bad feelings between herself and her young charge.

Yet Estelle was not chastened by her scolding. "Don't you? And why is that, I wonder? Could it be that you are jealous of my handsome guardian's mistresses, Miss Caitlynn?" She eyed Caitlynn curiously.

"Not at all. I simply feel such matters are . . . unsuitable for discussion between us. You are very young, after all, Estelle. Such a subject is inappropriate."

"Oh, I'm not so young as all that. I shall be sixteen on my next birthday. Most young women are married by my age, with children."

"So. You are considering marriage, are you, Miss Marsh?" Caitlynn said lightly, in an effort to ease the sudden tension that pricked like spikes between them. "And have you a man in mind for your husband, as yet?"

"Of course. Once he is done sowing his wild oats, I shall become Mrs. Donovan Fitzgerald. *Estelle Fitzgerald.* Don't you adore the way it sounds? I do." Her blue eyes shone, wide and innocent. Her expression was smug.

Caitlynn's jaw dropped. "You are to marry your guardian?" she whispered.

"Why, yes. It's been arranged for years. Didn't you know? Didn't anyone tell you?"

"No. I . . . I had no idea." In fact, the revelation had knocked the wind out of her. To think that Fitzgerald was to marry this pretty child, yet had calmly invited her companion to a dinner party right under his intended's nose, because of his betrothed's youth! And she, to her undying shame, had eagerly accepted his invitation! No wonder Estelle had seemed so upset.

127

Estelle's peal of laughter suddenly rang out. "Look how upset you are, you silly billy! But you have nothing to worry about, truly, Miss Caitlynn! Nothing at all. I was just teasing you."

"Teasing me!"

Estelle nodded. "Yes. Dr. Fitzgerald is my savior and my dearest guardian, but nothing more, as yet. As to whether he has mistresses galore, beautiful or otherwise, in Chelsea or Timbuktu, I really couldn't say." She shrugged airily.

The rush of relief that filled Caitlynn surprised even her. Anger was quick to follow on its heels. Why, that precocious little minx!

"Oh, don't look so cross, Miss Cait. It was only a game, after all. We invalids have so little to occupy us, you see. We are forced to invent new ways to divert ourselves."

"I'm sure you are. However, it is cruel to do so at the expense of others. You should think before you—"

"Cooo-eee! Oh, look!" Estelle exclaimed, cutting her off and waving madly, whether by accident or design, Caitlynn would never know. "There's Bridget and Rose! Rose! Bridget! We're over here!"

Chapter Ten

Big Ben was chiming ten as Donovan handed her up into the coach for the homeward journey after dinner at the small yet elegant Townsend mansion on Harley Street.

The Fitzgerald coach was dark. It smelled a little musty and damp, too. Feeling as fizzy as the champagne, of which she'd imbibed far too much in an effort to settle her nerves, Caitlynn seated herself with exaggerated care, hoping Donovan would not notice that her hands were shaking as she carefully arranged the folds of her cloak about her.

Springs creaked and the vehicle rocked as he sprang inside after her. But rather than taking the worn leather banquette opposite, as he had on the outward journey, he sat beside her. Rapping on the carriage wall, he signaled Tom to lay on.

The coach rumbled down Harley Street, passing palatial homes that belonged to some of England's finest physicians.

"I hope you weren't too bored this evening, my dear," Donovan murmured, turning to her as he leaned back in his seat.

She could feel his dark blue eyes upon her but did not look at him. The smoldering looks he had cast her over the candelabra at dinner had been more than hot enough to scorch the Battenburg tablecloth.

"All that talk about murder and mayhem. It upset you, did it not? You hardly said a word after the first course."

His thigh lay alongside her own on the seat, not touching hers but *there* nonetheless, radiating heat. Far too close, too masculine, for comfort.

"Miss O'Connor? Are you all right?"

He wanted her to talk? That was rich. She could hardly breathe, let alone speak!

"Of—of course. No, it didn't upset me in the least." Another lie, one of dozens she'd told since she left Ireland. She was becoming a mistress of deceit in her efforts to find Deirdre. "And dinner was superb. Thank you again for inviting me."

Her voice shook. The strain of trying to behave normally, coupled with her visceral fear of being alone with him, was beginning to tell.

"... *the brute is obviously an expert surgeon,*" Inspector Abberline of the Metropolitan Police had said with conviction over a delicious creamed asparagus soup, served by liveried footmen. Her flesh crawled now, as it had then. "*Mark my words! When we find our man, he will have M.D. after his name.*"

Conversation at the Townsends' table had turned almost immediately to the terrible murders in the East End, and to speculation about the identity of the Ripper. As she suspected, people all over the world were discussing the terrible crimes.

Some of the Townsends' guests had been key figures in the investigation from the very first. Two were detectives with London's Criminal Investigation Department. The same number were medical examiners. Three were fellow physicians from Harley Street or St. Bart's. There was also a scattering of high-ranking police officials and their wives.

That the guests were, almost to a man, intimately familiar with the infamous case, its victims and the suspects, was terrifying. Their very familiarity made the Ripper more real, more horrifying than any lurid account of his bloody doings in a newspaper or a penny-dreadful.

"It is impossible to believe that he mutilated those women without possessing considerable anatomical knowledge."

"Inspector, please! There are ladies present."

"The wretch is also a lunatic of the lowest, most depraved order," Sir Robert Anderson, Assistant Commissioner of Scotland Yard's CID, had added.

"One who is, moreover, very familiar with the rabbit warren of the East End," said another man whose name she forgot. *"How else would he make his escape so cleverly, when there are police patrols swarming all over Whitechapel?"*

"How indeed? I suspect he dons a disguise—perhaps one of several disguises—when he commits these atrocities. I believe a bonnet and other female attire were found burned on the last victim's hearth?"

"Yes," Inspector Abberline confirmed. *"That is quite correct."*

"I believe Kelly let him in, thinking he was a friend of hers. Just another woman. It was the last mistake

she would ever make. The murderer is also very fa-
miliar with the habits of the 'unfortunates' and thus
easily able to get close to them, despite their fear. One
of their bullies, perhaps, or someone who is just as
familiar in the East End, and therefore invisible . . ."

"Thank you for accepting," Donovan was saying.

His husky comment jerked her attention back to the
present. To the gently rocking coach, and the enigmatic man who sat beside her in the shadows, swathed
all in black, like an inky shadow himself.

"Wh-what?"

"The Townsends' invitation. Thank you for accom-
panying me. As I told you, Sir Charles and Lady Cecily
are old and dear friends of my father's. They've been
very good to me, too, despite the anti-Irish sentiment
here in England. However, their dinner parties can be
somewhat . . . trying." He smiled. "Tonight, however,
I actually enjoyed myself. For that, I have you to
thank."

"Me? How so?"

"Because of you, the view from my side of the table
was stunning. It more than made up for the topic of
conversation."

His voice dropped. Its timbre became low, sensual
and so intimate, she blushed. His face was very close
to hers now. So close, she could feel his warm breath
on her cheek, the tickle of his glossy black hair.

The hair on her own neck rose in response.

Attraction? she wondered, feeling a little faint and
unable to draw a proper breath, as if her stays were
too tightly laced. Or . . . something else? Fear or desire? Which was it? She sighed. The only thing she was
sure of at this point in time was her confusion.

How could she be drawn to a man like him? A po-
tentially dangerous man who could be stalking her at

this very moment, planning to make her his next victim . . . ?

"As I said, it was a very nice evening," she said again, louder than necessary. Surely Tom would hear her if she screamed, and come to her aid? Or would he? She frowned. Tom had been with Fitzgerald for years. He might simply do his master's bidding, even if that meant helping to dispose of a body . . .

A similar train of thought had been thoroughly discussed that evening: the possibility that the women were murdered elsewhere, their bodies dumped later from a closed carriage.

She swallowed nervously. "Lady Cecily is such a dear person."

He smiled. "Yes." Turning to face her, he cupped her face in his hands. His palm was warm as he cradled her cheek. "Enough, Caitlynn." His voice was stern yet gentle. "I can't keep up this charade anymore, even if you can. I'll be damned if I'll waste precious time in talking, when I could be kissing you."

Kissing her—or killing her? Was one a prelude to the other?

Her heart skittered nervously. Her mouth was dry. The blood roared in her ears.

Fear? Guilty excitement? Or . . . a little of both?

A lot of both, she corrected.

Danger and desire made potent aphrodisiacs.

She was afraid of him. She feared for her life. She should leap from the coach and flee into the night to escape him. She should be outraged at the mere thought of being alone with a man who might well have killed and would probably kill again—not want him to kiss her.

Instead, she was fascinated by him, excited by his Celtic good looks, aroused by his dark side. Intrigued

133

by the very fact that his true nature was hidden, a mystery to her. An enigma.

A reckless part of her wanted him to touch her, aye, and to hold all the wonderful masculine breadth of him in her arms. She knew herself to be a woman of earthy needs—needs she had never discussed or confessed to anyone, yet she sensed that this man would understand those needs, and not think less of her for having them.

She craved his lips, his kisses, his bed, with a dark and dangerous hunger that both thrilled and frightened her.

"Please don't say such things, Dr. Fitzgerald. We hardly know each other, after all—" She fell abruptly silent. He was so close, she could feel the heat of his body. If she closed her eyes, she could smell him, too, a mixture of shaving soap, of spicy bay rum, of cigar smoke. Heady, masculine smells.

"Call me Donovan."

"Very well." She sighed. "Donovan it shall be. Dr. Donovan, I do believe you are feeling a little the worse for liquor," she murmured, thinking to placate him. She tried to smile but could not.

"What I am, Cait, is hungry," he said thickly, looking not at all placated. His beautiful mouth was only a whisper from hers. She was lost, drowning in midnight eyes. Drowning in eyes like dark stars, in a voice like liquid silk. "Hungry for your mouth," he whispered as he linked his fingers through hers, still looking down at her. "Hungry for the taste of you."

Their fingers entwined, he lifted her hand to his lips and kissed the knuckles, then turned her hand over and kissed the well of her palm. "And if I'm drunk, as you claim, then 'tis you who intoxicates me. So shut up, Cait. Shut up and let me kiss you . . ."

So saying, he drew her into his arms.

"No!" She pressed her palms against his broad chest. Pushed him away. "Let go!"

"What is it? What are you so frightened of?" She was very pale. Her sable hair had escaped its pins and combs. It spilled in thick dark ribbons about her face. Her eyes were wide, the pupils dilated in the amber gaslight that slanted into the shadowed coach. Green pools of terror.

"Caitlynn? Tell me! What is it?" Holding her by the upper arms, he shook her slightly, searching her face for an answer. Surely such a spirited woman was not so afraid of being kissed?

Then his lips thinned in anger as understanding dawned.

"Aaah. I see. You think I had something to do with those women's murders. That's it, isn't it?" Abruptly he released her, almost thrusting her away from him.

"No, of course not," she insisted, shaking her head.

"Don't bother to deny it, damn it. It's not as if you're the first," he said, sounding bitter. "I sincerely doubt you'll be the last. I wonder. How many others think me capable of such butchery? Of hurting the people I'm sworn to heal?"

His harsh words struck home, for they had the ring of truth. Hearing him, seeing the hurt in his face, the anger, she was suddenly unsure of herself, doubted her suspicions.

Could the man who had spoken so . . . so . . . eloquently in defense of those poor women at dinner have murdered them? Could someone who spent endless hours at the hospital, doing rounds and holding clinics for the sick, the poor, the downtrodden, also be a ruthless killer, by night preying on the prostitutes he championed by light of day?

135

It was possible. But not very likely.

"How can you sit there in your comfortable chairs, your bellies full, a warm bed awaiting you, and condemn those poor women for what they were, for what they were forced to become? Tell me that!" he'd asked one man who, like Annie, suggested that the murdered women had got only what they deserved.

His lean, shadowed face was intent. His dark blue, almost black, eyes blazed in the light of the chandelier. His voice, its brogue more marked than usual, had vibrated with emotion as he added, *"It is the fault of our society that they are brought so low and made so desperate."*

"Society?" one man had asked. *"Why do you blame our society, sir?"*

"Because, in our prudish efforts to stamp out immorality, we passed laws that made mothers the sole providers for their illegitimate babes. This same law allowed their fathers to go scot-free, without giving a farthing to their care, or that of the mothers who bore them!"

"The point you make is valid, sir," said another man. *"Which is precisely why the laws you speak of were repealed several years ago. Yet most of these wretched women continue to sell themselves on the street! Why can they not seek honest employ as seamstresses in the sweatshops, perhaps, or in the match factories? Such work is poorly paid, true, but respectable nonetheless."*

" 'Respectable' does not put food in a family's belly, sir! How shall an unwed mother with a baby find such work as you speak of, when no decent employer will hire her, on account of her so-called 'immorality'? Laws may have been repealed, but public opinion is less easily changed.

Obsession

"Blame the laws if you must, sir. Blame the rakes and lechers who seduce, then abandon these young girls when they are with child. But for pity's sake, gentlemen, do not blame the women!"

There had been an awkward silence after his impassioned speech in defense of the 'unfortunates.' Some of the female guests had muttered under their breath, clearly shocked by the young doctor's unexpected stand on the matter, or by the subject of the discussion itself. The men's faces had been pinched in open disapproval or wreathed in scowls.

Lady Cecily Townsend had quickly made some witty comment or other, cleverly turning the tide of conversation to other, less controversial topics, but the damage had been done. The conversation at table resumed, but Donovan was given no opportunity to participate. When those at dinner adjourned to the drawing room for the evening's entertainments, Donovan announced that they would be leaving. She had not been surprised.

"I'm very sorry, Doctor. I was mistaken. I hope you will accept my deepest apologies. That you would harm those women is . . . well, it's unthinkable."

As she spoke, she said what she thought he wanted to hear, hoping it would calm him, turn aside the anger she'd generated. But when she finished, she realized it was true.

The dedicated, passionate man who had spoken in defense of the downtrodden at dinner tonight, and the 'saucy' Jack who delighted in destroying the same women, were not one and the same man. Like so many others, she had simply succumbed to the mass hysteria that had been rampant in the East End since September and had jumped to conclusions.

From somewhere she found the courage to reach out and touch his hand with her gloved fingertips. "Dr.

137

Fitzgerald? Donovan? Forgive me. Please?"

Taking her hand in his, he lifted it to his lips and kissed it. Their eyes met.

"Caitlynn. Beautiful Cait. I would forgive you anything for the price of a kiss." With a low murmur, he cupped her chin. "Will you pay my forfeit?"

"Yes."

He lowered his dark head and covered her lips with his own, savoring the sweetness that was her mouth.

"Blessed Mary," she murmured when she recovered her breath. His kisses drove the thoughts from her head. She was a trembling mass of emotions. Of feelings. "You should not, sir. Truly. I am not that kind of wo—aah."

To her shame, her halfhearted protest ended on a sigh as he grasped her firmly by the shoulders and took her mouth again. This time he kissed her even more deeply, more lingeringly, more thoroughly than he had before.

"Aah, Cait." He stroked her flushed cheek, tousled the soft tendrils of hair that framed her sweet face. "Darlin' Cait. You've no need to fear me. Ever."

He kissed her closed eyelids, first one, then the other. The tip of her nose. The dimpled corners of her mouth. His tongue traced her lips, then slipped between them to touch her own.

It was the most erotic kiss she had ever been given. She felt it in every part of her, in her mind, in her breasts, between her thighs. Perhaps even in her heart.

Cradling her head, Donovan bore her down, so that she lay across the banquette beneath him.

Hard hips angled across hers, he deepened the kiss, crushing her mouth beneath his, her body beneath his, as his knee pressed between her thighs.

She moaned as heat rippled through her loins, a liquid undulating warmth. *Desire?* What else could it be? But desire was for fallen women, for widows and those of the demimonde, not decent Catholic girls!

"Beautiful Cait. Lovely Cait," he murmured thickly in her ear. "I've wanted to kiss you ever since that day in the park." He nuzzled her throat, his lips pressed to the dancing pulse at its base. "To hold you. To awaken you to pleasure. Would you like that, my innocent Cait?"

She shuddered with the promise of undreamed-of pleasures. Of heady delights that glimmered like flashes of sunlight on water.

Feeling wild and reckless, she lay across the banquette beneath his hard male body, his to touch, to taste, to caress at will. A reckless hoyden without morals, without propriety, all sensibilities forgotten.

Devil take sensibilities! she thought. To Hades with propriety and decency! They were for the old Caitlynn. For the foolish woman who'd believed she loved Michael Flynn. Tonight . . . just this once . . . she would be someone else. A woman who was no stranger to passion. A woman who was not afraid to explore her desires . . .

Her fingers kneaded the shabby leather beneath her as he scorched kisses over her creamy throat. His hand inside her cloak, he splayed his fingers over her breast and whispered her name.

"Caitlynn. Caitlynn."

She moaned softly, a breathy sigh that thickened in her throat, like the guttural purr of a she-cat. She was melting, and she didn't want it to end.

Ever.

Drawing down the neck of her gown, he bared her collarbones, pressing his lips to the silky flesh.

Through the coach window, fireworks were exploding with crackling explosions of sound, spangling the frosty sky with glittering starbursts of gold, ruby, white and emerald. Yet their magical beauty paled beside the way she felt. Compared to the singing of the blood in her veins, the wild throbbing of her heart, they were nothing . . .

"*Here we are, sir!*"

Tom's voice!

She stiffened. The rosy euphoria shattered like glass.

"Stop!" She tried to sit up. To neaten her hair and straighten her clothing. "Doctor, please!"

"Drive around the park, Tom," Donovan ordered thickly. "Take it slowly."

"No! Please. I really must go in."

He froze. "Very well. If that's what you want." He ordered Tom to halt. "Here. Let me help you with those combs. Your hands are like ice."

She did not trust herself to speak as he helped her to neaten her hair, to draw the folds of her velvet-lined cloak tidily about her. His ease and familiarity with female attire and hair made her wonder, fleetingly, if Estelle had not been telling the truth about his countless mistresses, after all.

"There." He planted a farewell kiss on her cheek that was almost brotherly. He smiled. "Once again you are the very model of propriety."

He had kissed her. What had she been thinking of, to let him? She closed her eyes, willing the ground to open up and swallow her whole, as the whale had swallowed Jonah. How could she face him after this? How could she continue her employ in his household as if nothing had happened, let alone continue her search for Deirdre?

"Do you . . . are you mocking me, sir?" she asked stiffly, forcing herself to meet his eyes.

"On the contrary, Miss O'Connor," he said. "Had I not the deepest respect for you, we would even now be dizzily circling the square." His lip curled in mockery. "Come. Let us go inside."

Chapter Eleven

"Something's not right, sir!" Caitlynn heard Tom exclaim as he opened the coach door for them. "Every lamp in the bloomin' 'ouse is lit."

"So it is!" Donovan agreed, springing to the ground. He handed Caitlynn down after him. "What the devil's going on?"

Number 13 blazed like a golden beacon, the only house on the darkened square that was still lit at this late hour. Dark shadows could be seen through the sheer lace curtains as people moved about in one of the upper rooms.

"It's Estelle!" Donovan exclaimed. Taking Caitlynn's elbow, he ushered her up the pathway, let them both into the house, then took the steep, curving staircase to the upper story two steps at a time. Caitlynn hurried after him.

"What is it, Henry?" An elderly white-haired man was coming out of Estelle's room with Mrs. Montgomery. He was plucking a pair of gold-rimmed spectacles off his nose, which he tucked into his waistcoat pocket.

"The usual, I'm afraid, my boy. Your young miss has been quite feverish this evening. Fortunately, her temperature's on the way down now. Your girls have given her a sponge bath, and I've given her some medicine. I expect she'll sleep well tonight and awake feeling much better in the morning. Your Mrs. Montgomery had the good sense to send young Annie for me about an hour ago."

"Quite right, Mrs. Montgomery," Donovan said approvingly, patting a rigid shoulder. "Well done. Your quick thinking is to be commended."

"Not at all, sir. Besides, somebody had to do it," Mary Montgomery murmured, her hands tucked primly in front of her, "when them that have the care of the young lady are off gallivanting till all hours." She shot Caitlynn an accusing look.

"May I see her?" Caitlynn asked Donovan. They both ignored the housekeeper's snide comment.

"Of course. Go on in," Donovan urged. "Mary, take Dr. Geoffries down to my study. See that he gets a drink. I'll be with you shortly, Henry."

The maids, still in their nightclothes, were stripping rumpled, sweat-sodden linens from the bed and replacing them with fresh ones when Caitlynn entered the room, followed by Donovan.

Estelle was propped up on the chaise longue, looking wan and tiny in a voluminous white nightgown, from which her sparrow legs protruded like matchsticks. Her face was pale except for two spots of bright red in her cheeks. Her fair curls were damp and clung to her head. Her eyes still glittered with fever.

"My poor poppet," Donovan murmured, bending down to kiss Estelle's head. Holding her left wrist, he

143

took her pulse, using the gold watch he took from his waistcoat pocket. "Feeling wretched, are you, poppet?" He pulled down her lower eyelids and inspected her eyes.

She nodded.

"Do your arms and legs hurt?"

"I hurt everywhere," she whimpered, licking cracked lips. "I ache so much."

"Doc Geoffries has given you some medicine to help with that. It will start to work in just a little while. Soon you'll be fast asleep."

"Promise?"

"I promise."

"Are you thirsty? Would you like some lemon-barley water?" Caitlynn offered. She desperately wanted to do something for the ailing girl. *Anything.* Like it or not, Montgomery's words had struck home. She felt awful that Estelle had fallen ill while she was out enjoying the evening with the girl's guardian.

Estelle nodded wanly.

"In a second, Caitlynn. Let's get her back into bed first." Leaning down, Donovan lifted Estelle and placed her on the fresh sheets. "There you go, sweetheart."

Bridget pulled the bedcovers up, covering her to her chin in a snowy froth of *broderie anglaise.*

Caitlynn poured some lemon-barley water into a glass. Supporting Estelle's head, she pressed the glass to her lips. "There you go. Does that help?"

"Mmm. Yes. Thank you." Estelle took a few sips; then her head fell back on the pillow. She sighed heavily, as if even so small an effort had exhausted her.

"Sleep, sweetheart. Get all the rest you can. You'll feel much better in the morning," Donovan murmured.

"Dr. Geoffries gave her something for fever and

joint pain," he said, leading Caitlynn out onto the landing. "She should sleep for several hours, now that the fever's broken. There's nothing else we can do for her tonight."

"Perhaps not, but I'd like to sit with her, if I may. That way, if she wakes, someone will be here."

"By all means, do." He frowned and shook his head. "When Estelle was a little girl, I used to hold her on my lap all night long when she was having these attacks. It was the only way she would be comforted. Her nanny despaired."

She hesitated. "Dr. . . . Donovan, what's wrong with her?"

"She has rheumatic fever. She was already a very sick little girl when I . . . well, when she became my ward. It is a disease that recurs periodically, with fevers, night sweats, severe pains in the joints. It also damages the valves of the heart."

"Then it is serious?"

"Very, I'm afraid."

"And she will never recover completely?"

He shook his head. "No. You see how she is. She's much too weak to walk. Too frail to ever lead a normal life."

"I see." Her eyes filled with tears.

"I have a few things to discuss with Dr. Geoffries. If you should need me during the night—if there's anything, however small, that concerns you—ring for Bridget or Annie. Have them wake me immediately."

"I will."

He took her hand, lifted it to his lips and kissed it. "Tonight was very special, Caitlynn. Thank you."

"Yes. Good night," she said quickly, looking away, for once at a loss for words.

After he went downstairs, she let herself into her

room. She would change into her nightgown and robe, then take her book into the adjoining room and sit with Estelle for an hour or two.

Fresh guilt washed over her. That poor girl. Had Estelle rung for her while she was gone, and received no answer? Caitlynn wondered guiltily. Her heart ached. She had let Estelle down. Abandoned her without ever realizing until tonight, how fond of her she had become.

She changed, then retrieved her book from the night table. She was heading for the connecting door to Estelle's room when she froze in her tracks, frowning as she looked about her. Someone had been in her room while she was gone!

At first glance, everything looked as she'd left it, but on closer inspection, small details were subtly changed. The way the counterpane draped at the corners of the bed was not quite as she'd left it, as if someone had lifted its folds to peek underneath and hurriedly replaced it. The notepaper, blotter, nibs and inkwells on her desk had been subtly rearranged. The armoire door was ajar instead of neatly closed.

Deirdre's diary! Oh, no! Had whoever searched the room found it? Was the diary what the intruder had been looking for?

She scrambled across the room, dropping to her knees on the hearth, not caring if her dressing gown was ruined by coal dust and ashes.

Thank God. Deirdre's diary, wrapped in the sooty shawl, was safe in its hiding place, as it had been all summer. So it would remain, unless an enormous fire was lit. She left the diary there and stood up.

It was only then that she caught the sparkle of glass on the hearth. She picked up the shard. It was scorched and black and left soot on her fingers. Crouching

146

down, she frowned as she turned the glass shard over in her hand. It looked familiar. What could it have come from? Had one of the maids broken something and been afraid to tell her? Had the person who searched her room broken something?

Hurrying to the desk, she pulled out a drawer and almost wept at what she found—or rather, what she didn't find—there.

The silver frames were gone, as were the three glass ambrotype plates they held. The only family picture that remained to her was the one of Deirdre she kept hidden in her drawstring bag. The one of Mama and Da on their wedding day, taken on the steps of St. Patrick's Church, was missing. So was the picture of her brothers and sisters a few years ago, following Patrick's baptism.

Her eyes filled. The picture had shown the older boys in their Sunday best coats and trousers, the younger ones in caps and knickers, every one of them with the spark of mischief in his eyes. Little Maggie had been wearing her best pinafore and hair ribbons, holding baby Patrick in her arms. Her infant brother had been wearing the one-hundred-year-old heirloom christening gown they had all worn in their turn.

She swallowed. Bad enough that the thief had stolen the silver frames. Shattering the precious ambrotypes in the hearth had been unnecessarily spiteful. If a sparkling chip of glass had not slipped through the rungs of the grate, Bridget or Annie would have shoveled out the fragments in the morning along with the ashes, and she would never have known what became of them.

Angry tears scalded her eyes. Who would do something so spiteful, so cruel? Obviously, she had made a bitter enemy in this household. But who? she wondered. Mrs. Montgomery? Annie? Bridget? No, not

Bridget. Bridget was not evil, and evil had been here in her room. It lingered still.

She shivered and cast a wary glance over her shoulder. Evil clung to the draperies, hovered in the shadows, even though the evildoer was long gone. That evil was as real, as palpable, as any miasma.

She gathered up book, shawl and pillow and went through the connecting door into Estelle's room.

Her charge was deeply asleep, bless her, her lashes long and surprisingly dark against her flushed cheeks, her breathing deep and even.

Caitlynn gently felt Estelle's cheek with the back of her hand. Good. Dr. Geoffries's medicine was working. Her cheek felt warm to the touch, but not overly so. The fever was gone, for the time being. "Sleep well, darlin' girl," she murmured.

Caitlynn carried the oil lamp away from the bed, keeping the wick trimmed low so that the light would not wake the sleeping girl.

Tucking herself into one of the wing chairs drawn up to the fire, she stuck the bolster behind her neck and tried to read. But the words blurred and ran together like rain down a windowpane. She could not concentrate on the moors, on Cathy and Heathcliff or their torment, not tonight. She had torments of her own.

Her thoughts kept returning to Donovan, to his kisses and her startling response to them. To the Whitechapel murders and the identity of the killer. To the intruder and the shattered ambrotypes. To Deirdre's disappearance.

Question after nagging question churned around and around in her mind like clabbering butter, without any answers, until her head ached and she was utterly exhausted.

Obsession

From staring into the glowing coals of the fire, she drifted into an uneasy sleep, sitting upright in the chair. In the distance, Big Ben chimed two. It was the last sound she heard.

The next thing she knew, it was daylight. The scrap of sky she could see between the draperies was pale with the promise of snow. Annie and Bridget were bustling about, bringing the morning tea for her, broth for Estelle, a scuttle of coal to lay on the fire.

Another day had dawned, but she was still no closer to finding Deirdre. Still no closer to learning the truth.

Chapter Twelve

"Well, hello, there! 'Tis Miss O'Connor, is it not? I thought so. I never forget a pretty face. Merry Christmas, my child."

"Merry Christmas, Father Robert."

"Tell me, have you found your missing sister?" the assistant priest asked, looking serious as he walked beside her up the steps of St. Anthony's Church.

"My missing cousin? No." Caitlynn's smile faded. "It's as if she vanished off the face of the earth, Father."

"I'm sorry to hear that. You might ask Father Timothy if he's seen her. He was away from the parish the last time you visited us. But he's much more likely to remember your cousin than I am, as he's been the parish priest here for almost thirty years. Please, let me carry that basket for you."

Her basket was piled high with mysterious packages, wrapped in brown paper and tied with string.

"Thank you, but it's not at all heavy. I thought I'd show Father Timothy my cousin's picture, if he's here."

"He is. And feeling much recovered from his illness, thank the good Lord. You'll find him in the vestry, Miss O'Connor." Father Robert nodded to the rear of the gloomy church, lit only by the flicker of votive candles. "Go on through. I hope he's able to help you."

"Thank you, Father. So do I." She made her way between the rows of wooden pews, past the altar to the vestry, beneath the agonized eyes of the crucified Christ.

Wintry gray light slanted through stained-glass panels that portrayed the temptations of Anthony in the desert, the saint distributing his wealth amongst the poor, and miraculously healing those afflicted with erysipelas, or St. Anthony's Fire as the disease was called in honor of the saint.

"Yes, my child?" Father Timothy asked wearily, peering up at her through wire-rimmed spectacles. He appeared quite frail, dwarfed by the mounds of paperwork strewn across the desk in front of him. "Have you a loved one in need of the final sacrament?"

"No, Father. Nothing like that." Caitlynn quickly introduced herself and explained her reasons for wanting to speak with the elderly priest. When she was finished, she withdrew the one-quarter ambrotype of Deirdre, framed in silver, from her drawstring bag. "This is a likeness of my cousin, Father. She was last seen in July. Do you recall ever seeing her among your congregation?"

Father Timothy's lips pursed in thought. He studied Deirdre's picture for several moments. "Such big dark eyes—the windows to the soul, 'tis said. A lovely young woman like that would be difficult to forget.

151

And as it happens, I do remember her, quite clearly."

"You do!" The excited words burst from her.

The elderly priest nodded. "Yes. But not as a member of my congregation, I'm afraid. No. Quite the contrary. This young woman used the house of God for her romantic . . . assignations."

"Assignations?"

"Yes. At least, so I assumed. Assignations, trysts, rendezvous, call them what you will. Last April or May, I think it was, this young woman started coming to my church every Thursday afternoon, regular as clockwork. She would visit the confessional, then return to her pew to sit and pray. Before long, she was joined by a gentleman. Within a few moments, they left together, arm in arm, like sweethearts."

"Was the man anyone you knew?"

The old priest shrugged. "No. But I assumed they were sweethearts, using God's house for their meetings."

"You disapproved." His tone said as much.

"I did, yes. There was . . . a . . . a certain furtiveness about them that made me think they did not want to be seen. I wondered if the gentleman was perhaps a married man. Or someone the young woman's parents did not approve of. She was too well-spoken, too well-dressed, to be from the East End, you see. As was he."

"I see. And what did the man look like?" Caitlynn asked breathlessly. Her heart was skittering about like a dervish.

"Let me see." He pursed his lips. "Quite tall. Wavy black hair. Medium build. Oh, and he was Irish—educated Irish, I'd say, by the way he spoke. Not from the East End, either of them."

"Could he . . . is it possible he was a doctor?" She almost held her breath as she awaited his answer.

152

Please don't let it be he. Please oh please oh . . .

"Very possibly," Father Tim said, and she died a little inside. *Ah, Caitlynn. Had that night, that stolen kiss, meant so much, then?* "Although I don't recall ever seeing him carrying a physician's bag. He was obviously quite smitten with the young lady, judging by the way he always handed her up into the hack—"

Caitlynn's head snapped up. "They took a cab?"

"Why, yes. Every Thursday."

"You wouldn't know where they went?" she asked eagerly, praying he would.

He shook his head. "I'm sorry . . . But perhaps you could find the cabby. I understand they cover roughly the same general area every day, looking for fares. Very territorial fellows, these cabbies."

"Do you remember when you saw the couple last, Father?"

"Oh, let me see. At the end of June or the beginning of July, it must have been. You see, my assistant, Father Robert, was sent here in late June, when I first began feeling my age." He smiled. "I only recall seeing the couple a time or two after his arrival, so that would make it the early part of July." The priest polished his spectacles on the hem of his black cassock. "I'm afraid that's all I can tell you, Miss . . . ?"

"O'Connor. Caitlynn O'Connor. You've been a great help, Father. Thank you. Just one more question before I let you get back to your paperwork. Have you seen the man since?"

"I have not, no."

"You've been very helpful, Father Timothy. Thank you. If you remember anything else, please, please contact me at this address." She handed him a calling card on which she had written the address of the Fitzgerald residence.

153

"I will." He hesitated. "Miss O'Connor, have you asked Our Blessed Lady to guide your search?"

"I have, Father. Each and every day. Thank you again for your help."

There was a mounting sense of urgency inside her as she flagged down the empty hackney carriages that passed through the St. Anthony's area, showing Deirdre's picture to every startled cabdriver that would stop to listen to her.

Yet each cabby had the same disappointing answer. No. They had not seen Deirdre, either alone or with a male companion. Or if they had, they didn't recall having done so.

Determined not to find herself alone in Saucy Jack's territory after dark this time, she paid the last cabby to take her to the far side of Huntington Park. It was early yet—too early to go straight home. She would go the rest of the way on foot, despite the cold. A brisk walk would warm her, and give her time to think; to accept that Deirdre had been meeting a man who sounded very much like Donovan Fitzgerald. . . .

Although she'd suspected something of the sort all along, Father Timothy's apparent confirmation was a shock. Was Donovan really the beloved 'D' Deirdre had written about in her diary? Probably. Who else could he be? Then 'D' was the same man who had kissed *her* with such ardor in the coach, barely six months later.

Her heart ached, yet her body simmered with a disquieting broth of rage and sorrow. She would have given anything she possessed for Deirdre's lover . . . friend . . . sweetheart to be someone else. *Anyone* else. But another part of her—the realistic part—knew that that was unlikely, and raged at life's injustice. The man she thought she was falling in love with might very well hold the key to her cousin's disappearance. Even worse, he could be directly responsible for it.

She walked briskly, her breath forming puffs of smoky vapor on the cold air, telling herself as she went that, even if Donovan *had* been meeting Deirdre on her Thursday afternoons off, it did not follow that he had anything to do with her disappearance.

Nevertheless, such a possibility tainted her new and fragile feelings for him. Replaced her deepening affection with confusion, suspicion—even fear.

She turned in through the park's east gates, following the looping pathway between an alley of trees whose leafless branches met above her head, and whose trunks stood silent vigil on a wintry world.

She walked stiffly, limbs rigid, spine straight, like someone just awakened from a nightmare. Her boots scuffed the path as she walked blindly, like a sleep-walker, her vision blurred by tears.

It was damp and bitterly cold. Curls of mist rose from the brown grass, so that it seemed she waded knee-deep through a silvery fog. Above her, the sky was a dead charcoal, flat, barren. The ornamental lake mirrored its color, a looking glass of polished pewter that winked slyly in the last glints of daylight.

She shivered and quickened her pace, for some reason eager to be gone from there. Today the park was not a pleasant place in which to while away a lazy afternoon, but sinister. Unwelcoming.

The ducks' wings had been clipped. Unable to fly off to warmer climes like their wild counterparts, they instead huddled in disconsolate groups along the lake's banks with their feathers fluffed out for warmth, half in and half out of a low wooden shelter.

An old man tended a brazier on the path ahead of her. He wore a long, threadbare black coat, a flat cap

155

that he politely tipped to her, and green knitted gloves with the tips of the fingers cut out, showing his sore fingers covered in chilblains. His ears, nose and cheeks were so reddened by cold, he looked like a goblin.

"Some roasted chestnuts for you, mum? Just the thing for a bitter day like today, they are!"

The aroma of roasted chestnuts, hot and salty on the blustery wind, stirred her numbed senses, slicing through damp and cold. Her stomach growled appreciatively.

She bought two paper twists of the nuts, counting out the correct coins mechanically, receiving the cones of brown paper and the old man's thanks in the same manner.

Had Deirdre been having an affair with Donovan? she wondered as she continued her walk through the park to the main Huntington Square gates. Almost certainly, if what Father Timothy had told her was true—and it was hardly likely a priest would lie.

Perhaps they had been lovers. Perhaps Deirdre had discovered she was with child. Perhaps when she told Fitzgerald of her condition, he had tossed her aside, refusing to acknowledge that it was his child she carried. Distraught and ashamed, what would Deirdre have done?

Fled into the East End, probably, hoping to find anonymity amongst the Irish poor. One thing was certain: Deirdre would have been too ashamed to contact her family. Though they were loving parents, Caitlynn doubted that Aunt Connie and Uncle Daniel could ever have accepted that their unwed daughter was with child. But if that was what had happened, surely Deirdre would have written to tell Caitlynn of her predicament. They had always been so close.

Caitlynn sighed. Was that where she would find her

cousin? In the slums of the East End? Alone and, by now, surely, huge with child, eking out a sorry existence by whatever means she could—perhaps even selling herself for a penny or two to earn money for food? One of Liam O'Sullivan's girls?

None of that mattered, Caitlynn told herself. Finding Deirdre, alive and well, was all that mattered. If she was with child . . . well, then they would just come up with some story or other to satisfy Aunt Connie and Uncle Daniel.

Deirdre could claim she was a—a grieving widow, perhaps, left to bear her child alone following her husband's tragic death. Her aunt and uncle might suspect the truth, but they would not question the lies too closely, not as long as they had their beloved daughter home, safe and sound, her reputation intact, and a grandbaby to adore.

Or perhaps Deirdre could stay here, in London, with her child. Caitlynn would willingly donate her own income as a lady's companion toward her cousin's support. Her board and lodgings were provided for. She needed very little else. They could find decent lodging for Deirdre and her child, surely?

Somewhere . . .

As she turned through the park gates onto Huntington Square, she was brought up short by the sight of number 13 across the street.

By the light of day, the house looked like a fairy-tale castle, with its conical towers, its wrought-iron gates, its stone walls and its mossy rockery and overgrown gardens. But by late afternoon, with a darkening sky and brooding dark clouds for a backdrop, number 13 changed. It became Hansel and Gretel's nightmare cottage. A sinister place that something evil called home. . . .

She shook her head to clear it. What on earth had given rise to such an unsettling thought? Nevertheless, filled with foreboding, she shuddered and drew her cloak more closely about her.

"Holly! Get your holly 'ere! Ivy! Fill your 'ouse with the spirit o' Christmas, laidy! Ho, Christmas holly! Holly and ivy, ho!"

On the square, a few houses down from number 13, a street crier was selling holly and other seasonal evergreens. The lad's wooden handcart was heaped high with branches of fir and prickly green holly boughs, hung with bunches of scarlet jewels. Folklore said that the crown of thorns worn by Christ before his crucifixion had been made of holly, and that its berries were scarlet to remind us of the blood He spilled for all mankind. She frowned. The street crier looked familiar. Where had she seen him before?

"I'll take half of whatever you have, boy. There'll be an extra penny-ha'penny for you if you'll carry it over to number 13."

"That I will, mum," he mumbled. "Merry Christmas, and thank you kindly, mum."

He took her money in a grubby, bony hand, darting her a furtive glance as he dropped the coins into the leather money pouch at his waist. His eyes were big and very blue in his pinched face, startlingly bright beneath the ragged carroty hair that stuck out from beneath his cap.

"Selling holly's a far cry from poaching ducks, is it not, boy?" she murmured teasingly as recognition dawned. She smiled to show the young poacher she meant him no harm.

Nevertheless, terror filled his eyes. His bony shoulders tensed, as if he was thinking about making a bolt for it. She could have kicked herself for her thoughtless comment.

"And I venture to say 'tis the safer of the two endeavors. Oh, come, now. Don't look so frightened, lad. I promise I won't call the bobbies—cross my heart and hope to die." She drew the sign of the cross on her chest with her finger.

He obviously did not believe her, for he dumped the holly on the doorstep of number 13 and quickly fled without his promised penny-ha'penny, trundling the wooden handcart ahead of him around the square with a haste that would have been amusing under other circumstances.

Wishing she'd never mentioned the blasted duck, she gingerly gathered the prickly holly into her arms, hefted up her basket and rang the doorbell to be let in.

The sound echoed hollowly within the house.

Rose, Bridget and Annie were preparing dinner when Caitlynn went into the kitchen. She greeted them, set down her basket, then carried the evergreens through to the scullery sink, where she stood them in icy water.

Two plum puddings hung from pegs there, ready to be steamed for Christmas dinner. The aroma of rum, brandy, sultanas, currants and spices was strong. The puddings looked for all the world like cannonballs with ears, wrapped in white pudding cloths with the ends knotted, she thought with a smile. Hidden inside the puddings were silver charms: rings, sixpences, thimbles and buttons. According to tradition, whoever found a ring in his or her portion of Christmas pudding would be wed within the year. The man or woman who found a sixpence would receive great wealth. The silver thimble predicted a spinster's life for the recipient, a silver button, a bachelor's solitary existence.

"Can I pour you a cuppa, love?" Rose asked when Caitlynn went back into the kitchen. The cook stood, wiping her hands on her apron.

A beefsteak-and-kidney pie with a perfectly crimped crumbly golden crust was keeping warm on top of the black range. Gravy bubbled up through the pie slit. The savory aroma of steak, kidney, carrots and onions made Caitlynn's mouth water.

"Mmm, please. Brrr. It's freezing out there!" She rubbed cold hands together. "Just let me change out of these damp clothes, and I'll be right back down."

"What's in your basket, Miss Cait?" Bridget asked cheekily as she went out.

"Oh, nothing much. Just a few knobs off chairs and pump handles," Caitlynn said over her shoulder, laughing.

The nonsense phrase had been her mother's favorite answer to her children's questions, which had ranged from what she was cooking for supper to what present she'd bought them for Christmas.

"Remember, Bridget? 'Twas curiosity killed the cat. Don't ask, and if you're a good girl, you'll have a treat from Father Christmas on Christmas morning—though it won't be number fifteen's handsome new groom, alas!"

Bridget pouted, murmuring, "Aaah, Sean, he's a darlin' boy, he is," and the others laughed. That Bridget had her eye on young Sean Kennedy was no secret to anyone.

Caitlynn hurried upstairs to hide her basket of treasures. She brushed off her damp bonnet, hung up her cloak, then changed into dry indoor shoes and went to look in on Estelle in the adjoining room.

Obsession

She found her charge napping, as Estelle often did before dinner since her attack two weeks ago. Her gold ringlets streamed across the pillows, gleaming like old gold in the dim firelight. Her angelic face was flushed from the warmth of the fire, but her breathing was deep and regular. Normal.

She seemed to have completely recovered from her attack of rheumatic fever, with the exception of being much more listless than before, Caitlynn thought, stroking her brow. She bent down and kissed Estelle's forehead. "I'm home, darling girl," she murmured. "Don't get up."

As she was drawing Estelle's draperies against the fading light, she caught a movement on the square below.

Curious, she pulled the lace curtain aside for a better look and saw the young holly seller and his cart. His flight had taken him only to the far side of the square, by the lofty park gates. She smiled, relieved.

Apparently, her comments had not frightened the enterprising lad off, as she'd feared. He was presently engaged in earnest conversation with another prospective customer, a thin woman dressed in the gray uniform of a domestic servant. Carroty hair stuck out from beneath her white cap as she handed something to the boy.

The woman's shoulders were hunched. She was hugging herself about the arms and shivering with cold, for she wore no shawl or cloak as she handed him something wrapped in a white cloth. A pillowcase, perhaps? The boy hastily took whatever it was and shoved it beneath the load of holly in his cart.

With no further exchange of words, the woman turned and scuttled toward number 13. But it was not until she let herself in through the wrought-iron gate that Caitlynn recognized the woman's frightened up-turned face. *Annie Murphy!*

Abruptly Caitlynn stepped away from the window, hoping she had not been seen. She did not want Annie to think she'd spied on her—even if, in a manner of speaking, she had.

What had Annie given the holly seller? And why, she wondered, frowning, had the pair behaved as if they had something to hide? What business did Annie have with the blue-eyed lad?

But when Caitlynn went downstairs, Annie was seated at the scrubbed kitchen table, peeling potatoes as if butter wouldn't melt in her mouth. She looked as if she hadn't moved in ages, and certainly hadn't been outside just moments before, up to no good.

Was I mistaken? Caitlynn wondered. Had the thin woman been someone else? No. Annie Murphy's cheeks were redder than usual, as if stung by a cold wind—or flushed with guilt.

Bridget smiled up at her. "So, Miss Caitlynn! Did ye have another of your exciting afternoons off? Sit down and tell us all about it, do."

"Exciting? Noo, it wasn't exciting at all," Caitlynn denied, firmly pushing what she'd learned about Deir-dre and the unknown gentleman to the back of her mind. She took her seat at the table. "But I *did* buy some roasted chestnuts, among other things."

She paused for emphasis, smiling mysteriously and laughing at their expectant expressions. She was not about to show them what else she'd bought that after-noon, or even tell them where she had shopped. Her purchases were Christmas presents, intended as a sur-prise. She opened the paper cones. "Here. Have some hot chestnuts, all of you."

The others, Annie included, eagerly helped themselves to the hot, salty treats, juggling nuts from hand to hand.

"There was a lad outside," Caitlynn said casually, "selling holly and evergreens from a cart. Did any of you see him? His hair was as bright as yours, Annie!"

But they all shook their heads. Caitlynn frowned, puzzled. What reason did Annie have to lie about such a thing? she wondered. Unless . . . Could the white-cloth bundle Annie had given the holly seller contain the silver frames stolen from her desk drawer? It was not only a possible answer, it was a plausible one.

"His—er—his evergreens looked freshly cut," she carried on. "They smelled heavenly, too, and the holly berries were so plump and bright, I bought some to decorate the house for the season. I thought Estelle and I would make wreaths and garlands tomorrow, if she's feeling up to it. Is there anything I can help you with here, Rose?"

"Not a blessed thing, thank you, love. We're almost done. Sit yourself down. Have a nice hot cuppa and a warm-up by the fire, while I put these 'taties on to cook. Get a move on with that cauliflower, Bridget, love. It's for supper tonight, not New Year's Eve. . . ."

Chapter Thirteen

"The master has asked you to join him and Miss Estelle for dinner tonight. See that you dress appropriately, O'Connor," Mrs. Montgomery instructed sourly the following afternoon.

Not for the first time, Caitlynn wondered about the hardy mister who had dared, at some point in the distant past, to take his courage in both hands and make prickly Mary Montgomery his bride.

One of her father's gardeners had been overheard to remark that his own somewhat bad-tempered wife surely had barbed wire in her drawers. So, it seemed, did Mary Montgomery.

Biting back a retort, Caitlynn murmured her acceptance as she anchored a pine garland to the newel post at the bottom of the stairs.

Much as she loathed the thought of dining with a man who might well have seduced and abandoned her cousin, she could hardly refuse his invitation, given her position in his household.

"How kind of him," she murmured without sincerity. "I'll be there promptly at seven—and dressed appropriately, never fear, Mrs. Montgomery."

"Be where?" Estelle asked, looking up from the table, which was spread with old newspapers, as Caitlynn went into the dining room. She was adding bunches of holly, ivy, pinecones and fat gold ribbons to a large pine wreath.

"At dinner this evening, with you and your guardian," Caitlynn said, wrinkling her nose.

"Donovan asked you to join us?"

"Uncle Donovan," she corrected by rote. "Yes. Or so Mrs. Montgomery says."

"But you don't want to?"

"Not particularly, no."

"Whyever not? I thought you liked my guardian."

"Dr. Fitzgerald is my employer, nothing more." Her voice sounded oddly flat even to her own ears, but she couldn't help it. "Besides, I don't have to like him. I just have to do what he pays me to do, which is to keep you company and out of mischief, miss!"

"I see. Did something happen?"

"What makes you think that?"

"You. You're different. Ever since you went to that dinner party with him, your face has looked . . . dreamy whenever you speak about my guardian. But now, all of a sudden, you just look cross."

"Do I?" Estelle was a most observant young woman. "Does your guardian have that effect on every woman?"

"Yes. All of them."

"Even Miss Riordan?"

"Especially Miss Riordan. She was in love with him, you know."

"No, I didn't know that," she lied. "How do you know?"

No answer.

"Did she tell you she was in love with him? Did she talk about it? Did you see them kissing, perhaps?"

"No. But she didn't have to tell me. She would get this . . . this funny look in her eyes sometimes, and sigh. Then she'd excuse herself and spend ages in her room, scribbling in her stupid diary. I notice these things. You know. Like that Annie," she added in a sly tone.

"What about Annie?"

"The wretched creature has sticky fingers! I saw her going through my things when she thought I was asleep. I shall have to talk to her about it soon. Or better yet, I'll make Mrs. Montgomery dismiss her."

"Perhaps it was Annie who took your rings the other time, and not Miss Riordan at all?"

"No. I'm certain it was Dee Dee." She shrugged slender shoulders and looked up at Caitlynn, smiling the sweetest smile. "But I suppose we'll never know for sure, will we, Miss Cait?"

"Probably not. Did Miss Riordan seem upset when you came back from the park that last day, do you remember?"

"I remember. Yes, she did. But then, she seemed worried all morning."

"But she didn't tell you why?"

Estelle shook her head.

"And when you got home, what happened?"

Estelle fiddled about, apparently intent on tying a bow with wide gold ribbon.

"After she drove the pony cart back to the carriage

house," Caitlynn nudged; "did she say anything— anything at all—before she went inside?"

It was obviously not easy for Estelle to talk about that day. "No. She just jumped down and ran into the house. I was very cross with her, because she left me to wait in the hot sun for Tom alone. I needed him to carry me upstairs, you see."

Though she could not have explained why she thought so, Caitlynn had the feeling Estelle was lying.

"I see. And had she ever done that before? Left you alone to wait for Tom, I mean?"

"No, never. There! That's it. It's finished. Do you like it?" She held out the finished wreath.

"Yes, it's beautiful. Clever girl! The way you looped the ribbon around and around the evergreens is charming. And just look at that great big bow! We'll hang it in pride of place on the front door, shall we, where everyone who comes to call can see it?"

Estelle beamed with pride and pleasure.

Caitlynn hesitated before asking, "Estelle, getting back to Miss Riordan. Did you see her again, later that day?"

"No. I never saw her again. Ever. Not that day, nor that evening, nor any other time." Her lower lip quivered.

"Perhaps you heard her moving around in her room that night?"

"Not that I recall, no. Aren't you going to get Tom? He'll hang the wreath for us now, if you ask him."

"Yes. I'll see to it right away; then we'll tidy up our mess, shall we? It's past time for your rest, darlin' girl." She frowned as she stroked Estelle's fair hair. "You look a little pale. Do you feel poorly?"

But despite looking pale and wan to Caitlynn's eyes, Estelle insisted she was fine. Caitlynn carried the handsome wreath through to the kitchen, in search of Tom.

When not driving the master's coach, Tom Larkin worked in or around the carriage house, polishing the vehicle or caring for the master's two horses, Buster the pony and Turk the carriage horse. He could also turn his hand to any number of repairs that needed doing about the house.

The wreath was the last of the seasonal decorations to be made, with the exception of the Christmas tree, which would be brought home, put up and decorated on Christmas Eve, and the ball of mistletoe, which would be hung in the foyer. The last two items—according to Estelle—were her guardian's and her Uncle Declan's provinces.

Tom had been dispatched to Covent Garden market early that morning to buy armfuls of pine and fir boughs to mix with the holly and ivy Caitlynn had already bought.

She and Estelle had spent all day fashioning garlands and door-toppers with the evergreens. Now, pine garlands looped with gold ribbon and studded with gold-dusted apples and lace-trimmed pears decorated the balustrade and the drawing room, spreading the fragrance of fresh pine everywhere.

A wicker cornucopia, overflowing with oranges, apples, nuts, sweets and sugarplums, held pride of place on the massive sideboard in the dining room. It was flanked by squat brass candlesticks holding stout bayberry-scented candles. The first dozen or so Christmas cards to arrive were displayed, elaborate with chubby cherubs and jolly pictures of Father Christmas with his sack of tin whistles, drums, hobbyhorses, nuts and oranges.

The scents and colors of Christmas were everywhere, filling the rooms with seasonal Yuletide cheer, banishing the uneasy atmosphere that seemed so often to grip number 13 in its spell.

She found Tom Larkin out in the carriage house. Seated on a stool, he was cleaning the master's shoes while he puffed on his pipe. Her own muddy button boots and Estelle's scuffed slippers awaited his polishing rag and brushes, as did a pair of the master's boots. A heap of harness and tack also awaited cleaning.

"Miss Caitlynn, good afternoon. What can I do for you?" Tom asked. Removing the pipe from his mouth, he squinted to see her.

"Miss Estelle has made this wreath for our front door, Tom. Will you hang it for us?"

"That I will, miss." Standing, he set his polishing rag and the shoes aside. "Well, well. Will you just look at this beauty!" he exclaimed, taking the wreath from her and holding it out at arm's length to admire. "It's a handsome one, isn't it? Clever with her hands, the young miss is."

"Isn't she? Wait until you see the stairway and the entry hall. The house looks so beautiful, and it smells wonderful, too."

"Does it, now?" Taking up hammer and nails, Tom said, "Come along, miss. I'll put that wreath up for you right now, if you'll show me where you want it."

At Caitlynn's direction, Tom centered a hook on the front door with just a couple of blows of the hammer. He carefully positioned the wreath on it, then stepped back to admire his handiwork.

"Perfect, Tom! Thank you!" Caitlynn exclaimed.

"Not at all, miss. My pleasure." He puffed on his pipe. "Anything else needs doin'?"

"No, nothing. Estelle will be so pleased." She paused. "Tom, do you remember the last time you saw Miss Riordan?"

169

He thought about it before answering. "I do. It was in the morning, before she and the young miss went off to the park. Nice little thing, she was, Miss Riordan. Always thanked me for helping her with this or that, just as sweet as pie. You remind me of her sometimes, miss, if you'll pardon me saying so."

Caitlynn smiled. Her mother had always said she and Deirdre could have been sisters, they were so alike in manner if not in looks. Tom missed very little. "Did you see her at all that last afternoon, after she returned from the park?"

"Not Miss Riordan, no. I only saw the young miss. Aye, and in a proper tizzy, she was, an' all." Tom shook his head. "That one can be a right little madam at times. She's been quieter since Miss Deirdre went away. Misses her, I suppose. But that day! Well, Miss Estelle had a right tantrum!"

"Oh? What was she so upset about?"

"About being left outside alone—or so she said. Claimed she had to sit in the hot sun waiting for me to carry her inside, she did. She said Miss Dee Dee'd gone inside, and that she waited for ages for me to carry her in, but that was an out-and-out lie, miss." He chuckled.

"Why do you say claimed?"

"Because I was currying Turk right here in the carriage house, keeping a weather eye out for the dogcart to come back, that's why! Miss Estelle *couldn't* have been sitting there for more than a minute—two at most—because I'd just popped my head out to check for the cart, and the yard was empty!"

"So you didn't see Miss Riordan at all?"

He shook his head. "No. Then the next morning, Mrs. M. was saying she'd scarpered, just like that!" He snapped his fingers. "Done a moonlight flit with some of the young miss's pretties, or so everyone was saying. Me and the missus don't believe a word of that nonsense, though. We reckon Mrs. M. made up that bit about her stealing to explain why Miss Riordan left so sudden. If you ask us, harsh words was exchanged between the two, but Mrs. M. won't own up to it."

"Did Miss Riordan have supper sent up to her room, as usual?"

"Yes. The girls left her dinner tray outside her door for her, but it was still untouched the next day, they said. Rum doings all around, if you ask me."

Rum doings indeed, Caitlynn thought. "Tom, are you sure Miss Riordan came back from the park with Estelle that day?"

He shrugged, his white brows beetling. "Well, the young miss said she did, didn't she?"

"I suppose so, yes." Another blind alley.

"And we've got no reason to doubt her, have we, miss?" Tom continued, voicing Caitlynn's own thoughts. "Loved Miss Dee Dee like a mother, Miss Estelle did. Never seen a body so upset as she was after she left." He slapped his thighs. "Now, then, Miss Caitlynn. If there's nothing else I can do for you, I have the rest of the shoes t'polish and a coal cellar to set to rights. Coalman's deliverin' tomorrow . . ."

After thanking Tom again, she went inside, exchanging a few words with Rose before returning to Estelle in the dining room.

Her hand on the doorknob, she heard angry voices from inside the room, and hesitated before going in.

"—this game you play is a dangerous one," she heard Estelle say, her low voice laden with menace. Some words Caitlynn couldn't make out followed. "You've had fair warning, my girl. There will be no next time, do you . . ."

171

Penelope Neri

Her voice dropped, becoming so low Caitlynn could not make out the rest of what was said through the door. And although she strained her ears to hear, she did not recognize the low, urgent voice that answered Estelle. Determined to discover the identity of the other speaker, she opened the door and went inside.

Estelle and Annie. Both young women turned toward her, startled by her sudden entry. Annie's face was streaked with tears, while Estelle's was blotchy with anger.

"Estelle? Is everything all right?" Caitlynn asked quietly, frowning as she glanced from Estelle to Annie. The atmosphere in the room was crackling.

"It is now, thank you, Miss Caitlynn," Estelle said sweetly, but cast Annie a dark glance nonetheless. "You may go now, Murphy. But remember what I told you."

"Oh, I will, miss." Annie bobbed a curtsey that bordered on insolent. "I won't forget—and no more should you."

With that, the maid rushed past Caitlynn and out the door as if hounds were snapping at her heels.

"That impudent creature! She is a thief and a liar, and insolent to boot!" Estelle exclaimed, shaking her head in disgust. She appeared very much the mistress of the house in that moment. "I decided to speak to her about her pilfering. Remember, I told you?"

Caitlynn nodded. "Yes. And did you?"

"Oh, yes. Indeed I did." Estelle bit her lip. Her sky-blue eyes were guileless, her expression angelic. "And I believe, although I say so myself, that I was more than fair in the way I handled the matter. I gave Annie every opportunity to confess. I even offered to be lenient, if she would only admit her wrongdoing, but no. She denied all knowledge of it." She sighed. "There is

172

nothing else for it. She has left me no choice. I shall ask Mrs. M. to let her go."

"Must you?" Caitlynn soothed. "I hate to see anyone sacked this close to Christmas. Please wait a week or two, Estelle. Knowing she's been found out will convince Annie to stop stealing, I'm sure." If the girl really had been stealing. Or would Annie simply disappear one night, as Deirdre had apparently done, too shamed by the accusations, founded or otherwise, to stay?

"Hmm. I shall have to think about it," Estelle said thoughtfully. "Just because it is the holidays does not excuse her," she added, giving Caitlynn a stern look that reminded her of Donovan.

"I know. You're being very grown-up and gracious about the whole thing. But I do believe it has made you quite exhausted. You look very pale." She frowned. To her eyes, there seemed to be a bluish tinge to Estelle's lips. "I'll ring for Tom to take you upstairs, shall I?"

"Yes, please. I do feel tired."

While Estelle slept away her exhaustion that afternoon, Caitlynn wrapped the Christmas gifts she had bought everyone on her afternoon off. She hid them in the bottom drawer of her dresser, beneath her folded nightgowns and undergarments.

For Tom, there was a handsome tapestry pouch to hold his pipe when it was not in his mouth, and his baccy. For Rose, a pretty paste brooch shaped like a peacock with its magnificent tail spread. For Bridget, a burgundy feather collar to spruce up her simple dresses and catch Sean's eager eye. For Annie and Mrs. Montgomery, there were gilt boxes of pretty handkerchiefs, edged with lace and embroidered with pansies, roses and a curling initial.

The most expensive present of all, however, was the jewelry box she'd found for Estelle. It was the perfect gift for her charge! The hinged lid held a three-dimensional winter's scene of exquisitely carved and painted wood and plaster. There were little gaslights, miniature fir trees hung with colorful garlands and tiny candles, and porcelain snowdrifts that sparkled with glitter.

In the center of the snowy scene was an oval mirror. When the key was wound, two little skaters circled the frozen 'lake,' whirling around and around to the tinkling strains of a Viennese waltz.

Caitlynn had fallen in love with the music box immediately. She just had to buy it, whatever the cost, for the pretty scene on the lid was the image of Estelle's favorite place, the lake in Huntington Park, while the jewelry box it decorated was exquisitely crafted of rosewood, cushioned with plump royal-blue velvet.

She couldn't wait to see Estelle's face when she opened her present on Christmas morning, she thought, tying a wide red ribbon around the wrapped parcel.

Tucking the finished gift in one of her hatboxes, she carefully arranged a bonnet over it, closed the lid, and returned the hatbox to the top of the wardrobe.

A glance at the tiny ormolu clock on the mantel confirmed that she was running late. She must start her evening's toilette immediately or she would be tardy for dinner with the doctor and his ward.

With a grimace, she took the porcelain jug from the dresser and hurried downstairs to the kitchen to fill it with hot water for washing. As she went, the first giddy quivers of excitement flickered through her.

You're a hypocrite, Caitlynn! A bloody fool! Are you quite mad, is that it? she asked herself. Ah, yes.

She must be all of that, and more. For despite her belief that Donovan was a callous seducer of young women, her spirits soared at the prospect of spending the evening with him. Her heart sang.

Like the reckless moth that courts the naked flame, giving no thought to burning its wings, she was drawn to him, obsessed, fascinated, and too bewitched to flee.

She dressed that evening as if she were going to her wedding rather than sharing a simple meal with her employer and his ward. Sweeping up her hair, she applied hot tongs to curl the ringlets—a task she normally hated—in an effort to tame the unruly dark mass into an elegant coiffure.

After beating her hair into submission with the tongs, she bit her lips to redden them, then pinched her cheeks until they turned as pink as the silk roses she pinned in her hair.

She turned this way and that, green eyes sparkling, her complexion glowing as much with inner excitement as from pinching fingers. Perfect, she decided, smoothing down the folds of her favorite gown, a deep rose silk that left most of her shoulders bare. The dropped puffed sleeves showed off her graceful arms, while the bustle and narrow skirts drew the eye to her slender waist.

She was pleased with the sophisticated reflection the dresser mirror threw back. Yes, that was the word, the look, she wanted. *Sophistication.* The city of London was no place for sleepy Irish ways or country charm.

Drawing a lace shawl with long fringes over her bare shoulders, she went downstairs.

As she went in through the double doors of the dining room, she realized Donovan and Estelle were already there.

The doctor's eyes ignited with pleasure as they met hers.

"Miss Caitlynn. Thank you for joining us." Donovan crossed the room to meet her. He was tall, sternly handsome, his coal-black hair gleaming like polished jet in the sparkle of the gas chandeliers.

Taking her hand in his, he drew it to his lips; kissed it far too ardently. Held it far too long. But in her heart, she did not want him to stop, no matter what propriety dictated.

"You are charming this evening, as always, lovely Cait," he said softly, impaling her with his sapphire eyes, compelling her to look up at him—and to keep on looking at him—by the sheer force of his will. "Your gown becomes you. 'Tis the color of a wild Irish rose."

He was remembering that night, she could tell. The darkened coach. The stolen kisses. The desire that had exploded between them, and oh, so very nearly had been sated. It was all there, all of it, in his smoldering eyes, in his challenging half-smile, in the lingering heat of his fingers.

"And you flatter me, sir. As always," she murmured quickly. Her voice was husky with nerves. How should she respond to him? What did one say under such circumstances? Was there even a proper way to respond?

She didn't know what to do, or how to behave, for in truth, she was fascinated by him. Drawn to him like metal to magnet, yet wary of him at one and the same time. Irrationally, the edge of fear, of doubt, of danger and mystery, only fueled her attraction. He was becoming an obsession—and a dangerous one, at that.

"Please, won't you be seated?" Taking her chill hand, he led her to the dining chair closest to the pink

Italian marble mantel, where she could feel the warmth of the crackling fire.

She allowed him to seat her, toying nervously with the fringes of her shawl. He remained standing, his back to Estelle.

"I have missed you," he said softly, for her ears alone.

From the corner of her eye, Caitlynn saw that Estelle watched them like a hawk.

"I believe you have been avoiding me these past few weeks. Is there a reason for it? Have I offended you in some way?"

"No! No, of course not. You are wrong about that, Doctor. I didn't—I mean, I *haven't* been avoiding you." Her breathing became shallow and unsteady. Because of him, she could not draw enough air into her lungs to take a proper breath. Because of him— because of the way he was looking at her—she wasn't making sense. Didn't know what she meant anymore.

She stared at him but could not read his enigmatic features, nor decipher his closed, dark expression. *Where is she?* another part of her screamed silently. *Do you know? Is my answer there, hidden behind those sinfully long lashes? Locked away behind those sensual, soulful eyes, in which I long to lose myself?*

"I'm relieved to hear it," he said. "As soon as Mrs. Montgomery joins us, I'll have Rose begin serving dinner." He smiled, the charming host. "Will you take a glass of something while we're waiting? I'm afraid we don't have your favorite, champagne . . ." Here he smiled, remembering the Townsends' dinner. "But there's a decent port or sherry—"

"I'll have a small porter, please. Or a—"

Estelle's head snapped around. "Donovan, no!" she exclaimed, cutting Caitlynn off in mid-sentence. "Tell me I misunderstood you—that awful Mrs. M. isn't dining with us?" she demanded rudely.

"Oh, but she is. At my request."

"How could you! She's such a bad-tempered old stick. She does nothing but complain and complain, and always considers herself above everyone. Why did you ask her?"

Estelle's sulky expression probably mirrored her own, Caitlynn thought ruefully. Montgomery would not have been her choice of dinner companion, either.

"You are being rude, Estelle," Donovan said sternly, "not to mention childish. It doesn't become you. Yes, Mrs. Montgomery will be joining us. And, as with any of my invited guests, you will be gracious and polite to her, the perfect hostess. Or . . ." He hesitated.

"Or what?" Estelle demanded.

"Or you may leave us, and your supper will be sent up to you on a tray."

Estelle's small fists were clenched in her lap. Her pretty jaw and chin jutted with anger. Her blue eyes glittered. "You scold me. You tell me not to be childish, but then you treat me like a child and send me to my room!" she exploded, shaking with anger. She would have stamped her foot, Caitlynn thought, were she able to stand.

"Estelle, please—" Caitlynn warned in a low voice.

"Have you forgotten?" Estelle demanded recklessly, flinging the words across the table, ignoring her. "I'm almost sixteen years old! A woman, not a stupid child."

"Then act like it," Donovan replied quietly. His icy tone promised there would be hell to pay if she continued to defy him.

Estelle's lower lip jutted, wobbled. To Caitlynn's eyes, she looked perilously close to tears.

"I hate you! You never have time for me anymore! You're always too busy with your horrid patients and your—your hateful dinner parties!" She shot Caitlynn a murderous look, making it quite clear that it was not really the dinner parties she resented, so much as her guardian's choice of companion.

"You don't care what happens to me, either of you. You never have. You only pretend to care. I hate you! I hate you both! You should have left me where you found me. You should have let me d-die in that p-place!"

Donovan stood and jangled the bellrope to summon Tom. He appeared in a matter of seconds, dabbing his mouth on the corner of a handkerchief. He had probably been enjoying his own supper in the kitchen when Donovan rang.

"Ah, there you are, Tom. Miss Estelle would like to be taken back to her room, if you would be so kind."

"Very good, sir." If Tom was surprised or annoyed by his master's request, he carefully hid it. "Miss?"

Estelle was stiff and unyielding in Tom's arms as he lifted her and carried her from the room. She refused to look at either Caitlynn or her guardian as Tom swept her past them, yet her eyes were suspiciously bright, her chin defiantly set.

"Excuse me. I'll just be a moment. I really should make sure she's all right," Caitlynn murmured. She started to get up.

"No. Please, sit down," Donovan snapped. "It will do Estelle good to spend the evening alone, regretting her behavior. She will not learn if you coddle her."

"Very well." He was right. She knew that in her heart. Yet even so, she could imagine how devastated, how alone and abandoned Estelle must feel, exiled to her room, sent away by her beloved Donovan, leaving the field free—or so she probably believed—to her rival: none other than Caitlynn herself. Her soft heart went out to the girl.

"Doctor . . ."

"Yes?"

"I have no wish to pry into personal matters that do not concern me, but may I ask what she meant?"

"About leaving her where I found her?"

"Yes."

He frowned and appeared to be weighing whether to confide in her as he went over to the sideboard. There, he poured her the promised glass of port, and himself a whisky, adding a third glass, this of sherry, for Mrs. Montgomery as she joined them.

The housekeeper thanked him, apologizing profusely for being late as she accepted the drink. Her nod of greeting for Caitlynn seemed somewhat sheepish. No doubt she was embarrassed about being tardy, after cautioning Caitlynn so strongly to dress appropriately.

Mary Montgomery looked surprisingly handsome. She wore a gown of bronze wool, trimmed with jet beads, that Caitlynn had never seen before.

"Mrs. Montgomery knows the story, don't you, Mary?" Donovan said easily, much to Caitlynn's surprise. He seemed very comfortable with the old battle-ax, as if they were fast friends. "It happened several years ago. One night I was called away from St. Bart's by a priest to attend a sick infant in the East End. Apparently, a distraught woman had sent for him to baptize her infant son, who she believed was dying. Father Timothy was appalled by what he found in that house."

"Father Timothy? The Father Timothy from St. Anthony's Church?" she asked faintly.

"Yes, that's right," he confirmed.

Her mind raced, latching onto the fact like a dog to a very welcome, very juicy bone. Surely Father Timothy would have recognized Donovan as the man who had met with Deirdre, would he not? And if that was the case, then Donovan could not have been Deirdre's mysterious gentleman.

"Why?" he asked, frowning.

"Oh, no reason." Her heart thudded. "Please, go on."

"A woman named Lily Perkins owned the boarding-house to which the priest led me," Donovan was saying. "The woman's dying infant was but one of several we found in her wretched care. Lily Perkins was a baby-farmer, you see. Are you familiar with the term?"

"Not really, no." Her mouth was filled with saw-dust.

"Baby-farmers are unscrupulous women, quite without conscience or morals. They take money from un-wed mothers who can ill afford it each month. And in return for their ten or twelve or more shillings, these women promise to care for the mothers' newborn ba-bies as if they were their own, while the mothers work in the sweats or the factories.

"Instead, they feed these tiny helpless infants a witch's brew of lime and spoiled milk. In a matter of weeks, they sicken, their little brains swell, and they die."

"Lime! Oh, my God!" She covered her mouth with her hand.

"The dead infants are then tossed aside, to be quickly replaced by other newborns. And so the pro-cess repeats itself, over and over again. Each year, thousands of babies are killed in this fashion in London alone—and the baby-farmers grow rich as Midas."

"But . . . those dreadful women are guilty of murder!"

"That's true. But although baby-farming was outlawed almost twenty years ago, and although women have been tried for murder because of it, the practice continues to flourish until this day.

"I found seven such infants in Lily Perkins's care that night. Four were dying, or very close to it. I had all seven taken to an orphan asylum. Not a vast improvement over their original lot, I admit, for such places are notoriously reluctant to take in illegitimate babies, but it was the best I could do for them at the time. At least in an orphanage, they would have milk, and a chance at life.

"I also found Estelle there—or should I say, Stella Marsh, as she was called then. I believe she was Lily Perkins's own daughter.

"She was just nine years old, and already a victim of rheumatic fever. She was filthy, covered in sores, dressed in rags. Her hair was matted, her scalp crawling with lice. She spoke not at all, except to whimper in pain. Yet despite the filthy conditions in which I found her, she was beautiful. A lovely, innocent little angel. Her beauty shone like a candle in that hellhole of a room.

"I could only imagine what Lily Perkins planned to do with such a pretty child. There was but one reason she would keep her alive that I could think of."

"Oh? And what reason is that?" Caitlynn whispered. She had an awful feeling she would not like his answer, but felt compelled to ask.

He sighed heavily. "There are men in this world, this city—depraved, often very wealthy men—who frequent brothels that specialize in supplying young children for their clientele. They traffic in little boys, as well as little girls. Such monsters would pay royally for such a beautiful little girl to serve their perverted pleasures. Need I say more?"

Caitlynn shuddered, struck almost speechless with horror. "Indeed you need not, sir. But please, go on. What happened to Stella—Estelle?"

"I told the Perkins creature I would remove the child from her care, by force if need be. I threatened her with the law. She laughed in my face. She said no magistrate would part a child from its natural mother.

"I knew then what I had to do. I offered her five guineas for the child. She said I could have her for ten. 'No questions asked, Doc.' Then the bloody bitch winked at me, as if it was all some twisted game we played."

Grim-faced, Donovan shook his head, then drained his whisky in a single swallow.

"She sold her own child to you, a stranger? Without knowing—or caring—what sort of man you were? Or what would happen to her little girl?"

He nodded. "Just like that." His eyes were dark with sorrow as he remembered that night. "In the following months, it became apparent to all of us that the little girl—we changed her name from Stella to Estelle, a new name for a new life—was very clever. She learned quickly, and soon began to talk, copying whatever she heard or saw like a little parrot. Unfortunately, she was also sexually precocious for her age."

"Sexually precocious?"

"Yes. She flirted with me, behaved seductively to get her way if I attempted to set limits, or to discipline her, much as a grown woman might do with her lover."

Their eyes met, and she knew exactly what he was

183

thinking, and which grown woman he was imagining with her lover. Flustered, she looked away. She could feel a blush rising up her throat, to burn in her cheeks.

"She was grateful, you see. To me, for taking her away from her former life. But because of the life she had led, she did not know how else to show me, or any man, that she was grateful, or that she loved me. It was all she knew—all she'd been taught.

"If I brought her a new toy—a doll, say, or a dollhouse—she would throw her little arms around my neck and rub herself against me, kiss me and tell me over and over again that she would be good, that she would do whatever I asked, *anything I asked,* if only I didn't send her back to Lily.

"She believed—quite wrongly, of course—that I had bought her to be my—er—um—plaything, and that if she ceased to please me, I would rid myself of her." His embarrassed expression became a scowl.

"But—she was only a little girl. An innocent child. Why would she think such a thing?"

"Because she knew nothing else. She was a child in years, perhaps, but an ancient in her knowledge of men. God only knows what depravity she had witnessed—perhaps even experienced—in her short life with Lily Perkins! In many ways, she was more . . . knowing, shall we say, more worldly, than women twice her age." He sighed.

"Anyway, I brought her back here, to number thirteen, where she quickly grew more attached to me than was healthy. I engaged a nanny, then a governess, and later Mary, here, to see to her education and her daily care. Finally, Miss Riordan, and now yourself, became her companions. For the reasons I explained, I have myself maintained a prudent distance from her over the years. Gradually she has recovered, and has since

184

quite outgrown her infatuation with me."

"Are you quite certain about that?" Caitlynn asked.

His dark blue eyes caressed her, like a lambent blue flame whose heat she felt upon her cheek. Her fingers still tingled where he'd kissed them.

"I am, yes. Quite sure. She considers me nothing more than an indulgent uncle now. One she has no qualms about defying or manipulating at every opportunity, as do all nieces! Against all odds, and despite such awful beginnings, I am happy—and proud—to say that Estelle has grown into a lovely young woman, if at times a spoiled one, prone to temper tantrums when crossed. As she was this evening."

"You love her."

"Yes. I do. *As a daughter.* I could love her no more were she my own flesh and blood."

He grinned, the very picture of the indulgent guardian. The proud papa. His love for the child he had saved was very much apparent, but it was the unconditional love of a parent, nothing more.

"Now. Shall I ring for dinner, ladies? Over the fine meal Rose has prepared for us, I have a small favor to ask of you. . . ."

Chapter Fourteen

Over dinner that evening, Donovan persuaded Caitlynn and Mrs. Montgomery to arrange a small party for him on Christmas Day. His twenty or so guests would be mostly unmarried medical residents, bachelor doctors from St. Bart's who had no family in London with whom to spend the holidays, and several of his older friends who had single daughters, like the Marchants, the Priors and the St. Germains.

Lacking a wife to act as his hostess, Donovan enlisted their help in preparing the guest list, sending the invitations, choosing a menu and so forth.

To Caitlynn's surprise, she discovered she enjoyed the opportunity to act as hostess. She found herself remembering the dinner parties she'd helped her mother to arrange at home in County Waterford, and drawing upon those earlier experiences.

Much to her amazement, Mrs. Montgomery deferred to her on questions of style and correct etiquette, whereas Caitlynn found the older woman a wizard of organization, highly effective at delegating tasks and getting things done quickly and well.

Together they made an excellent team, if not an overly amicable one.

The morning of Christmas Eve found the two women with their heads together in Donovan's study-cum-library. They were having a final meeting to go over the guest list, write the place cards and check off the last items on their 'to-do' list.

"Am I correct in thinking everyone has accepted except for the Misses St. Germain, who claimed a prior engagement?" Mrs. Montgomery said.

"No, no, that's the Priors. The St. Germains will be here—and so will Dr. Christopher Donahue, who apologized for not being more definite. He may join us late, perhaps not until the evening," Caitlynn confirmed, "depending on his ailing mama's state of health. One more or less won't make much difference. Now, what about our Christmas tree! We don't have one yet."

"Hmm, I know." The housekeeper frowned. "Doctor always brings the tree home on Christmas Eve, while Master Declan brings the mistletoe, the young rogue, as well as a bottle of something. . . . warming."

Mary Montgomery actually blushed, perhaps remembering past Christmas tipples and teasing mistletoe kisses stolen by the dashing Fitzgerald brothers, both of whom had set her stone heart thumping like a giddy young girl's.

"Can we rely on the doctor to bring the tree this year, do you think?" Caitlynn wondered, chewing the end of her pencil. "He's been so preoccupied with that new clinic of his."

"Normally, I would say yes. But this year, I think

you're right. He's so involved with his patients, he might well forget."

"And by the time he comes in, it will be too late for us to find one. We can't have a Christmas party and guests without a tree, Mrs. M! I know. We'll ask Tom to find us one."

"We can't. Tom's not here. He's running errands all over the city for Rose, for the feast tomorrow."

In the end, it was decided that Caitlynn would go to St. Bart's personally to remind Donovan to bring home a tree.

"Wrap up warmly," the older woman cautioned. "There's the scent of snow in the air."

"Why, Mrs. Montgomery, I do believe you care!" she teased gaily, surprised. It was the closest Mrs. M. had ever come to a kind word for her, and Caitlynn was touched. She grinned, and Montgomery's lips pursed. "But I think you're wrong about the snow."

She pulled the draperies aside. The sky was almost white, and it was bitterly cold, but there was no sign of snow. Not a single snowflake spiraling down like a solitary feather. "I doubt very much we'll have snow today."

"We will. You mark my words. I'm never wrong when it comes to the weather. It's my knees, you see. If they tell me it will be a white Christmas this year, it will be."

Donning a warm cloak, muffler, rabbit-fur muff and gloves over a warm woolen gown and several petticoats, Caitlynn left Estelle by the drawing room fire, engrossed in wrapping the little Christmas gifts she had either made or else instructed Caitlynn to purchase for her, according to her own explicit instructions.

Caitlynn set out at a brisk pace, passing houses

whose windows were amber rectangles of welcome and seasonal good cheer.

In many drawing rooms on the square, the Christmas tree—a charming German tradition first brought to England by Prince Albert, Queen Victoria's husband, only a few years earlier—held pride of place in the bay window. The decorated trees were dazzling, with garlands of tinsel looped in elegant swags about their green boughs, the tips of the branches hung with glittering glass balls, blown-glass birds, orange pomanders and tiny flickering candles. On the highest bough of each shone a brilliant star, like the Star of Bethlehem that had led the Magi to the Christ Child's place of birth in a humble stable.

Salvation Army carolers congregated on the street corner outside the gates of St. Bart's hospital. The singers reminded Caitlynn of a flock of crows in their smart black uniforms, trimmed with narrow burgundy ribbons.

The robust strains of "God Rest Ye Merry Gentlemen" and "Wassail, Wassail" filled the cold air, putting smiles on the faces of passersby as they hurried home through the fading light, heads down, hands tucked under their armpits for warmth.

She passed several fathers dragging home Christmas trees, the trees tied to a sled or a small cart or wagon. Children skipped along beside some of them, bundled against the cold, their little cheeks rosy-red with cold, eyes bright with excitement and the promise of a gift from Father Christmas.

With a pang, she thought of the children she had seen in the East End. Grubby, ragged, painfully thin, they had no warm clothes in which to be bundled by loving mothers, nor a proper home in which to decorate a tree, nor a seasonal feast to look forward to.

Most of them would be lucky to get a meal at all, let alone have a delicious Christmas dinner like the one Rose was already preparing.

Nonetheless, Caitlynn's feet fairly skipped past the monument to the monk Raherus, who had founded the hospital centuries earlier after receiving a vision of St. Bartholomew, who told him to build a hospital for the needy there. The surrounding fields had served as a livestock and meat market over the centuries, as well as a site of public executions up until the beginning of the century. Now only busy Smithfield Meat Market survived, a stone's throw from Billingsgate Fish Market.

St. Bart's was actually four huge buildings, surrounding a courtyard with a fountain at its heart. It was only a stone's throw from St. Paul's Cathedral across the street.

Caitlynn's feet kept time with an old carol sung by the carolers, who were accompanied by the lively beat of drums and the tooting of a trumpet. She dropped a coin in the collection box at the conductor's feet as she passed.

"God bless you, miss! Merry Christmas!" the conductor called after her.

"And you!"

Grinning like a bearded gnome, the conductor saluted her with his baton as she made her way past the hospital porter and into the huge hospital.

Donovan's clinic was a single enormous room.

The waiting-room side of the clinic was furnished with scarred wooden benches and a few rickety rattan chairs, partitioned off by a dark green curtain that hung from brass rings that rattled whenever the curtain was whisked aside by the nurse.

It was behind this curtain that the doctor examined his patients, one by one. They waited until their names were called, then were shepherded into his presence by the nurse wearing a starched gray gown, white apron and head covering. The uniform made her look like a nun, and did nothing to soften her frosty, no-nonsense expression.

"Merry Christmas, Dr. Fitzgerald."

"Merry Christmas, Nurse Phillips. I'll see you again on the twenty-seventh, shall I—? Why, Caitlynn!" he cried as he emerged from behind the curtain in his shirtsleeves to see her sitting there. "What a pleasant surprise! What are you doing here? Is something wrong?"

"Nothing. Nothing's wrong. Everything's wonderful, in fact," she assured him. "Mrs. Montgomery and I were worried you'd be so busy with your patients, you'd forget the Christmas tree—"

"Damnation!" He thumped his forehead with his palm. "Thank God you came to remind me. I completely forgot. The clinic was packed all day. I've never seen so many babies, children and mothers with coughs and colds."

"I know. I've been here watching for quite some time."

"You have? You should have had Nurse tell me you were here. I'm so sorry you had to wait so long."

Clad in only his shirtsleeves and waistcoat, he grabbed his jacket and overcoat from a peg by the door as they left the clinic.

He shrugged into his coat as she fell in step beside him. Footsteps echoing on cold stone floors, they walked briskly down long corridors with vaulted ceilings. Caitlynn's nose wrinkled. Everywhere was the faint whiff of age, sickness and despair that was common to hospitals everywhere, underscored by the unsubtle reek of carbolic soap.

"I didn't mind waiting at all. In fact, I enjoyed watching you work." She smiled shyly. "You looked so . . . engrossed in what you were doing." *Tired but content*, she added silently.

He smiled, a charming smile that made his eyes twinkle, and her heart gave a crazy flutter in her breast.

"Aaahh, that's the Irish in me. I always put my heart and soul into everything I do. Doctoring. Kissing pretty women. *Everything*." He winked at her. "Come along, my dear Miss O'Connor. Let's put our hearts and souls into finding the grandest Christmas tree in London for number thirteen. We'll be the envy of every house on the square. Shall we?"

He offered her his arm, and after a second's hesitation, she slipped hers through it.

They set out, arm in arm, laughing companionably. Their good humor was infectious and drew the smiles of doctors, nurses and patients alike as they made their way out of the hospital, across the courtyard, past the fountain and out through one of the little postern gates used by nurses coming and going to their quarters on various shifts.

She had watched Donovan for close to an hour as he saw a seemingly endless tide of sick people, touching their hurts, their fevered faces and limbs, and—or so she fancied, their hearts—with gentle yet competent hands. One was a mason covered in blood who had fallen and struck his head. Another, a child with a rash and a runny nose who cried weakly and irritably the entire time he was being examined. A little boy, his arm severely bitten by a dog, was too deeply shocked to cry at all.

Poorly dressed, none too clean, defiant or good-natured, sullen, even drunk, they were all treated alike by Donovan. He showed them all the same unfailing patience, the genuine respect, the burning desire to help, to heal.

What she'd seen from her vantage point was a dedicated, caring man. A man who worked himself to the bone to provide badly needed medical care for the needy, the poor, the underprivileged. A man who loved what he did and would be desperately unhappy doing anything else.

Every baby had been jounced on his knee or rocked gently in his arms. Every child who was old enough was given a striped peppermint humbug or a lollipop on a stick, selected from the fat-bellied sweet-jar on his desk and gravely presented. Their mothers were given humbugs, too, if they seemed in the least bit envious.

The women, all thin, all heavy-eyed, all with the tired, downtrodden look so common to working-class mothers, accepted the sweet with either broad grins or shy smiles, along with the envelope in which the doctor tucked their precious pills, or their iron tonics, or ugly bottles of dark brown medicine.

As Donovan and she left the clinic, anxious mothers, feverish babies riding on their hips, called after him, "God bless you, Doc. God bless you. Have a happy Christmas!" Then they pulled their shawls about themselves and their children and plunged back into the freezing rabbit warren of the East End.

It was while they were selecting a Christmas tree from the seller on a nearby street corner that Montgomery's weather forecast was fulfilled.

First, a few flakes swirled down out of the colorless sky. In minutes, those few flakes became millions, swirling and eddying like feathers emptied from a pillow.

"Will you look at that! Sure and the angels are having a pillow fight," Caitlynn declared, laughing, her face upturned to the fluffy flakes. Her cheeks glowed with the cold.

"If you ask me, the loveliest angel is right here helping me choose a Christmas tree," he said huskily. In her velvet bonnet and cloak of hunter green, with her dark hair framing her pretty face, her green eyes sparkling, she was truly a vision. One that made the breath catch in his throat and his heart ache.

"Hardly an angel, Dr. Donovan," she shot back. Although embarrassed by his compliment, she couldn't seem to stop smiling. "What about this one?" she said quickly to hide her emotions.

"Hmm? Oh, the tree! That one's far too small. This one, however . . . this one is perfect," he declared, selecting a tree from the stack that leaned against the building.

As Donovan stood there holding the tree like a fisherman displaying a trophy trout, the branches shook themselves out in a pleasing, even cone shape. "There. What do you think?"

"Yes! That's the one." The fir tree was a good six inches taller than the man holding it. Its branches were dark green, thick and furry with needles, and it smelled heavenly, of pine woods and deep, dark forests.

"Home, Miss O'Connor?" he murmured while the tree seller trussed their chosen tree with string. His eyes were warm as they lingered on her mouth. Warm enough to melt the thin layer of snow that was already blanketing grimy London in pristine white.

"Home. Yes," she murmured with a delicious shiver.

Obsession

It would be a white Christmas after all, she thought as she slipped her hand through Donovan's. With, God willing, the promise of a happier New Year to come. . . .

Chapter Fifteen

Estelle linked her hands around Tom's neck as he carried her downstairs to join the others. He wouldn't be able to carry her much longer, she thought. He was breathing heavily and she could feel his limbs trembling from the strain of carrying her. Soon he would be just another old man. Useless.

At the turn in the staircase, Tom paused to catch his breath, leaning against the balustrade for support. His position gave Estelle a clear view of the entryway below. Too clear, she thought, biting her lip. Her fingers tightened around Tom's neck.

Donovan and her so-called companion were kissing beneath the mistletoe posy that Uncle Declan had hung from the chandelier earlier that afternoon. Standing so close that their bodies almost touched, they were blind to what was going on around them. Lost in a private world of their own.

A world in which she had no part.

Donovan was cupping Caitlynn's face between his hands. The expression in his dark blue eyes, in his handsome face, was unbelievably tender . . .

. . . as if he loved her.

Estelle knew that couldn't be true, but even so, her chest hurt. She felt as if she might be sick.

Miss Caitlynn's eyes were closed. She was hanging on to the ends of Donovan's muffler as if they were lifelines, her face glowing as if she were in heaven, or something. Imagine, looking like that after just a stupid kiss!

She tried to swallow but couldn't. Tears stung behind her eyes. There was a lump in her throat that hurt so much, she could hardly swallow.

"Well, I'll be!" Tom exclaimed softly. "So that's the way the wind's blowing."

"It is not! Don't be so stupid, Thomas," she flared, hating him. "Mistletoe kisses don't mean anything," she said scathingly. "Now, hurry up, do! I don't want them decorating the tree without me."

"Oh, they won't be doing that, miss. They can't, not even if they're ready to—which, by the looks of things, they ain't." He chuckled. "I still have to stand the tree in a bucket of stones. Um, begging your pardon, miss! My neck?"

"So? What about your stupid neck?"

"Your fingers, miss! They hurt!"

"Oh!" Her fingernails were sharp. She hadn't realized just how sharp until Tom winced in pain. Her fingers had dug into his flesh so deeply, she could see half-moon gouges in his saggy old neck. "Ohh, poor Tom," she cooed. "I'm sorry."

His wind recovered, her choke-hold slackened, Tom continued down the steep staircase. His arrival in the entryway below, with Estelle cradled in his arms, burst the bubble that enclosed the couple beneath the mistletoe.

"Merry Christmas, sweetheart," Donovan murmured to Caitlynn, releasing her. He raised his dark head, yet was still looking down at her.

"Merry Christmas to you, too, Donovan," Caitlynn said softly. "I'll change out of these damp things, and be right back down."

"All right. But be quick."

She smiled. "I will. Promise. Estelle, there you are! Ready to trim the tree, darlin' girl?"

Caitlynn stepped away from Donovan, peeling off her gloves finger by finger. She was smiling as she went to greet her charge and Tom at the foot of the stairs.

"I'm ready. Are you?" Estelle shot back. Her curdled smile never warmed her eyes, which were blue ice.

"Quite ready. I've been looking forward to this evening all day," Caitlynn said blithely. "We found the most beautiful tree you've ever seen, Estelle! Over six feet tall, with the thickest, furriest branches. It's going to look wonderful in the window."

Donovan gestured for Tom to carry Estelle over to him. When she was directly beneath the mistletoe, he grinned, dipped his dark head and kissed her cool cheek. "Merry Christmas, poppet."

Estelle did not return his kiss, or look up at him. Rather, she kept her face averted, cheek pressed against Tom's shoulder.

She's jealous, Caitlynn thought with a sigh. *The poor child is green with it. She must have seen us kissing and didn't like it one bit. Donovan can try to make it up to her, but I doubt he'll succeed, not with Estelle. She's far too possessive, too deeply attached to him, unfortunately.*

"Did Mrs. Montgomery have the ornaments brought

down from the attic?" Donovan asked, unwinding his muffler from about his throat and draping it over the hall stand.

"You'll have to ask Mrs. M. I'm sure I don't know."

"Estelle?" Donovan's eyes narrowed at his ward's clipped tone. "Are you upset about something?"

Caitlynn groaned silently. *Couldn't he see? Hadn't he guessed? He still saw Estelle as the little girl he had rescued, but that little girl was a woman now.*

"Noo, not at all, *Uncle* Donovan," Estelle lied sweetly. "It's just that I really don't know whether Mrs. M. brought them down or not. I slept all afternoon, you see."

"You did?" There was concern in his tone now.

Caitlynn glanced at Estelle. Her expression was smug. She knew exactly what to say and do to draw her guardian's undivided attention.

"Yes."

"And why was that? Are you feeling unwell? Do you have a fever? Should I send for Dr. Geoffries?"

"Oh, there's no need for all that fuss. I'm quite all right now. I was just a little . . . tired, that's all."

"You're certain that's all it was?" He felt Estelle's brow.

She managed a brave, tremulous smile. "Quite certain. Besides, I don't want to miss all the fun. Rose has made mulled cider and eggnog for us to drink while we're trimming the tree. And Bridget says there are mince pies and sausage rolls, too, straight from the oven."

"Sausage rolls? Mince pies? What can Rose be thinking of? We'll ruin our appetites for supper!" Donovan declared teasingly. His wicked grin said he didn't give a jot about their appetites, ruined or otherwise.

Caitlynn laughed, too. His grin was infectious. Her

green eyes sparkled in the light of the gas chandeliers. Her cheeks glowed, the aftereffects of Donovan's long and lingering kisses as they rode home through softly falling snow and his ardent embrace beneath the mistletoe. She felt beautiful, adored, special. Right or wrong, she didn't want this glorious feeling to end. Ever.

Estelle's lips tightened. "No, we won't. Rose said supper will be only soup, meats and bread, because we're having roasted turkey and all the trimmings tomorrow. She's not serving supper until eight-thirty at the earliest so we'll have lots of time to decorate the tree. How many guests are coming for dinner tomorrow?"

"Nineteen, plus the three of us, so there'll be twenty-two for Christmas dinner, in all."

"Twenty-two!" Estelle exclaimed softly, watching Donovan's face. She sighed. "So many. I liked it better when it was just the two of us. Remember, Donovan? We had so much fun." Her look was calculated to make Caitlynn feel like an outsider.

Caitlynn flinched. She knew the girl's behavior was the result of jealousy, but being excluded hurt nonetheless.

"Miss Estelle?" Tom cut in with a discreet cough. "Begging your pardon, but if I could just carry you into the drawing room, miss? Me old arms aren't what they once was, ye see."

While they'd chattered on, poor Tom had been standing there holding Estelle in his aching arms.

"Oh, my goodness! Tom, you poor man!" Caitlynn exclaimed. "Why didn't you speak up sooner?"

"Oh, he's all right, aren't you, Tom? Onward! To the tree! The tree!" Estelle commanded, waving her arm like a general leading her troops.

Caitlynn frowned as Tom carried Estelle into the drawing room. Despite her attempts at gaiety, the girl's laughter sounded forced, shrill and false. Caitlynn suspected the girl was, in reality, perilously close to tears. She sighed. She hoped Estelle wouldn't make herself upset and come down with another bout of fever, not on Christmas Eve. She'd been looking forward to the holiday for weeks.

"Miss?"

"Yes, Annie?"

"Could I have a word with you, miss?" the maid asked later that evening as she ladled steaming beef and barley soup into Caitlynn's bowl.

"Why, of course you can, Annie. What is it?" She had never liked the maid very much, finding her secretive and sly. But Annie was so pale, so nervous tonight, she felt a twinge of pity for her.

"Not now, miss," Annie murmured, brushing carroty hair off her freckled face. "Not now, and not here, either. Later. I'll come to your room later tonight, shall I, miss?"

"Of course. Annie, this isn't about tomorrow, is it?" She frowned. "I know you want to be home with your family for Christmas dinner, but we really need your help to serve; then you may take the rest of the day off. In fact, we're counting on you. Dr. Fitzgerald has promised that you and Bridget will be well rewarded for your trouble."

Annie looked over her shoulder. She seemed edgy, afraid of being overheard. "No, no. It's got nothing to do with that, miss. I'll be here. Promise! It's—will ye have more soup, miss?" she asked in a louder voice.

Caitlynn looked in the direction Annie was staring. The maid was so white, Caitlynn thought she might faint. *Why?* she wondered. Who was she so afraid of? Surely not Declan Fitzgerald?

Declan was pulling a cracker with Estelle at the other card table. They were both laughing uproariously at their silliness, paying no attention to either herself or Annie, that Caitlynn could see.

Donovan's teasing younger brother, the respectable lawyer, was wearing a silly red-paper crown, one of the prizes from his cracker. He was tooting a tiny gilt horn as he and Estelle tugged on opposite ends of another paper cracker.

There was a sudden sharp snapping sound as Estelle's cracker tore in half, showering tiny favors over the tablecloth. A rolled paper hat. A small toy of some kind. A printed fortune.

"Listen to my fortune. It says, *'Beware the thief amongst you,'*" Estelle read aloud in an ominous tone. She glared pointedly at Annie, who turned scarlet to the roots of her hair.

"Aha. That must mean me!" Declan declared. He theatrically clutched his hands to his chest. "Declan Fitzgerald, lawyer extraordinaire—and thief of female hearts! *A votre service, ma belle* Estelle!"

"You, a thief of hearts?" Estelle giggled, putting her paper crown on at a jaunty angle. "Hardly!"

She gave a shrill experimental blast on her prize, a small silver whistle, and tossed her blond ringlets. Her eyes met Annie's. Usually wide and innocent, tonight they were hard as nails as they met the maid's.

Annie froze, then quickly looked away, before moving on to serve Donovan. Her hands shook as she carried the heavy silver soup tureen, so that the soup slopped against the sides of the serving bowl and the ladle rattled. The tureen seemed far too big, too heavy for such a thin young woman to carry.

What was all that about? Caitlynn wondered. Was Annie afraid of Estelle? Worried about Estelle's threats to have her fired? Yes, that must be it. She probably wanted Caitlynn to speak to Mrs. Montgomery on her behalf. What else would she want to talk to Caitlynn about in private?

Serving platters took up the centers of the three card tables Tom had set up for them by the fire. One table held slices of buttered bread. Another held an array of meats for the sandwiches that included cold chicken, roasted beef, sliced ham and wafer-thin morsels of tender tongue. There was also an assortment of small pots containing mustards, relishes, chutneys or pickles.

After the delicious mince pies and sausage rolls they'd enjoyed while trimming the tree and singing carols to Mrs. Montgomery's robust piano playing, sandwiches and soup were more than enough.

In fact, a truly wonderful time had been had by all of them.

After they finished eating, Declan danced around and around the drawing room with Estelle until she was giddy, her feet resting on his feet, his arms wrapped tightly about her waist to support her.

"You dance divinely, my dear Miss Marsh," Declan declared.

"I know. But you have two left feet!" Estelle tossed back at him, giggling as he growled and whirled her around the room until she was dizzy and begging him to stop and let her catch her breath.

As they danced, Caitlynn caught a glimpse of the lively, vibrant young woman Estelle would have been were it not for the childhood infirmity that had made her an invalid and threatened to still her damaged heart forever.

With her beauty, Estelle could have enjoyed an array

of eager suitors, made a comfortable if not brilliant marriage, and lived a full and happy life with a husband who adored her, the mistress of a small but pleasant household. Her life would have been a far cry from Lily Perkins's sordid house in St. Giles, and Lily's wicked plans for her daughter's future.

But alas, marriage and a long and happy life as wife and mother were unlikely. Rheumatic fever had robbed Estelle of her future. According to Donovan, it was only a matter of time before it also claimed her life.

Caitlynn swallowed, tears filling her eyes at the injustices of life. But then, life was filled with injustices, she reminded herself. What of her cousin, gentle Deirdre who had never harmed a fly, yet had nonetheless vanished without a trace in this wicked old city?

Estelle was glowing when the music stopped. Her pearly teeth were very white against her full red lips. Perspiration glistened on her brow. Simple exertion— or the signs of impending fever? Caitlynn worried.

"Estelle, perhaps you should rest for a little while," she suggested, withdrawing a lace-edged handkerchief from her skirt pocket to dab at Estelle's brow.

Estelle shrugged her off. "Stop fussing, do, Miss Caitlynn! I'm quite all right. Dance with me again, please, Uncle Declan?" Estelle cajoled.

"Are you propositioning me, brat?" He grinned.

"I certainly am, sir!"

"Ah! And what sort of proper young lady asks an older gentleman to dance with her, instead of waiting for the gentleman to do the asking, hmm?" Declan demanded, smiling down at her. His dark brows were arched. Warm brown eyes twinkled in his attractive face.

Estelle gave Declan a playful thump on the chest.

"An impatient one, Lawyer Declan. Mrs. M? Do be a dear and play us a waltz!"

Caitlynn frowned as she watched the pair together. Something didn't fit. Something . . . something was wrong about the scene, as out of place as the wrong piece in a child's jigsaw puzzle. But what? What could it be?

Something about the pair had struck some chord in her memory. It worried at her like a pup worrying a bone. But, try as she might, the elusive memory flitted away, like a butterfly dancing over a meadow.

In the end, she stopped trying to think what it could have been and idly watched the others as she sipped eggnog from a silver mug, basking in the fond smiles and smoldering glances Donovan sent her way from time to time.

Estelle's peal of laughter rang out again and again. She had obviously recovered from her earlier fit of jealousy, and now seemed to be determined to have a good time. The latter included flirting outrageously with Declan. Caitlynn could hardly blame her for that! Estelle was almost sixteen, practically a grown woman, and Declan was a very handsome young man. More handsome, perhaps, than his older, more serious brother.

Not for the first time, Caitlynn wondered how the two Fitzgerald brothers, both attractive, both successful men in their own right, had both avoided marriage for so long. Then again, perhaps they were too successful, too dedicated to their professions, to enter into marriage.

While Donovan spent long hours doctoring the Irish poor and starting clinics for the sick, Declan did *pro bono* work for their countrymen in need of legal representation. He was also a staunch advocate of Irish home rule.

Penelope Neri

After several waltzes, followed by a lively polka, Declan collapsed into one of the overstuffed armchairs beside the fireplace. His chin on his chest, his long legs stretched out before him, he declared himself done in.

"Done in! So soon? Why, you are getting as crotchety as old Tom!" Estelle declared scathingly. "Uncle Donovan? What about you? Won't you dance with me?"

Estelle cajoled Donovan to take Declan's place as her dance partner, pouting prettily when at first he refused, then smiling in delight when he reluctantly gave in.

But in the middle of the second dance, Donovan abruptly declared himself worn out, and asked Declan if he'd care for another drink.

Estelle, her lower lip jutting, shot her guardian a look of pure venom as he returned her to her chaise.

Well, well. What had brought about his abrupt change of mind? Caitlynn wondered. Had Estelle said something the rest of them had not heard?

Rather than meet Estelle's angry glare, Caitlynn turned her attention to the Christmas tree, which stood in pride of place in the drawing room's bay window.

The Christmas tree was over seven feet tall, its thick branches aglow with the tiny flames of over a hundred miniature candles set securely in silver-gilt holders. With every candle lit, it was a magical sight.

Each long-needled bough was elegantly trimmed with colored glass balls, orange pomanders studded with fragrant cloves, then wrapped in lace and ribbons, and papier-mâché pears dusted with gold glitter. There were colored blown-glass birds with tails of trailing feathers, chubby gilt cherubs blowing trumpets, fat red-satin bows and more.

At the topmost point of the tree shone a beautiful

star. Of course, the usual water-filled buckets had been discreetly hidden behind the draperies, on hand in the event of a fire.

Christmas Day would be wonderful, Caitlynn thought happily. The tree and the decorations throughout the house were festive and beautiful. Special presents had been chosen, wrapped and hidden, ready to appear beneath the tree on Christmas morning. Invitations had been sent, and replies received. A fine Christmas feast was already being prepared, complete with flaming plum pudding. If it were not for feeling homesick and missing her family at this time of year, and her lingering sorrow that she had not yet found Deirdre, it would have been the perfect Christmas, she thought, remembering Donovan's kisses.

Ah, yes. Perfect. . . .

The last to retire that evening, Caitlynn moved about the drawing room, extinguishing the lamps. The carol she was humming was cut off as she stifled a yawn. Although the clock on the mantel was only chiming nine, she felt pleasantly exhausted.

She was just about to blow out the last lamp when she noticed a tiny roll of green paper beneath Estelle's chaise. Her fortune, or motto, forgotten in a fit of temper.

Picking it up, Caitlynn idly unrolled the strip of colored paper and read, "*Many good friends surround you.*"

She frowned, surprised. Not Estelle's fortune, after all, but someone else's. Estelle's fortune had been a warning about thieves, she recalled, remembering the look Estelle had cast Annie, and the expression on poor Annie's face.

She shook her head. Whomever it belonged to, the prediction would undoubtedly prove correct at this time of year. After all, who wasn't surrounded by friends in this merry season?

Caitlynn was about to retire for the night, feeling full, happy and pleasantly exhausted by the exciting day, when she heard a knock at her door.

Expecting Annie, she pulled on her dressing gown and hurried to open it.

It was not Annie, but Bridget.

"Did I wake you, miss?" the girl whispered as she peered through the open crack. The long landing behind Bridget was as dark as any cavern, except for the candle the maid carried to light her way, which guttered in the draft.

"No, not at all. I was just getting into bed. What is it?" she murmured.

"It's Dr. Fitzgerald. He's been called to a lying-in in the East End. He said to tell you that, if you've a mind to see a baby born this Christmas Eve, you can go with him, but ye'd best be quick! Oh, and mind ye dress warmly."

Bridget smiled doubtfully. Coming from the heavily populated stews of the East End herself, she'd seen her share of babies born, several of them her own little brothers and sisters, of which there were eleven, not counting herself. She couldn't imagine someone like Miss O'Connor wanting to see a birth.

"Oh, yes! I'd like that," Caitlynn said after only a moment's hesitation. The exciting prospect quite banished her fatigue. "Please ask him to wait for me, will you? I'll be right down."

As she closed her door, Caitlynn distinctly heard the soft click of another door closing farther down the shadowed hallway.

Nosy Mary Montgomery, she decided. Then again,

perhaps the older woman wasn't snooping at all but waiting for Father Christmas, she thought with a muffled giggle. It was impossible to imagine the housekeeper as an impatient little girl, eager for gifts.

She dressed in record time, layering several petticoats over her drawers, wool stockings and boots, then adding her warmest gown and a short fur-trimmed jacket, before throwing her cloak over the lot.

Within minutes, she was downstairs. Donovan grinned with delight as she joined him. She grinned back, unable to keep a straight face in her pleasure.

"That was quick. I'm glad you decided to come with me."

"How could I refuse? A baby coming into the world on Christmas Eve! Why, it's what Christmas is all about!"

He frowned. "Perhaps I should warn you. Childbirth is bloody. No sight for the squeamish."

"Then I'll be fine, Dr. Donovan," she said pertly, grinning up at him. "For I don't have a squeamish bone in my body."

"I'm happy to hear it. Don't you need your bag?"

"No, I didn't bring it. I'll have no use for it tonight."

"Good. Then let's be off. I've found that babies have an annoying habit of coming fast when you want them to come slowly, and of taking their time when you want them to come quickly. Contrary little creatures, all of them!"

His hand against the small of her back, he ushered her outside to where Tom, muffled to the gills in greatcoat and several scarves, waited with the coach.

Snowflakes were falling as the carriage lurched forward, rumbling away from the square and into the snowy night.

Chapter Sixteen

Being invited to accompany Donovan to a confinement was only the first surprise in store for Caitlynn that night. The second was the identity of the woman who was in labor—and a woman less like the Christ Child's mother would have been difficult to imagine.

The woman on the bed, wearing a fraying petticoat for a nightgown under her shabby shawl, was none other than Kitty Abbott, she realized, shocked. The same sly baggage who had tricked and robbed her at the Britannia public house weeks ago, making promises she had no intention of keeping before she took her pound note and vanished into the slums.

"Well, well! Will ye look what the cat drug in!" Kitty said with a wry grin, between contractions. "Evenin', Doc. Your Majesty!" She inclined her head to Donovan and Caitlynn in turn.

Caitlynn flushed.

"Evening, Kitty," Donovan began. "This is a fine

210

time to be brought to childbed, is it not? Christmas Eve!" He shook his head. "How's Mrs. Abbott doing, Moll?"

"Ohh, well enough, sir," the frowzy bundle of rags in the corner answered him. "I'm thinking we didn't need ye after all, sir."

On closer inspection, Caitlynn realized that someone was sitting on a stool, half hidden in the shadows of the single sorry room that was Kitty Abbott's doss.

The old woman, obviously the midwife, was huddled against the chimney breast, where it was warmest. She continued, "When I sent the lad for ye, the babe was minded to come breech. But me and Sal, we was able t'turn the little bastard." She chortled with laughter, as if she'd made a great joke.

"Bloody lucky for me it did an' all," Kitty muttered, panting as another contraction drew her belly up to a great peak. "And it ain't a bastard, I'll have you know, Moll Jackson," she panted. "M-married proper, me and Billy were. At St. Anthony's . . . *Aaah!*"

She caught her lower lip between her teeth as pain engulfed her. Beads of sweat popped out on her face and slid down her cheeks, bright amber beads in the flicker of the fire.

"Lucky indeed," Donovan soothed when the contraction ended. He felt her belly and seemed pleased. "You're doing well, Kitty. Your baby's head is down and ready to be born. Not much longer now and you can start pushing. Is this your second?"

"Not bloody likely. My first. And, God willing, my last! One kid's enough, you ask me." Despite her hard words, her expression told Caitlynn that this baby was wanted, by its mother, at least.

Donovan removed his coat and hung it on a peg beside the door. He rolled up his shirtsleeves, baring powerful forearms shadowed with a sprinkling of hair. "Hot water, if you please, Moll. And strong soap. If you have none, there's some in my bag. Remember what I told you? You must wash your hands each time you examine a mother," he warned in a sterner voice. "Then wash them again when you are done."

"I remember, for all the good that washing nonsense does a body," the midwife muttered with a disdainful sniff.

Lifting the black kettle that hung over the fire, she poured hot water into a chipped basin. Steam billowed into the smoky room as she carried the bowl over to the battered table.

"Where's your man tonight?" Donovan asked Kitty as he washed his hands and a good six inches of his forearms.

"Billy Abbott's where he always is at this hour, Doc. Down at the pub with his bloody cronies. This your missus, then?" she asked cheekily, nodding at Caitlynn as he quickly examined her. "Don't look like no nightingale to me, she don't."

Donovan continued his examination without answering her. When he was done, he pulled down Kitty's petticoats and drew the yellowed bedsheet up, restoring her modesty and dignity as carefully as if she were a vicar's wife rather than a sometime dolly-mop and con woman.

"Not exactly, no," he answered Kitty at last. "She's my . . . sweetheart, shall we say?" He winked at Caitlynn, then withdrew his pocket watch from his waistcoat and lifted Kitty's wrist to count her pulse. "I've given up hoping you'll leave your wretch of a husband and run away with me, Kitty, my lass," he teased.

"Ah, my Billy's good enough when he's sober. He don't knock me about much, like some do. He's promised me he'll keep this job, too, 'n' take care of me and the little 'un."

"You mean to keep this child, then?"

"Aye." Her hard yet pretty face softened. "No orphan asylum for this little nipper. It'll be mine, see? An' Kitty Abbott don't give away her own, like they was kittens t'be drowned."

"I'm glad to hear it. What sort of job does your Billy have?"

"One that's hard to come by. A bummeree at Smithfield's, he is." There was pride in her voice.

Donovan nodded, suitably impressed. The powerful men who hauled the meat carcasses were well paid and guaranteed steady work. Consequently, any openings at Smithfield's were quickly snapped up.

"Good for him, Kitty. And good for you, too," Donovan said with genuine pleasure. "Then you won't be going back on the streets?"

"No, Doc, never. Not if I can help it." She shuddered. "Especially not with them five women dead and the Ripper still at large! Knew 'em all, I did, too. Polly. Annie Chapman. Long Liz. Kate Eddowes. Mary Kelly. . . . No, Kitty Abbott's no fool. There's other ways to make a bob or two, if a gel's clever." Despite her labor pains, she winked saucily at Caitlynn. "And I'm clever. Right, Queenie?"

Caitlynn glared at her. "If you say so."

Donovan's dark brows lifted as he looked from one to the other. "Have you two met before?"

"Yes," Kitty said.

At the same time Caitlynn said, "Never!"

"Well, which is it?" Donovan asked, amused. "Have you or haven't you?"

"On second thought, I think perhaps we have met. At St. Anthony's Church, wasn't it?" Caitlynn said desperately, shooting Kitty a warning look.

"I think it was at the church, yes," Kitty agreed with an impish grin, imitating Caitlynn's educated brogue. "You were looking for your—*aaagh!*"

Whatever she was about to say was cut off by another labor pang, to Caitlynn's enormous relief. The time was coming when she would have to trust Donovan enough to tell him who she was, and why she had come to number 13 Huntington Square masquerading as a lady's companion. But she would much rather tell him herself than have him find out from Kitty Abbott that Deirdre Riordan was her missing cousin. She had the uncomfortable feeling that Donovan would not take kindly to being lied to.

Kitty's labor ended at seven minutes past midnight, Christmas Eve. She gave a last bellowing cry, then pushed William Fitzgerald Abbott out into the world, and into Moll Jackson's waiting arms.

The midwife tied and cut the cord, swaddled the baby in a square of worn linen, then held the squalling, bloody infant up for his mother's inspection.

"Here's a fine healthy boy for you and Bill, Kitty," Moll crowed. "A mite on the scrawny side, but strong for all that."

"Aww, he'll grow, God bless 'im," Kitty vowed as she looked at her bloody newborn. Tears flowed down her tired face. "Give him here for a bit of a cuddle with his mum, the poor little sod."

Although Caitlynn had no fondness for Kitty, it would take a far harder woman than she was to remain unmoved by the miracle of birth, or the joy of motherhood, which had so transformed the con woman.

Kitty's face was radiant, beautiful as she looked down at baby William. The birth had turned a grimy, sad little doss in an East End rookery into a joyful place filled with love, as the birth of a special baby had once transformed a stable in Bethlehem.

"Congratulations, Mrs. Abbott," Caitlynn murmured. "He's a beautiful boy."

"He is, i'n't he? My Billy will be right chuffed when he sees 'im. Wanted a boy, he did, same as most men. That's why I'm calling him William, for his dad, see, and Fitzgerald after you, Doc! Will you hold him for a bit?" she asked Caitlynn.

Surprised, Caitlynn nodded. She took the red-faced infant in her arms. Although almost asleep, the baby was gnawing at his tiny fist with a rosebud mouth, making loud, juicy smacking sounds. He was whole, innocent, perfect in every way from his tiny eyelashes to his tiny toes. "Will you look at him!" Caitlynn murmured. "Oh, he's a wonder! Not two minutes old and already hungry!" she exclaimed, deeply moved.

"Just like his blooming father. Greedy sod, Billy is. I'll put him to the breast in a bit. Make us a cup o' tea, will ye, Moll? Worn out, I am." Kitty sighed. "Will you take a cuppa, miss?"

"If there's enough, yes, please. I'd love one."

"I must leave you ladies for just a moment," Donovan said, going to the door. "I won't be long, nor far away."

Before Caitlynn could protest, he left her alone with Kitty, the baby and the old midwife, who was brewing tea in a brown pot with a chipped spout. The Sally that Moll mentioned had yet to put in an appearance.

"Right. We've only got a minute before the doc comes back, so listen up, Queenie," Kitty told Caitlynn quickly, all business now. "What you asked me that night at the Britannia? About the missing woman?"

"My cousin Deirdre. Yes! What about her?" she demanded eagerly, her heart thumping.

"I know you think I scarpered with yer money, and I 'spose I did. But I got t'feeling guilty for it—stow what you're thinking, Moll Jackson!—so I asked around, later. About her, I mean. I've been meaning t'come and tell you, but—well, there was never time."

Caitlynn nodded. She believed Kitty. The woman had probably been too busy trying to put food in her belly, she thought, feeling an unexpected twinge of sympathy, to give much thought to anything else.

"Go on. Tell me what?" Dread lay in her belly like a heavy stone.

"Word on the street is that Annie Murphy knows about the Riordan woman. Ask her. Last I heard, she was in service on Huntington Square."

"Yes, yes. Annie's in service at the doctor's. But why Annie? Why would she know where my cousin is—"

"I don't know nothing about nothing, I don't. *Ask Annie.*"

Kitty abruptly fell silent as Donovan returned, a blast of cold air following him into the warm, smoky room before he closed the door behind him. He was carrying an orange crate piled high with food. There were a string of pork sausages, a roasted chicken wrapped in greasy brown paper and string, eggs, a wedge of cheese, a bottle of milk, some mince pies and jam tarts, an apple, an orange and a jar of the striped humbugs he kept on his desk at St. Bart's.

"This is for you, Kitty. A Christmas present! I want you to eat and rest until you recover your strength. The baby has taken all the nourishment from your body. You need to eat properly or your breasts won't make milk to nurse your son. And drink plenty of fluids. Tea and milk, as much as you can, as often as you can. If you have only water to drink, drink that, but you must boil it first."

The water pumps and wells in the East End were often unsanitary.

"Oh, and here. This is for your William, from his namesake." He thrust something into Kitty's hand. "A little something for his birthday, and to pay his mam's doss for a night or two, at least." He winked as he closed Kitty's fingers over the crackling bank note, smiling at her slack jaw, her teary eyes.

Caitlynn swallowed. The 'little something' he'd given Kitty was a five-pound note—a fortune in this part of London. "God bless you, Doc," Kitty thanked him huskily, clasping his hand and kissing it. Tears overflowed her eyes.

"Oh, don't bless me, Kitty. Bless Mr. Dickens. Mr. Charles Dickens, God rest his soul. Before his *Christmas Carol*, we were all tightfisted Scrooges, without an ounce of Christian charity or conscience among us."

"All right, then. But you tell your Mr. Dickens Kitty Abbott says God bless him, too, wherever he is."

"I shall indeed, Mrs. Abbott," Donovan promised solemnly, slipping Moll Jackson a paper twist of tobacco from his coat pocket. His grin deepened as her rheumy old eyes lit up with glee. "When you've finished your tea, Miss O'Connor, we'll be off home."

"I'm ready when you are, Doctor."

Fresh snow had fallen while they were with Kitty. The pristine white blanket glistened, cloaking the shabbiness, the filth, the soot, the abject poverty, the despair that was the East End. Under a dark blue canopy of clearing sky, spangled by a few frosty stars, the snow-covered scene actually looked quite pretty.

Almost.

Try as she might, Caitlynn could not forget that the purity of the snow concealed the bloodstains of five brutal murders.

An image of those bloody bodies lying in the virginal snow like fallen flowers, their scarlet petals mutilated, filled her mind. It was such a vivid, unsettling image, she shuddered.

The Ripper had claimed his fifth victim on November 11, just forty-five days ago. Had Mary Kelly truly been his last, as everyone was saying, or was it still too soon to tell?

Resolutely she set her jaw and forced such thoughts from her mind. They had no place there, not tonight. . . .

"Evening, Constable," she heard Donovan murmur, nodding to someone in greeting. "A Merry Christmas to you."

Peering around Donovan, Caitlynn saw the caped and helmeted silhouette of a bobby. He stood alone in the gloomy doorway of a building off Kitty's court—a men's social club that was dark and deserted at this late hour.

She could not make out the constable's features in the gloom as he returned Donovan's greeting with a grunted word. Even so, she could feel his eyes on her. Watching her. Following her from the deep shadow of his helmet.

Empty eyes, devoid of emotions and feelings.

It was the same bobby. She was sure of it. The same police constable she'd seen on the evening she became lost in the East End. That night, he'd been standing on the street corner, alone, as the hired hack in which she was riding passed by him.

For a fleeting second, their eyes had met. His had been quite empty then, bottomless black pits, as devoid of emotion as they were now. The unnerving feeling that she had come face-to-face with pure evil was one not easily forgotten.

Although she could not see his features any more clearly now than she had that night, it was the same man; she was certain of it in her heart. He was patrolling alone tonight, as he had then. At least, there was no sign of any partner. Only a single black-caped apparition.

One is for sorrow. . . .

The macabre thought stirred an uneasy flutter in her belly. What if he was the one? she wondered. *Oh, God, what if the p.c. was—?*

Refusing to continue her frightening train of thought, she shook her head to clear it, then uttered a silent prayer for the 'unfortunates' forced to walk the streets this Christmas Eve. Those poor women were little more than helpless prey for such a nameless, faceless predator, like goats tethered by a hunter to bait a hungry tiger.

In his uniform garb, a p.c. could move at will through the maze of the East End. He was a familiar, trusted, even beloved authority figure to all. Who would suspect the local bobby, paid to protect and serve the people, to fight crime and apprehend the criminal, of being a pitiless killer himself? A diabolical monster who butchered helpless women?

"You're very quiet tonight, Miss O'Connor," Donovan observed, squeezing her hand. "A penny for your thoughts."

"I was just wondering. Does Rose know you raided her pantry?" she asked, thrusting her silly suspicions aside as Donovan lifted her up into the coach for the ride home.

"Hmm, not exactly, no," he said, clambering in after

her and slamming the coach door behind them. "But you can rest assured she will find out, first thing in the morning."

At that moment, the coach rumbled past a gaslight. In its light she saw that he was grimacing.

As they quickly left the policeman and Kitty's court behind them, Caitlynn forced herself to laugh. To put all thoughts of sadness, death and sorrow aside on this night of love and peace. "Indeed she will. And what will you tell her, sir?"

"Why, the truth, of course." He grinned and crossed his heart. "The truth and nothing but the truth, so help me God."

"And that is?" She cocked her head to one side.

"That we have mice! Do you think she'll believe me?" he asked hopefully.

"Not a chance. Unless, of course, they were very *large* mice."

"Ah, yes. Mice as big as cats. But, enough of rats and cats. Where were we? Ah, yes. Come here, my lovely, and kiss me."

So saying, he drew her into his arms and ducked his dark head to kiss her. To nuzzle her slender neck until she moaned softly in delight.

"You know, it *is* Christmas Day. We could always blame the missing feast on a greedy Father Christmas," he suggested when he came up for air. He toyed with her hair, twining a thick lock of silky sable around his finger. His warm breath in her ear made her shiver.

She smiled. "We could. And pigs might fly, too— *Mmmm*," she murmured, her voice muffled by his lips as he kissed her again.

This time his kisses were deeper, more sensual, than ever before, melting her, crumbling her reserve in ways his earlier kisses had not.

She surrendered utterly, going limp and heavy against him, letting his arm support her weight as he bore her down across the leather banquette beneath him, while his other hand supported her head.

"Dear God, Caitlynn. I want you so much." His voice was husky against her hair.

And then, to her amazement, he slipped his tongue inside her mouth to touch and tease her own.

She tasted him, *really* tasted him, for the very first time. A thrilling, exciting taste. His deeply erotic kisses touched off a chain of responses throughout her body.

She parted her lips on a sigh, letting pleasure sweep her away. He felt so exciting, so strong, pressed against her. This close, she could taste him, inhale his exciting scent, feel the heat of his body, the thunder of his heart against her breast. Feel what she was almost certain was his arousal as a hard ridge pressed to her lower belly.

Excitement rippled through her, spreading along her veins like a silvery wine. Mere kisses were no longer enough for her. Not anymore. She wanted more. Right or wrong, good or bad, angel or wanton, she wanted him as a woman wants a man. One she is growing to love.

Unconditionally. In every way.

Sliding her arms around his neck, she kissed him back, pressing her lips fiercely to his with a feverish, breathless hunger that took him by surprise. Delighted him. He groaned and held her a little closer, a little tighter, his thigh pressed against her womanhood. Incredibly, she pressed back.

"Sweet Lord, mavourneen," he swore softly. "Do you know what that does to a man?"

"No. But I can guess," she said. Fitting her lips to his, she plunged her fingers into the raw-silk midnight

221

waves that brushed his collar. Gripping his dark head, she demanded more.

"Because I want you, too," she whispered. "I do. I do. I do. Oh, Donovan, *please....*"

Her hunger was like a glowing cinder touched to a dry haystack. He'd been so wrapped up in the clinic, he hadn't made love to a woman in . . . well, far too bloody long. Come to think of it, he hadn't met a woman he *wanted* to make love to in a very long time. Not until now . . . not until Caitlynn burst into his life.

"Aaah, Cait, my love," he whispered raggedly, pressing his lips to her scented throat as she clung to him. "I will. I promise. But not here. And not like this. Later."

He cupped her breast as he kissed her again. His thumb circled the hardened nipple that sprang stiffly to attention. He ached to bare the creamy breast it crowned, buried now beneath layers of cloth; to take it in his mouth. To watch her eyes darken to emerald fire as he suckled it.

To shower her with kisses. To kiss and caress her everywhere, in a hundred delightful ways. Only then, when she lay in his arms, warm and languorous with surrender, rosy with desire, would he claim his prize. Only then would he make love to her all night long.

"We're almost home," he murmured between kisses.

"Yes," she whispered back. There was a world of regret in that single word.

"Will you come to me, Caitlynn? To my bed? 'Tis where you belong. Or if you like, I'll come to you."

She hesitated, then shook her head, lifting green eyes to his in the shadowed coach. "I want to, more than anything. I really do. But . . . I—I cannot. Not yet. Please don't ask me again. You see, there's something I must do first, before you and I can be together. . . ."

It was no lie. God knows, she wanted him. Wanted him so badly, she ached for him. Somehow, without noticing when or where or how, or even why, she had fallen in love with him, little by little, against her will and despite all her suspicions. But until she knew every detail of his relationship to her cousin, what they had meant to each other, if anything, and where Deirdre was now, doubt would permeate every moment they were together. Mistrust would taint every joy. Mistrust, and—yes!—even fear.

Gripping her chin, he forced her to look up at him in the shadows. His dark blue eyes smoldered. "It's not what you think. I'm not the lecherous master of the household, seducing the maids and the lady's companion. Dammit, Cait, I'm in love with you. Do you hear me, darling girl? *I love you.*"

Chapter Seventeen

"I love you."

His impassioned vow would echo through her dreams that night.

"God help me, I love you, too, Donovan," she whispered in her darkened room. Stirring restlessly, she remembered how she had run inside the instant the coach rolled to a halt before number 13, thrusting open the carriage door and leaping out before either he or Thomas could help her down.

Had she been running from Donovan, or from her own feelings? she wondered. Was her need to be sure of him real, or just a welcome excuse, as Michael Flynn's desertion had been welcome?

"How can I trust you, how can I believe in you, with Deirdre still missing? When I have no idea what happened to her, or whether you played some role in her disappearance?" she asked the shadows. True, she was almost certain he wasn't the man Deirdre had been meeting on her afternoons off, but that didn't mean he had had no part in her disappearance.

Nonetheless, she fell asleep still flushed with the memory of his lips on hers, the sensation of his gentle hand cupping her breast.

She remembered Donovan holding Kitty's baby in his arms, smiling as sweetly as any dark angel as he looked down at the infant.

Remembered Donovan slipping a toothless old woman a twist of tobacco for her pipe.

Remembered Donovan passing out peppermint humbugs to tired mothers and sickly children.

Could the same man have seduced an innocent young woman? Could he have driven her away? Abandoned her? Perhaps even worse . . . ?

Everything she knew about Donovan said no. And yet . . . the wolf often appeared in the guise of a sheep. Great beauty often concealed the beast within. Even the rosiest apple could hide a squirming maggot at its heart.

Until she was certain, one way or the other, she would make no declarations of love. Nor would she share Donovan's bed, however tempted she might be.

It was safer that way.

As she drifted off to sleep, she remembered that Annie had wanted to talk to her.

Had the maid come to her room while she was gone, leaving when she received no answer to her knock? Caitlynn wondered guiltily. Never mind. She would make a point to speak with Annie privately first thing in the morning when she came in to lay the fire, she promised herself. And she would do all she could to keep Estelle and Mary Montgomery from sacking the girl, if that was what Annie wanted to speak to her about. Surely Annie would think twice before pilfering again, after almost losing her position? *If*, as Estelle claimed, she had been pilfering.

She smiled. She couldn't think of a better Christmas present to give the girl than peace of mind. And in return, God willing, and if Kitty Abbott could be trusted, Annie would tell her about Deirdre.

Despite her best intentions, Caitlynn had no opportunity to speak with Annie the following morning. Instead, it was a furious Bridget who brought the morning tea tray. She also carried in the coal scuttle to lay the fire.

"Merry Christmas, Bridget," Caitlynn greeted her sleepily.

"Merry for some, perhaps," Bridget grumbled. "But not for them that have the work of two to do, thanks to that bloody Annie Murphy!"

Bridget noisily rattled the coal scuttle as she shoveled coal into the grate. She made no secret of her anger.

"What's Annie done now?" There had never been any love lost between the two maids.

"What she's done is scarpered, Miss Caitlynn, and left me to do my work and hers, too! Today, with all those people coming t' Christmas dinner, and all!"

Bridget appeared close to tears as she dropped to her knees before the grate. She began energetically raking the cold ashes out of the hearth, making a great deal of noise in the process. "I don't know how I'll manage, I don't, what with the master at home, and Mrs. M. breathing down my neck, and all them people coming, too!"

"What do you mean, she's scarpered?" Caitlynn demanded, trying to squelch the panic rising through her. If Annie was gone, how could she ask her about Deirdre? Her only chance to find out what had happened to her cousin had disappeared with the maid, if Kitty Abbott was to be believed.

"She's run off, that's what," Bridget snapped with a furious toss of her brown curls. "*Scarpered*. She must have brought the coal up from the cellars early this morning as usual, then decided she'd had enough. She left a full scuttle right by the cellar door for poor Rose t' trip over when she came in. Oooh, I'll box her bloody ears for her, I will, if she ever shows her face here again—which I doubt! I almost forgot." She withdrew something from her apron pocket and gave Caitlynn a tentative smile. "Here you are, miss. Merry Christmas. It's nothing very grand, just a little something I made for you. Sorry about me going on, and all."

While Caitlynn, numb with shock, tried to absorb the news that, like Deirdre, Annie had left number 13, taking her secrets with her, she forced her unwieldy fingers to unwrap the small package Bridget pressed into her hand.

Bridget's gift was a strawberry pincushion, beautifully sewn and stuffed, with leaves of green silk and small strawberry flowers cut from scraps of stiff white buckram. Black seeds and the veins in the leaves had been meticulously embroidered.

"Why, it's lovely, Bridget. Thank you! Now I'll always remember you when I'm sewing."

Bridget's smile faded. "Remember me, miss? Why? You're not leaving us?"

"No, no, I didn't mean that. Just that it will always remind me of you." She went over to the armoire and withdrew a small decoupaged box. "Here. I have a present for you, too. Merry Christmas."

She watched as Bridget unwrapped the box. The young woman withdrew the collar of burgundy feathers with a cry of pleasure.

"Oh, miss! You shouldn't have! Really, it's much too grand, it is!" She fastened it around her neck with what bordered on reverence, then went to preen in front of Caitlynn's dresser mirror, stroking the soft down feathers with exclamations of delight.

The collar looked incongruous against the maid's plain gray wool dress and bibbed apron, but drew attention to her pretty features and fresh complexion, just as Caitlynn intended.

"Oh, miss, I've never owned anything near as fine, I'm sure!" Bridget exclaimed, tears welling. She blushed. "This'll turn that Sean's head, and no mistake. Thank you, miss, and may God bless you!"

Caitlynn's smile faded the minute Bridget left the room, her present clutched to her chest.

She should never have gone to see Kitty's baby born last night, she told herself. She should have stayed here instead and waited for Annie. What had she been thinking? If Kitty was right, Annie knew where Deirdre was! Perhaps that was why Annie had wanted to talk with her. Perhaps it had nothing to do with pilfering at all, nor her fear of being sacked.

But no sooner had that thought occurred to her than she realized such a thing was unlikely, since no one at number 13 knew she and Deirdre were cousins.

She bit her lip, angry at herself nonetheless. If Annie really was gone, as Bridget said, she would never know what the girl had meant to tell her. Unless . . . ! Tomorrow she would have to go to Annie's home on some pretext or other and ask her, she decided.

Feeling better now that she had a plan of action, she washed, then dressed for the day in one of the simple day gowns she favored. She would come upstairs to change shortly before their first guests arrived at noon.

To that end, she took a green velvet gown out of the

wardrobe and hung it on the door so that any wrinkles in the skirts would fall out.

As she bustled about the room, brushing her hair, twisting it up into a tidy chignon, fastening it in place with hairpins, she suddenly noticed small details that had gone unnoticed in her fatigue as she'd readied herself for bed last night.

For the second time since her arrival on Huntington Square, someone had searched her room. Someone had opened drawers and cupboards, moved things about. There was nothing missing, as far as she could tell. Her drawstring bag was still on the desk where she'd left it last night, but her writing things had been rearranged, her drawers opened and not completely closed. Small details, perhaps, but telling ones for someone as observant as herself.

She remembered then the soft click of a door down the hallway last night as Bridget delivered the doctor's invitation.

Who had still been awake? Who had been curious enough about Bridget's late-night summons to eavesdrop? Mary Montgomery? Annie? Or had it been Declan, who had stayed over last night instead of returning to his lodgings? And why in the world would any one of the three have wanted to search her room? What could the intruder have been looking for?

Dropping to her knees on the hearth, as she had done before, she reached up the chimney and was filled with relief as, yet again, she withdrew Deirdre's diary, unscathed.

Removing its sooty wrapping, she carried the diary to her desk and sat down to reread its entries while she sipped her morning tea. In a few moments, she would have to solve the dilemma of who would serve their guests if Annie failed to return, but for now, she had a few moments to herself.

Most of the entries were about the everyday happenings in Deirdre's life. Her worries about her father, Daniel Riordan, who had been ailing when she left Ireland. Her homesickness. Her wish that she could see Caitlynn, whom she affectionately called 'coz,' again.

One entry in particular brought tears to Caitlynn's eyes. It had been written only days before Deirdre disappeared.

"What I would give to be able to talk to you, my dear cousin," she had written, *"as we once talked away long summer afternoons in the orchard, with the smell of apples and freshly mown grass heavy on the air. If you were here, coz, I would tell you all about him, and how it feels to be loved, and to be in love. Ah, yes, it is true, coz. I love him to distraction! D. loves me, too. There is such tenderness in his brown eyes when he looks at me. He will propose very soon. I know he will. And I shall accept. Oh, coz, I'm truly the happiest woman alive."*

Hardly the words of a woman who intended to run off into the night, never to return.

Caitlynn read through the same entries she'd read before, in which Deirdre said she needed to talk to someone, obviously a woman. After that final entry, only blank pages remained.

She closed the diary and pursed her lips in thought. Like last night, as she watched Declan and Estelle dancing, she had the strangest feeling that she was missing something important. That a key to Deirdre's disappearance was right there under her nose. Or at least, some clue as to what had happened to her. But, try as she might, she could still not fathom what that answer could be.

Returning the diary to its hiding place, she went downstairs.

Chapter Eighteen

To Caitlynn's relief, the dilemma of who would take Annie's place was solved by Bridget, who suggested that her younger sister, fourteen-year-old Maureen, be sent for.

Caitlynn conferred briefly with Mrs. Montgomery, and soon after, Tom and the carriage were duly dispatched to the family's lodgings in the East End, to bring Maureen to Huntington Square in fine style.

A younger, plumper version of Bridget, Maureen was a shy yet capable girl, delighted by the opportunity to earn some extra money for her large family.

"Mam taught all of us girls how to wait table, miss. You needn't worry about a thing," Maureen declared in her lilting brogue, bobbing Caitlynn a curtsey. "Me and Bridget will take fine care of the doctor's guests, won't we, Bridie?"

"Aye," Bridget agreed with a grin. She flashed Caitlynn an I-told-you-so look. "That we will!"

Penelope Neri

"You're a lifesaver, Maureen," Caitlynn said with feeling. "You, too, Bridget. If all goes well, I'll talk to Mrs. Montgomery about making the position permanent, if you like. Even if Annie comes back, she'll be sacked for going off without telling anyone."

Maureen and Bridget's smiles and the way they hugged each other were answer enough. The pair reminded Caitlynn of Deirdre and herself. *Merry Christmas, wherever you may be, coz, and may God bless you,* she thought sadly.

It had been decided that Caitlynn and Mary Montgomery would take breakfast with the family, since it was Christmas morning.

Afterwards, the usual formalities were abandoned. Everyone in the household, including Tom, Rose, Bridget and Maureen, gathered about the tree in the drawing room to open gifts and sing carols, as was the Christmas-morning custom in the Fitzgerald household.

Estelle was elected 'Father Christmas,' with Declan as her helper. He handed out the gifts while she read the names written on the tags. Apparently, the pair took the same roles every year.

"Mrs. Montgomery, this one's for you," Estelle declared bossily, seated on a plump footstool next to the Christmas tree, the beautiful princess issuing royal commands from her velvet throne. "It's from . . . Miss Caitlynn."

Estelle looked far older than her fifteen years in a gown of scarlet velvet with long fitted sleeves. A matching red ribbon pulled her fair hair back at the sides, baring her angelic face and small pink earlobes, from which heart-shaped garnet earbobs sparkled like drops of blood.

"Why, Miss O'Connor, what a charming surprise—

232

and how kind of you to think of me. Thank you!" Mary Montgomery exclaimed as she opened the box of dainty monogrammed handkerchiefs Caitlynn had chosen for her. Her usually severe face was pink, almost girlish as she surveyed the small pile of gifts before her. "Hankies are always useful, but lace-edged *and* embroidered? Delightful!"

Tom's eyes grew moist when he opened the tapestry tobacco pouch from Caitlynn. It was perfect to hold the excellent cut of pipe tobacco the doctor had given him. His gruff thanks ended in an impromptu hug on Caitlynn's part. "Oh, Tom, enough! Stop it, do! You're very welcome!"

Rose was similarly delighted with her peacock brooch. She pinned it to the bib of her apron, beaming like a duchess in her new finery as she turned from side to side so that the sparkling stones reflected the light in a dazzling rainbow of colors.

"Oooh. This one's for you, Miss Caitlynn. I wonder what it can be," Estelle wondered aloud, gently shaking the long, narrow box wrapped in gold foil and decorated with gold bows and cream silk roses. When it rattled, her brows rose questioningly. "Hmm. I wonder . . . A pen, do you think? No, no, the box is far too long. A bracelet, perhaps?"

"Who could it be from?" Caitlynn asked, mystified as Declan gravely presented her with the foil box. She had, of course, received Christmas cards from her family and friends in Ireland, but had certainly expected no gifts.

"The master of the house," Donovan confessed gruffly, coming to perch on the arm of her chair. There was just a hint of a twinkle in his eyes, and his usually stern expression was softer this morning, more relaxed.

233

He looked so handsome, so lighthearted, the breath caught in her throat.

"Well? Go on, slow coach," he urged. "Open it!"

"From you, Doctor? But I . . . I didn't get you anything," she admitted, crestfallen. "I didn't think it would be . . . well, appropriate, what with you being my employer."

"Devil take propriety," he said softly for her ears alone. His dark blue eyes were tender as they met hers and filled with warmth. "Come on. Everyone's waiting. Hurry up!"

"Hurry up and what?"

"Hurry up and open the damned thing!" He grinned, exasperated.

The 'damned thing' proved to be a black lacquered box, lined with pale pink velvet. Inside was a white silk fan, delicately painted with Oriental flowers and small birds. Cherry blossoms, she thought, and rice birds or finches. It must have been very expensive, for its ribs were made of carved, wafer-thin ivory. A pink silk tassel decorated the looped carrying cord.

"Ohhhh!" she exclaimed. "It's exquisite! Thank you so much, Donov—Dr. Fitzgerald!" Her green eyes shone. "I shall treasure it always." *Because it came from you.*

"I'm glad you like it. It has a fine history, too. The antique dealer said it once belonged to the Empress Josephine. A Valentine's gift from Old Bony himself!"

"Napoleon? Really? Oh, my!" She opened the pretty piece with what bordered on reverence and gracefully fanned her flushed face, unaware of the charming picture she made, like a pretty butterfly fluttering its delicate wings.

Donovan was not nearly so unaware of her charms.

He stared at her hungrily, his heart on his sleeve for all to see.

Estelle cut in, glaring at Donovan. "This is a very nice musical box. Don't you think it's nice, Donovan? Thank you, Miss Cait!"

Her comment had the desired effect of drawing their attention away from each other, back to the goings-on.

"You're very welcome, darlin' girl," Caitlynn declared, going over to Estelle and fondly kissing her cheek. "I just knew you'd like it the minute I saw it. Does it remind you of anywhere special?" she asked, smiling down at her.

"Noo, I don't think so. Should it?" Estelle set the box aside with a dismissing shrug.

"The lake in the park," Caitlynn explained, crushed with disappointment. "Remember? I thought the lake was your favorite place." She'd imagined a delighted Estelle realizing immediately why she had given her the gift. She certainly hadn't expected the girl's bored expression, nor her lukewarm reaction to the music box. Then again, perhaps she had expected too much.

"Oh, yes," Estelle said at length, placing the music box on the Aubusson rug at her feet. "The lake in the park. It does look a little like it. Now, come along, Uncle Donovan! Your turn. You haven't opened my present yet."

With that, Caitlynn's gift was forgotten.

"Ah-ha. That's because I'm saving the best for last," Donovan assured Estelle, tweaking her nose. "What will it be? I wonder. A dozen of the best Virginian cigars? New scalpels of the finest Sheffield steel? That stethoscope I've been wanting? Or—aha! I've got it! A glass eye!" He winked horribly, his mouth hanging open. "So I'll have a spare one to keep on you, minx."

She giggled. "Don't be silly, Donovan. You don't give me nearly enough allowance for expensive presents like glass eyes."

"Is that right? Well, I'll have to fix that little matter before next Christmas, won't I?" He was laughing as he unwrapped her gift.

It was the silhouette she had made for him weeks earlier, now framed in gilt. It was unmistakably Estelle, a lovely young woman, even in silhouette. Who could blame Donovan for loving her as dearly and unconditionally as any father? And love her he did. Any fool could see it.

"Beautiful," he murmured, his eyes softening, his smile deepening. "And almost as precious as the one who made it." Leaning down, he kissed Estelle's cheek. "Thank you, poppet. This will take pride of place in my study."

Estelle beamed, clearly delighted by his response to her gift.

At last, only a single package remained beneath the tree, wrapped very simply in brown paper and tied with string. It was almost lost amidst the torn wrapping paper and bright ribbons that littered the Aubusson carpet.

"Who can this last present be for?" Estelle wondered aloud, looking around the circle of expectant faces as she brandished the last gift. She inspected the name tag and pouted prettily. "That's not fair! It's another one for you, Uncle Donovan! You must have been a very good boy this year," she teased, her blue eyes dancing with merriment.

"For me?" Donovan asked, surprised. "Who's it from?"

"Umm, let me see." She turned the package this way and that. "It doesn't say."

Obsession

The name of the gift giver was not written on the tag, nor on the brown paper wrapping. Nor would anyone own up to giving it.

"Ah-ha! An anonymous admirer!" Donovan declared, looking around the circle of expectant faces. Laughing, he untied the string and tore off the wrapping paper. "Now, then. Let's see what we have here."

Inside was a rectangular yellow tin. The advertisement SWAN VESTA MATCHES was stamped across the lid in red lettering. Beneath it was the picture of a swan. "Matches? Splendid! Matches are always welcome, are they not, Mrs. M."

"They are indeed, Doctor," Mary Montgomery said gravely. "Welcome and . . . um . . . very practical."

Donovan opened the tin. He lifted out something that was heavy for its size, wrapped in layers of tissue paper. "Not matches, after all. How very mysterious. . . ." he said in a deep voice, peeling away the tissue. "There. Now let's see what we've got here."

Chapter Nineteen

Inside the tissue was an ambrotype, a glass photographic image, framed in silver. Donovan's smile quickly turned to a scowl.

"Is this someone's idea of a joke?" he asked. Sapphire eyes piercing, he looked around the circle of curious faces. "Because if it is, I'm not amused. Speak up! I want to know who gave me this. And why."

"Look, Caitlynn. It's her! That's Miss Dee Dee!" Estelle exclaimed in delight. "Didn't I tell you she was pretty? Oh, dear. I still miss her so much." Tears welled in her eyes.

Caitlynn said nothing. She could not speak. Could not move. She felt stunned, as if she'd been slapped in the face. Her chest was tight, as if there weren't enough air in the room anymore. So tight it was difficult to breathe.

"Miss Caitlynn? What is it? Are you all right?" Estelle asked. "You've turned so pale!"

Caitlynn cleared her throat. But when she managed to speak, only a whisper would come out. "The picture. It's mine."

"*Yours?*" Donovan's saturnine brows rose. A nerve ticked at his temple.

Her jaw came up defiantly. She had done nothing wrong, after all. Whoever had removed the ambrotype from her drawstring bag was the wrongdoer. The thief. "Yes."

His jaw tightened. "I see. Then may I ask why you had a picture of this woman in your possession? And why the devil you chose to give it to me? Here? Now?"

She primly clasped her hands in her lap, an unconsciously defensive gesture. "I can explain. Deirdre was—Deirdre *is*—my cousin, you see."

There. It was out.

It was as if she'd thrown cold water on a hot griddle. Shocked gasps followed her announcement.

"No, Miss O'Connor, I don't see at all," Donovan said with great severity.

Springing to his feet, he paced back and forth, a cold and distant stranger who appeared more than a little perplexed, she sensed, and angry.

The others continued to watch them, like theatergoers watching a stage drama unfold. Their expressions were uncomfortable yet fascinated, with the exception of Estelle's. Unlike the others, she seemed completely absorbed by her music box, examining its mirror lake and tiny ice-skaters. Her low humming and the silvery tinkling of the Strauss waltz as the painted figures whirled around and around their glass lake were unnerving in the suffocating silence of the room. Caitlynn had the sudden irrational urge to shake the girl, to scream at her to stop.

"Why did you give me a picture of your cousin?

239

What did you hope to achieve by it?" Donovan de-manded, granite-jawed. His eyes flashed. "Answer me!"

"I didn't say I gave it to you!" she corrected, springing to her feet. "I said it *belonged* to me. I had no idea it was missing until just now. It must have been taken from my room last night while I was with y— while I was—while we were—elsewhere," she finished hastily. She bowed her head as color flooded her cheeks, like crimson ink seeping through a blotter.

Mary Montgomery's head jerked up at the latter. Caitlynn could feel the woman's gray eyes boring into her, icy with disapproval, narrowed with curiosity, the thin, bloodless lips pinched in spinsterish disapproval. It was obvious the housekeeper could guess the in-tended ending of Caitlynn's sentence. After all, last night there had been the telltale click of a door closing farther down the landing.

"Taken?" Donovan echoed. The single word was like the crack of a whip.

She nodded miserably but said nothing more. Even to her ears, the truth sounded trumped-up. False.

Donovan sighed. He looked perturbed. "Miss O'Connor, if you are suggesting there's a thief in my household, it is a very serious matter that needs to be discussed further. Please accompany me to my study, if you will. I'm sure it will take only a few minutes to clear this up. Meanwhile, all of you, go on about your business. It's Christmas morning, after all!"

"All right. Let's hear it. Is there a reason you never mentioned that Miss Riordan was your cousin?" Don-ovan asked, turning to face her as soon as they were alone in his study. She shot him a mutinous look but said nothing. "Caitlynn? Miss O'Connor? *Is* there a reason?"

She nodded. "Yes. Yes, there is."

"Ah. And would you care to share it with me?" he asked. His tone dripped sarcasm.

In that instant she hated him. Loathed him with every fiber of her being. She shook her head. Set her jaw. Squared her shoulders as if bracing for a fight. "I'd rather not, no."

"Aah. Then I would be correct in assuming your reason has something to do with me?"

"You would, yes." She sighed, exasperated, and threw up her hands, all the fight seeping out of her. "I suppose I have no choice but to tell you."

"I think it would be for the best," he agreed gravely.

She paused to collect her thoughts for a second or two before continuing. "According to your letters to my uncle and aunt—that would be Daniel and Constance Riordan, if you recall—my cousin left your household last July under a cloud of suspicion, following your housekeeper's claims that she'd pilfered some items belonging to Estelle."

"That's what I was told, yes."

"Told?"

"Yes. I was only informed of the situation after the fact."

"No one—either here or in Ireland—has seen Deirdre since her last visit to the park with Estelle. To all intents and purposes, Doctor, my cousin vanished off the face of the earth that night without a word to anyone, including me, although she and I were closer than sisters. Her family has heard nothing from her since July—nothing, in five long months! Such behavior is completely out of character for Deirdre. Fearing the worst, we decided that I would take her place and try to find her."

"I understand your concern. And I have every sympathy with you and your family. But why give her picture to me? What reaction were you hoping to elicit from me?"

Her eyes flashed with anger. "I told you, I was not responsible for giving you the ambrotype! Nor do I know who was. The last time I saw that picture, it was in my drawstring bag. In my room." She would not meet his eyes.

"Good God! You think that woman and I were involved, somehow!" he exclaimed, correctly reading her expression. "That's why you said nothing sooner, isn't it?" Stunned, he abruptly sat down in the chair behind the desk. "You think that we were—"

"—lovers? I think it's quite possible, yes."

Normally, he would have been amused that a well-bred young woman like Caitlynn would have referred to such an illicit situation, but he was beyond amusement.

"Oh, you do, do you? And I think it's quite possible you've been reading too many penny-dreadfuls, madam! The bloody scandal sheets have given you ridic-ulous—outrageous—ideas!"

She met his eyes without flinching, unperturbed by his angry outburst. "Perhaps. But you haven't answered my question, Doctor," she said softly. "Were you lovers?"

"That's been it all along, hasn't it?" he ground out, still ignoring her question. "That's why you stiffen in my arms when I hold you. Why you hold back when we kiss. You think your cousin and I were having an affair," he ground out. "That's why you don't trust me, isn't it, Caitlynn? You think I had something to do with her disappearance, too, I'll wager!"

"Yes, yes, I do," she flung back. "Well? Am I right? Did you have an affair with Deirdre?"

"No, damn it!" He stood as he said the latter. Palms braced on the desktop, he leaned across it for emphasis. "*No.*"

Was he lying? She didn't think so, but there was always the chance that Father Timothy had simply not recognized the man he saw meeting Dee Dee as Donovan. He could have taken pains to disguise his appearance, perhaps. Or simply worn a hat that cast his features in shadow, either by accident or design.

"We were never anything more than employer and employee," he went on, reading the doubt in her expression. "I liked the woman. I considered her attractive, with that fair hair and those great dark eyes. But more than anything, she seemed intelligent. Principled. *Kind.* In short, an excellent companion for Estelle. Sorry to disappoint you, Miss O'Connor, but as you know, my taste runs to women with a little more . . . fire. More spirit. A woman, for example, who would go with me into the seamiest courts of an East End rookery to witness the beginning of a new life." There was a biting edge to his tone now.

"Believe him, Miss O'Connor. He's telling the truth. Donovan wasn't having an affair with Deirdre. I was," cut in a weary voice from the doorway, which stood ajar.

Declan came into the study. He carefully closed the door behind him, rubbed a hand across his brow and muttered, "Oh, God, what a mess," before he dropped bonelessly into a leather wing chair by the fire.

"I was about to come in when I overheard you," he explained simply, looking up at Caitlynn. "I loved her, Miss O'Connor. I loved her with all my heart and soul.

And I'm proud to say she returned that love. Last May, I moved out of Huntington Square into my own digs solely to preserve Deirdre's reputation. You see, I intended to marry her, if she would have me."

"Good God!" Donovan exclaimed, clearly as surprised as Caitlynn by his brother's revelation. "I assumed Estelle—"

"No. Not this time. It was solely because of Deirdre. I would have done anything for her, Miss O'Connor—moved heaven and earth if she asked me to. I had every reason to believe she felt the same. But two days after I proposed, she went away without giving me her answer, or telling me she was leaving. I have neither seen nor heard from her since, although I have scoured this wretched city looking for her."

"*You?*" Caitlynn whispered. "You and Deirdre—?"

Then again, why was she so surprised? she wondered. Deirdre's beloved 'D' could just as easily be *De*clan Fitzgerald as it could *D*onovan. "That's it! Your eyes. They're brown! Of course!" she blurted out as one of the missing puzzle pieces dropped into place. "How could I have been so blasted stupid?" she wondered aloud, her brogue thick in her upset.

That was what had seemed wrong the other evening. The jarring note. The puzzle piece that didn't fit. Deirdre's diary entries had spoken glowingly of her beloved D's brown eyes. *Donovan's eyes were dark blue.* Declan, not Donovan, was the dark-haired young man Father Timothy had seen meeting Deirdre at St. Anthony's on Thursday afternoons.

"Of course what?" Declan and Donovan both asked.

"I found Deirdre's diary hidden in my room. There were some entries in it about the man she was falling in love with. The man who'd asked her to marry him, and whose proposal she was going to accept." Her voice was husky, her eyes swimming with tears as they met Declan's. "She called him only by his initial, 'D,' so I assumed . . . well, I thought the 'D' stood for . . . Donovan."

Declan's face lit up. "She was going to accept?" His smile abruptly vanished. "But if that was the case, why the devil would she leave here without telling anyone—especially me—where she was going?"

"That's the question I've been asking myself, over and over. She was troubled, I know that much. But I don't know what about, exactly, except for Montgomery's accusations that she was light-fingered." Her jaw hardened. "I've never heard such nonsense! My cousin would no sooner have stolen a farthing from someone than she would fly to the moon."

"I'll second that," Declan murmured with feeling. "Deirdre was as honest as the day is long. She even agonized about meeting me in secret on her days off, the poor love. She said our rendezvous made her feel deceitful. That's why I moved out and found my own lodgings."

He shook his head, then sprang to his feet and went over to the portable globe bar, intending to pour himself a stiff drink. Deciding it was too early to be drinking hard liquor, he turned away and took his seat again.

"Deirdre didn't have an underhanded bone in her body, bless her." His eyes were moist. His shoulders sagged. He hung his head in his hands, a man destroyed by loss. "Where the devil is she, Don? Where?"

But Donovan and Caitlynn could offer him neither comfort nor answers. His were the same questions Caitlynn had been asking herself for months, with the same lack of answers.

"I can't help you, Dec. I wish I could," Donovan said at length. He shot an accusing glance at Caitlynn. There was a world of hurt in his expression, too. "Perhaps if someone had seen fit to confide in me . . . to trust me, long before this, we could have found some trace of her before the trail grew cold."

Caitlynn bristled at this thinly veiled accusation, but chose to ignore it. "Kitty Abbott might be able to help us. She told me last night that Annie Murphy has some knowledge of Deirdre's whereabouts."

"Kitty Abbott?" Both men turned to look at her, as if she'd sprouted horns.

"When?" Donovan demanded, frowning.

"When you went to get the box of food."

"I see. And what has the redoubtable Kitty to do with all this?" Donovan inquired in an icy tone.

"I've been going into the East End on my afternoons off to look for Deirdre—"

"You've been what?" he exploded. He looked angrier than she had ever seen him before. Frighteningly so.

"—trying to find someone who might have seen her. That's why I kept her likeness in my bag, you see. So that I could show it to everyone. I met Kitty Abbott outside the church one afternoon in October. She claimed she knew someone who might be able to tell me where . . . well, let's just say she didn't. She was lying. But apparently, she had an attack of conscience after she conned me out of my pound at the Britannia!" Her green eyes flashed. She tossed her dark head.

"Aaah. That would be the afternoon I saw you? The night I surprised you rifling my study."

"Rifling!"

"Hadn't you just rifled my desk? I thought you had.

246

Nothing was quite as I left it. Papers had been moved about . . . But go on."

"Yes, well, when I saw Kitty again last night, after she had her baby, she told me Annie Murphy knows where Deirdre is. Then this morning, Bridget tells me Annie's run off, so I'm going to her lodgings tomorrow to talk to her."

"All right. I'll come with you."

"No! You can't! I have to go alone. Annie won't talk to me if you're there."

He clamped his jaws together, his black brows like thunderheads. "May I remind you, Miss O'Connor, that five women were slaughtered in the vicinity of the courts where Annie Murphy and Kitty Abbott have their lodgings? An unaccompanied woman in that area is asking for trouble."

"But there hasn't been a murder in weeks!"

"All the more reason to be extra careful now. I forbid you to go there alone. Do I make myself clear?"

Caitlynn set her jaw. "Perfectly. Now, if I may go, Doctor?" she said frostily. "Your guests will be arriving soon. I must prepare myself to welcome them."

"Very well. But rest assured, we will discuss this matter in greater detail after my guests leave."

"As you wish."

Caitlynn left the study, her chin carried high, her spirits at an all-time low. This morning she had not only lost Deirdre; she had lost Donovan, too, she thought miserably. Lost his trust and with it, his growing affection, which had become infinitely dear to her— as had he, the wretched man. Dearer, perhaps, than she had ever imagined possible.

"You're in love with her," Declan said softly after Caitlynn closed the door in her wake. It was a state-

247

ment rather than a question. "If not, she wouldn't be able to get under your skin."

"I was beginning to think so, yes," his brother admitted gruffly. "Now I'm not so sure. Blasted woman! She's too bloody headstrong, too willful for her own good!"

"In a word, perfect for you." Declan laughed. "Exactly what you need! She'll keep you from getting too immersed in your bloody patients, or I'm a Dutchman."

"The devil she will! I want nothing more t'do with the woman. You heard what she said. She's been sneaking around behind my back for the past three months. She doesn't trust me. Good God, Declan, at one point she admitted she thought I was the Ripper!"

"She wasn't the only one, Don—not by a long chalk! Dozens of men have been taken in as suspects— some with far less cause, I might add. Some came under scrutiny merely because they were Jews. Or Irish. Or Poles. Or Americans. Others have come under investigation because of what they do for a living— butchers, or slaughterers, even surgeons or doctors. Good God, man, there are even rumors flying about Sir William Gull and the prince! The queen herself has expressed her concern that this case be solved as quickly as possible."

"Gull? The royal physician, you mean? Good Lord!"

"Exactly. No one is above suspicion. Not the royal family's doctor—and not you. One"—Declan counted on his fingers—"you have the anatomical knowledge that the Ripper is thought to possess in order to perform his mutilations. Two, you come and go in the East End at all hours of the day and night. Three, you return home disheveled, sometimes with blood on your shirtcuffs or shoes, according to Rose, who sorts your laundry. Four, when we ask you about it or where you've been, you give us one of your darkling looks and bluntly refuse to talk about it! Can you blame Miss O'Connor for what she thought? Can you blame any of us for wondering?"

"You sound like Sir Charles. Damn it, it's bad enough that I have to deal with the terrible things I see without having to talk about them. I cannot believe that my own household—my own brother, damn it!—could think me capable of such butchery!"

He shook his dark head. "There's unbelievable misery in this dark city, Declan. Unimaginable poverty and squalor. Brothels. Starving children selling themselves to the highest bidder on street corners. Women forced into prostitution to put food in their bellies. The gin sots. The opium dens. The diseases. You name it!" He snorted in disgust. "Jack the Ripper is the least of the terrible faceless killers stalking Whitechapel, if you ask me! And you wonder why I refuse to talk about what I do and see there, man?" he demanded, furious. "Let me give you an example, shall I?

"Back in September I was called to a court in Whitechapel late one night to tend a patient who once lived in our own little village in Ireland. My patient's name was Polly. A pretty red-haired girl, cheeky as any sparrow." Remembering, he smiled, but the smile quickly faded.

"Not Polly Doolan who went to St. Dunstan's primary school with us? The cheeky one whose da worked for old Ryan over at the pub?"

"That was her."

"The brat used to stick her tongue out at me whenever we passed her cottage." Declan grinned. "I heard she ran off to England with a bricklayer."

"That's the one. When her ne'er-do-well husband abandoned her, Polly took to the street corner. In due course, she found herself in the family way by another man—one of many, I suspect. She had to live, and it was the only way she knew to survive.

"But rather than have the child, this nice Catholic girl tried to rid herself of it. She scraped together ten shillings—just enough to pay an old woman for the privilege of perforating her womb with a knitting needle. Kitty Abbott came and got me less than a half hour after she found her. But by then it was too late. Polly had aborted her child and bled to death."

Declan was deeply moved. He frowned. "I understand how you feel, Donovan. You care deeply for these people. You work yourself to the bone to help them, and I admire you for it, I really do. But can you blame your Miss O'Connor for thinking the worst, under the circumstances? Look at it from her point of view, man! It may come as a shock to you, but you're not always the most . . . approachable . . . person, you know!" His brown eyes twinkled.

"Really?" Donovan shot back sarcastically. "Well, I doubt it matters anymore," he declared with an air of finality. "If there was ever the chance of anything between us, it's finished now. Nipped in the bud." And with luck, he would quickly forget how right she'd felt in his arms, and how lovely she was, he told himself. Yet his heart ached for what might have been between them but now would never be. A love that, quite unknown to him, had been building, slowly, surely, since the moment he first saw her.

He scowled. Right now, he wasn't sure if he wanted to kiss her speechless or throttle the blasted woman.

"It's finished only if you let it end, Brother. Only if you let it," Declan said solemnly. "Learn from my mistakes. Don't wait. Don't let pride stand in your way. Go after her, and mend things between you. And when you have, never let her go again."

Declan went over to the globe, opened it and poured himself a double shot of good Irish whisky.

"One for you?" he offered his brother, raising the Waterford decanter.

"No, thanks, Dec. I thought you didn't believe in drinking before noon," he observed, aware of the play of intense emotions on his brother's face. His attempt to make Declan smile failed miserably.

"I don't, as a rule. But today I think I'll make an exception and drink to absent lovers. It's noon somewhere in the world, after all, is it not?" He lifted his glass. "To absent friends."

The first of their guests arrived at a very proper fifteen minutes past twelve, carrying presents that ranged from baskets of nuts and fruits to bottles of excellent sherry or wine.

Cries of "Merry Christmas!" echoed through the house as they trooped into the hall, snowflakes clinging to eyelashes, bonnets and boots. The sounds of deep male voices, silvery laughter and song rang through Huntington House, filling its cavernous rooms with festive sound.

The spicy scent of bayberry candles burning on every mantel perfumed the air. Fires of fragrant applewood and coal roared behind gleaming black grates, adding seasonal cheer and welcome warmth. Garlands of pine-cones dusted with gold glitter, fir branches and sprigs of shiny green holly with clusters of scarlet berries twined in and out of the balustrades and outlined the doors, accented every few feet by fat bows of red velvet or by gilded bisque cherubs blowing miniature trumpets.

The doctor, looking elegant and urbane in formal jacket and trousers, snowy wing collar and knotted tie, greeted his guests in the entryway with Caitlynn at his side acting as his hostess. Though neither of them had planned it, Caitlynn assumed the role with effortless grace and style.

Silent and frosty-eyed where the doctor was concerned, she was nevertheless the perfect hostess, charming his colleagues and friends with her wit and gaiety, setting his guests at ease with a gracious word, a smile, a touch.

The hunter-green velvet gown she wore, with a deep lace collar and cuffs, accented the color of her eyes. She had never looked lovelier than she did that Christmas morning.

Watching her, Donovan determined that he would take his brother's advice. He would mend the rift between them at the earliest opportunity. He could hardly blame Caitlynn for not trusting him, under the circumstances. He was not a man given to confiding every detail of his life, after all.

If she believed him to be a heartless lecher, the seducer of young women, he could well imagine what she'd thought when he'd made it known that he was attracted to her. That she had not rejected his advances toward her spoke volumes. On the contrary, she had responded, initially. Whether she would admit it or not, she was as attracted to him as he was to her.

By one-thirty the last guest had arrived. Maureen and Bridget whisked the ladies' coats, capes, gloves and hats away to one of the bedrooms, which had been pressed into service as a cloakroom, while Tom, dressed in his Sunday best, took the men's greatcoats and capes and hung them on the mahogany hall stand.

"Everything all right, Tom?" Caitlynn asked. The man was patting his pockets as if he'd lost something.

"Quite all right, miss. Just thought I'd go and have a smoke, now that the last guest has arrived, but I've left my pipe in the flat. The pouch you gave me, miss, well, it's perfect for baccy, it is."

"I'm glad to hear it. Now go and enjoy your smoke before Rose finds you something to do."

Tom chuckled and headed toward the kitchens. "Good at that, my missus is!" he said over his shoulder.

The guests adjourned to the drawing room to gather about the fireplace and warm themselves while enjoying a glass of sherry or porter, engaging in lively conversation or singing carols to Mrs. Montgomery's enthusiastic piano accompaniment as they awaited Rose's announcement that Christmas dinner was served.

It was all delightfully informal, like the gathering of a large and somewhat boisterous family, the family of St. Bartholomew's. The young doctors called Donovan 'sir' and treated him with deference, clearly delighted to have been invited to their hero's home for the holiday. The young female guests simpered and blushed and flirted with the doctor and his young colleagues, while the older guests discussed the weather, the royal family, politics and the state of the British Empire.

"What a wonderful get-together, Miss O'Connor." Lady Cecily Townsend looked thinner, more fragile than Caitlynn remembered. The lines that bracketed her mouth were deeper, the shadows haunting her eyes darker, although there was still that teasing sparkle in their depths. "I understand we have you to thank for it?"

Before Caitlynn could respond, the older woman continued, "Lord knows, that young rogue would never allow himself any time away from that wretched hospital to have fun, unless a pretty young thing like you talked him into it. I've lost count of the number of times I've told him, 'Donovan, dear boy, life is short! Leave yourself time to fall in love, to find yourself a wife and father some children.' " She patted Caitlynn's cheek, and Caitlynn was shocked by the lightness of her hand, gentle as a feather, without strength or substance. "I'm so glad he's finally taken a silly old woman's advice."

Caitlynn did not bother to correct Lady Cecily's impression. What was the point in doing so? It would only disappoint her. Let her assume whatever she wanted, since it so obviously gave her pleasure. To her eyes, the fragile Cecily Townsend seemed as if she were fading away.

While Mrs. Montgomery played, the guests gathered around her to sing carols, eyes smiling as they sang the familiar refrains—"God rest ye merry gentlemen, let nothing . . ." "Silent night, holy night, all is calm . . ." "The holly and the ivy, when they are . . ."

Assured that all of the guests had drinks, Caitlynn drew apart from the others, badly needing a quiet moment to herself.

She went to the bay window that overlooked the square, and rubbed a circle in a steamy windowpane with her finger.

Peering through the peephole she'd made, she saw that it was snowing again. A light layer of flakes drifted down to blanket the square like eiderdown, emptied from a feather bolster. More flakes were collecting in the corners of the windowpanes. By the park gates, a group of carolers had congregated, all of them warmly cloaked and muffled against the cold.

" 'God bless us, every one,' " a familiar voice quoted from the much-loved Dickens novel. "But especially you, sweet Cait."

Startled, she looked up.

Donovan had left the group to join her. He smiled as he looked down at her—a little uncertain, for once, she thought.

"You and Mary make an excellent team. It's a fine party you've made for me, and I thank you for it."

"It was my pleasure," she said stiffly. "Everything seems to be going well doesn't it?"

"It does. Very well. But what about us, Caitlynn? We're not going well at all, are we?" He spoke very gently.

She turned away, staring at the foggy glass and the spyhole she'd drawn there. "I'd rather not discuss it, if you don't mind."

"That's too bloody bad," he ground out, "because I do mind. I mind terribly. 'Tis going to be discussed, right here and right now, one way or the other, my lass, whether you like it or not."

"I really should see if Rose is ready to serve dinner. Excuse me." She tried to brush past him, but his hand snaked out, steely fingers clamping around her wrist like manacles. They were gentle restraints, but restraints nonetheless.

"Let go! You're hurting me!" she hissed, although it was a lie.

"The devil I am." His jaw was hard as granite. Set. Stern. "I would sooner cut off my right hand than harm a hair on your head."

"But dinner—"

"To hell with dinner," he rasped, leading her after him, out of the drawing room and into the empty hallway. "You and I must talk. About us. The bloody dinner can wait. Our guests can wait. What I want to say is more important than any of that. I need you, Caitlynn, even more than I need my practice. Even more than my patients. My clinic. Medicine. *Everything.*"

"But I—"

"I'm not finished. Although I'm surrounded by people each and every day, from all walks of life, I never realized how lonely I was in the middle of that crowd until I met you. Darlin', I understand how it looked, and why you couldn't trust me, but Declan has explained all that. I had nothing to do with your cousin's disappearance. Let me help you find her, Cait. Let me be a part of your life. Don't build a wall between us because of some silly misunderstanding, darlin' girl. For the love of God, don't."

His gentle, earnest tone, the sincerity in his eyes, the way his finger lightly traced the curve of her cheek, down over her throat to her collarbone, were her undoing. It was as if he held her heart in his hands, warmed by his love, soothed by his touch. Involuntarily she covered his hand with hers. His hand was solid, comforting, and yet . . . "Please, you must not."

"You don't mean that, Cait. Let me hold you. Let me love you—as you love me. Admit it."

"No. It's not true. I don't. I cannot!"

"Why not? Give me one good reason."

"I don't have a reason. I just . . . I don't know what I mean anymore, nor what I feel," she cried. "Dear God, I'm so confused."

"Well, I'm not. I'm clearheaded and rational enough for both of us. All these weeks I've been wondering what was eating at Declan. What could explain the sadness I sensed in him. Now I know. And, Cait, I don't want to be like him. I don't want to lose you, as it seems he's lost Deirdre. Not now, not ever." His tone was harsh with emotion. "Darlin' girl, you fill up all the empty places in my life. When the terrible things I see at the hospital seem unbearable, I hurry home because I know you'll be here. I need to know that you'll always be here waiting for me, Caitlynn. *Always*."

He drew her to him, holding her close, cradling her against his broad chest. His fingers, his lips, his breath, were lost in her fragrant hair. "God, Cait. Sweet Cait. Say you'll be there. I want you so much. Let me be with you, Cait. Tonight. I'll come to you. We can be together," he whispered urgently.

Desire smoldered in those lambent sapphire eyes. She stared at his mouth, his sensual mouth, wanting him to kiss her, aching for the whispering caress of his lips on her skin.

"Very well. Tonight. Yes. *Yes*." Eyes closed, she went into his arms, whispering his name again and again. It was the only word she could utter—yet it was the right word, for her. Besides, she was too moved to say more. Trembling, weak-kneed with arousal, she tilted back her head and surrendered to his mouth.

"Um, Don?" There was a polite cough. "Um. Dinner's served."

A figure stood in the drawing room doorway.

"Hmm? Oh, right. Thanks, Dec. We'll be right there. Miss O'Connor? Please allow me to escort you." Ignoring Declan's broad and knowing grin, he broke away from her and gallantly offered her his arm.

Mastering her chaotic emotions with admirable composure, she inclined her head and slipped a white-gloved arm through his. "Why, thank you, Doctor," she murmured, smiling up at him; a smile that was filled with invitation—and seductive promise.

"It's Donovan. Or Dr. Donovan, if you insist." His

eyes twinkled. The corners of his mouth twitched with
the beginnings of a smile.

"Yes, Donovan. Thank you."

Their eyes met and held, sparkling kelly green to
sapphire.

"Shall we?"

"Oh, yes, let's."

Arm in arm, Caitlynn and Donovan led their guests
into the dining room.

There, they discovered that Rose had outdone herself. The table was beautifully set, with colorful red,
black and white tartan tablecloths layered over a more
traditional snowy white cloth. Matching serviettes
were tucked into silver napkin rings etched with a
snowflake, holly and ivy pattern. Arranged at intervals
down the long table, extended by several leaves today
to accommodate their number, were three centerpieces
of miniature 'pear' trees set in sturdy earthenware pots.
Their branches were hung with painted papier-mâché
partridges, gold rings, turtledoves, French hens and so
on according to the traditional "Twelve Days of
Christmas" song. By every place setting lay a paper
cracker, with mottoes, favors, paper hats and 'crack-
ers' hidden inside.

Creamy cock-a-leekie soup, served flawlessly by a
beaming Bridget and Maureen, was followed by
mouthwatering turkey roasted to a golden brown and
plumped with chestnut stuffing. There were also a
large roasted pork loin with crackling, and a leg of
lamb, the leftovers to be minced the following day for
the traditional Boxing Day mutton pies. Accompany-
ing the meats were fresh bread, roasted potatoes, brussels sprouts and creamed parsnips.

But the dishes that drew the most cheers were the
two huge plum puddings that Rose and Tom trium-

phantly carried in on silver platters, topped with sprigs of holly and haloed with dancing blue flames, courtesy of a full jigger of Donovan's lighted brandy.

"Bravo, Rose! Bravo!" Donovan declared, standing to applaud the arrival of the puddings.

"Well! Well! This is quite a spread!" young Christopher Donahue declared with a broad smile. "I haven't eaten so much in—"

"—two days, or was it three?" joked his friend Dr. Nelson, thumping Christopher on the back. He grinned. "Don't believe a word of his blarney, Miss O'Connor. Loves to exaggerate, does our young Dr. Donahue. Now, Bob Sullivan, down there on your left, he's the trencherman among us."

"Me? Don't talk, Nelson! Look at you with your stuffed cheeks bulging, like a squirrel gathering nuts," Bob, a rather rubicund young man, declared indignantly.

Everyone laughed.

"Oh, no! There's a thimble in my pudding!" cried one of the St. Germain twins in dismay. Caitlynn couldn't remember whether it was Amy or Annabel. The young women, both pretty but lamentably mousy-haired, were identical, except that one wore a deep blue gown and the other wore burgundy. "That means I'm going to remain a spinster, doesn't it?"

"A charming lady like yourself? I doubt that, Miss St. Germain," Christopher gallantly assured her. "Men must surely be waiting in line to offer for your hand."

The young woman blushed. "How kind of you to say so, Mr.—?"

"Donahue, Miss St. Germain. Dr. Christopher Donahue."

"See here? I found a silver button in mine." Bob Sullivan held up the silver 'bachelor's' button for all to see. "All those thimbles and buttons in the pudding just mean the cook must be more careful when she's sewing, else we'll all choke on 'em! It has nothing to do with divination!" He laughed at his own joke.

Those who heard him laughed, too.

"Mama says putting charms in the pudding is superstitious nonsense—a silly tradition," the other St. Germain twin declared with a sniff of her pretty nose. "I found a thimble in my pudding last Christmas, but it didn't bother me a jot. I don't intend to remain a spinster, thimble or no thimble!"

She tipped her head so that her mousy ringlets bobbed to their best advantage, quite dazzling Christopher. He stared at her, a man smitten, the other twin forgotten.

"Isn't it nonsense, Mama?" she asked her mother, simpering and playing to her adoring audience while pretending Christopher didn't exist.

"Oh, yes, Amy," declared her mother, elegant in navy with osprey feathers in her hair. "Complete and utter nonsense. But it's still great fun, for all that, don't you agree, Miss O'Connor? There's nothing we—oh, lucky you, my dear! You've found the wedding ring!"

"So I have." Caitlynn stared down at her plate in dismay. The coveted silver charm lay half hidden in the crumbled ruins of her plum pudding.

"There! Now do you see? That just proves it's nonsense," Estelle said crossly, "because Miss Caitlynn will never be married—will you, miss? She's already been jilted once in her life, you see." Estelle said to no one in particular, yet every person within earshot turned to study Caitlynn with renewed interest, obviously looking for some glaring flaw in her. "She won't chance it happening again."

Caitlynn wished that the floor would open up and swallow her.

"Estelle, please. I'm sure the matter is not something Miss O'Connor cares to discuss at table," Cecily Townsend cut in. Her voice was low but very firm. She shot Caitlynn an apologetic smile. Then in a low whisper to the girl she added, "A lady never mentions such private matters in public, except to be spiteful, miss."

Caitlynn blushed to the roots of her hair as Estelle scowled at the sharp reproof, looking daggers at the older woman, then at Caitlynn.

Estelle continued blithely, "It's not my fault. I had nothing to do with it. Besides, Miss Caitlynn doesn't know any men she could marry. It's not as if she attends balls or soirees to meet eligible bachelors, is it?"

Donovan caught the latter half of the conversation. He smiled and cast a fond glance at Caitlynn, reaching for her hand beneath the folds of the tablecloth. "I'm sure there's a very presentable husband right beneath Miss O'Connor's nose, should she care to wed, without her having to resort to balls and soirees. Well, well! Look at this. There's a sixpence in my plum pudding. I was a spoonful away from swallowing it!"

"A sixpence in your pudding means you'll be rich, Doctor," Amy St. Germain explained on his left side. At this, her mama sat up a little straighter and gave the doctor a speculative stare.

Donovan grinned. "A doctor, rich? I doubt it, if he's good at what he does! And I certainly won't be rich if I eat any more of this pudding. I suspect there's more silver in it than sultanas. Am I right, Rose? Are you giving away the Fitzgerald silver?"

"Oh, go on with you, sir!" Rose denied from the doorway, blushing yet smiling nonetheless as the maids served their guests under her and Mrs. Montgomery's watchful eyes.

Caitlynn, still stunned by his comment about finding a husband right under her nose, said nothing. She could not have done so even if her life depended on it. For once, she was struck speechless.

His soft knock at her door that night sent her pulse leaping out of control, for all that it was expected. Would she be making the biggest mistake of her life by answering that knock? she wondered. But mistake or not, she knew she would respond. She could not help herself.

She wanted him.

Flying to the door, she pressed her flushed cheek to the jamb. "Yes? Who is it?" she asked, breathless.

"Me, ye wee idiot! Who were you expecting? Good King Wenceslas?"

Laughing softly, she opened the door just wide enough for him to enter.

He was inside in an instant, laughing, too, his cold hands framing her face, his lips hot and hungry, eager as he backed her up against the closed door and held her there for his kiss.

"Mmmm. You taste wonderful." It was as if she were a lush red wine and he a man dying of thirst.

"Never has a day gone on so bloody long. I thought our guests would never leave. Here. Let me look at you," he whispered. Holding her at arm's length, he rubbed a swath of loose silky dark hair between his fingers, eyes kindling as his gaze raked her.

"Ah, yes. Exactly as I thought."

"What? What did you think?" she asked, nervous.

"That you're glorious," he breathed. "That's what

you are, did you know that, Cait? A vision. My green-eyed angel."

" 'Glorious' I'll accept," she whispered back, her green eyes dancing with laughter, her voice shaky with a mixture of nervousness and desire. "But I'm no angel, Fitzgerald. Trust me. What I've been thinking . . . imagining . . . all day—well, it's hardly the sort of thing that angels think about." Her voice shook at the latter, for they had been erotic images indeed. Images of the two of them together in various stages of undress, too carnal, too vivid and far too intimate to recount.

"Was it not? Why, I'm delighted to hear that," he said with a wicked little grin, roguishly cocking his dark head to one side. This was a playful teasing side of him she'd never seen before. "Because I've had a few such wayward thoughts myself, miss. So come here t'me, my lovely sinner. Tell me what it is you've been imagining while we get you out of that nightgown."

Smiling, a little shy, she stepped into the circle of his arms, shivering in anticipation.

Taking one end of her sash in each hand, he pulled.

Her flannel dressing gown fell away. She stood before him like an unwrapped gift, wearing only her silk nightgown. The robe she'd worn over it was now a puddle of white flannel at her feet.

Fire and lamplight limned every feminine curve through the silk, casting erotic dark shadows at her breasts and the juncture of her thighs.

"Sweet Lord!" he breathed, his voice thick with desire. "You're glorious."

She'd known instinctively what seeing her like this must do to him, he thought. Oh, yes, she'd known, innocent or nay. He could see it in her eyes, in the way she moved as she pirouetted slowly before him, lifting her tumbling hair high above her head, then letting it fall in wanton disarray over bare shoulders.

She carried herself like a woman who wants to be noticed by a man. A woman who wants that man to want her. As, unless he was mistaken, she wanted him, though it was quite possible she did not fully understand what was happening inside her. That it was desire she was feeling.

She wanted him, as he wanted her, by God!

"You're so bloody lovely," he murmured. Lifting her into his arms, he kissed her throat, her silk-clad breasts as he carried her to the bed. "As lovely as the morning. And the way you smell . . . fresh . . . delicate. Like summer rain."

Breathing shallowly, she lay there looking up at him, an invitation in her eyes, on her parted lips, as the warmth of arousal stole through her.

Her face was framed by a cloud of long hair that was the color and texture of Russian sable. Her supple body was swathed in clinging white silk that molded to the peaks of her breasts and the curves of her hips, like a fluted lily that had yet to open its moonflower petals to the sun.

The sight, the feel, the taste, the scent of her intoxicated him. He wanted her, more than he had ever wanted any woman.

Another man would have taken what she offered quickly, roughly, his only thought to slake his lust. But he could never do that, not to his Cait, nor, come to that, to any woman. He would instead lead her slowly down passion's path, awakening her, step by lovely step, to pleasure. He would feed her desire, whisper by whisper, caress by caress, until spark became inferno, and her virginity a gift she surrendered freely, lovingly, as was her right.

He swept his hand down over her body, lightly skimming its slender curves until his hand covered hers. He drew it to his lips, brushing each knuckle, each fingertip, then the well of her palm with lips and tongue until she shivered in delight.

"Sinner or angel," he murmured, nuzzling her earlobe, burying his fingers deep in her hair, "I mean t'take you to heaven tonight, mavourneen."

Her low moan nearly cost him what little control he had left. He trailed his fingertips over her collarbone, hooking the lace-trimmed silk of her nightgown and pulling it down, down, to bare one perfect breast, tipped rosy pink. As he feasted his eyes upon it, both nipple and aureole ruched like crumpled velvet.

"Lovely," he whispered, taking that crest gently in his mouth, plying it with kisses and feathery caresses.

His fingers, his lips, his tongue whispered over her delicately perfumed skin, cupping, smoothing, suckling, claiming inch by delicate inch, each swell, each curve, each hollow as his own; learning its taste and texture, until she was naked in his arms, her bare skin pressed to his, both of them as nature intended.

She drew a breath as his fingertips stroked her inner thighs, caressing the silken hollows before sliding higher to brush the dark fleece where they joined and stroke the folds of her womanhood.

Her breath caught on a gasp of delight. She licked her lips, her pulse racing as he caressed her intimately there. She was trembling, and her limbs were filled with a lovely languor, as if her bones had melted away.

Liquid, languid, fluid—she was floating on a sea of pleasure when at last he eased himself over and, finally, inside her.

She cried out, first in pain as he quickly breached the delicate barrier, then in delight as he possessed her fully; cries that were muffled by his kisses as he filled her again and again, each time more deeply, both of them moving instinctively together in the ancient dance of love.

Moving as one.

Hearts beating as one.

Fingers entwined. Bodies joined.

Braced on his palms, he looked down at her, watching her eyes darken to the deep green of the primal forest, seeing her lips part on a gasp of delight as he made love to her.

Each carnal kiss, every intimate caress, every breathless moment, every erotic thrust of his flanks brought them ever closer to heaven on earth.

It came as a bolt of lightning that arched her up off the bed like a drawn bow, then rippled through her in velvety echoes that left her breathless and clinging to him, raggedly uttering his name like a prayer.

He threw his head back, gritting his jaw to muffle the roar of release that fought to escape him as he gripped her hips and spent himself deep inside her, thrusting one last, silvery time before he fell forward across her body, his face buried in the perfumed angle of her throat.

"You're glorious, woman," she heard him murmur as she stroked his dark head. "Bloody glorious!"

Chapter Twenty

"Holy Mother of God! What the devil was that?" Caitlynn exclaimed at dawn, clutching her pounding heart. Still half asleep and disoriented, she sat bolt upright in bed.

"A banshee," Donovan supplied, stepping from the bed and into his trousers in what seemed like a single move; pulling on a shirt as he stood up. "Or a woman screaming bloody murder."

Caitlynn supposed doctors were used to dressing in the half-dark, a skill acquired after years of urgent summonses to emergencies or lying-ins in the middle of the night. She, on the other hand, was still only half awake, her thoughts fuddled, eyes bleary.

"Stay here while I find out what's going on."

"No, I'm coming with you," she insisted, throwing aside the sheet. "If it's a banshee, I want to see it, too!"

"All right. But put some clothes on first, darlin'," he suggested, leaning down and dropping a kiss on her brow. "Personally, I much prefer you as nature made you, but you could give poor old Tom quite a turn."

Startled, she realized that she was naked, and hastily pulled the blankets up to her chin.

"Don't worry. I'll see that the coast is clear before I go outside."

"Why?" she inquired cheekily.

"One of us has to protect your reputation, madam, since you obviously don't give a jot." He grinned, his teeth very white, his sapphire eyes very bright in the half-light from the fire. "Cait? Last night was . . . well, it was . . ."

". . . truly memorable?"

"More than just memorable. Unforgettable. Indescribable." At the door, he paused. "Oh, and by the way, Cait?"

"Can there *possibly* be more?" she teased, giddy with the afterglow of their lovemaking.

"Did I mention that I love you?"

With that, he was gone, leaving a stunned Caitlynn staring after him, wondering if she'd heard him properly.

"Whist! Will ye look at me—sitting here as naked as a plucked chicken," she muttered. "A very sleek, contented chicken, but a naked one for all that."

Rather than feeling ashamed or contrite over the heavenly night she and Donovan had shared, she was warmed through and through by the glow of their lovemaking. It was a sense of well-being quite unlike any other.

"Did I mention that I love you too, Fitzgerald?" she asked her reflection as she pulled her flannel dressing gown on, over her nightgown, and knotted the sash firmly about her waist.

Quickly combing her tangled hair with her fingers,

she plaited it into a single thick braid, hurried to the door and peeked out.

There was no one on the landing, but she could hear raised female voices and anguished cries from below. She glanced at the clock. Not quite five. And it was Boxing Day—a holiday. She would check on Estelle first, then go down and investigate.

"Caitlynn! Miss Caitlynn? Where are you?"

Estelle. The screams must have woken her, too. Caitlynn unlocked the door that connected their rooms and went through to her charge, turning up the oil lamp as she went.

"Yes, dear. I'm here. It's all right."

"I've been calling you for ages. Why didn't you come?" Estelle's eyes were enormous in the lamplight, and somehow accusing—or was it just her own guilt that made it seem so?

"I heard something. A scream, I think. Did you hear it, too?"

"Yes, darlin', I did. Something's happened downstairs. I was just going down to find out what it was."

"It was a scream, I think. I expect Bridget saw a mouse. She hates mice." Estelle giggled sleepily.

Caitlynn smiled, smoothing a lock of fair hair off Estelle's brow. "I expect so, too. Go on back to sleep, if you can. It's early yet."

Estelle shook her head. "No. I'll wait for you to come back up and tell me what's going on. I'd love a cup of cocoa, if someone has the kettle on," she wheedled.

"Cocoa it shall be, my lady," Caitlynn teased gently. "I'll be back before you know it. Be good."

"I'm always good." Estelle blew her a kiss, then snuggled under the covers, her eyelids heavy.

Halfway down the stairs, Caitlynn was brought up

short by the sight of Donovan and Declan hefting what looked like a rolled-up carpet out of the kitchens and into the front hallway. They carefully lowered the object to the floor.

As Donovan stepped aside to take something from the open Gladstone bag that Bridget held out to him, Caitlynn saw something ruffled and white at his feet. A maid's mobcap. A shock of carroty hair spilled onto the polished wood floor after it.

She went cold all over. A hand flew up to cover her mouth in horror. It was not a rug they were carrying, but a *person*, wrapped in an old blanket. And there was only one woman in the household with hair that color.

Annie Murphy.

The blood drained from her face. Her heart was pounding so loudly, she could hear it in her own ears.

"What's going on?" she asked as she joined the others in the entryway. "Has Annie been taken ill?"

Bridget and Maureen were clinging to Rose, sobbing into the bib of her apron. Tom was clasping his cap to his chest in a solemn way. He kept patting his pockets, as if looking for something. Declan and Donovan looked graver than she had ever seen them. Only Mrs. Montgomery seemed unmoved.

"When did Annie come back?" Caitlynn asked. "Has there been an accident?"

"She didn't come back, miss. Annie's been here all along. Poor Bridget found her at the bottom of the cellar steps—she just about tripped over her when she went down to fill the coal scuttles," Rose explained. "There, there, now, Bridget, don't take on so, lamb. Nobody's blaming you. Shoo, shoo, there's a good girl." To Caitlynn, she added in a low voice, "Annie must have been lying there since yesterday morning, miss, the poor girl. Forgotten and all alone in that nasty, cold old cellar." Rose shuddered. "Let's pray she recovers."

"I'm afraid she won't be doing that, Rose," Donovan said heavily, unhooking the stethoscope from around his neck. "Annie's dead. She's been dead for at least twenty-four hours, from what I can tell."

"She's dead? Holy Mother of God, no!" Bridget crossed herself. Maureen followed suit. Rose's lips clamped tightly together, as did the housekeeper's.

"You mean, all the while we were celebrating yesterday, enjoying our Christmas fare, poor Annie was . . ."

". . . down there? Yes, I'm afraid so, Rose. Tom, summon the ambulance, if you will." He turned to the maid. "Bridget, who filled the coal scuttles yesterday morning?"

"Annie, sir. All four of them, same as every morning."

"Where were they when you came down?"

"Sitting right at the top of the cellar stairs, sir. I was terrible cross with her because . . . well, because she didn't help me lay the fires before she ran off." Bridget's lower lip wobbled. "I didn't know. I thought she'd run away, sir. She always said as how she hated it here and wanted to be gone."

"Bridget's right. I almost broke my blessed neck tripping over the scuttles she'd left in the way," Rose confirmed.

"So Annie brought up all four scuttles of coal, but only fell and broke her neck after they were safely brought up and the cellar door closed?" Donovan asked.

"She broke her neck?" Caitlynn exclaimed. "How awful! Oh, that poor, poor girl!"

271

Bridget sighed noisily, sniffing back tears. "I hope and pray the Blessed Virgin forgives me, but I never liked her. She was a sly one, Annie was. But I would never have wished such a thing on her. Never." She knuckled fresh tears from red, swollen eyes. "Little Timmy will be all alone now, the poor lad."

"Timmy?"

"Her little brother. He was all she had left. She didn't much care for anyone else, but she'd do anything for Timmy, she would."

"Bridget, when you came into the kitchen yesterday morning, was the cellar door open or closed?" the doctor asked again.

"I'm sure I don't remember, Doctor."

"Think very hard. It's important."

Bridget considered, her face scrunched into a frown. "It was shut," she said at length.

"You're sure?"

"I am. The scuttles were sitting right in front of the kitchen door, weren't they now? That's why Rose almost tripped over them when she came into the kitchen from the carriage house."

The Larkins lived in quarters above the carriage house, across the stable yard.

"Bridget's right, Doctor. The cellar door was shut," Rose confirmed.

He nodded. "Did either of you notice anything out of place in the kitchen? A rolling pin, say? Or a heavy soup ladle?"

Rose pursed her lips to think about it. "Bless you, no, Doctor. Not a thing. Why do you ask?"

"You know how doctors are, Rose. We always ask a great many questions." He smiled. "Now go on, all of you. My brother and I will stay with Annie until the ambulance arrives."

272

As the others dispersed to the kitchen or went back upstairs to their rooms, Donovan knelt alongside Annie. He turned her head to one side and pointed something out to Declan.

"Do you really think she fell and broke her neck?" Caitlynn asked quietly, joining them. Something wasn't right here. She could tell by Donovan's expression and tone.

Although she did not want to look at the dead woman, she felt compelled to do so.

Annie's skin was the color of whey, her freckles paler than they had been when she was alive. Her bright hair spilled across the polished wood floor in a tangle of carroty red curls, except for an ugly darker area above the left temple.

Dried blood, Caitlynn thought. Annie's eyes were open, flat, the sheen of life gone as she stared blindly up at the chandelier and beyond.

Donovan reached over and gently closed them, then drew the blanket up to cover her face. Caitlynn's last thought was that Annie had been surprised to find death so close at hand. Her mouth was slightly ajar.

Caitlynn swallowed, eyes filling with guilty tears. Ah, yes. They were tears of guilt rather than pity. Like Bridget, she'd never liked Annie, but liking or no liking, she'd let Annie down very badly by not being there for her to talk to, as she'd promised.

Had Annie, desperate to unburden herself, knocked at her door that night but received no answer? Had Annie ever really known where Deirdre was, or had Kitty Abbott been wrong? Caitlynn would never know, not now. Annie had taken her secrets with her to the grave.

"See here, Declan," Donovan murmured. "This bruise on the temple? And there's another large contusion here, at the base of her skull. I believe that one was from the fall. This one . . . well, this one was caused by something else."

"They could both have been from the fall, don't you think?" Declan suggested with a frown.

"Not a chance, unless she turned completely over on the way down. But there are only nine steps. I doubt that was enough of a drop for the body to turn much. One bruise or the other, possibly, but not both."

"Aah. Then you don't believe it was a falling accident?" Caitlynn asked.

Donovan looked up at her as if he'd only just realized she was still there. "Far from it. I didn't want to say anything in front of the others, but it's my belief she was hit on the head with sufficient force to knock her backwards down the stairs. The fall snapped her neck and finished the job. Whoever killed her then closed the cellar door, knowing she probably wouldn't be found until the maids went to fill the coal scuttles the following morning."

Declan gave a low whistle. "Murder?"

"Murder." Donovan frowned. "Fetch the police for us, Dec. Once they've taken her away, I'll let her family know."

"Timmy Murphy. Her little brother," Caitlynn supplied absently. "Bridget says he's all the family she has. *Had.*"

"Murder," Declan repeated, shaking his head. Although a lawyer, he was clearly stunned that such a crime had been committed in his brother's home. "But who would do such a thing?"

"God knows," Donovan said heavily. "But I found this in Annie's hand."

He was holding Tom's pipe.

* * *

274

Caitlynn wondered what to tell Estelle as she hurried back upstairs, carrying the girl's steaming mug of cocoa.

That Annie had fallen, she decided. There was no earthly reason for Estelle to be told otherwise. The suggestion that someone in the household was capable of murder was terrifying.

To her surprise, Estelle's door was locked. She knocked. "Estelle?"

Receiving no answer, she went back down the hall to her own door and went inside, intending to get into Estelle's room by the connecting door. But what she saw there stopped her dead in her tracks.

Chapter Twenty-one

Estelle was standing by the dresser.

Standing unaided. On her own two feet.

In one hand she held a pair of sewing shears, and in the other, the white silk fan Donovan had given Caitlynn the day before.

Shreds of hand-painted white silk littered the rag rug at her feet.

She stared at Caitlynn, eyes wide with surprise, cheeks hot with guilt, all movement frozen by Caitlynn's unexpected entrance. "Miss Cait! I—I didn't expect you back so soon."

"That much is obvious," Caitlynn retorted, green eyes snapping. "How long have you been pretending you can't walk, Estelle?" Her hand shook so badly with outrage, she had to set the mug of cocoa down on the desk before she spilled it. "And what the devil are you doing in my room, destroying my things? Answer me! What can you be thinking, to do such a spiteful thing?"

A guilty flush rose up Estelle's throat, but she continued to glare at Caitlynn, her lower lip jutting in defiance, saying nothing.

Caitlynn went across to her, barely resisting the urge to shake the girl or box her ears. "Say something, you wicked girl!"

"I—I don't know what I was thinking, so I can't tell you, can I?" Estelle blurted out, throwing the shears down on the desk with a clatter. "I—I was jealous, I suppose. I—I wanted to hurt you."

"Jealous! Of what?"

"That Donovan gave the fan to you and not me."

"But he gave you a charm bracelet!"

"And then you found the silver ring, too," Estelle carried on in a rush. "It was supposed to be mine, not yours! Rose promised me. *I* was to be the one married within the year, not you!"

Caitlynn was astonished. "Finding the ring was luck. Who gets which charm in the plum pudding—It's only a silly nursery game! A foolish but harmless tradition. It's not meant to be taken seriously. You know that, Estelle, so stop being silly. As for the fan . . ."

Shaking her head, she bit her lip as she looked down at the ruins of her gift. "It was given to *me,* whether you like it or not, miss. You had no right to destroy my belongings so—so willfully."

"I want him to look at me the way he looks at you. Donovan, I mean. He likes you. He *really* likes you." Her eyes brimmed with tears, turning them to glittering crystal, like a porcelain doll's glass eyes. Pretty, yes, but emotionless. "Everyone at the party heard what he said about you finding a husband. They were all talking about it."

She was sobbing uncontrollably, but then, she could always make herself cry at the drop of a hat, Caitlynn thought, unimpressed by her tears.

"I wanted to h—hurt you, that's wh-why I did it . . . that's why I always do—do the—things." Tears rolled down Estelle's perfect cheeks and dripped onto the yoke of her nightgown.

A child's mind trapped in the body of a beautiful young woman, Caitlynn thought. A selfish, willful, jealous child.

Was it possible that she was also a dangerous child?

Possible, yes. But unlikely. Estelle was volatile by nature. She would soon get over her jealousy and return to her normal sunny self.

"Don't look at me that way! Say something, Miss Caitlynn."

"What would you have me say? What you did—well, to be honest, it has left me speechless."

"Can't you say you'll forgive me? That you won't go away, like Miss Dee Dee did? I couldn't bear it if you left us, too!" she pleaded. "Don't be cross, Miss Caitlynn. Please don't! I'm sorry. I'm so very sorry."

"I'm sorry, too, Estelle," she said frankly. "All this time I thought we were friends, but—"

"We *are* friends. The very best of friends!" Estelle insisted.

Caitlynn frowned. "Are we? I'm not so sure about that anymore. A friend doesn't do this to another friend's belongings, Estelle. I don't know what to say, except that I am very disappointed in you."

"You're right. I deserve to be punished. Lock me in my room. Whip me. I'll do anything. Just—just don't go away."

"I shall have to think about a suitable punishment—but rest assured, it won't include a whipping." She shook her head, bemused by the girl's overactive imagination. "For now, I want you to go back to bed, drink your cocoa and get another hour's sleep. We'll discuss this matter later."

"Yes, Miss Caitlynn," Estelle murmured meekly, bowing her head. Her lower lip wobbled. Tears welled in those innocent blue eyes. "But first . . . I—I'll need your help getting back to bed."

"Of course. I'm amazed you had the strength to walk this far." Beneath her long nightgown, the girl's legs were as spindly as matchsticks. She supposed jealousy had given Estelle the strength to take her revenge.

"I'm not crippled, Miss Cait. Nor paralyzed. Just very weak because of the rheumatic fever," she mumbled. "And I haven't been pretending! My muscles don't work very well because I don't use my legs very much. That's what Donovan says."

She curled an arm around Caitlynn's neck and kissed her so hard on the cheek, Caitlynn winced in pain and tried to pull her head away. "Stop it, Estelle!"

"Not until you say you'll forgive me," Estelle wheedled. "I'll buy you another fan with my allowance, just like the one he gave you, I swear I will. But first you must promise you won't tell Uncle Donovan what I did."

"As I said, we'll discuss it later." She took Estelle's hand and placed it on her shoulder, then did the same with her second hand. "There. Now hang on to me and we'll get you back to bed—"

"*No!*" Estelle hissed. "I won't! Not until you promise. You're going to tell him, aren't you? I can see it in your face! I know you will." Sharp fingernails dug into Caitlynn's shoulder. Punishing fingers bit down, bruising soft flesh. "If you tell him, he won't love me any-more. He'll hate me and love you!"

"Nonsense, Estelle. Your guardian thinks of himself as your father. He loves you with all his heart—"

"No, he doesn't. He'll marry you and send me back to that dreadful Lily Perkins, I know he will!"

"Send you back! Now you're really being silly."

"No, I'm not. Ask Montgomery. She'll tell you. She and I will be sent away once the doctor marries. When he does, he won't need either of us. So you must swear you won't tell Donovan about the fan. Swear, or you'll be sorry!"

Estelle's face was contorted, her hands clamped over Caitlynn's shoulders. It was as if a fluffy kitten had suddenly become a snarling tigress.

Gripping Estelle's hands, Caitlynn broke the girl's painful grip on her shoulders and slapped her hands away.

"Stop it immediately! I shan't allow you to hurt me. Nor will I make promises I cannot keep. Remember? I told you that my very first day here," Caitlynn said quietly, standing her ground, although her bruised shoulders throbbed. "I do promise to think about it, however. Does that help? And if I decide to tell your guardian, I promise I'll tell you first. That's the best I can do."

Estelle shot her a sulky look. Her blue eyes were murderous. Her lower lip stuck out. Her creamy com-plexion was covered in angry red blotches and tears, her features twisted into a horrid expression that Cait-lynn had never seen before. It was as if there were someone else behind Estelle's eyes. An evil imp. Some-one—or some*thing*—evil lurking there that had peeked out for a fleeting second, then darted back behind its veneer of angelic beauty.

Caitlynn gave an inward shudder. It was a veneer that seemed perilously thin at times.

"I suppose it will have to do, won't it?" Estelle managed stiffly, tight-lipped. "Now I know where I stand and what must be done. Thank you, Miss Caitlynn."

Her woebegone expression softened Caitlynn's resolve. "Dr. Fitzgerald loves you like a daughter, Estelle. Why won't you believe that?" she asked gently. "He could love you no more if you were his own flesh and blood. You needn't worry that he'll send you away, because he won't, ever, no matter what Mrs. Montgomery has told you."

That meddlesome old bat! It was very possible the housekeeper would be dismissed if the master of the household were to marry. After all, very few married doctors needed housekeepers. Their wives were able to run their households. But a bachelor doctor was quite another matter.

"That's what you think!" Estelle flared. "What if he marries, what then?"

"He would never marry anyone who was not prepared to love you, too," Caitlynn soothed in a firm yet gentle voice, her initial anger dispelled by the girl's obvious terror and upset. She sometimes forgot that in many ways, Estelle was more child than woman. A frightened child who reacted to anger, jealousy and fear by striking out at those she loved the best, without heed for the consequences, terrified she would be sent away.

"Even after what I've done?" Estelle whispered.

"Even then."

She licked her lips. "What if he knew, though? What if he found out that I was a wicked, *wicked* child? What then?" She held her breath, waiting for Caitlynn's reply.

Did she mean the fan? Caitlynn wondered. Or something else entirely? "You destroyed something that belonged to someone else. An old and expensive piece that you should be made to replace. But a silk fan, however pretty, is still just a thing, Estelle. An object. A trifle. We can replace things. What we cannot replace are the people we love. People like you, Estelle.

"Either I or Donovan will decide on your punishment, but then he will forgive you, darlin' girl, as will I, because *we love you.*"

Estelle's lower lip wobbled. She threw her arms around Caitlynn's neck and hugged her fiercely. "Oh, Miss Caitlynn, I love you, too! I really do! It was horrid of me to do that to your present. I'm very sorry, really I am."

"And so you should be, you darlin' wicked girl!" She laughed, helping Estelle back into her own room. "Now come along, dry those eyes, then back into bed with you. I expect your cocoa will be cold by now." She hugged herself about the arms, suddenly chilled, as if someone had walked over her grave.

"What is it, miss? You look sad all of a sudden."

"I am. I almost forgot." She bit her lips and could not meet Estelle's now guileless eyes. "I have some bad news."

"Oh. Is it about Annie?"

"I'm afraid it is, dear. She's dead. We found her down in the cellars, poor girl."

"Dead? Oh, dear! But how?" Estelle asked, sliding under the covers, then propping a pillow behind her back. When Caitlynn retrieved the mug, Estelle took a sip of cocoa, leaving a milky brown 'moustache' on her upper lip. She licked it off with obvious relish, like a cat lapping cream. "Was she covered in blood?"

"No, thank God. Doctor thinks she fell down the cellar stairs and hurt her neck."

"You mean, she broke it, don't you? Like Tom, when he wrings the chickens' necks?"

Caitlynn shuddered. "In a way, yes. Now, the ambulance will be here for her very shortly, so I want you to stay upstairs and rest until they take her away, all right?"

Estelle nodded, licking her lips as she sipped her cocoa. "Mmm. This cocoa is very good. Nobody makes cocoa like you. What shall we do until Annie's gone, Miss Cait? Play cards?"

"Yes. Or draughts. Either one. We'll make a lazy morning of it, shall we?"

Estelle nodded eagerly.

And while they played, Caitlynn would try to forget that a young woman had lain at the foot of the cellar stairs with her neck broken all day yesterday, while they were calmly sitting down to their Christmas dinner—and that yet another young woman had not been heard from in over five months.

Were the two incidents connected? Caitlynn felt sure they were somehow. Call it female intuition—what men called 'gut instinct'—but there was a link between the two somewhere. Find that link and she would find Deirdre, she was certain of it.

Annie could tell her nothing now, but perhaps her younger brother could.

This afternoon, while Estelle was resting, she and Donovan would find out.

Chapter Twenty-two

Caitlynn decided to spend Boxing Day afternoon reading by the drawing room fire while Estelle rested and Donovan made his afternoon rounds at the hospital.

Mrs. Montgomery had mentioned she had some letters to write in her room. She promised to look in on the girl from time to time, leaving Caitlynn free to spend the afternoon downstairs as she pleased. When Donovan came home at half past three, they would go and find Timmy Murphy.

For what must have been the umpteenth time, Caitlynn read the address that Bridget had scribbled on a scrap of butcher's paper: 9 *Farrier's Lane, Whitechapel, London.* The maid's expression said volumes about the Murphys' choice of lodging house.

"Is it so very low?" Caitlynn had asked.

" 'Tis worse than low, miss," Bridget exclaimed, shooting her a darkling look. " 'Tis a wicked sinful place it is, with wicked sinful women and terrible men goin' in and out at all hours—is it not, Rose? Tom, tell Miss Caitlynn! Ye should not go there, miss. Really, you shouldn't."

"It's all right, Bridget. I'll be perfectly safe with the doctor," she assured the girl.

But thinking about their conversation now made her edgy, unable to concentrate on her book. Her mind kept drifting off to other things, anxiously wondering what Timmy would tell her about Deirdre, or whether he knew anything to tell. In all honesty, it was not likely Annie had confided in her little brother. After all, how often had Caitlynn told her own little brother, Patrick, her secrets? Never, that she could remember.

Huntington House dozed, lost in the drowsy spell common to great houses on high days and holy days once the feast has been devoured and a good fire is blazing in the hearth, making cheeks ruddy and eyelids heavy.

The combination of a full belly, the fire's warmth and a sleepless night proved irresistible. One moment, Caitlynn was yawning sleepily, mesmerized by the words that skipped and danced on the page before her. In the next, Donovan's light touch on her shoulder woke her.

"My dear?"

"Hmm? Oh! I'm sorry. I must have nodded off. What time is it?" She covered her mouth to stifle a sleepy yawn. "Are we leaving soon?"

"I'm afraid not. I just stopped by to apologize before I left. I can't go with you yet, Cait. I have an emergency. But don't worry. We'll find Timmy Murphy later."

"But Timmy's the key to finding Deirdre! The only key!" She didn't mean to sound so complaining, or so disappointed, but she couldn't help herself. Ever since

Penelope Neri

Kitty Abbott had told her that Annie had information about Deirdre's disappearance, one thing after another had conspired to keep her from finding out what that information was. And now this.

"I know, darlin', and I'm sorry, but it can't be helped. A messenger came to the clinic to fetch me. There's a very sick woman who needs me." Even as he spoke, he was striding out into the hallway again, forcing Caitlynn to run to keep up with him.

Taking his greatcoat down from the hall stand, he thrust first one arm, then the other into its sleeves. The heavy wool was still cold and damp from the outside, she noticed as she handed him his muffler and gloves, which were also damp.

"Here. It's bitter out."

"So it is, sweetheart. Thank you. *Bridget! My bag!*"

"We really do need to find Timmy as soon as possible," Caitlynn pleaded in a last effort to talk him out of going. "Couldn't another doctor take the call just this once? Please? Timmy Murphy could disappear when he hears about his sister's death—if he hasn't already. You know how it is. There are precious few secrets in the East End. Bad news spreads like wildfire."

He frowned. "Cait. Sweet Cait." He framed her face between his hands and kissed her full on the lips. His eyes were sad and very earnest when he held her at arm's length again. "If it was any other patient, I'd say yes without thinking twice about it, my darlin' girl. But I can't, not this time. You see, it's Lady Cecily."

"Oh, no! Is it very serious?" But she knew without hearing his answer that it must be. Why else would he look so grim, so very sad?

"Very, unfortunately." He ducked his head and planted a quick kiss on her forehead. "God willing, I'll

286

be home as soon as she's out of danger. If it's not too late, we'll see if we can find Timmy then. Wait for me, Cait. You're not to go there alone, not on any account. Promise me?"

She nodded, and crossed her heart with her finger. "I promise. Cross my heart and hope to die. Please take care."

"And you." He chucked her beneath the chin. "I love you, Caitlynn O'Connor. If I were to propose on New Year's Eve, might you accept?" he asked huskily.

"That depends on what you intend to propose, sir," she answered, her green eyes sparkling. "I do have my reputation to consider."

"Marriage, of course. What else?" But his wicked grin said he knew exactly what else—and relished the memories they'd made. "Would you? Say yes, I mean."

The look in his eyes thrilled her. "Ohhh. You mean *marriage!* There's only one way you'll ever know the answer to that question, Doctor," she teased, her heart all aflutter. "You will have to ask me it and see! Now go, go quickly! Oh, and tell Lady Cecily she's in my thoughts and prayers. And Sir Charles, too. The poor man must be beside himself with worry," she added in a more somber vein.

"I will. Until tonight?" he added in a low, caressing tone that left her weak with need and longing. It was as if he had touched her intimately instead of that long, lazy stroking with voice and eyes alone.

"Tonight," she echoed.

"And be careful. We don't know who . . . well, you know. Until the police determine who pushed Annie, we all need to be careful."

"I will be. I promise."

She stood on the front steps hugging herself about

the arms and shivering as Donovan sprang into the hackney.

How very lucky she was that such a fine, handsome man, such a good, decent man, should care for her as much as she cared for him. Their future together promised great happiness. To think of it! She had her entire life ahead of her. A lifetime to spend with the man she loved and admired. Donovan was a man who cared about others, whether rich or poor, more than he cared about himself, or about money and material things. He had high ideals and principles, did her Donovan. All she needed to make her happiness complete was to find Deirdre.

She lifted her hand in farewell. Donovan returned the salute by blowing her a kiss; then the cabby clicked to the horse and lightly flicked the whip across its broad rump.

The vehicle rumbled smartly away from the gaslit square, the horse's hooves clattering over the icy cobbles.

"Promises or no promises, I doubt you'll see the doctor back until the wee hours," Mary Montgomery said with an air of finality as she joined her by the doorway. "If then."

"I beg your pardon, Mrs. Montgomery?" she asked, closing the front door behind her against the chill draught. She'd only heard half of what the woman said. But how much of the exchange between herself and Donovan had the housekeeper overheard—or seen? she wondered, embarrassed. Remembering Donovan's fond kiss, his wicked farewell, she blushed.

"I said the doctor won't be back until very late, if then," the housekeeper explained. "I'm sorry, but I couldn't help overhearing, dear. You and the doctor were going to find that young scamp, Timmy Murphy, were you not? To tell him that his sister's passed on?"

"That's right. Someone has to. It's the proper thing to do. The boy shouldn't have to learn about it from someone else."

There had been no time to find Timmy before the detectives arrived from Scotland Yard's Criminal Investigation Division. Once they had, the police insisted nobody leave number 13 until they'd questioned everyone about Annie's fatal fall. When had they seen Annie last, the detectives wanted to know, calling them into Donovan's study, one by one. Had Annie quarreled with Tom, whose pipe was found clutched in her hand? And then there was poor Tom himself, as white as the proverbial ghost, shaken and trembling at finding himself the center of their investigation.

Tom was able to tell the police only that he didn't much like the girl, but that he'd never had words with her, nor had much to do with her at all, except at mealtimes in the kitchen. His pipe had been missing since Christmas Eve, as far as he could remember. And no, he had no idea how it could have been found in the dead woman's hand, since he always carried it in the breast pocket of his jacket.

After the police left, Donovan gave Tom a dose of laudanum to calm his nerves, and insisted he take the remainder of the day off to recuperate. The poor man was so upset and agitated, he was quite unable to do his duties anyway. Donovan was more concerned that Tom would have a seizure or a heart attack than he was about him working.

"Well, there'll be no money from young Timmy to bury the chit," Montgomery said with great relish. "Paupers' field, that'll be Annie Murphy's grave, same as the rest of her kind. I always knew that one'd come to a bad end, I did."

289

"On the contrary. The doctor said he would arrange for her burial himself. At St. Anthony's cemetery."

Her announcement wiped the smug smile from Montgomery's face. "Oh, did he, now? Well, there, you see? You needn't worry about letting the boy know, Miss O'Connor. She'll be properly laid to rest. Besides, there's every chance young Timmy's heard by now, don't you think? You know how servants are. There are no secrets below stairs. None at all. Bridget or that new girl—"

"Maureen."

"Maureen, yes. One of them only has to remark on Annie's death to someone, and word will spread through the East End quicker than the plague."

"You know a great deal about the East End, Mrs. Montgomery," Caitlynn murmured, amused.

"Well, we didn't all start out in comfort and plenty, did we, dear?" The housekeeper smiled. "Perhaps you'd like to share a pot of tea with me in my little sitting room while you're waiting for the doctor. I must admit, I do enjoy a bit of company at the holidays. We can get to know each other."

"What a lovely idea."

"My position as housekeeper here is a little . . . well, it's lonely at times, you know. And uncertain." Those piercing gray eyes met Caitlynn's. "It's difficult being neither a member of the family nor a domestic servant—especially after a woman reaches a certain age and her choices are fewer."

"I hadn't thought of it like that."

"Well, you wouldn't, would you? But you know what I mean, don't you, dear, a pretty young thing like you? You didn't let any grass grow under your feet, eh, you clever girl! But that's beside the point. The hard truth is that there are very few options left to older women. Like myself."

Caitlynn hid her surprise. She would not have expected Mary Montgomery to admit to being lonely, let alone discuss her position in the Fitzgerald household so frankly. Working together to plan Donovan's Christmas dinner must have brought about these overtures of friendship—or perhaps it was just the goodwill of the holiday season.

"A cup of tea would be just the thing," she accepted warmly. "Thank you for asking me, Mrs. Montgomery. I'll just look in on Estelle first."

"By all means, do, but I'm sure the dear girl's fast asleep by now. She was yawning when I left her."

"Left her?"

"Yes. I took her up a cup of cocoa. You know how she loves her cocoa, bless her."

"She does, doesn't she? How kind of you. I'll just be a moment."

Sure enough, Estelle was fast asleep, her cheek cradled on one outflung arm, her breathing deep and even. Her cocoa mug stood on the night table beside the bed, drained to the last drop.

The excitement of the holidays had exhausted the girl, Caitlynn thought as she made her way to the housekeeper's small bed-sitting room. News of Annie's tragic death, followed by their games of cards and draughts all morning until the police finally left number 13, hadn't helped.

Estelle was fiercely competitive and hated to lose. As a consequence, she'd insisted on playing until she won. But by then, she'd been exhausted and short of breath. Caitlynn thought Estelle seemed to tire more easily of late. Was her damaged heart growing weaker?

"One lump or two?" Mary's brows arched in inquiry as she held a sugar cube up by a pair of silver tongs.

"Just one, thank you." Caitlynn looked around. "This is such a charming room. What pretty touches you have given it."

The overstuffed wing chair by the fire boasted a beautiful lace antimacassar, with plump chenille and tapestry cushions tucked into the corners. The top of the dresser was adorned with porcelain and silver knickknacks that appeared to be of excellent quality, though her knowledge of such things was limited. "I'm not nearly so clever at making a place cozy."

"Oh, don't be so modest, Miss O'Connor. I'm sure you are. Besides, I cannot take credit for the beautiful pieces I have collected. All of them were gifts from my employers over the years, given in gratitude for my faithful service. Lemon or milk?"

"Milk, please. Just a little. Thank you." She took the delicate bone-china cup and saucer Mary handed her, and sipped the steaming tea. "Mmm. Perfect. It must be gratifying to be held in such affection and esteem."

"Oh, yes, very. May I offer you a ginger biscuit?"

"No, thank you. How long have you been the doctor's housekeeper?"

"Oh, for about six years now." Mary Montgomery helped herself to a biscuit. "Dr. Fitzgerald hired me to keep house for him the same week he brought Miss Estelle home. And what a wretched, unmanageable little imp she was, too!" She rolled her eyes. "That pretty hair of hers was filthy, and swarming with lice. She was dirty, too, with sores and bruises everywhere. Oh, and the language! It would have made a trooper blush. Such filth and profanity! The nanny engaged by the doctor quite despaired. In the end, he let her go and

292

hired a governess instead." She shook her head. "Ah, well, all that is water under the bridge now, and best forgotten, I dare say."

"You must be proud of the young lady she has become." It was impossible to imagine the lovely Estelle as a grubby urchin spewing profanities.

"Indeed I am, Miss O'Connor. Very proud. But then, I have been like a mother to that girl, haven't I, though I do say so myself. Precious few would believe it, the way she treats me now!" She sniffed and took another bite of her ginger biscuit. "Let me see, where were we? Ah, yes. I was about to say that Annie's little brother will take it very hard when he hears his sister is dead."

"I'm sure he will, yes."

"He's all alone in the world, the poor lad."

"You have met Timmy, then?"

"No, no, I haven't, not exactly. But he was always hanging about by the kitchen door, waiting for Annie to slip him kitchen scraps."

"Really?"

She nodded. "You didn't know? Rose has a bad habit of feeding young wretches like him. I have t'keep a sharp eye on her."

"That's Rose, bless her. So kind and softhearted."

"Kind! Softhearted!" She snorted in disgust. "It's no skin off Rose Larkin's nose to play Lady Bountiful, when the poor doctor's paying for every bite she puts in the little blighters' ungrateful mouths. Besides, lads like Timmy Murphy are hard as nails. Turns himself to any number of ventures, lawful or otherwise, does Timmy, all with an eye to making an easy penny here, a fast ha'penny there.

"And as for his sister . . . well, Annie was always light-fingered, right from the very first. If you'll forgive me saying so, she was no better than she should be, that one. She'd as soon help herself to what she fancied as pay for it. Oh, will you listen to me—and I call myself a good Christian woman!" She shook her head, as if disgusted with herself. "I shouldn't be going on like that. I hate to speak badly of the dead."

"So do I. I wouldn't know about Annie stealing, though." Estelle had dropped hints that Annie was a sneak thief, but Caitlynn wasn't about to share that information with Mrs. Montgomery.

"Well, I dare say she couldn't help herself. Just like magpies, some people are," Montgomery continued in a conversational tone, nibbling her ginger biscuit like a water rat gnawing at a moldy cracker. She swigged her tea with more gusto than delicacy. "Can't resist the temptation to help themselves to whatever they fancy, they can't. A sparkly bauble here, a shiny bit o' brass there." Gray eyes gleamed. "I'm afraid our dear Miss Riordan was cut from the same cloth, if you'll forgive me for saying so. What a disappointment! Oh, no reflection upon yourself or your family intended, my dear. Every family has its black sheep."

"Ours certainly did not," Caitlynn responded, bristling with indignation. The housekeeper appeared not to notice her tone, however, or—far more likely— deliberately chose to ignore it.

Apparently, the nasty old woman saw no reason for Caitlynn to take offense, although she'd blatantly accused her cousin, who was not there to defend herself.

"Besides, it's not really known who has taken what. Or if anything was actually taken at all, is it?" Caitlynn added.

"Oh, but it was!" the housekeeper said. "You have only to ask the doctor—"

"I did ask the doctor, weeks ago, Mrs. Montgomery," Caitlynn countered smoothly. "According to him, my cousin left this household before any accusation of pilfering was brought against her. He knew only what he was told about the matter by you, after the fact."

Montgomery sighed and smiled indulgently. "The poor man. He's so very busy with his patients. He must have forgotten our discussion after all this time. More tea, dear?"

"No, thank you. This has been delightful, but I really should go downstairs and wait for Dr. Fitzgerald now."

"Young ladies nowadays! So impatient. So very anxious to do the proper thing. But the boy's sister is dead, is she not? An hour or two—a day, come to that—can make no difference to Annie or the lad's situation, surely? Not now."

Caitlynn's lips tightened, but she said nothing.

"On the other hand . . . if it is so urgent that he be told today, some special reason it cannot wait, perhaps you could go on ahead of the doctor? If he returns sooner than expected, I would be happy to tell him where you have gone."

"There is a special reason, yes. One I'd rather not discuss, I'm afraid. But I can't go alone, Mrs. Montgomery. I gave Dono—I gave the doctor my word, you see. And a promise is a promise."

"Oh, I quite understand. Dr. Fitzgerald is concerned for your safety. And rightly so. I couldn't agree with him more. The East End is a cruel place, unkind to its own, pitiless to outsiders. Besides, that wretched Jack hasn't been caught yet." She paused. "I don't suppose I could . . . no, no, don't mind me. It's none of my business, I'm sure. I was just thinking out loud. I'm sure you'd rather wait for the doctor to return."

"No, please, go on. What were you going to say?"

"Only that . . . well, that I would be happy to accompany you, if you must go this afternoon. That way, you could keep your promise to the doctor and still let little Timmy Murphy know about his sister's death." She beamed.

"You would accompany me?" Caitlynn's brows rose in surprise.

"Of course. It would be my pleasure to be of help to you in some small way. I know we did not get off to a very good start when you first came here, but I so enjoyed planning the Christmas dinner party with you, Miss O'Connor. I believe the two of us are going to become the best of friends. Besides, if we leave within the half hour, we could be home before it gets dark."

It would be dusk by four-thirty, full dark well before six in these winter months. She had a little over an hour, two at most. But it might mean the difference between talking to Timmy Murphy, telling him about his sister and learning what he knew, if anything, about Deirdre, and finding him long gone, swallowed up by the courts and rookeries of the East End.

Besides, it wouldn't really be breaking the promise she'd made to Donovan, she reasoned, since she wouldn't be alone. Mrs. Montgomery would be with her. The housekeeper was a pillar of respectability, her very appearance intimidating. The old bat would scare even Saucy Jack himself!

"Of course, if you'd rather wait for the doctor, I quite understand," Mrs. Montgomery murmured. "And I hope you won't think I overstepped my position by offering to accompany you."

"Why on earth should I think that, Mrs. Montgomery?"

"Mary, dear. Please, call me Mary. Well, it's no secret that you and the doctor are . . . well, that you have a fondness for each other, is it? It's quite obvious to everyone in this household, including myself. Oh, the way the doctor looks at you, and you at him! So romantic! Why, in the servants' hall they are even taking wagers on it."

"Wagers on what?"

"On when he will ask you to marry him, of course. In which case, if you'll forgive me for saying so, you will go from being a lady's companion to becoming the mistress of Huntington House and a doctor's wife overnight, you clever girl." She smiled in conspiratorial fashion. "When that time comes, I should not like you to think badly of your husband's old housekeeper. Or for you to forget our . . . friendship."

"Oh, what nonsense, Mary! But yes, I accept your offer. We'll leave as soon as you finish your tea," Caitlynn decided. "Thank you for offering."

"It's my pleasure, dear. I'll just tell Rose we're going out, shall I?"

Chapter Twenty-three

"I must say, it came as quite a surprise to hear that Miss Riordan was your cousin. Close, were you?" Montgomery asked as the hired hack carried them through the darkening streets of London like a great black beetle, trundling east. Headed from light to dark . . .

. . . from good to evil?

"We are, yes. Very close. More like sisters than cousins."

"And I expect she wrote to tell you about all of us here and our boring little lives at Huntington House. Amusing little anecdotes, perhaps?" Her hard eyes gleamed like wet stones as she eyed Caitlynn questioningly. The broad brim of her felt hat cast most of her face in heavy shadow, making the glitter of her eyes oddly bright.

"She wrote about Estelle and the doctor a little, yes." *But nothing about Declan, with whom she'd fallen in love. And certainly nothing about you, if that's what you're so worried about, my dear Mrs. M.!*

"Aah. I thought so. Good things for the most part, I hope?" she pressed.

Caitlynn smiled. There was an unmistakably anxious note to Montgomery's voice. Obviously, she suspected she was far from popular with the rest of the help, and wondered if Deirdre had written about it to her. "Oh, good things, yes, of course. My cousin *only* had good things to say about others. That's the kind of person she was. If Deirdre couldn't say something nice about someone, she didn't say anything at all."

"How very admirable." It was said sourly, however.

"She is, yes. A saint, almost." Caitlynn laughed. "Not like me. I'm far too outspoken and forward to ever be a candidate for sainthood."

"Saintly or not, your Miss Riordan had her sights set on Dr. Fitzgerald," Montgomery confided in a sly tone. "Did she tell you about that in her letters? Saw herself as the mistress of Huntington House, that one did."

"With all due respect, you're quite wrong about that, Mrs. Montgomery," Caitlynn said coldly. She could not let the woman's assumption go unchallenged. "My cousin imagined no such thing."

"Oh? Why do you say that?" the woman asked carefully.

"Because I have it on excellent authority that Deirdre was in love with . . . with someone else. In fact, she was about to accept this man's proposal of marriage when she vanished."

"You mean when she left?"

"No. I mean when she vanished. Went away. Disappeared. Still, whatever word I use, it all comes down to the same thing, does it not? My cousin is missing.

What do you think happened to her, Mrs. Montgomery?"

"Who knows, dear?" She shrugged her shoulders. "Perhaps she ran off with this other man you mentioned. Eloped. Or perhaps she was caught in the family way, and left because she was too ashamed to tell anyone her dirty little secret." The gray eyes gleamed. "It's a possibility, wouldn't you say?"

Caitlynn's jaw tightened. "Anything's possible, yes. But I happen to know that she did neither of those things. You see, her sweetheart is even more desperate to find her than I am."

"Tch-tch. Sounds fishy to me, that does. I do wish I could help you, my dear. All of this must be such a worry for you. And now, just to top it off, we have Annie's murder!"

"Who said Annie was murdered?"

"Oh, nobody, dear. But then, nobody had to. I was just putting two and two together. After all, it's obvious what the doctor suspects, isn't it? He wouldn't have summoned Scotland Yard unless he suspected foul play, now would he?"

"No, I suppose not."

They soon left behind the more affluent neighborhoods of the West End, with its graceful red-brick Georgian mansions, whitewashed front steps and polished brass knockers, clustered around charming little squares with lampposts, trees and elegant wrought-iron fences.

The cobblestone streets through which the coach now clattered on worn springs were seedy and dilapidated. The peeling-paint-and-brick facades of the buildings were stained by time and weather, and blackened by soot and grime, like jagged teeth in a rotting mouth. Some windows were shattered, allowing bitter

wind to whistle through the cracks. Others were
boarded up. The few glass panes that survived were
murky, crusted with decades of soot.

Between some of the tenements squatted abandoned
factories and derelict warehouses, converted into
countless cramped lodgings known as doss houses,
each room no bigger than a prison cell, where the rent
was fourpence a night.

From some of the buildings were strung sorry bits
of washing, makeshift laundry lines lacing window to
window like a spinster's corset.

The doss houses mushroomed around damp, dark
courts that had a pump and little else. Bony children,
raggedly clothed despite the bitter weather, and their
equally threadbare families were everywhere. Many of
them huddled around makeshift braziers set up on the
street corners, or in the little courtyards between the
buildings, either warming cold hands by their heat,
roasting the few potatoes or chestnuts they'd been
lucky enough to scavenge from the markets of Covent
Garden, or drinking scalding coffee from battered tin
mugs to keep hunger at bay.

Everywhere Caitlynn looked there were people with
pinched, hungry faces and crafty eyes. There were none
of the smiles, the ruddy cheeks, the cheerful season's
greetings exchanged in the West End. The people here
swarmed like hungry rats through the darkening
streets, piling out of doors and leaning out of windows,
or rubbing shoulders, often as many as eight to a single
tiny room.

Here in the East End lived the poorest of the city's
poor. The diseased. The foreign. The outcasts. The unwanted. The 'unfortunates.' The thieves, tricksters and
murderers, all of London's pariahs crowded into an
area whose very name was synonymous with hell, only

a stone's throw from the West End environs of the wealthy and the privileged.

Many people jeered at the passing hack and screeched obscenities when Caitlynn looked out. A few even hurled stones at the hack until the cabby threatened them with a taste of his whip and cast their parentage in doubt with a string of colorful cockney curses.

"Miller's Court," the cabby sang out at last. "Whoa, there, Ned." The coach lurched to a standstill. "This is it! As far as I go, ladies. Out!"

"Out? But this is only Miller's Court! You said you'd take us to Farrier's Lane!" Caitlynn protested. If she remembered correctly, Miller's Court was where one of the Ripper's victims was found murdered in her own doss; Mary Jane Kelly was the only prostitute to be slaughtered in her lodgings. She'd been so horrifically mutilated by Jack's blade, she was almost unrecognizable.

"Happen I did, miss. But this is as far as I go t'night. Farrier's Lane's that way, six, mebbe seven courts down. Easy walking distance. Ye can count yerselves lucky I brung ye this far. Not many cabbies 'ud take a fare inter the East End proper after noon, since them whores was murdered. Why, 'Black' Mary copped it not ten yards from this very spot, she did! I'll show ye her doss wiv the bloodstains runnin' down the walls for an extra tuppence!"

He shot them a ghoulish grin that reminded Caitlynn of the gargoyles that leered down from St. Anthony's eaves.

She shuddered. "Thank you, that won't be necessary. I suppose we could walk the rest of the way, if we must." *Even if it means taking our lives into our own hands.* "What do you say, Mrs. Montgomery?"

She'd gone this far, come this close, she refused to just give up and go home with her tail tucked between her legs and her questions unanswered. "Shall we walk?"

"I don't believe we have much choice, do we, my dear? You have the Murphys' address?"

"In my pocket, yes. Will you wait for us here, driver?" Caitlynn asked hopefully but with a sinking heart.

"Aye, but only for a bit, mind. It ain't healthy here after dark, it ain't. Pay me for me trouble first, laidy."

"Oh, all right." She sighed. "A shilling if you'll wait. Sixpence now and the rest when we come back." It was an outrageous sum, but what choice did she have?

"Not likely, miss. The whole shilling now, else I'm orf home!" He gathered the reins into his fist, and when she seemed to hesitate, slapped them across his horse's back. "Giddy-up, there, Ned!"

"Wait!" Caitlynn cried breathlessly, grabbing the bony horse's bridle to keep it from trotting off. The startled animal tossed its head and nervously rolled its blinkered eyes. "If we pay you in advance, how do we know you'll still be here when we come back? Do you take us for fools?"

The cabby grinned. "You pays yer money and you takes your chances. Now, then. What'll it be? Do I go or do I stay? Make up yer mind, laidy, and make it sharpish!"

"Good day to you. We're looking for Timmy Murphy. Is this where he lives?" Caitlynn asked the blowzy woman with hennaed hair who answered her knock at 9 Farrier's Lane.

Despite the bitter weather, the woman's neckline was cut low, her shabby gown too thin for the season. The cheap garment bared a generous expanse of doughy white bosom, now blue with cold. Raucous female laughter, cigar smoke and the clinking of glassware drifted out of the rooming house behind her.

"Who wants to know, then?" the woman demanded, fists on hips, her pointed jaw jutting in a belligerent way. She reeked of mother's ruin, and her eyes were flinty and bloodshot from hard drinking.

"Caitlynn O'Connor. That's Miss O'Connor. I was a—a friend of Timmy's sister, Annie. We were in service together at Dr. Fitzgerald's house in the West End. I'm afraid I have some bad news for him."

"If you've come t'tell 'im Annie kicked the bucket, you're too bleedin' late. The poor li'l sod already knows. And if you were really Red Annie's friend, you'd know she weren't his sister, like she claimed. She was Timmy's mum, she was."

"His mother!"

"That's right. Looked young for her age, our Annie did, which is more'n I can say for the rest of us tarts. So bugger off, Miss Hoity-Toity, 'cos there's not a bloody thing you do-gooders can say t'help Tim now. Just bugger off and leave the poor little sod alone." She started to close the door in Caitlynn's face.

"Wait!" Caitlynn cried, planting her foot between the door and the jamb. "Annie's employer wants to give Timmy a little something. You know, to—to tide him over." It was a lie, as far as she knew, but if it worked, so much the better. She'd find the money to give him herself, and make good on her word.

Slowly the door swung open again. "Somethin'? You mean, money?" The faded eyes brightened with greed. "How much money? Timmy owes me for two nights' doss, he does, the li'l bastard. Eightpence!"

"I'll pay you the eightpence he already owes you, and another fourpence for this evening's doss, if you'll just let me talk to Timmy. Just think," she coaxed. "A whole shilling, just for letting me talk to him."

"Deal!" the woman crowed. A hand like a piece of raw meat swooped down to scoop up the coins.

But before the woman could grab them and drop them down her bodice, Caitlynn whipped her hand out of reach. "No, you don't. Not until I talk to Timmy."

The woman looked daggers at her. "Wait for him outside, then. I won't have your kind in here, dearie. Bad for me business, you two are, if you know what I mean." She grinned slyly, showing gaps in her teeth.

"All right. Where's Timmy now?"

"Out. Only comes back here t'sleep, he does, 'cos he knows he's safe at Big Betty's." She stared at Montgomery, and her hard eyes narrowed. "Don't I know you from someplace, dearie?"

"*When*? When will he be back?" Caitlynn interrupted, thrusting half of the large copper coins into the woman's reddened hands.

"Sometimes eight. Sometimes nine. Could be later." Betty shrugged broad shoulders. "Depends on what tricks the li'l bastard's up to, if ye know what I mean." She chortled with laughter. "Now bugger off, both of you. Go wait in the court. An' don't go tuppin' me customers fer free, if you know what's good fer you." Her coarse laughter followed them out into the dark court.

They discovered very quickly what line of 'business' Big Betty was in as they waited, shivering and stamping their feet to get warm, in the dark, damp court between the run-down lodging house and the darkened Jewish social club next door.

From time to time, a disembodied cry, or a shout, or even a squeal would float from a broken window out into the night. Or the furious shouts, obscenities and bloodcurdling screams of a violent quarrel would erupt, accompanied by the harsh sounds of blows. It was frightening enough to lift the fine hairs on the back of Caitlynn's neck.

A steady stream of roughly dressed men strutted into Big Betty's house. All of them had a certain look. The same men shuffled back out a short time later, their eyes downcast now. They looked furtive and ashamed of themselves, eager to be gone.

When one of Big Betty's patrons took more than a cursory interest in Caitlynn on his way in, she drew her cloak tightly around her and shrank back inside her bonnet, like a tortoise retreating into its shell, looking past the men with their hungry eyes and their leering smiles.

Mary Montgomery chose a far more direct approach to get rid of unwanted attention. "Bugger off!" she snarled at them, much as Betty had done.

As methods went, it was crude but effective.

"You should have worn a big felt hat like mine," the housekeeper said, glancing at Caitlynn's pretty green bonnet. "Something with a broad brim would hide your face. You oughtn't to be seen in a place like this."

Montgomery was right, Caitlynn thought. Imagine, a decent Catholic girl like herself loitering in the shadows of a dirty courtyard, outside what could only be a—a brothel! Thank the Blessed Virgin the sisters at the convent couldn't see her now, she thought, fighting an insane urge to giggle. Donovan would be furious if he ever found out about this.

She sighed heavily, tucking her gloved hands under her armpits to keep them warm. The wait for Timothy Murphy was going to be a long one.

* * *

From the mouth of a dark alley across the street, I watch her as she paces back and forth before the house of ill repute. She stamps her feet as she paces, as if trying to get warm. But I know it is an act. A lie. A sham. Once again, she is displaying her tarnished wares, using her foul woman's body to entice innocent men and their coin.

This one is not like her sisters, however. She is younger, prettier, without the bloodshot eyes and reddened nose of the drunkard. Still, this is the third time I have seen her on these streets, and there are no innocents, not here. Not in hell. Like Sodom and Gomorrah, the East End is for the fallen. The damned.

Her eyes are green. A she-devil's eyes in an angel's face. Yet her heart is black and full of sin, like the hearts of those sacrificed before her. So must she be sacrificed, before she proves the instrument of my destruction. Twice she has looked me full in the eye. Both times I saw in their depths the dangerous spark of recognition.

She knows what I am.

She knows what I have done. What I was sent here to do.

She is not blinded by the beam of my bull's-eye lantern. No. This one sees beyond the wink of brass buttons, beneath the concealing bucket helmet and raincape. She knows my soul. Knows me for what I truly am. The Instrument of God. His Chosen One.

Jack the Ripper. Leather Apron. The Whitechapel Butcher.

It is as if she plumbs the very depths of my soul with those emerald eyes.

I shiver and touch myself down there, in that sinful part of me. I am hard again. The tide is rising, and she is dangerous.

I cannot let her betray my identity.
I cannot let her live.
I cannot.
One last sacrifice before I leave London forever.
Look lively, Green Eyes. Jacky's back—and saucy as ever!

"Hello, Bridget. Where is everyone?" Donovan asked as he let himself into Huntington House. The place was deserted, hushed except for the measured tick-tocking of the clock in the hall and the light footfalls of the little maid, who was flicking a feather duster over the mahogany hall stand with more gusto than skill.

"Why, Miss Estelle's fast asleep, she is, sir. And Rose is in the kitchen, taking her afternoon nap, too. Sure, I don't know where everyone else is, sir. But Mr. Declan says he's coming to dinner tonight, he is, and for Rose t'be sure t'set him a place at table." She smiled shyly. "He's very fond of Rose's mutton pies, is Mr. Declan."

"Aren't we all, Bridget!" Donovan grinned. "Aren't we all!" The lightheartedness that had caught him up when Cecily Townsend rallied unexpectedly still lingered. But then, keeping death at bay always made his smile more ready, his footsteps lighter, whether the reprieve lasted for six hours, six days, six months or six blessed years. Victories against the Grim Reaper, even temporary ones, were few and far between, and deserving of celebration. He could hardly wait to tell Cait.

"Where's Miss O'Connor?" He tried to sound casual but failed, judging by the maid's quick, knowing smile.

"I really don't know, sir. Sure, Miss Caitlynn was

308

reading in the drawing room earlier, was she not? But she's gone now."

"She didn't go out, by any chance?" He held his breath as he waited for Bridget's reply. Caitlynn wouldn't have gone into the East End alone, surely? Not after his warnings?

His jaw tightened. As much as he loved her, he would be the first to admit that Caitlynn was a headstrong woman, single-minded in her quest to find her missing cousin.

She'd been badly disappointed that their little mission had been postponed this afternoon—he'd seen it in her face. Had she gone after Timmy alone? Anything was possible with Caitlynn! She was not like other women, who were prisoners of their sex, and of the structures society placed upon them. She would take matters into her own hands if push came to shove, follow her gut instincts, and the devil take what was proper!

Unfortunately, the independence, the single-mindedness, the free spirit he so admired in her were also her biggest shortcomings. Still, she'd promised him she would not go into the East End alone, and he had believed her. Surely she would not take a promise she made him so lightly?

"I don't believe so, sir, no. Miss O'Connor always tells Rose when she's going out. Perhaps she's up in her room taking a wee nap. Would you like me to go up and knock, sir?"

"No, no. That won't be necessary. I don't want to disturb her if she's resting. I'll just look in on Miss Estelle. Thank you, Bridget."

He took the stairs two at a time, trying not to think about Annie Murphy lying dead and cold at the foot of the cellar steps all day yesterday, the victim of an unknown assailant. An assailant from this very household, or so the detectives thought, as did he. It was a sobering thought. Even so, he no more suspected Tom of murdering Annie than had the detectives. There was simply no motive.

He still couldn't shake the niggling suspicion that Deirdre Riordan's July disappearance was connected in some way to Annie's death. After all, Annie had wanted to talk to Caitlynn the night before her fatal fall. And, according to Kitty Abbott, the dead woman had information about Miss Riordan's disappearance. Was it possible that Annie had been killed to keep her from telling what she knew?

What had she known? he found himself wondering. *What could Annie possibly have known that was worth risking the hangman's noose to keep secret? Unless . . . had a second murder been committed to cover up a first?*

Despite what he'd told Bridget, he knocked at Caitlynn's door first. "Caitlynn? Are you in there?" he called, his ear pressed to the door, his knuckles urgent.

There was no sound from within, yet his apprehension mounted, fear for Caitlynn outweighing his concern for her good name or appearances. He knocked again, more loudly. "Caitlynn?" There was still no answer. Trying the knob, he discovered her door was locked.

Quickly moving down the hall to Estelle's room, he knocked and called her name. Again receiving no answer, he wasted no time and let himself in.

The room lay in heavy shadow, the draperies drawn, the lamps unlighted. The fire had burned down to a heap of white and orange ashes and was barely alive.

He turned up the lamp, flooding the darkened room with light. "Estelle?"

His ward was deeply asleep. When he gently shook her shoulder, she still did not stir.

He frowned. The way she looked disturbed him. Her sleep was too deep to be natural, surely? Moisture glistened on her upper lip and brow, and she was very pale and clammy to his touch. Frowning, he lifted her wrist and took her pulse. It was barely palpable.

"Estelle!" he called loudly, patting her face, then firmly shaking her by the shoulders. His expression was concerned. "Wake up!"

She remained as limp as a rag doll.

"Doctor? Did ye call me?"

He hadn't, but he needed her anyway. "Yes. Fetch my bag, Bridget. Hurry!"

To her credit, Bridget flew from the room without questioning his order, returning, breathless and flustered, with his black bag. In the few moments she was gone, he went through the connecting door into Caitlynn's room. Empty. The bed was neatly made, the fire banked. The faint scent of her soap hung in the air.

Returning to Estelle's bedside, he selected a phial labeled 'paregoric' from the bag, then drew a measured quantity of it into a dropper. Squeezing Estelle's cheeks together, he forced her lips apart and dripped paregoric into her mouth.

"Is it her heart, Doctor?" Bridget asked tremulously, wringing her hands.

"I don't believe so, Bridget. Not this time, anyway." He picked up the empty mug on the nightstand and sniffed. Cocoa. "Will you go down to my study for me? Inside the medicine cupboard you'll see a brown glass bottle marked laudanum. Fetch me the bottle and a basin, would you?"

"Right away, sir. Oh, and I asked Tom if he'd seen

Miss O'Connor, and he said he had. He said the miss
and Mrs. Montgomery left together a little before four,
sir."

Dark brows came together in a frown. "Mrs. Montgomery and Miss O'Connor?"

"Yes, surr."

Odd. Caitlynn had not seemed particularly friendly
toward the woman . . . unless—? His jaw hardened.
Could Caitlynn and Montgomery have gone to the
East End to find the Murphy boy together?

Perhaps Caitlynn had not told anyone she was going
so he would not learn of her expedition; he had asked
her not to go without him. But despite his request, she
had gone anyway, he thought, lips thinning in displea-
sure.

Estelle stirred and moaned.

"There's a good girl, Estelle. Wake up now. Come
on, poppet, sit up for me."

He hefted her up, holding her against his chest while
he arranged pillows and bolsters behind her back.
"You're going to be very sick in a little while, darlin'
girl; you have to sit up so you won't choke. But afterwards, you'll feel much better."

As if on cue, the paregoric started to work. Estelle
began to retch and gag horribly, although her eyes remained tightly shut. Fortunately, Bridget arrived on the
run with the basin.

"Aah, good! And in the nick of time, as always,
Bridget," he said, smiling his approval as he held Es-
telle's forehead and shoved the bowl under her chin.
"Where's the laudanum?"

"Here it is, sir. But the bottle's almost empty, it is."

The maid held up a large brown bottle with a cork
stopper.

As he expected, it was practically empty.

Obsession

Laudanum, a medicinal derivative of the poppy plant, from which opium also came, was prescribed by physicians as a sedative and painkiller. The bottle Bridget was holding had contained a good two inches of liquid when he'd dosed Tom earlier that same day to calm his nerves. Now, the same bottle was practically empty.

There was no longer any doubt in his mind that Estelle had been drugged. The only unanswered question remaining was, by whom? And *why*, for God's sake? *Why?*

"He's not coming, dear. I think we should go on home, don't you?" Mary said gently after an hour. "We'll come back another time."

"I suppose so." Caitlynn had never been so cold, nor so miserable—nor so beaten down by disappointment and an odd sense of dread. Her last hope of finding Deirdre, after all these weeks of looking and asking with no result, had ended here in failure and defeat, and yet another dead end.

Mutely she nodded, and let Mary take her elbow and lead her away from the sordid little court of number 9 Farrier's Lane, out onto the cobbled street.

Her numbed feet were lumps of ice. It was all she could do to put one in front of the other and walk. Indeed, if it were not for Mrs. Montgomery guiding her, she might have stumbled like a toddling infant.

"Blessed Mary be praised," she breathed as they rounded the street corner. By some miracle, the cabby was still there, despite his threats to abandon them.

"Huntington Square," she told him as Mary climbed into the coach and settled herself. "And thank you for wait—"

She stopped in mid-sentence, transfixed by the sight

Penelope Neri

of a now familiar carroty head, the jaunty bantam-cock walk, of the scrawny lad coming toward them down the street. It was the holly-seller! The young duck poacher from the park! And—she realized belatedly—Annie Murphy's son, *Timmy Murphy*.

He darted across the street, obviously headed back to Big Betty's house for his night's doss.

"Timmy!" she cried. "Wait!"

His head jerked around. He saw her, obviously assumed the worst, and took to his heels. Or was it a guilty conscience that made him break into a run?

She sped after him like a bat out of hell, her booted feet skidding on the icy cobblestones. "Wait, Timmy, stop!" she panted. "You don't have to run away! I just want to talk to you. Please, come back! It's about your—your mother!"

To her surprise, he stopped dead and swung around to face her like a cornered wild animal. The blue eyes blazed with hate in his narrow, foxy face. His hands were knotted into white-knuckled fists at his sides, painfully bony beneath too-short sleeves. "Don't talk about me muvver—me muvver's dead!" he warned, wagging a bony finger in her face like a stick. "They pushed her down the bleedin' stairs, they did!"

"I know, Timmy. And I'm so sorry for your loss. But the—the doctor—Dr. Fitzgerald, he wants to help you," she said quickly, the words spilling out in her desperate need to persuade him. Whom had he meant by 'they'? she wondered absently. "Really, he does, if you'll let him. He just wants to ask you a few questions first. Then he'll give you some money, and—and food, too. Whatever you need to tide you over. You know, until you can stand on your own two feet. Your mother had money coming to her. A week's wages, not

314

to mention today's Christmas box from the master. That money is rightfully yours now."

The mention of Boxing Day money and food worked. The lad's closed, hate-filled expression changed to a guarded one. "Food *an*' money?"

"Yes. Both. And whatever else you need."

"And all I 'ave to do is answer 'is bloody questions?" His accent was half Bow Bell's cockney, half Irish.

"Yes. That's all."

"Like wot?" he asked suspiciously, hopping about from one dirty bare foot to the other. "What sort o' questions?"

"Nothing difficult," she hedged. "You'll see. I have a hack waiting back there. Come back to the square with me, please, Timmy. I'll have Rose give you something to eat, and then we'll talk."

"If I come, you'll tell the sawbones t'gimme a coat?" he bargained, standing his ground like a fighting cock. "A wool one. An' a pair o' boots. An' a muffler. Not just the grub."

"You shall have food and money—whatever you need, I swear it. I always keep my promises, Timmy. Ask anyone."

He hesitated. "I'll do it, then."

"Good. Come on. This way," she coaxed, as if she were gentling a small, frightened animal. She offered him her hand, but he ignored it and she let it fall.

"Wait! Wot about the Marsh woman?" he asked warily, his blue eyes suspicious now.

"You won't have to have anything to do with Estelle, Timmy. You don't even have to see her." God only knew what lies Annie had told the boy about Estelle. But from the terrified look in his eyes, and the way he'd bolted when he saw them in the park that

315

time, whatever he'd heard could hardly have been favorable. "We just need you to answer some questions."

"Who's 'we'?"

"The doctor and I."

"I answer 'em, then I get the coat an' stuff? That's all?"

"That's all."

"You swear it, on yer muvver's grave?"

She nodded. "I do. Cross my heart and hope to die."

He ducked his head, just once, to signify agreement. Then, teeth chattering, his scrawny shoulders hunched against the bitter wind, bony arms thrust into the pockets of his too-small threadbare jacket, he followed Caitlynn back across the street to the horse-drawn cab and scrambled inside.

"Hello, Timmy," greeted Mary Montgomery from the shadows of the hack.

Chapter Twenty-four

"Please don't send me away, Donovan. *Please*. I'll do anything you say—I'll be so good, you won't even know I'm here. Just don't—just don't send me back to Lily's place," Estelle sobbed. "Please, don't!"

"What are you talking about, darlin'? Wake up and dry your tears. No one's sending you anywhere. I won't let anyone take you away from me, my precious girl," Donovan crooned, smoothing Estelle's hair as he rocked her.

The paregoric had rid her stomach of the laudanum, but she still sounded delirious to him, although she didn't seem to have a temperature.

"Ye're safe with me, darlin' girl."

"No, no, I'm not. She swore it. She swore you'd send me away, because of . . . of . . . Miss Caitlynn," she sobbed almost incoherently through her tears, then heaved a gusty sigh. "Because you l-l-love her. She said if you found out what a wicked girl I was, you'd send me back to Lily and marry Miss Cait. That if you marry her, you won't need either of us anymore."

"Who said I'd send you away? Miss Cait?"

"No, no. Mrs. Montgomery. *Her*. She told me you'd send us *both* away if you found out what I did. But I didn't mean it to happen, really I didn't. I swear it. I didn't! I loved Dee Dee, too. I didn't want to hurt her. It was all an accident, but I was so frightened. . . . I've been frightened for such a long time, Uncle Donovan! So very s-s-s-cared."

She threw her arms around his neck and hugged him so fiercely, he could scarcely breathe. "Please, please help me. I don't want to be af-f-fraid anymore."

Donovan gently untangled her arms and cupped her face between his hands. She was trembling violently.

"Listen to me, mavourneen, and listen well. *I love you*. Perhaps not in the way you'd like me to love you, as a sweetheart, but as a father who cherishes his daughter and will protect her come hell or high water! There is nothing you could ever say or do that will change that, Estelle, or the love I feel for you. Nothing that would make me send you away. *Nothing,* d'you hear me?" he asked sternly. "No matter what anyone has told you to the contrary."

Tears rolled down Estelle's cheeks and plopped off her chin, but she managed a small nod between her hiccupping sobs.

"Good. Now, then. Trouble's never as bad when it's shared with a friend. Why don't you tell me what the devil it is you're so upset about? Take a deep breath, darlin'. Start at the very beginning, and go on from there."

"I can't. I can't," she whimpered.

"Aye. You can and you will, because I'm here with you, and I won't let anyone hurt you," he said sternly. "Tell me, poppet. Tell me everything."

Holding his hands as if they were lifelines, Estelle began.

"*No!*" Timmy exploded. He hurled himself across the coach's interior and clawed for the door like a wild animal fighting for its very life. His eyes were stark with horror, almost popping from his head.

The coach door flew open with the force of his kick, but before he could leap down to the cobbles and vanish into the East End, Montgomery's gloved hand snaked out. Fingers closed over his shabby jacket and twisted.

The lad wrenched himself free so violently, the threadbare cloth screamed as it tore and gave him up.

"Ye lying bloody bitch!" Timmy snarled, turning on Caitlynn like a cornered feral cat. "Ye promised! Not Marsh, ye said. And I believed, damn ye!" He spat in her face, then slid free of his shirt and waistcoat, plummeting out of the moving coach, bare-chested. "Devil take yer bloody promises!"

"Timmy, wait!" Caitlynn screamed, banging on the coach wall to halt the hackney cab as Timmy's bare feet gobbled up the cobblestones in his desperate bid for freedom.

"He won't be back, dear. Let him go. If he knows what's good for him, we've seen the last of Master Timmy Murphy." It was said with great relish.

"Tell me something. Why was he so afraid of you?" Caitlynn asked softly, looking Mary full in the eye.

The housekeeper could not meet her questioning stare. Her eyes slid away from Caitlynn's. "I have no idea."

"Oh, but I think you do, Mrs. Montgomery. I think you've known all along why I was looking for Timmy. You admitted you'd eavesdropped on the rest of my conversation with the doctor. And by the way, why did Timmy call *you* Marsh?"

"Because it's my name, I expect, dear. Mary Marsh Montgomery. I'm Estelle's mother."

"Her mo—!"

"Wot's goin' on in 'ere, then?" the cabby demanded, flinging open the hack door and sticking his head inside. His cheeks were fat, shiny and very red, probably from too much strong drink. Stick an apple in his mouth, and he would have been at home at any feast, Caitlynn thought. He glared at both women, his piggy eyes cruel. "Wot's all this bloody racket, then, Mary? You up t'yer tricks again?"

"There's been a change in plans, Alf. Take us to Chapel Lane, if you please, luv. And sharpish!"

"Change in plans, is it? La-de-da!" Alf chortled. "Righto, then, ducks!"

"Don't listen to her. Go back to Huntington Square as quickly as you can!" Caitlynn pleaded.

"Gawd alive! First it's Huntington Square, then it's Chapel Lane! Make up yer bleedin' minds," the cabby growled, clambering back up onto his perch. "Stupid bloody tarts. Where to, Mary?"

"Chapel Lane, Alf. You heard me."

"Don't listen to her!" When Caitlynn tried to stand, Mary Montgomery grabbed her by both shoulders and pressed her down.

"Sit down and shut up. And don't make me angry, Miss O'Connor. *She* made me angry—but she was soon sorry," she said through gritted teeth.

"Who's she?" Caitlynn asked sullenly.

"Annie, of course," Montgomery said in an irritable tone. "Who else? Thought she and her scrawny little bastard could blackmail Mary Marsh, she did. But Annie was wrong, wasn't she?" The gray eyes gleamed. "Dead wrong."

"And my cousin, Deirdre?" Her knees were trembling uncontrollably now. She wanted to be sick. "Was she 'dead wrong,' too, Mary? Did she make you angry?"

"As a matter of fact, she did. Very angry. Runs in the family, eh?"

"What happened that last day, Mary? When Estelle and Deirdre went to the park?"

"Nothing out of the ordinary," Montgomery said levelly as if the matter were of no importance whatsoever. "Not at first, anyway. Estelle told me she and Miss Riordan had a little picnic in the arboretum. Then they fed the ducks with some stale bread, and decided to take a skiff out on the lake. They often did that. Estelle and that meddling bitch were always out on the lake. Estelle enjoyed rowing, you see. Her arms are very strong, you know. Much stronger than the Riordan woman's."

"I'm sure they were. Go on. What happened next?"

Montgomery smiled. "Can't you guess, a clever girl like you? Your Miss Riordan told Estelle she knew what I'd been up to. Claimed she knew all about the pretty bits and pieces I've taken for meself from my employers over the years. Said she knew I was setting her up t'look like a thief, too. Trying to get rid of her, she called it.

"She threatened to tell the doctor exactly who and what I was." Montgomery shrugged. "Well, Estelle panicked, didn't she, the silly little bitch."

"Oh? And what did Estelle do when she panicked, Mary?"

The housekeeper smirked. "I really shouldn't say."

"Oh, but you must. I insist," Caitlynn whispered, her mouth dry with dread.

"What she did was . . . well, it was a very bad thing. But you can't do anything to me on account of it. No. It was Estelle's doing, not mine, you see?" She smiled slyly. "She started it."

Her smile lifted the hairs on the back of Caitlynn's neck. Holding her breath, she leaned forward. "What did she do, Mary? Tell me what Estelle did!" Caitlynn wanted to shake the truth out of her—to shake her until her teeth rattled.

"She pushed her, that's what she did. She was afraid Riordan would tell the doctor. That he'd send her back, see? You know, to Lily's? So she pushed her to shut her up."

"Into the lake, you mean?" Caitlynn asked, confused. "She pushed her into the lake?"

"Where else?"

"But Deirdre swims like a fish."

"That's right. Estelle pushed her in. Then she drove the pony cart back to the house t'tell me what she'd done, all in a panic, like. It was left to me t'finish the job proper, just like always, wasn't it? But that's what mothers are for, am I right, Miss O'Connor?" she added with a vicious smile. "Cleaning up the nasty messes their dirty, snot-nosed little bastards make."

"And exactly how did you finish the job, Mary? What did you do to 'clean up' the mess Estelle had made of everything?" She felt sick to her stomach as she waited for Mary to answer her, for there could be only one answer that made sense.

"I ran back to the lake from the house. Miss Riordan was standing in the water by the bridge. She was soaked through. Just standing there, looking all wet and forlorn, with water running off her elbows and

322

her fine straw boater all dripping wet." She laughed, enjoying herself. "I told her Miss Estelle had sent me to help her."

" 'Oh, did she now?' she says in that way she had. 'Well, I don't want help from the likes of you, thank you all the same.' That's what she told me, the uppity little bitch. 'I know what you are doing to Estelle,' she says, 'and what you are trying to do to me, and I give you fair warning. I intend to put a stop to it all. This evening I am going to tell the doctor everything. You have done enough to that poor child,' she says.

" 'He won't believe you, not a word of it!' I told her. 'I'll tell him the truth, I will. I'll tell him that you're a sneak thief and a liar!'

" 'Oh, will you?' she says. 'Will you really? And whom do you think he'll believe? You or me? This cruel charade has gone on long enough, Mary Montgomery. Or should I say Mary Marsh? Your luck has run out. If you know what's good for you, you'll leave Huntington House immediately.'

"Well, I couldn't let that happen, could I?"

"What did you do to Dee Dee?" Caitlynn screamed at her. Lurching across the coach's shadowed interior, she grasped the woman by the upper arms and shook her furiously. "Tell me!"

"All right, then! Let go of me, do, and get a grip on yerself, dearie! I pushed her into the water again. That's what I did! Satisfied?"

"The water—? No. That's not what you did. There's less than four feet of water in that lake. Deirdre couldn't have drowned. What else did you do to her? You must have done *something* else."

"The oar." The woman spoke so softly, Caitlynn had to strain to hear her. "When she tried to come back up, I hit her on the noggin. Over and over, I hit her."

Caitlynn's mouth was so dry, she could not swallow. "How many times?"

"As many times as it took."

"What do you mean?" Caitlynn demanded brokenly. "As many times as it took to do what?"

"Why, to make her stop moving, of course."

"Holy Mother of God," Caitlynn whispered, crossing herself. Her hand flew up to cover her mouth, which had dropped open in horror. Tears streamed down her cheeks uncontrollably. "You killed her. You murdered her. Oh, Deirdre, Deirdre. I'm so sorry. So very sorry." She hugged herself, rocking back and forth in her grief.

Montgomery shook her head impatiently. "You weren't listening, were you, O'Connor?" she said sharply. "I *had* to do it. I had no choice! It was a matter of survival. Me or her—and it wasn't going t'be me! I'd read her stupid diary, see? She was in love with the doctor—and he with her! He would have listened to whatever she told him.

"Well, I couldn't take a chance on that happening, could I? My Estelle's going to marry the doctor, she is! Then she can take care of her old mum for the rest of her days, bless her li'l heart."

"That will never happen," Caitlynn whispered hoarsely. "You know why not? Because the doctor considers Estelle his *daughter*. Truth is, you've been wrong about a lot of things lately, Mary. Deirdre was never in love with the doctor. She loved *Declan*. He was the 'D' she wrote about in her diary. That's why he moved out of Huntington House. To protect her reputation. They were to be married, and you killed her, you godless, hateful bitch!" she shouted. "You killed a wonderful, loving person, a good sweet person—and for what? To keep your stupid position!" she shouted. "To hide your pilfering, your deceit!"

"Stop it! Stop it this instant!" the housekeeper hissed. "Someone will hear you."

"I don't give a bloody damn who hears me!" Caitlynn shouted. "It's high time someone knows what you are and what you've done. I'm going to tell the whole bloody world, and when I'm done, you'll swing for what you've done, Mary Marsh, or whatever your bloody name is. You'll hang from the neck until you're dead!"

"Shut up!"

"No! I won't shut up! Tell me, did you tell Estelle what you did, Mary? Or did you let your own daughter believe she'd killed Dierdre? And how did Timmy and Annie Murphy find out about it? Was Timmy by the lake that day, poaching ducks? Is that what happened? Did he see you kill Deirdre? Yes! That's exactly what happened, isn't it?"

But even without confirmation, Caitlynn knew the truth.

Someone like Mary Montgomery wouldn't care what private hell her daughter suffered, believing herself responsible for the death of a woman she'd loved and considered a friend. Mary had already killed at least twice. She would not hesitate to kill again, to keep her dirty secrets safe. Timmy Murphy would have to run and keep on running if he valued his life.

As would she. . . .

Again, there was that sly, darting look. That snaky hint of the evil that lurked behind Mary's homely facade. Caitlynn almost expected a long forked tongue to dart out of her mouth, flickering between thin, dry lips as she hissed, *"What do you think, Miss Clever Drawers O'Connor, eh?"*

325

"That's how you controlled Estelle, isn't it?" she demanded, her grief replaced by anger. "By telling that poor child she'd be sent back to Lily's if the doctor ever found out what she'd done, or if she told him about you."

"So what if I did?" Mary sneered. "I'm entitled. I'm her bleedin' mother. I gave that little bastard life, I did. She owes me! She was my ticket out o' the East End, thanks to her pretty looks and them golden curls she got from her father, the drunken bastard. I knew the minute the doctor saw how his pretty little angel 'took' to dear Mrs. Montgomery that I was in! Hired me t'be his housekeeper on the spot, he did. No questions asked!"

She chuckled. "The stupid doc thought me 'n' the brat had never set eyes on each other until that day, but we had. Oh, yes. And I told Stella—Estelle—she'd be sent back to Lily's t'play nicey-nice with the rich old gents wot came 'round, if she didn't play along."

And in just days, the terrified child who'd thought she'd escaped a living hell found herself trapped in another kind of purgatory; living a lie, tortured by the ever-present fear of discovery and abandonment by those she had grown to love but was not allowed to trust, thanks to her mother, Caitlynn thought, sickened.

"And who is this Lily, anyway?" she asked casually, playing for time, trying to lull Montgomery into thinking she would go with her willingly.

"Lily? She's me sister, that's who she is. Lily Perkins, she calls herself. But you'll be meeting her soon enough, so don't go—*hey!*"

Caitlynn lunged for the carriage door. It swung open with the impact of her body, just as it had with Timmy's.

She shot through it, landing hard on the wet cobbles below with a grunt of pain, tangled up in her unwieldy skirts and full cloak.

Montgomery followed her out, landing only feet from her. Caitlynn had no time to catch her breath, no time to think or plan. She could only react.

Scrambling to her feet, she picked up her skirts, took to her heels and ran, her booted feet slapping the wet cobblestones.

Every breath she drew was agonizing. Every move she made, every step she took, caused a stabbing stitch in her side that made her whimper in pain. Nevertheless, she raced on, dodging through alleys and around tiny dark courts, trying always to keep the looming black mass of the railway bridges in sight. Running toward the only landmark that was even remotely familiar.

Running for her life down a blind alley that literally led nowhere—and ended abruptly in a blank brick wall too high for her to scale.

It was the end of the road, she realized.

She was trapped.

No way out.

Flinging herself around, her back pressed to the rough brick wall, Caitlynn lifted her head and braced for Montgomery's headlong attack, determined to meet it with a well-placed knee, a hefty kick.

There was a sudden rush of movement toward her, like the strike of a deadly cobra that came out of the night with its hood spread. A blinding pain knifed through her skull. It was followed by utter blackness, Stygian and absolute. . . .

She is breathing heavily as she leaves the alley, stumbling along the gutters like a drunkard and tying the strings of her bonnet as she goes. There is no sign of the other whore in the big hat. Whatever their quarrel, I sense she has won this round, and that the other is vanquished.

Like me, Green Eyes has become the hunter! The stalker! The sacrificer!

Instinct tells me she is going after the Murphy lad now. That she has old scores to settle with him, as do I with her foul kind. In that, we share a common bond, she and I. Sacrificer and sacrifice. Damner and damned. Hunter and hunted.

My fingers curl lovingly around the virgin blade. I shiver as I caress its frigid steel, so pure, so cleansing. "Soon, my precious," I croon. "Very soon, my beloved one."

It is almost time. The tide has risen.

Come to me, Green Eyes . . .

"Evenin', copper," the woman says, pretending she is looking for men to lead astray.

I cannot see her eyes in the shadow of her bonnet.

"All alone tonight, are ye? Where's your partner, then?"

I smile a little and let the knife slide smoothly down my sleeve. The handle fits my fist like the scalpel fits the hand of a surgeon.

Gripping her by the throat, I force her backwards into a small dark courtyard that stinks of cat piss. It is only then that I see her face. Her eyes.

Too late to turn back now—!

What will be will be. It is inevitable, just as day follows night.

The wheels are already in motion.

The die is cast.

"No partner, dearie," I tell her with a breathless grunt as the knife catches on bone. Humming, I begin my handiwork. "I do my best work alone. . . ."

Chapter Twenty-five

Donovan abandoned Tom and the coach and set out on foot to find Caitlynn, dread mounting as he sprinted down one dark street after another, through drizzling icy rain, without any sign of her.

He came at last to the address Bridget had given him, a run-down boardinghouse next door to a Jewish social club. *Number 9 Farrier's Lane*. This was it. Raising his fist, he beat upon the door.

"All right, all right, handsome. There's no need fer you t'be so impatient. There's lots t'go around. What's yer pleasure?" the madam asked, stroking his lapel before she'd hardly opened the door.

"I'm looking for a woman," he began, but before she could fix him with that knowing look, he added, "No, not just any woman, Betty. This one's young and pretty. Dark hair. Green eyes. A lady."

"Aren't they all, handsome?"

"I don't have time for games, Betty. Have you seen her?"

Betty's lips jutted sulkily. "Ye missed 'er by a good half hour, ye did. O'Connor her name was, right? *Miss* O'Connor?"

"That's her."

"She and Mary Marsh was both here. They was waitin' for Timmy Murphy t'come home, or so they claimed. Said they wanted t'tell him about his muvver dyin'—a likely story, if ever I've heard one. I told them they was wastin' their time. He already knows." Betty fluttered her lashes. "Sure you aren't lookin' for me, handsome?"

"Sorry, sweetheart. Not tonight. Do you know where she went, this Miss O'Connor?"

Betty shrugged. "I don't know. What's more, I don't bleedin' care. If you're not interested in me nor me gels, then bugger orf!"

Donovan needed no second urging. Unless he was mistaken, or Estelle had lied—and he didn't think she had—Caitlynn was in grave danger in Mary Marsh's company. The sooner he found her, the better.

He was no stranger here in the East End. There were many who recognized him and called out greetings as he strode the darkened streets without fear. The people here remembered his past kindnesses. The babies he had delivered for free, the hurts and illnesses he had healed, both big and small, whether here in their sorry lodgings or at his clinic in St. Bart's.

Workingmen doffed their caps. Women bobbed him sketchy curtseys. Bullies and the girls they ran on the street corners gave him respectful nods. He asked all of them the same question, growing more and more desperate each time he asked it, but the answer they gave him was always the same. No. They had not seen a green-eyed slip of a girl. A pretty Irish girl with dark hair who did not belong in these parts.

"Evening, cabby." The man was leaning against a wall, his fat face and bulbous nose bright red in the puddle of light cast by a nearby gaslight. His belly bulged beneath his braces. A drinker, Donovan guessed, with a liver as pickled as an onion. His spavined horse hung its sorry head, half starved and dejected. " 'Tis a powerful bad night for fares, I'm thinking, what with this blasted cold rain we're having."

"Not so bad as all that, gov'na. I've made meself a pretty shilling t'night, I have," the man said with a smug smile. "An' it's early yet."

Donovan pulled up short, the fine hairs on the back of his neck prickling. A shilling was no small sum in these parts. The cabby's fare had not been from the East End. "Have ye now, cabby? So tell me. Who'd be leaving a warm hearth to go out on a wretched night like this? Sure, 'tis piddling down, it is." He forced a grin. "Tell me what I want t'hear, and I'll double that shilling for ye."

"You a copper?" the cabby asked suspiciously. "From the Yard?"

"That depends."

"On what?"

"On whether you tell me what I want to know."

"So you set them down here?" Donovan asked as the hackney coach shuddered to a poorly sprung halt at Miller's Court.

"I told yer, gov'na, I didn't let no one down," Alf whined. "They said as how I was ter take 'em to Chapel Lane, or else t' Huntington Square—they never did make up their bleedin' minds about which, but

331

that's women for yer. Then the Murphy boy just flew
outta my hack. Took to his heels like a bat out o' hell,
he did! Then the women jumped out, one arter the
other. The one in the bonnet jumped up and started
running that way." He pointed toward the looming
shadow of the railroad arches. "The other one—the
one in the big hat—followed her. That was the last I
saw of either of 'em."

Donovan nodded. "Good man. Here's your shilling.
And here's another threepence for the loan of your lantern."

"Done!" the cabby declared, handing the lighted
lantern down to him.

Donovan began searching the rabbit warren of cobbled alleys systematically, one by one, the cabby's lantern carried aloft to light those inky courts not lit by
gaslight.

He heard squeaks and the pattering of feet as he
disturbed rats about their nightly foraging in the gutters. He saw the slippery slink of alley cats on the
prowl, heard their eerie mating yowls, like crying children. But of Caitlynn there was no sign.

He was about to retrace his path back to the cab
when he heard what sounded like labored breaths behind and to the left of him. Slowly he swung around.

The arc of the lantern lit a lurid tableau, straight
from the pages of a penny-dreadful.

A bobby, rain-caped and helmeted, crouched over
what looked like a bundle of rags in a corner of the
dark court. He was breathing heavily.

As Donovan took a step toward him, he turned.
Lantern-light winked off the man's glassy, unfocused
eyes.

"What is it, Constable? What have you found
there?"

"Another present from our friend Saucy Jacky, sir," the man explained hoarsely, turning his face away from the light. "Looks just like the others, she does, too, God have mercy on her soul. Bloody 'orrible mess." He shuddered. "That—that butcher! I'd give my right arm t'see the Ripper swing!"

Something's not right here, Donovan thought. Gut instinct confirmed it.

"Where's your partner, Constable?" The men always patrolled in pairs.

"Bill's gone for the horse-drawn ambulance, sir. I was just about to whistle for reinforcements when I came over all peculiar, like. Wasn't meself for a moment, I wasn't." He shook his head. "Thought I might make a fool of meself and be sick, but I'm all right now, sir."

The constable put the silver whistle to his lips and blew. The three strident blasts carried loudly in the damp and darkness. Donovan heard the alarm taken up and instantly relayed by other whistles in the distance.

"Are you quite sure she's dead?"

"No doubt at all, sir. He's very thorough in his work, is Jacky."

Donovan shuddered. There was an awed quality to the constable's tone that was chilling. He could not see the man's face, as it was shadowed by the brim of his bucket helmet, but his eyes gleamed like wet black stones.

Donovan hardened his jaw. "I think I'll have a look anyway, poor woman. I'm a physician, you see. There might be something I can do for her."

"Of course, Doctor," the man said softly, standing and stepping away from the victim's huddled body and the dark pool of blood in which it lay.

Donovan carried the lantern over to the brick wall

and the ghastly bloodied corpse. He rested the light on the edge of the wall, then knelt to feel her wrist, knowing long before he found the spot that there would be—could be—no pulse, not with such great blood loss.

It was only then that he saw the bonnet—a familiar bonnet of hunter-green velvet, trimmed with a single ribbon bow.

That bonnet had once framed a pretty green-eyed face.

A face he had come to love, now hidden by blood.

A woman he'd cherished and planned to wed, her ravaged body now cooling in his arms.

The love he had searched for all his life but never found, till he found her—

—only to lose her. Here. Like this.

The gorge rose up his throat. His hands began to shake. Denial ripped through him.

Cait. Cait. Caitlynnnnn—!

"*Noooo!*"

Reeling with shock, he flung himself away as the first shout of denial, the first savage wail of grief, tore its way up from the very depths of his being. "Nooo!" he roared.

But there was no one to hear his cry. The bobby who'd found her was gone, melted into the dark night as if he'd never been.

In his place there were only shadows. And, in the distance, the strident blast of police whistles, drawing closer by the minute.

It was there that they found him, on his knees beside the murdered woman, his sleeves soaked in her blood.

"Dr. Fitzgerald, isn't it?" Inspector Abberline said.

Obsession

"Dr. Donovan Fitzgerald, of thirteen Huntington Square?"

Abberline asked many more questions before the Black Maria came to take him away, with his wrists cuffed behind him.

Chapter Twenty-six

Detective Inspector Frederick Abberline frowned as he peered over the wire rims of his gold spectacles, tugging on the thick moustache which, combined with mutton-chop whiskers, made up for his receding hairline.

On the battered desk before Scotland Yard's C.I.D. officer lay the Metropolitan police blotter that the desk sergeant had just set in front of him. Slips of paper jutted from between its lined pages, marking dates or entries that were of particular interest to the detective.

He opened the blotter to the second such slip and ran a stubby finger down the inked entries on that page.

"Let me see here. August thirty-first. Buck's Row. Does that date or address mean anything to you, Doctor?" Abberline asked, leaning back in his chair with his fingers steepled on his chest.

Donovan ran an exhausted hand through disheveled

black hair. He had been clean-shaven when they took him into custody the evening before, but was not any longer.

Overnight, a heavy shadow of scratchy black stubble had sprouted. Dark circles of fatigue—and sorrow—ringed his eyes. Those, and his bloodstained shirt cuffs, gave him a disreputable appearance.

They had taken his blood-soaked coat away, along with his bloody shoes and laces—evidence, they claimed, that he had murdered 'the woman,' as they kept referring to Caitlynn. Not that he gave a damn about his clothes, or what they believed, or anything else, come to that! He squared his jaw. Devil take the bloody lot of them! Nothing mattered anymore, not with Caitlynn gone.

Nothing.

"As I told McNaughton's goons last night, no. Should it?" he growled, answering Abberline's question.

"I would have thought so, yes. You see, Doctor, according to the notes taken by a Police Constable Peter Reece that same evening, he encountered you in the Buck's Row vicinity at about midnight, under suspicious circumstances. You claimed to have been visiting an injured man, one . . . Joseph Casey, a slaughterer . . . who had lodgings in the area. Does that name strike a bell?"

"Indeed it does, yes. Joe Casey worked at Mulhaney's Slaughteryards. He was gored by a bull earlier that day, and in terrible pain from a belly wound. His wife sent one of the children to fetch me. Unfortunately, the poor devil died of gangrene two days later. He left behind a wife and five children."

"Aaah. A true tragedy. You are to be commended for your good works, Doctor. Noble errands of mercy, done by dark of night." His tone belied his flowery compliments.

Despite the shock and apathy into which he had fallen since discovering Caitlynn's body, Donovan's jaw tightened. "You asked, Inspector. I merely answered. If I sought recognition for what I do, let me assure you, I would be practicing medicine in the palatial surgeries of Harley Street, Buckingham Palace or Windsor Castle, not a—a makeshift curtain clinic at St. Bart's."

"Forgive me if I offended you, Doctor," Abberline murmured with little sincerity, scribbling in his notebook. "And you say you went directly to your home on Huntington Square after you'd attended this . . . this injured man? This Joe Casey?"

"I didn't say so, no. But yes, from what I remember of that evening, that's exactly what I did. What I always do, in fact. You must realize that I see a great many patients. It is not possible to remember them all, after so many months have passed."

"Then you had no idea that—while you were saving a man's life!—a prostitute was being savagely murdered and her body mutilated just a few streets away? A Whitechapel whore named Mary Ann Nichols?"

"No idea whatsoever, no. I did read an account of the murder in the newspaper the following day, however."

"Hmmm. I see." More scribbling. "And what of the night of September thirtieth? It says here that you were seen near St. George's church at around eleven o'clock."

"It was St. Anthony's church, but yes, that's correct. That was the night Polly Doolan had a . . . a miscarriage, poor woman." It would serve no purpose to tell the inspector that Polly had tried to rid herself of the babe she was carrying. "Alas, she bled to death before I could help her."

"You seem to remember this patient far more clearly than you do the last."

"I do, yes."

"How so?"

"Polly was from my own village back in Ireland, and yet there was nothing I could do to save her. You don't forget the ones you lose, Inspector. Polly had no family here in London, so I reported her death to the first police constable I met. I also asked him to fetch the hand-ambulance to her lodging house, to take her body to the workhouse. The workhouse women pepare the bodies of the poor for burial, you see. I then went home and wrote a letter to her family, to tell them of her passing."

It had been a letter of lies, he recalled. A masterpiece of deception, written for all the right reasons, but lies nonetheless, for it had implied that poor Polly had died respectably, in childbirth, along with her stillborn infant. That she had been a cherished wife to the bitter end, and deeply mourned by her bricklayer husband. Nothing could have been further from the truth.

He would have to write similar letters to Caitlynn's and Miss Riordan's families at some point in the near future, he thought heavily, wondering if he would be permitted writing tools and stationery in his prison cell.

How the hell would he find a way to tell the two families that their beloved daughters had been murdered? No words could blunt the piercing agony of such terrible news.

"I'm well aware of that, Doctor," the chief inspector was saying. "There were two—I repeat, *two*—

prostitutes murdered that night. The first was Elizabeth Stride, on Berner Street."

" 'Long Liz' Stride. Yes."

"Soon after her body was found, Catherine Eddowes was found murdered, just off Mitre Square. A 'double event,' just as the Ripper promised."

"Promised?"

Abberline nodded. "In his letter to the newspapers."

"I know nothing about their murders."

"But you knew the women?" Something in the young doctor's tone had suggested that he had. Besides, he had known Stride's nickname. A tall women, her cronies had called her 'Long Liz.'

"By sight, yes," Donovan admitted. "I make it my business to know these women."

"By 'these women,' you mean the prostitutes? The unfortunates?"

"Yes."

"And why is that, Doctor?" Abberline asked, speculating. Fitzgerald was Irish, unlike the last physician suspect they'd had in custody, an American quack, Dr. Francis Tumblety. The American had been arrested in November for acts of gross indecency. That arrest, and his medical background, had made him a prime suspect in the Ripper murders, until he'd managed to post an enormous bail and left the country posthaste just a few days ago. Fortunately for Tumblety, this latest murder had cleared him.

Although Fitzgerald was some thirty years younger and did not appear to be a quack, he *was* Irish—a people reputed for their violent tempers. Abberline had decided he disliked Fitzgerald when he met him for the first time at the Townsends' dinner a few weeks ago. But despite his dislike, the doctor hadn't struck him as the sort to commit murder.

Obsession

Still, Fitzgerald had been found crouched over the woman's butchered body, which had still been warm to the touch when the first p.c. arrived. The doctor had been distraught, and his hands had been bloodied.

When asked what had happened to the woman, he claimed she had been murdered by a bobby. One whose name and badge number he had neglected to take, and whose face, coloring and build he could not describe, except for the eyes, which he'd claimed were black and as cold as wet stones.

By his own admission, Fitzgerald enjoyed the company of prostitutes. He had ready alibis to explain his presence in Whitechapel at all hours of the day and night. Too ready, perhaps. . . . He also possessed the razor-sharp scalpels and medical know-how to have performed the mutilations and the organ removals of the six women. Witnesses claimed the Ripper wore a swirling black cloak, a black slouch hat, and carried a physician's black bag. With the exception of the hat, Fitzgerald fit their description to a T.

Despite the inspector's gut instincts, honed by a lifetime of such investigations, Fitzgerald was the perfect suspect, with one notable exception: Where was the murder weapon? How—and where—had he disposed of it so quickly?

No knife or blade had been found on him, or in the vicinity of the murder scene, although the police had cordoned off several courts in all directions, and searched house to house without success. Nor had he carried a black bag containing scalpels.

And where was the police constable Fitzgerald had described?—the bobby who had blown his whistle to sound the alarm? The constable who'd discovered the body had not come forward.

"Tell me again, sir. Why is it you help these women?"

"I help them because, unlike others of my profession, I take my physician's oath seriously," he said. "Because their lives are sorry, wretched, difficult ones, for the most part. They have precious little money to spare—certainly nothing left for medical care, even when they badly need it. I have made it known throughout the East End that they can always come to me, or to my clinic, without fear of being turned away or preached to."

"Despite the censure of your peers in the medical profession?"

"Yes, indeed. These women need to know that they can trust me. That I will help them, or their children, or their menfolk, whenever they are in need of help, or in trouble, in whatever way I am able."

Abberline sprang to his feet, his face red. "You speak about them as if they were silly, misguided schoolgirls—but they are *whores*, Doctor! Fallen women, quite beyond any form of redemption, whether it be yours or God's."

"On the contrary, Inspector—they are not fallen women, but desperate women. Frightened women. Struggling women. Women who, without men very much like you and me, would be out of work and off their backs in no time, would they not? The hypocrisy of our society sickens me. Poor women are forced to sell themselves just to live or to feed their little ones when their husbands or fathers callously abandon them. But the very men who avail themselves of their services and their bodies turn around and condemn them for it, while suffering no social stigma themselves.

"These women are to be helped and pitied, Inspector. Not condemned for what they must do just to stay

342

alive. They do not need imprisonment or moral guidance. They need food, decent jobs, a chance for a decent life for them and their children."

"A liberal attitude on your part, Doctor."

"I prefer to think of it as sound common sense, Inspector. A decent attitude—a truly Christian attitude, leading by example—rather than a liberal one."

"Let's talk about last night, shall we?" Abberline said, trying to throw the suspect off guard by adroitly changing the direction of his questions.

"I think not." Fitzgerald's fists clenched. His shoulders squared.

"I must insist, Doctor. That is, after all, why we are here at this ungodly hour. Tell me, what were you doing in Whitechapel? Tending another sick patient, perhaps?" Abberline raised a sardonic brow.

"No."

"No? Then why were you there, if not on yet another heroic errand of mercy?"

"Not last night. Last night was different."

"How, then? In what way? Tell me."

"I don't want to talk about it."

"But I insist."

He heaved a sigh. "All right. I was looking for Miss O'Connor."

"Miss O'Connor?"

"Yes. My ward's companion. We were to be married. I returned home from my clinic on Boxing Day to find her gone—"

"Gone?"

"Yes. I went to look for her. I had every reason to believe she was in danger, you see."

"In danger from what?"

"Not from what, Inspector. From *whom*. A woman. The woman she was with. A very dangerous woman named Mary Marsh, who has been my housekeeper for the past six years."

"I see. And because this Marsh woman posed a danger to your Miss O'Connor, you killed her?"

He blinked as if awakening from a long and horrible nightmare. "I didn't kill anyone, Inspector. In fact, I believe I should speak to my solicitor before I say anything further. Would you send for Declan Fitgerald? He's my brother, as well as my legal counsel."

"All in good time, Doctor," Abberline said smoothly. "First, tell me more about the dead woman."

"What is it you want to know? What can I tell you, except that I found her dead, with the bobby kneeling at her side? I had nothing to do with her death, nor do I know who killed her, unless it was he. The p.c. His eyes—there was something about them. They were so . . . so *empty*." He shuddered. "I can't explain it. Besides, nothing I tell you can bring her back! Nothing at all."

"All right. Then tell me how you knew where to find her?"

"Estelle—my ward—told me Caitlynn had gone with my housekeeper to Whitechapel. She thought they might go to Farrier's Lane. When I got there, they'd left. The cabby, Alf, told me he'd seen her running after the boy."

"What boy? I'm afraid you've lost me."

"Annie's son, Timmy Murphy."

"Annie Murphy. That's the young woman who was found dead in your coal cellar on . . . December twenty-sixth?" Again he referred to his notes.

"Yes. It was Marsh who killed her! I borrowed the cabby's lantern and started searching for Caitlynn, street by street. Nothing. Then I turned a corner and saw something lying against the wall of a sordid little court. A bundle of dirty rags, I thought. A bobby was kneeling beside them. 'Twasn't rags at all, but a body. Smaller, somehow. Shrunken by death. Butchered beyond recognition. No more human than a piece of raw meat. I didn't know who it was—or even what it was." A shudder ran through him. "I thought—I thought I could help, and so I went over to her. I felt for her pulse, fool that I was." He covered his face with his hands. "Oh, God, so much blood! And there was I, expecting a pulse! 'Twas then that I saw her bonnet. The fetching green one with the ribbon bows. . . ." He closed his eyes, reliving the horror of it. The shock. The grief. The rage. And, finally, the blessed numbness.

"Whose bonnet, Dr. Fitzgerald?" Abberline pressed. "Whose?"

"Caitlynn's, of course. My Cait's. Miss O'Connor's. It was her bonnet."

"I see. And do you have any idea why the dead woman was wearing Miss O'Connor's bonnet?"

"Why the dead wo—?"

Donovan stared at him, not daring to hope.

She opened her eyes with a groan to find herself looking up at a gargoyle. A gargoyle with a shock of ragged carroty hair, pale blue eyes in a pinched grubby face, and snot running from his nostrils.

"Timmy Murphy. Please don't run away," she whispered hoarsely. "Not again. I won't let her hurt y—"

"*You* won't?" He snorted. "That's a good 'un! Like you did somefink to help me in the coach when she grabbed me! Don't matter. I can take care of meself, I can!" Timmy Murphy said fiercely. "Which is more'n I can say fer you."

"So why did you come back?"

345

" 'Cos me muvver said you was always straight wiv her. Hoity-toity, but straight. Soo, I came back for ye. Come on. Get up. We gotta hide before Marsh finds us!"

Although badly nourished, Timmy was as wiry and tenacious as a young terrier. He hauled her to her feet, chivying her along despite the tears of pain that streamed down cheeks grown numb with damp and cold.

Every breath she took drew a stabbing pain from her cracked ribs. Every move she made created fresh waves of pain in her throbbing skull, injuries courtesy of her fall from the carriage, and the brick with which Mary Marsh had tried to brain her.

Timmy helped her along with a stream of curses until they reached the pitch-black arches under the railway bridges.

"Wait 'ere," he whispered. "An' don't come out till mornin'—not for nuffin', y' hear me? Not if ye know what's good fer ye!"

"Wait! Don't go! What if she catches you?" she hissed, hanging on to his bony elbow. "You saw her kill my cousin. She won't give up until she catches you."

He shrugged her off. "She won't catch me."

With that, he was gone.

Nauseated by the pounding in her skull, unable to draw a deep breath without crying out in agony, Caitlynn slid down the damp, grimy wall until she was crouched in a sitting position on the dank ground.

She closed her eyes and leaned her head against the rough, sooty brick of the railway arch, staring into the inky blackness in which things squeaked and scurried, moisture dripped, and heaven-only-knew what monsters lurked, human or otherwise.

Timmy had seen Mary Marsh use an oar to batter her poor cousin to death in the park.

No wonder Estelle had been so odd about the music box she'd given her for Christmas. The gift, with its mirror lake and tiny lead skaters, must have seemed like a curse to the poor child—a reminder of the terrible crime she thought she'd committed, and a place that drew and repelled her at one and the same time.

Armed with the knowledge of what Timmy had witnessed that day in July, Annie had been blackmailing the housekeeper, taking small items of value from Mary Marsh—such as Caitlynn's own silver picture frames—in return for her and Timmy's silence.

Those items had ultimately been fenced to the East End's criminal element for cold hard cash. But instead of turning a lucrative profit, Annie had been killed to shut her up. Now Marsh would have to silence Timmy and Caitlynn for the very same reason. . . .

Caitlynn decided she would stay here, where she was safe, even if it was cold and uncomfortable, beneath this horrid, smelly arch tonight, as Timmy had insisted. But at first light, she would go straight to the closest police station—Bow Street, she thought—to tell the authorities everything she knew. Then, and only then, could she return to Huntington House to face Donovan.

Would he still love her? she wondered. Would he forgive her for breaking her promise to him? For going after Timmy Murphy without him?

She would find out, come morning. . . .

Donovan looked up as Abberline entered the holding cell.

"Dr. Fitzgerald?"

"Inspector."

"You're free to go. My sincere apologies for any inconvenience we may have caused you."

"You're releasing me? Just like that?"

"We are. The desk sergeant will give you your belongings. Good day to you, sir."

"But . . . what changed your mind? Has there been another murder?"

"No, sir." The suspicion of a smile played about Abberline's mouth. He tugged on his moustache. "If it were up to me, I'd lock you up and throw away the key. However . . . you have several very strong advocates outside who insist that you are innocent." He lowered his voice to add, "The most vocal of whom, I might add, is a very attractive young lady, who claims to have . . . personal knowledge of your exact whereabouts on both the nights and the times in question, you lucky bastard! Your—um—*friends* are waiting for you outside, sir. Constable, unlock the cell door for the doctor, if you please," he finished in a louder voice.

"Right away, Chief Inspector."

"You heard him. Get out of my police station, Fitzgerald!"

His coat hooked over his shoulder, like a rake returning home from a night on the town, hair disheveled, eyes dark-ringed, Donovan walked out of the police station. Although dazed, he was a free man.

Waiting for him were his brother, Declan Fitzgerald, a beaming Sir Charles Townsend, Kitty Abbott and her infant son—and, of course, Caitlynn.

He barely noticed the others as he strode quickly toward her.

"Donovan!"

"Ah, Cait. My sweet Cait, thank God! And thank you!"

Tears streaming down her cheeks, she ran to meet him. Seconds later, she was in his arms and he was twirling her about, kissing her fiercely in his joy at finding her unharmed.

"I love you," Caitlynn declared, not caring who was watching or who might be listening. She framed his face between her hands and planted a smacking kiss full on his lips. "Do you hear me? I love you so much!"

Passing police constables grinned appreciatively. It wasn't often they saw a pretty girl kissing a man in public.

Sir Charles chuckled. "I say! Jolly good show, Miss O'Connor. Cecily will be delighted. This young devil will have to make an honest woman of you now, my dear. Your reputation's been badly compromised, don't ye know."

"Do I know, Sir Charles? On the contrary, I was *counting* on it!" Caitlynn said with a laugh that had her clutching her side in sudden pain.

"Rest assured I have every intention of marrying Miss O'Connor, sir," Donovan said softly, his eyes only for Caitlynn. "Come on, sweetheart. Let's go home. Unless I'm mistaken, you need to see a doctor for those cracked ribs—and for once, I don't mean myself."

Chapter Twenty-seven

It was New Year's Eve, and the gardens of Huntington House were spun in a sugary web of frost that glittered like strands of crystal beneath the full moon.

Their breath made little puffs of vapor as they strolled arm in arm away from the house and through the wintry gardens, their boots crunching on the frosty grass.

The tiny gazebo with its wrought-iron gingerbread was their destination. The summer-house reminded her of a tiny white palace as Donovan led her up its three steps.

"Well, here we are," he began, gesturing as if they were in an elegant ballroom. For once, he seemed uncertain, not his usual bold self at all.

"Ah, yes. Here we are," she agreed, giddy laughter in her voice as she linked her hands with his. "What now, sir?"

She knew very well why he had brought her here.

What it was he intended to ask her. Her excitement had been building all week. The next few moments were ones they would cherish forever. Happy moments, devoted solely to joy, to hope. *To their love, and to their future.* They had no connection to the sad revelations of the week before—not to poor Deirdre's death, nor to Annie's, nor to Mary Marsh Montgomery's murder by person or persons unknown.

Telegraphs and letters had been sent to poor Aunt Connie and Uncle Daniel, telling them of the tragedy that had befallen their daughter. As Caitlynn told them in her letter, Donovan had ordered a proper headstone from the stonemason's to replace the numbered marker on the pauper's grave in which Deirdre had been buried, the unidentified victim—or so the authorities had believed back in July—of a vicious beating and robbery by an unknown assailant in the park.

For six months, Deirdre's and Annie's murderer had gone scot-free. But by now, Mary Marsh Montgomery, herself the victim of a brutal murderer, had surely been tried and found wanting by a higher court and a sterner judge than any found at London's Old Bailey.

Rather than Estelle being upset over her mother's death, she was relieved, Caitlynn believed. The enormous burden that Marsh's dangerous obsession had heaped upon her was now gone forever, as was her terrible fear of being found out. All of that belonged in the past. Estelle was now truly free. In just a few short days, the young woman had blossomed beyond recognition.

And, although Caitlynn would grieve for and miss the dear cousin she'd loved like a sister, life must go on, she reminded herself.

Donovan inspected his pocket watch. "In about two

minutes it will be 1889," he declared. "Think of it, darlin' Cait! The birth of a new year."

"A wonderful new year! One of new beginnings and fresh starts," she agreed softly. "One in which we put the past and old sorrows behind us and move bravely forward, without looking back."

He nodded, too moved to speak as he drew her into his arms. He simply held her there, her dark head cradled against his chest, his handsome face serious as he tenderly stroked her hair.

"I love you, Caitlynn," he said in his lilting brogue. "I love you with all that I am, and with all that I shall be. I believed my life was over that night when I saw your green bonnet. With my beautiful Cait dead, nothing mattered to me. *Nothing*. My heart only began beating again when I learned the truth. When I saw you standing there before me, alive and lovely as ever."

"Lovely? With cracked ribs and a lump on my head the size of an ostrich egg?" she teased, yet her eyes sparkled with tears. "Hardly!"

"Shh. I meant what I said. *Lovely*," he repeated, pressing his finger against her lips. "You are, you know. So blessed lovely." He caressed her cheek.

She kissed his admonishing finger.

"I vowed then that I would never let you go again. That I would make you my bride as soon as was humanly possible. We'll be wed in Ireland—a great big noisy wedding that folks will talk about all over the county for years t'come! There'll be your family and mine, darlin'. Dancers, fiddlers and singers— everything! Just say you'll marry me, darlin' Cait. Say you'll make me the happiest man alive by becoming my wife."

"I would be honored, sir," she said quickly, the acceptance spilling eagerly from her as she looked up at him with love and joy in her shamrock eyes. There was no hesitation, no second thoughts, as there had been with Michael Flynn. "I can think of nothing on this earth that would give me greater happiness than to share my life with you and our children."

"And your . . . conkers?" he demanded gravely, and in precisely the same grave tone in which he'd just proposed to her. "Will you share those with me, too, hmmm?"

"My *what*?" She blinked in surprise, then giggled and thumped him on the chest, remembering that long-ago day in the park. "Share my *conkers*? I'll have to think about that, won't I? Conkers are a very serious matter, I'll have you know, sir—owww! My ribs!" she squealed.

"Devil take your ribs. Say it, minx!" he growled, pulling her roughly against him and holding her there. "Say it! Your life, your love *and* your conkers! I'll take you no other way."

She curled her arms around his neck, linking her fingers through the crisp black waves of his hair. "Liar," she breathed, her green eyes dancing with amusement. "My dear, darlin' lunatic, you would take me with or without my bloody conkers, and you know it. Admit it! You're madly in love with me."

The serious facade cracked. He grinned. "All right, woman. So I am—madly, passionately in love! Especially passionately. . . . Now, enough of yer blatherin'. Come here t'me."

As Caitlynn went into his arms for the kiss that would seal their union, the church bells of London rang out in a glorious carillon.

She laughed in delight. The bells were ringing because it was New Year's Eve—the moment of midnight on December 31, 1888. But it seemed they rang for her and Donovan alone, in glorious celebration of their engagement.

The old year was dead, and a brand new year was being born. Ships anchored in the Pool of London were blasting their whistles and foghorns to welcome its birth. Big Ben was chiming. Voices singing "Auld Lang Syne" drifted from houses all around the square, rivaling the pop of champagne corks, kazoos and glad cries of "Happy New Year!"

Last year's autumn of terror was over. There would be no looking back, no brooding on what had gone before, Caitlynn promised herself. The past was gone. Finished. Over. Done. It could not be changed by so much as a jot.

She and Donovan would instead look forward to their new lives together. To marriage, to children—and to endless summers of love.

CHRISTINE FEEHAN
SUSAN GRANT
SUSAN SQUIRES

THE ONLY ONE

They come from the darkest places: secluded monasteries, the Carpathian mountains, galaxies under siege. They are men with the blackest pasts—warriors, vampire monks, leaders of armies—but whose passions burn like dying stars. They have one purpose: to find those women who fulfill them, complete them, and make them rage with a fire both holy and profane. They seek soul mates whose touch will consume them with desire, yet whose kisses will refresh like the coolest rain. And each man knows that for him there is only one true love—and in finding her, he will find salvation.

- -